KAT FRENCH

Undertaking Love

AVON

AVON

A division of HarperCollins*Publishers*
77–85 Fulham Palace Road,
London W6 8JB

www.harpercollins.co.uk

A Paperback Original 2014

1

First published in Great Britain by
HarperCollins*Publishers* 2014

Copyright © Kat French 2013

Kat French asserts the moral right to
be identified as the author of this work

A catalogue record for this book is
available from the British Library

ISBN-13: 978-0-00-757692-0

Set in Sabon LT Std by Palimpsest Book Production Limited,
Falkirk, Stirlingshire

Printed and bound in Great Britain by
Clays Ltd, St Ives plc

MIX
Paper from
responsible sources
FSC C007454

FSC™ is a non-profit international organisation established to promote
the responsible management of the world's forests. Products carrying the
FSC label are independently certified to assure consumers that they come
from forests that are managed to meet the social, economic and
ecological needs of present and future generations,
and other controlled sources.

Find out more about HarperCollins and the environment at
www.harpercollins.co.uk/green

UNDERTAKING LOVE

Kat French lives in England with her husband, two little boys and the world's oldest cat.

She also writes erotic romance as her USA Today best-selling disreputable alter-ego, Kitty French.

Keep up to date with Kat's news at www.katfrench.co.uk or follow her on twitter @katfrench_

Thanks first of all to you for reading *Undertaking Love*, I truly hope it will give you a few hours of escapism and pleasure.

Huge thanks to my lovely editor Sammia Hamer for making me feel so welcome, and for loving Gabe, and for helping me to bring out the best in the story. Thank you also to Eleanor Dryden and the whole Avon team, it's a complete thrill to join the Avon family. I'm still pinching myself.

I'm indebted to Scott Pack for loving lighthouses enough to read my manuscript in the first instance, for being a super-hero, and for setting me on the path to publication. Thank you!

Many thanks also to Rachel Faulkner and all at Authonomy for your unending patience and holding my hand throughout my first experience of the publishing industry. Thanks also to the Authonomy on-line community for support and advice, and special love to Caroline Batten and the chick-lit girls for your friendship and help.

Much love to my minxy writing sisters, Maya Blake, Sally Clements, Catherine Coles, Lacey Devlin, Tara Pammi, Suzanne Ross Jones, Romy Sommer and Lorraine Wilson. Thank you for not flinching when I said I was going to try something different, and for being the coolest kids on the writing block. You know I love you all to bits.

Big thanks to the beautiful Bob girls for the many years of friendship and encouragement. You're a lovely, lovely bunch of ladies.

Much love and thanks to the fantastic ladies of Facebook and twitter and blog-land, you make me laugh every day and I'm super-grateful for your support.

Last but never least, thank you to my own special people. My fabulous folks who have been unstintingly interested, encouraging and proud, even when it seemed that I had no news to report!

Thank you to my little boys for being the best kind of distractions, and last but never least, to James, for believing in me even when I didn't, supplying endless coffee, and for allowing me the occasional diva strop without divorcing me. I thank my lucky stars.

For my brilliant, funny sister, for terrible plot advice and excellent encouragement. xx

CHAPTER ONE

Marla squinted at her new neighbours from the upstairs office window and fumbled around on the desk behind her for her glasses.

'Holy crap, Emily . . . Emily, quick!'

'Where's the fire?' Emily appeared around the doorway, puffed-out from sprinting the length of the aisle and up the steep, rickety chapel staircase.

'Oh, it's worse than that. Come and see this.'

Emily joined Marla, and the two women stood shoulder to shoulder at the window, gazing out in silent, duplicate horror. Before them were two nervous-looking workmen balancing on stepladders, inching brand new shop signs above their heads as a huge, bald guy yelled instructions at them from across the street. He was flinging his arms around him like a possessed windmill, and his hairy beer belly was sliding in and out from underneath the hem of a tea-stained T-shirt that had clearly not seen an iron in the last decade.

Marla slid her glasses up her nose and cracked the window

open a little, all the better to eavesdrop. Not that they needed much extra help, because the bald guy was bellowing at the top of his Irish lungs.

'Up a bit. Not that much!' He hopped from foot to foot and clutched his bowling ball of a head in exasperation. 'Down a bit! Feck it, man, it's practically vertical!'

Marla squinted to read the freshly painted signs and then turned away and pressed her hands against her flushed cheeks in panic. This had to be a joke. Had someone called that TV show where they turn your worst nightmare into reality, and then expect you to laugh when they reveal it was all a big set-up?

'Umm . . . that doesn't look much like a cupcake bakery . . .' Emily ventured.

'You don't say.'

'It's . . . er, it's a funeral directors, I think, isn't it?'

Marla closed her eyes as Emily voiced her worst fears. Her heart banged around behind her ribs like a panicked bird trying to escape, and she laid a hand over it as she tried to steady her breathing.

'Cupcakes. It was *supposed* to be cupcakes, Emily. Not dead bodies.'

Emily grimaced. 'Maybe there's some mistake?'

Marla's head spun with the implications of going from the sublime to the ridiculous in terms of her new neighbours. None of them were good. Wedding limos fighting for space in the street outside with hearses. Brides bumping into widows. Wreaths instead of bouquets. And how many happy couples would run the risk of ending up with a party of sobbing relatives huddled in the back of their wedding photos for all eternity?

2

'It better be a mistake, or we're ruined.'

Marla had shed blood, sweat and tears over the last three years to turn Beckleberry Little White Wedding Chapel into a national smash hit, and the idea of it suddenly being under threat made her shiver with fear. And anger.

'I'm going over there.'

'Excuse me! Er . . . Hello . . .'

Marla marched up to Guinness Guts, who had finally allowed the workmen to hang their signs and shambled his bulk back across the road.

'Are you in charge here?'

He screwed up his chubby nose and shrugged a non-committal shoulder before reaching for the mug of tea that he'd balanced on the narrow window ledge.

'Some might say that, darlin'. Depends entirely upon who's doin' the askin'.'

'I'm Marla Jacobs – from the wedding chapel? You know, *that* wedding chapel.' She jabbed a finger towards her beloved premises. 'The one *right there*.'

'Aaah. The new neighbours.' He glanced down at her empty hands. 'No cup of sugar, then?'

Marla narrowed her eyes. Was he joking?

'*Where* is the cupcake bakery?' she asked, enunciating each word with care.

His bushy eyebrows twitched as he looked at her. Then he shrugged. 'Don't ask me for directions, darlin'. I've only been here five minutes.'

The man was either winding her up, or he was an idiot. Possibly both.

'No, no, no . . . Mr?'

3

Marla glared and waited for him to supply his name. The smirk on his face told her he knew so too, yet he wasn't complying. She clenched her teeth and ignored his rudeness with considerable difficulty.

'Look. There must be some mistake.' She smiled, despite the fact that she actually wanted to knock the grin right off his face. 'These premises,' she waved her arm towards the shop currently bearing his ruler-straight new signs. 'These premises have been sold to a cupcake bakery. You know . . . for cupcakes? Cakes? For birthdays. And weddings. And all sorts of other *happy* events.' She emphasised the *happy* in the hope that he would finally cotton on to the thumping great problem. The blank expression on his face told her otherwise. *Maybe diplomacy was overrated, after all.*

'Happy events. Not sad. And certainly not events for *dead people*,' she hissed, her fists clenched into tight balls on her hips.

A look of understanding dawned across Guinness Guts' face. Or, *damn the revolting toad to hell*, was it amusement? His piggy eyes travelled slowly from her purple skyscraper Louboutins all the way up to her auburn waves.

'Look, Red. I've no clue about any of this stuff. You'll be wanting Gabriel when he gets here tomorrow. He's the organ grinder. I'm just the monkey.'

He made a frankly alarming attempt at something Marla could only guess was supposed to be a monkey impression, then slurped his tea and reached for a half-eaten packet of chocolate digestives.

Marla fought down the urge to grab the biscuits, hurl them to the ground and grind them into the pavement

4

beneath her shoe as she cast her eyes to the skies and drew in a measured breath. Guinness Guts. Monkey Man. Revolting Toad. Whoever this man was, talking to him any more today was obviously a pointless exercise.

'Right. Fine.' She huffed, throwing her shoulders back. 'Well, you can tell *Gabriel* to expect me bright and early tomorrow morning. And FYI, we don't need any organ grinders around here. We already *have* a perfectly good organist in the village, thank you very much.'

Guinness Guts nodded and tugged on an imaginary forelock. 'Gotcha. Not required. But hey, listen . . .' He jerked his head towards the shop window with a grin that revealed biscuit crumbs stuck between his teeth. 'We make good neighbours, you know. *Very quiet.*'

Marla shot him a withering look and stormed back to the chapel. Emily, who had been watching from the brick porch, flattened herself against the wall to let her friend steam by. Inside, Marla sank onto the nearest spindle-backed chair and scrubbed hard at her temples.

'This cannot be happening, Em. If they open up there, we could be ruined. No. Scratch that. We *will* be ruined.'

Emily sat down across the aisle from Marla. Pin tucks of anxiety folded across her forehead as she twisted her rings around on her slender wedding finger. She couldn't think of a single useful counter argument – as new neighbours went, a funeral parlour was just about as bad as it got for a wedding chapel. She clutched at the only available straw. 'Maybe this Gabriel guy will be a bit more approachable tomorrow.'

Marla snorted. 'You reckon? If he's anything like his henchman, then I seriously doubt it.' Her heart was hurting, as if someone had grabbed hold of it and given it a Chinese burn. The chapel wasn't just her business. It was her everything. She might not believe in marriage for herself, but she sure as heck believed in it for other people, especially those who chose her quirky American-style wedding chapel as the venue for their big day. She'd poured her heart and soul into the business from the first moment she'd laid eyes on the vacant little chapel. The 'for sale' sign had stopped her in her tracks, and she'd known without doubt that Beckleberry was the perfect village for her business and her big fresh start. And she'd been right, up to now at least. It had proved the perfect distraction from her own shambolic love-life, and she was far too business savvy to allow her personal feelings towards marriage to stop her from turning the empty, unloved little building into one of the most in-demand wedding venues in the UK. She glanced up at the clock. 12.30 p.m. Past the yardarm. *Thank God.*

'I need a stiff drink. Does Dora still stash brandy in the kitchen drawer?'

Emily nodded, then stood up and held out her hand. 'Come on. I'll make us some coffee with a nip of the hard stuff and we can make ourselves a plan.'

They both jumped as the back door of the chapel banged open.

'Did someone mention a plan? Faaaabulous! For what? When? Tell me everything.'

Jonny's made-for-the-West-End voice rang out around the chapel as he unclipped the lead from around the neck of Bluey, Marla's impractically huge and lovable Great Dane.

Decked out in a black shirt that clung lovingly to each perfectly sculpted ab, Jonny looked every inch the gay icon he was – in their sedate corner of Shropshire, anyway. He also happened to be the best wedding celebrant and creative director Marla could ever have dared wish for. She'd known the moment that he arrived for his job interview in full Elvis garb that he was the ideal man for the job, but she hadn't realised at the time that he'd also come to be one of her closest friends too. They were each other's perfect foil; she loved him for his exuberance and *joie de vivre*, whilst he adored her understated sense of humour and determination. He'd moved his life lock, stock and barrel from Brighton to sleepy Beckleberry on the strength of Marla's job offer, leaving behind a string of broken hearts and empty karaoke spots in his wake. In truth he'd been ready for the move, because he'd reached a stage in his life when the footloose-and-fancy-free lifestyle had run its course and left him wanting a little substance with his sex.

Emily decided to go for shock tactics and shepherded him to the window to judge the scale of their problem for himself.

'A plan to get rid of this bunch of jokers,' she whispered, gripping his muscled arm so hard that her knuckles popped out white against her skin.

Jonny gasped in horror as he took in their new neighbours' sombre signs, while Bluey loped over to sit beside his beloved mistress. Marla leaned her head against his and counted backwards from ten while she waited for the inevitable explosion. Jonny was nothing if not predictable, and liked nothing better than a good strop. He was the only person she knew who was desperate for a slot on *Jeremy Kyle*.

'A fucking Funeral Directors?? Next door to us? Errr,

helloooo?' Jonny snapped his fingers in the air, diva style. 'I don't fucking think so!'

Marla sighed as he strutted off towards the front doors. Much as she'd like to unleash Jonny on Guinness Guts, he would probably only make the situation worse.

'Hang on, hang on. I've already tried that. There's nobody in charge over there until tomorrow.'

'Hmmph.' Jonny's broad shoulders slumped. 'Well, when they do get here, they'll wish they hadn't bothered, because I'm going to kill them with my bare hands.' He made a throttling gesture with his hands, his eyebrows lost somewhere in his hairline.

Marla threw her shoulders back and painted on a determined smile. She was the boss, and her troops needed rallying. 'Come on, guys. Let's go and put the kettle on and get cracking on that plan.'

When the going gets tough, the tough put the kettle on. Marla might have spent her formative years in America, but after almost a decade in England, tea was a tradition she had well and truly taken to heart. Weddings permitting, the small staff of the chapel took a well-earned break most afternoons to drink tea and swap gossip. They'd been rather looking forward to adding cupcakes to that ritual, too.

Somehow, tea with a side order of formaldehyde didn't hold quite the same appeal.

Gabriel Ryan stilled the growling engine of his Kawasaki Z1300, restoring the sleepy early morning peace to Beckleberry High Street. The pavements still glittered with the dawn frost of early spring, and his breath hung on the icy air as he slid his helmet off. He sat stock still for a couple of seconds and drank in the sight of his perfectly hung shop signs for the first time.

Gabriel Ryan, Funeral Director. One thought consumed all of the others in his head. Mine. It's *my* name over the door.

Time to grow up, Gabe.

His father's last words had become his mantra over the last few months. If he'd ever needed to feel the warmth of his beloved Da's approval, it was now. He kicked the bike stand down and fished around in the pocket of his battered leather jacket for the front door key. *To his own front door.* This was it. Elated and scared witless all at the same time, he felt for his mobile as it buzzed against his chest. He didn't need to glance at the screen to know who would be on the other end of the line.

'Hey, Rory.' He slipped the key into the lock and turned it.

'You there yet, little brother?'

At forty-five, Gabe's eldest brother Rory's voice sounded heart-wrenchingly similar to their Da's. He'd appointed himself patriarch of the family after their father's heart attack last summer – a role he took very seriously.

'Sure am. Just arrived.'

Gabe cast a last glance up at his name as he passed underneath the sign and stepped inside.

'And?'

He looked around at the haphazard clutter of stepladders and paint pots that littered the reception area.

'And, yeah. It's looking pretty good.'

'Only Phil the Drill said it's an almighty mess.'

Phil the Drill has a big mouth, Gabe thought, but refrained from saying it, because he knew that Rory meant well, and would no doubt relay everything he said back to their mother and three other brothers. He brushed off Rory's concerns.

'It's nothing I can't handle.'

Besides, it wasn't a lie. He'd handle any amount of mess rather than go home and take his place in the family firm. He loved the bones of his family, but being back there had just been too hard on his heart since last summer. His dad was everywhere, and for Gabe, the only way to deal with his grief was to be somewhere else.

'How's Ma?'

Rory's rich laugh rumbled down the line. 'Same as ever. Bossy. Interfering. But she misses you.'

Guilt stabbed through him. 'Tell her I'll call her later.'

'Don't forget, okay?'

'Course not.'

'And Gabe . . .'

'Yes?'

'Good luck, little brother.'

Gabe clicked the phone shut and rested his helmet down by the door. He'd drifted from funeral home to funeral home since his father's death, unable to settle but unwilling to go back to Ireland. His heart might belong in Dublin, but he was going to make this place his home now.

It had all happened quite by accident really. He supposed some might have called it fate if they were given to believing in such things. Firstly, he'd turned thirty. His family had, of course, wanted to throw the customary huge bash at the club in Dublin, and Gabe had known perfectly well that once he was there they'd use every trick in the book to make him stay in Ireland and leave his days in England behind. He'd refused their pleas and opted to stay in

Shropshire with his best mate Dan, making plans for a weekend where the sole intention was to drink until they couldn't stand up anymore.

A weekend which, in turn, was devastated beyond repair by the untimely death of Dan's gregarious, life-loving grandmother. Gabe's funeral director instinct had kicked in hard as he'd leaned over to gently close Lizzie Robertson's eyes for the last time. He'd poured out generous measures of scotch for her family, and made the calls they were too shell-shocked to handle themselves.

Much later, over midnight brandies, it had struck him exactly how far away the closest undertakers were. Dan's family had waited a good few hours before anyone could reach them from Shrewsbury, the nearest market town to sleepy Beckleberry. Much longer than any family needed to wait at a time like that. And so the seed had been sown. A seed that grew with frightening speed, like a magic beanstalk leading Gabe towards his pot of gold at the end of the rainbow.

But I don't have any premises, and I can't afford it anyway, he'd reasoned, and he'd smiled with relief that there was a bona fide reason to let himself wriggle off the hook. Which was all very well, until his brothers finally wised-up to the fact that he really wasn't coming home and bought him out of the family undertaking business as a birthday gift.

Still, he'd laughed when Dan shoved property details into his hands for some place that had just come back onto the market due to a deal falling through with a cupcake company. *Cupcakes?* How could a company hope to survive just selling cupcakes? No wonder the deal had fallen through. It would be way too small, but he'd viewed the premises anyway to shut Dan up. Cupcakes didn't take up as much space as dead bodies.

Wrong again.

Gabe wasn't much given to mystical flights of fancy, but had he been pushed, he'd probably have agreed that it seemed as if the planets had aligned obligingly just for him. He had the money. He had the experience. And now he had the perfect premises. 'Go big or go home' had been Dan's sage advice over a pint in his prospective new local. And because going home wasn't an option, Gabe had climbed the beanstalk and signed on the dotted line before he could let himself back out of it.

'Time to grow up, Gabe.'

He picked his way between the stepladders and criss-crossed extension cables and let himself through to the back. In the kitchen, his eyes fell on the bright yellow note gaffer-taped to the bubble wrap around the newly delivered fridge.

'The Yank bird from across the way is on the warpath. Watch yer back, kid.'

Gabe read it over twice more, still none the wiser about the note's possible meaning. *What Yank bird? And why the hell would she be on the warpath already?*

He glanced out of the window, half expecting to see someone storming his way, but no warring harridans appeared to be beating a path to his door at this early hour. No doubt all would become apparent when Phil the Drill arrived. Late, of course. But what Phil lacked in time-keeping skills, he more than made up for in fitting skills. He'd worked for the family undertakers in Ireland for over twenty-five years and knew their business inside out. He'd been happy to bring his boys on a jolly across the Irish Sea on the promise of decent money, good digs and as much beer as they could drink.

Impatient for his first caffeine shot of the day, Gabe rummaged around and managed to unearth the kettle from behind a pile of half-eaten packets of biscuits.

A blur of red caught his eye outside as he sat down with the steaming mug cradled in his hands. He rocked back on his chair legs to watch the girl outside as she struggled to find something in the bottom of the huge bag she was balancing on her knee. Why did girls always carry such huge handbags? Her hair whipped around her cheeks, heavy red waves that irritated her enough to make her brush them roughly away from her mouth. She found what she was searching for, straightened up and disappeared around the back of the weird chapel place next door.

Interesting. He added 'attractive redhead working next door', to the growing file of positive aspects to his new venture. He grinned as the caffeine seeped steadily into his system. Phil the Drill was wrong. Today was going to be a good day. He could feel it in his bones.

CHAPTER TWO

Crap, crap and triple crap. Gabriel Ryan was divine. 'Are you selling lucky heather?'

Marla knew she sounded surly, but come on. Really?

What else could he expect when he turned up on her doorstep uninvited, all rumpled with come-to-bed eyes? The man might hold the future of her business in the palm of his hand, but right at that very moment the only question on Marla's mind was how on earth the sexiest man on the planet could *possibly* be an undertaker.

His gypsy-black hair would probably be given to curls if he let it grow, but as it was it had just reached that optimum run-your-fingers-through sexy length without veering too far into goth territory. Truth be told, there *was* something ever so slightly grungy about him. But cool, louche, stubbly grunge, rather than the patchouli-soaked rocker-in-need-of-a-bath kind.

He was smokin' hot, and Marla didn't have a fire extinguisher. Pity he was a funeral director. *Eeew*. Not to mention the fact that he was in danger of killing her business stone dead. The double reality check was enough to make his halo slip down to his throat, and Marla was only sad it wasn't tight enough to pose a full-on choking hazard. Gabriel Ryan might be easy on the eye, but as far as she was concerned, he was trouble in all the wrong ways.

His face cracked open into a big, easy smile as he lounged against the doorframe and held out a chipped, empty mug.

'Not heather, but any chance I could borrow a cup of sugar please?'

The 'cup of sugar' line again. He wasn't even original. Marla leaned ever-so-slightly forward and gazed into the empty, chipped mug for a long moment before raising her eyes back up to his.

'You must be Gabriel.'

He pushed his spare hand through his hair and assaulted her with that slow smile again.

Jeez, he had perfect teeth.

Marla was American.

Teeth mattered.

'Guilty as charged. But please, it's just Gabe.'

'Gabe.'

His name felt treacherously good on her lips. A shiver ran down her backbone as he held her gaze for a second longer than strictly necessary. Invisible to the naked eye, a gossamer spider web of attraction spun around them, and undetectable to the human ear, Mother Nature's wicked laugh tinkled off the chapel's stained-glass windows.

Marla swallowed hard. It was her move, but somehow it didn't feel safe to invite him over the threshold. He was like a vampire trying to glamour her into submission, and

15

right at that moment he was doing a pretty good job of it. She gave herself a mental slap and swung the door wide. 'Come on through.'

He stepped past her into the chapel, and as she closed the door she couldn't help but take a sly sniff of him.

Not a whiff of patchouli or dead bodies.

Phew.

In fact, he smelled really rather delicious, all lemony-spice shower gel and fresh coffee. Marla loved coffee. And lemons.

She led him into the small back kitchen and gestured for him to take a seat at the buttercup-yellow formica table. As she flicked the kettle on, she turned to him sceptically. 'Do you *really* need sugar?'

He grinned again. He needed to stop doing that. It was distracting.

'Not especially. But I could murder a coffee.'

Marla made no move to take his bashed-up mug from him, but instead took down two pretty duck-egg blue cups from the cupboard and heaped coffee into them. They needed to talk. It might as well be civilised, over coffee. And at least here she had the advantage of being on home turf.

'Sugar?' She held the jar up.

He shook his head and laughed. 'Never touch the stuff.'

Why oh why did he have to have a beautiful voice to match his beautiful face? His soft Irish lilt was full of gravel, as if the man had actually swallowed a bucket full of blarney stones. She placed the cups down on the table before dropping into the seat opposite him.

'I'm Marla.'

'Marla. That's unusual.'

Oh God. Her name sounded bone-meltingly good with his Irish lilt. He rolled the R in the middle, as if he were playing with it in his mouth, and deciding whether or not to let it escape.

He raised his cup in salute. 'To new neighbours.'

And there it was.

The perfect inroad into the most delicate of conversations. Marla sipped her coffee and eyed him over the rim, suddenly unsure how to begin now show time had arrived.

He lowered his cup and watched her steadily. 'So . . . a little bird told me you wanted to see me.'

Marla coughed at the description of Guinness Guts as a 'little bird', but at least he appeared to have passed on her message. It was no good; she couldn't put it off any longer.

'Look, this is awkward, so I'll just come right out and say it. I'm afraid you can't move in next door.'

She breathed out hard and registered the way his eyebrows inched upwards. He nodded and took a long, contemplative sip of his coffee. 'I know my line of business sometimes makes people a bit squeamish, but honestly, there's no need to worry. I'll make sure we don't cause you any bother.'

Did he really think that that was all there was to this? That she was simply being *squeamish*? Unfortunately for Marla, he chose that moment to smile at her again and temporarily robbed her of the ability to speak.

'Look. I promise you won't be suddenly seeing dead bodies all the time or anything. Scout's honour.'

He was trying to make light of it. The need to clarify the situation burned in Marla's gut until she finally regained power over her vocal cords.

'Gabe, I don't think you understand what I'm saying. *This*,' she spread her hands to encompass the building around them, '*this* is a wedding chapel. It's a *happy* place.'

Trouble seeped slowly into his dark eyes, but he held his tongue and let her speak.

'It's a place where people come to celebrate love, and life, and to enjoy the best day of their lives, you understand?'

He nodded, and for a second he looked as if he really might. Maybe there was hope, after all. Marla crossed her fingers underneath the table and waited.

'Okay.'

Okay? Even in her wildest dreams, Marla hadn't expected him to give in *that* easily.

'Okay. I can see that our businesses *are* very different, but I'm also pretty sure we can work something out. A little give and take, you know?'

Damn it. Either he hadn't listened, or he was being deliberately evasive.

'Give and take? Give and take?' She couldn't hold her voice steady as it helter-skeltered up several octaves. 'Gabe, people won't book to get married here if they see a dirty great hearse parked up in the street or a wailing family outside.'

His brows knitted together at her harsh words. Gabe, in turn, watched pink spots burn on Marla's cheeks.

'Look, that probably sounded heartless, and honestly, I'm *really* not, but I . . . I just won't let this happen.'

His expression was unreadable as he stared at her across the table. She went for broke.

'The bottom line, Gabe, is this. Your business will kill my business.'

18

Gabe steepled his fingers in front of him, and any trace of merriment died in his eyes when he looked up.

'Then we have ourselves a problem.'

Marla's stomach flipped over.

'Because here's the thing, Marla.'

His voice was soft enough for her to have to lean in close in order to hear him.

'People come to me to celebrate love too, it's just at the other end of life's spectrum. It might not be *happy*, or *frothy*, but my services are just as important as yours. More so, probably.'

Distaste dripped from his every word, and pure steel underscored his deceptively soft tone.

'You've made it very clear that I'm not your ideal neighbour, and trust me, I'll make every effort to minimise the impact I have on you.'

He shook his head with a look of derision and scraped his chair back. He crossed the tiny kitchen in a couple of paces, before turning in the doorway to deliver his parting shot.

'But make no mistake. Whether you like it or not, in a few weeks' time I absolutely *will* be opening for business next door.'

Emily slid down the bathroom wall, slumping to the floor, her back pressed against the radiator to ease the all-too-familiar ache. She hurled the unopened pregnancy test across the room. At least the tell-tale scarlet streak on the loo roll had saved her the bother of wasting eight pounds this month – not that she'd expected much else, given that she and Tom had barely seen each other, let alone made love.

What had started out as a crazy, exciting plan to make a baby had steadily turned into a monthly cycle of failure and heartache, that, month on month, was ripping the heart right out of their marriage.

Seventeen months, to be precise. Eighteen, including this one.

They hadn't expected to score a home run on their first month, of course not. Hoped maybe, but not expected. Nonetheless, Emily had passed that first month daydreaming of ways to tell Tom their happy news. Would she buy him a card? Spell out 'daddy' in alphabetti spaghetti? No, Tom hated tinned spaghetti. And anyway, he'd want them to do the test together, wouldn't he?

In the end, they'd perched side by side on the edge of the bath and passed the upside-down stick between them as if it might singe the skin off their fingers.

'You look. No, you! Please, you do it, I can't . . .'

In their defence, they had every reason to feel hopeful. Hugh Hefner himself would have been impressed with the way they'd dedicated themselves to their task over the month, but all they wound up with for their trouble was numb bums from the old ceramic bath and a stubbornly empty window where there should have been a blue line. Month two followed pretty much the same pattern. Month three involved a little less sex and a decent bottle of Rioja to drown their sorrows. Month four . . . well, suffice to say it had been one long downhill slide from there to here, eighteen months later on the bathroom floor.

Emily was just glad Tom was away on business. *Again.* At least this way there was no one around to have to paint a brave face on for. She could quite easily spend the entire evening curled up against the radiator. In the end she cried herself to sleep, and only the lure of a very large glass of Shiraz held enough incentive to make her drag herself downstairs some time just before midnight.

Three hundred miles away, Tom dropped down onto the bullet-hard mattress in his drab Brussels hotel room and kicked off his shoes. It had been a long day of ball-ache meetings, and he was hot and hassled. He needed to relax.

Guilt gnawed through his gut as he glanced at his BlackBerry on the bedside table. His hand even hovered over it for a second before he bottled it and reached for the TV remote instead. Emily would've called if there was good news to report, and he just couldn't muster up a long-distance supportive shoulder. This trying-to-conceive business, or the TTC club, as it was chattily called on the many message boards Em had signed up to, wasn't at all like those rose-tinted rom-com movies she adored. Oh no. This was more like some fright night, bloodthirsty Halloween movie being shown on nightmarish monthly repeat, and Tom was sick to the back teeth of the lot of it. He'd had a bellyful of Emily's brave attempts to raise a smile for his benefit with grey tear tracks on her cheeks, and he could practically recite his own predictable 'maybe next month' speech in his sleep.

How in hell had it got this bad?

God knows he loved her, and before all of this baby crap he'd known exactly how to show her, too.

'Let's make a baby.'

He wished he'd never uttered those immortal bloody words as he'd cradled her in his arms in bed, still buried deep inside her, knowing he wanted nothing else for the rest of his life.

21

Since then, somewhere along the way, sex had become less about impulsive lust, and more of an insert tab A into slot B, and then hope like hell that something sticks. And now, to make things worse, if things could possibly *be* any worse, Emily had started to mutter about going to the bloody doctor to get tests.

He sighed hard and dragged his weekend bag closer.

A fresh wave of guilt washed over him as he shoved his hand underneath the carefully folded shirts, feeling for the dog-eared porn mag beneath the baseboard. He tried to block out the thought of what Emily would think of him for wasting precious semen.

But then, she wasn't in her fertile window anyway, so what did it matter?

The bleakness of being more familiar with his wife's menstrual cycle than he was with the football fixtures wasn't lost on him. He pushed the whole sorry mess to the back of his mind and unbuckled his belt. He flicked the magazine open to his favourite page. At least he could rely on Candy from Arizona not to take her temperature before spreading her legs.

CHAPTER THREE

Jonny clanged his fork against the side of his wine glass.

'Order, mon chers, order!'

He looked from one face to another as they gathered around Marla's kitchen table. It had been a little over a week since Gabriel Ryan had thundered into the village on his motorbike, and this was the first official meeting of the hastily cobbled-together committee to get him thrown out again just as fast.

Emily paused with her fork full of lasagne midway to her mouth, and Dora, the chapel's octogenarian cleaning lady, fiddled with her hearing aid until it whistled furiously. As the self-proclaimed campaign leader, Jonny shot her a mutinous look. Dora's husband, Ivan, smiled benignly at his wife.

'You hum it, I'll play it, dear,' he muttered, and helped himself to a third glass of Merlot.

'So,' Jonny said with a theatrical flourish. He nodded pointedly at Ruth, village florist and gossip central, to start taking notes in the pad he'd thrust into her hands when she sat down. Taking a great slug of wine, she darted her eyes around the table, then picked up her pen and clicked the end a few times in a show of efficiency.

Satisfied that his every word would be recorded for posterity, Jonny cleared his throat and planted his hands on his snake hips.

'Right, so. We all know why we're here. The fucking Munsters are trying to set up shop next door to the chapel, and it's our job to get shot of them. Like, pronto.'

He glanced around at the suddenly hushed group, who looked slightly shell-shocked by his rousing opening gambit.

Ruth raised a hesitant hand.

'Er, Jonny? Do I have to write the "fucking" bit down?'

'Christ almighty, Ruth!' he exploded. 'Just get the general gist down, this isn't CSI fucking Shropshire!'

'Why is he reciting the alphabet?' shouted Dora, her hearing aid now whacked up to full.

'He isn't, Dora. It's a cop show,' Emily supplied.

'Oh. Oooh, you wouldn't half make a lovely Bergerac, Jonny.'

'Drove a Jaguar, you know.' Ivan nodded sagely.

'"Bergerac"?' Jonny seethed, askance. 'Fucking "Bergerac"? Pure Captain Jack Harkness or no one, thank you very much Dora.' If he could have donned a military overcoat and heavy boots to ram his point home, he would have.

'Captain Hairnet? Never heard of him,' Dora muttered, a gleam in her eye as she ran her hand over her freshly set hair.

'What did he drive, Jonny?' Ivan said, squinting at the

24

wine bottle to see if there was any left. 'Might jog my memory.'

'A goddamn bloody space ship!' Jonny all but shouted, sending Dora's hand straight to her ear to adjust her hearing aid again.

Ivan nodded. 'I know who you mean, now.' He leaned across to stage whisper to Dora. 'The one with the big ears, darling.'

Dora's face cleared into a smile that displayed her neat rows of false teeth to perfection. She looked at Jonny and tapped the side of her nose. 'Beam me up, Scotty.'

The mutinous expression on Jonny's face as he felt for his cigarettes made Marla drop her head into her hands, and Bluey flop his massive head onto her knees under the table in silent solidarity. This was hopeless. Gabriel Ryan was going to open up his funeral parlour regardless, and there was precious little they, or anyone else, could do to stop him.

'What we need is a plan of attack,' Jonny said, recovering himself and flapping a hand at Ruth to put her wine glass back on the table.

'Write that down. I'm thinking we should start with a petition. After all, lots of local businesses around here benefit from the chapel. Look at you, for instance, Ruth. You've never been so busy.'

Ruth looked up from her pad with a vigorous nod.

'It's true, Marla. The chapel's brought in so much new work. I mean, I do almost as many weddings these days as I do, er . . . funerals . . .' She tailed off, having inadvertently highlighted the fact that she could only benefit from Gabe's arrival. She was dying to meet the man himself. The villagers had talked him up into a cross between Heathcliff and the devil incarnate, and if that beast of a motorbike she'd seen parked outside his place was anything to go by then they might not be too wide of the mark. Thoroughly overexcited, she knocked back the rest of her wine.

'We could follow it up with a public meeting in the chapel,' Emily suggested.

She tucked a stray strand of her neat, jet-black bob behind her ear and glanced up the table towards Marla. She desperately wanted to help, not just because Marla was her closest friend, but because the chapel was her lifeline. The idea of losing it horrified her. Tom was away so much that she'd be unbearably lonely without work, and truth be told, it was becoming her bolt-hole even when Tom *was* at home.

A fact that she wasn't quite ready to dwell on.

'Thank. You. Emily,' Jonny said, banging his fist down on the table between each word in gratitude for a rational suggestion. 'Stellar idea.'

Marla's grateful smile didn't quite reach her eyes. The locals could be a fickle bunch. It had taken them a good year to accept the chapel into their midst, especially since the majority of weddings they held were not for local couples. The chapel's kitsch appeal and Jonny's colourful style as a celebrant ensured that it attracted more than its fair share of the weird and wonderful, usually rolling into town with a wedding party of even more weird and wonderful guests. It was never dull, and Marla loved it.

She gave herself a stern telling off for being so defeatist and vowed to try harder.

Besides, Jonny was right. Local businesses *did* benefit.

The chapel had given the local tourist trade a massive shot in the arm, but would it be enough for them to actively come out and support her now?

Ivan raised his hand.

'Think you should know, old boy. That Irish chappie has asked my Dora to clean a couple of times a week. Seems a decent sort, actually. Ate Dora's shortbread, and it's bloody awful.'

He nodded knowingly around at the others, clearly not feeling a jot of disloyalty towards Marla, nor to his wife for the slight to her cooking skills.

Jonny shot daggers at Dora.

'Well, I hope you've told him to stick his job where the sun doesn't shine.'

'She starts Monday week,' Ivan supplied merrily as he drained his glass in one gulp.

'I don't friggin' believe this!' Jonny howled. 'Is there *anyone* here who isn't planning to jump ship?' An uncomfortable silence settled over the table. Ivan scrubbed a hand over his tufty grey hair and twiddled with his bow tie.

'He's asked me to look after his garden. Bit of maintenance, like. Told him I might as well, seeing as I do yours and it's only next door.'

Marla, who'd stayed quiet throughout the meeting, finally spoke up.

'Look guys, it's okay, really.' She turned to Ruth. 'Ruth, of *course* you should do their flowers.'

Ruth smiled gratefully and wrote it down in case anyone forgot Marla had said it.

'Ivan, Dora, it's absolutely *fine* about the cleaning, and the gardening. If you don't do it, someone else will.'

'We can be your moles,' Dora offered, with a gleam in her eye.

'Hallelujah. We're saved,' Jonny muttered sourly.

Marla admonished him with a gentle frown and patted the older woman's hand.

'Hey, we've made an encouraging start, haven't we?'

She stood up and started to gather the plates. 'A petition and a public meeting seems like a good way to get the ball rolling.' She was tired suddenly and ready to have her home back to herself. 'Let's call it a night, okay?'

Emily carried the plates through as everyone else pulled on their coats and shuffled out in varying states of sobriety. Marla loitered on the doorstep whilst Bluey went for his constitutional evening stroll around the tiny garden. He was far too big a dog for Marla's cottage, but he was inherently lazy and content to be the unlikely master of his mini-manor. When she came back into the kitchen a few minutes later, Marla found Emily bent double, rooting through the freezer. She emerged with a triumphant smile and a tub of Ben & Jerry's.

'Still hungry?' Marla asked.

'Not really, but isn't ice-cream essential for American girly chats around the kitchen table?'

'You've watched too many re-runs of *The Golden Girls*,' Marla laughed as she placed a bottle of wine next to the ice-cream on the table. Emily's eyes moved from the wine to the ice-cream with a heavy sigh.

'This is my staple dinner when Tom's away.'

Marla found spoons and glasses and sat down. 'Which seems to be quite a lot these days?' She twisted the lid off the chilly Pinot Grigio.

'You noticed.'

Marla nodded and filled their glasses.

'He's just busy with work. You know how it is.'

Emily peeled off the ice-cream lid and sighed.

'Who am I kidding? He's avoiding me, Marla.'

'Surely not. Why would he do that?'

'Because we're trying to have a baby.'

Marla nodded, her face a study of sympathy. She'd been aware of Emily and Tom's decision to add to their family from fleeting conversations and casual remarks, but looking at her friend's miserable expression it was obvious she'd played it down, or else played it close to her chest. 'Well . . . I'm no expert, but I'm pretty sure that avoiding you isn't going to help make *that* happen.'

Emily's shoulders slumped. 'That's the problem. It *isn't* happening.'

Oh. Marla hated to see her friend so low, and cast around for something encouraging to say. 'They say it can take a while to catch, Em.'

'Yeah, I know. But it's been over eighteen months now.' Emily started poking her spoon gloomily into the ice-cream.

Marla couldn't believe her friend had kept this secret so long. 'Have you seen the doctor?' she asked.

Emily shook her head with a cynical laugh. 'Why do we, as women, know that it's okay to ask for help, but men see it as an insult to their manhood? Well, Tom does, in any case.'

Marla reached over and squeezed Emily's hand. 'Give him time, Em. He loves you. He'll come around.'

'You reckon? Think, Marla. When was the last time you even laid eyes on Tom?'

Marla cast her mind back. Actually, she couldn't remember. Tom used to visit the chapel almost daily, but now she came to think about it she hadn't seen him more than a handful of times in recent months.

'Exactly.'

'I never realised, Em. What are you going to do?'

Emily looked helpless. 'I've booked us in to start tests – or for Tom to give a sample, at least. I haven't dared bring it up again since I told him, because it always ends up in a row.'

'I'm sorry, honey,' Marla soothed. 'Bloody men. Mars must be a boring place with all of that testosterone swilling around making civilised conversation impossible.'

Emily rolled her eyes. 'I bet they play a lot of darts and live on beer and pizza.'

'Give me Venus anytime,' Marla said. 'Wine and ice-cream is much more fun.'

Emily clinked her glass against Marla's. 'I'll drink to that,' she agreed, pushing the ice-cream tub across the table. 'So. Marla.'

Something about the sudden speculative gleam in Emily's eyes put Marla on her guard. 'Umm?'

'Have you never met *the one*?' Emily pressed.

'The one?' Marla fidgeted in her chair, uncomfortable with the turn the conversation was taking. 'You're such a hopeless romantic, Em.'

'Is that a yes?'

Marla shrugged. 'I'm just not looking for Mr Right.'

'Everyone is, Marla.'

Marla sighed. 'Not me. I've no desire to tie myself down to some man, only to see it all go wrong a few years later and end up as another divorce statistic. No thanks.'

She winced as a shadow passed over Emily's face.

'Oh God, Em, I'm sorry. I didn't mean you, obviously.' She squeezed her friend's hand. 'It's just a personal thing, that's all. I've had more step-parents over the years than I have fingers to count them on. Us Jacobs just aren't cut out for all of that *forever and ever, amen* stuff.'

Emily sighed. 'I don't think divorce is a genetic thing, honey,' she said. 'You can't go through life avoiding commitment on the off chance that you'll get your heart broken.'

'I'm not saying I'm off men altogether,' Marla said, scraping a curl of ice-cream onto her spoon. 'I just don't see the point to all the forever and ever drama.'

'I'd keep that line out of the chapel's press-pack if I were you,' Emily laughed.

Marla lifted her shoulder with a smile, well aware that her own values flew in the face of her livelihood.

'Well, that's a shame, really,' Emily wheedled. 'Because if you *were* in the market for romance, I think I've caught our new neighbour making eyes over the coffins at you.'

Marla brandished her spoon across the table. 'Enough, Em.'

'But I have!' Emily laughed. 'Come on, admit it . . . he's easy on the eye, isn't he?'

Marla studied her fingernails. 'I haven't noticed.'

'Rubbish! Let's pretend for a second that he isn't an undertaker, and he isn't your arch enemy . . .' Emily's eyes danced. 'You would, wouldn't you?'

Marla looked her friend straight in the eye. 'Honestly? No. No, I wouldn't.'

And she meant it. The way her body reacted whenever

31

Gabriel Ryan was around frightened the living daylights out of her. Even without all of the barriers Emily had listed, Marla's biggest problem with Gabe was that he stole away her powers of self-control without even trying, and they were just about all she had to hold on to.

Half an hour later, Marla sloshed a measure of brandy into a tumbler and threw one last log on the fire. She'd finally managed to prise Emily away from the ice-cream and into a taxi, and had spent the last twenty minutes clearing and straightening the kitchen until the cottage was back to peaceful perfection again. Bluey loped in, well-fed and content to flop down onto the sofa he more than filled, and Marla curled herself into the armchair beside him. Companionable bookends, as always. This was all she wanted, all she needed. She reached out and stroked his gentle face as she sipped the nightcap in an attempt to settle her stomach. It seemed to be constantly jumbled up with nerves these days. She hadn't had a decent night's sleep since Gabriel Ryan had roared into the village. It had taken three years of hard work to carve out her place here in this community, and the sense of safety and peace it afforded her was precious beyond measure.

Gabriel. Even his name was a misnomer.

The man was no angel, that much was for sure. Hell's angel, more like, with that filthy great motorbike and James Dean sex appeal. Strange really, for an undertaker. But then, as a marriage-phobic wedding coordinator, who was she to judge?

Her eyes wandered over the small collection of family photographs on the fireplace.

Her sex therapist mother, birdlike in a flower garland and jewel-bright sarong, on holiday somewhere with Robert, one of Marla's varied collection of stepfathers. He'd been by far the best of the bunch, and for a while back there Marla had almost believed that her mother had finally settled. She'd been wrong of course, but by then Marla loved the gentle-giant English doctor she'd come to look on as almost as much of a father as her own dad. She'd felt the loss of him from her life like a bruise on her heart when her mother had declared herself unable to tolerate another English winter and decamped back to the States, and stayed in touch as much as their schedules allowed. But Marla had let contact slide when it became obvious that he seemed unable to stop himself from asking for news of Cecilia, even when hearing of her mother's newest beau was clearly painful.

A picture of her father stood alone in the next frame alongside it. Another serial aisle-walker, she'd long since lost track of his numerous wives and, no doubt, offspring, scattered across the States. He'd been a benevolent figure in her childhood, and an absent one in her adulthood. It wasn't that Marla wasn't fond of him, more that she knew very little of him besides his predilection for upgrading his wife for a younger model every few years.

Between them, they'd painted a very clear picture to Marla on love and romance.

Don't pin your hopes and dreams on one person, because soon enough you'll want to pin them on someone else. Or worse, they'll pin their hopes and dreams onto someone else and leave you behind to ask around for crumbs of news of them from mutual acquaintances.

Her mother would no doubt have a field day if she ever got to analyse the jarring juxtaposition between her daughter's personal and professional opinion on the sanctity of marriage. A deep, hidden yearning for a husband would no doubt be her dramatic conclusion, and she couldn't have been more wrong. For Marla, it was simple. She was playing to her strengths. Her American roots, her organisational skills, her ability to identify a niche market. It could have been any number of things; it just so happened to be weddings.

Bluey yawned, a clear signal that it was time for bed, and Marla fussed his ears as she stood up. He was all the male she needed.

'Just you and me, big guy. Just you and me.'

'A petition? Against a funeral parlour? That's bloody hilarious, mate.'

Dan laughed as he knocked back the last of his pint and raised his glass towards the landlord for a refill.

Gabe didn't laugh with him. It wasn't that he was worried that the petition might actually work. In fact, he was pretty certain that it would come to nothing, given that as far as he could see, it was based on nothing in the first place. But the fact that it existed at all was drawing unnecessary eyes his way, and that was the last thing he needed. He'd hoped to set up shop quietly, to slide into place in the community as if he'd always been there. His business wasn't about trumpet fanfares, or razzamatazz launches with crazy Elvis impersonators; it was understated and unobtrusive, just there ready and waiting for those who needed him.

'It's a pain in the arse, man. People are shoving their

34

noses against the window to get a look at the long-haired Irish bloke who's blown trouble into town.'

Dan raised his glass and his eyebrows.

'Don't forget the dirty great fuck-off, noise-polluting bike.'

He smirked as he tossed a peanut in the air and caught it in his open mouth with a snap. Gabe grinned despite his frustration. Every morning over the last week he'd watched Marla strut past the funeral parlour window with too many folders in her arms, her wild curls blowing around her beautiful, determined face. And each time she passed, she'd thrown a customary look of disgust at his motorbike.

'Have you met Marla, the girl from the wedding chapel?'

He balanced a beer mat on the rim of the table and flicked it upwards, then caught it mid-air in a show of nonchalance.

Dan wolf-whistled under his breath.

'Redhead, great legs? Not to speak to, but I've seen her around all right. I take it you've already had the pleasure?'

Something about the appreciative gleam in Dan's eyes rankled Gabe. His friend's lothario ways usually amused him, but normal rules somehow didn't apply when it came to Marla Jacobs.

'Yeah, we met last week.'

'And?'

'Oh you know. The usual. She told me to leave the village and never darken her door again. That sort of thing.'

Dan laughed.

'Doctor Death strikes again. You need a different job, mate.'

Gabe sighed. His difficulty lay in that, actually, he *could* kind of see Marla's point. The fact was he hadn't given any thought to the impact he might have on his new neighbours. Well, nothing beyond being mildly amused by the ironic symmetry, anyway.

Not that he'd ever expected anyone to put out the bunting and wave the welcome flags. He was more than used to the adverse reaction his profession drew from people. He'd learned many years ago that it was just about the biggest passion killer of them all to tell a girl you spend your days caretaking dead bodies.

But Marla was in a class of her own. She was being plain unreasonable.

Surely she hadn't thought she could issue him with his marching orders and expect him to roll over and limp out of town with his tail between his legs?

The truth was, the chapel's unique perspective aside, this community needed him. There wasn't a funeral director for more than twenty-five miles, and that was plain unacceptable. The only surety in life was that one day everyone was going to die, and that alone meant that every family in this village would be better off for him being here.

And *please*. A Las Vegas-style wedding chapel in Shropshire? It was a novelty, certainly, but it was hardly a necessity, was it? Who *really* used it anyway? From what he'd seen so far, he was pretty sure it wasn't the locals.

'Maybe she'd listen to your altogether-more-charming best friend instead. You know how persuasive I can be when I put my mind to it.'

Dan's cocky grin and conspiratorial wink pushed all the wrong buttons. Unwanted memories strayed into Gabe's head; countless girls wandering half-naked out of Dan's bedroom on Sunday mornings when they'd shared a flat in London.

'Stay away from her. I'll sort this out myself, okay?'

Dan laughed, a knowing look in his eyes. He shrugged and opened a second bag of peanuts. 'Suit yourself, sunshine.'

The silence between them lengthened.

'So . . . watcha gonna do about it then?'

'No clue.'

'Want me to go and ask her out for you?' Dan grinned. 'My mate fancies you . . .'

Gabe rolled his eyes. 'Fuck off.'

Dan laughed but didn't push the point. He knew Gabe better than most people, and sensed something different about his friend's demeanour. He made a mental note to keep a close eye on him where the redhead from the chapel was concerned.

Gabe shrugged and picked up their glasses. 'Same again?'

He leaned against the bar and waited as the landlord placed a shot in front of a guy who looked as if he had the weight of the world on his shoulders. Gabe didn't mind the delay. He was still trying to work out the answer to Dan's question.

On a purely practical level, the last thing he wanted was a dispute with his neighbours. God knew he needed the goodwill of the community to help his fledgling business off the ground.

But there was a lot more to this than practicalities.

There was a far more pressing reason for Gabe to pour oil onto the troubled waters between him and Marla Jacobs.

Because the simple, inescapable truth was that from the moment Marla Jacobs had opened the chapel doors and deliberately insulted him, Gabe had known with utter certainty that he wanted to spend the rest of his life with her.

It was just a shame that she couldn't stand the sight of him.

A few feet away from Gabe, Tom was leaning against the bar, his BlackBerry in one hand, a glass tumbler in the other. He wasn't usually given to drinking after work, but then today wasn't the usual kind of day. He looked from the flashing message icon on his mobile to the whisky, and after a moment's pause he tipped the twelve-year-old malt down his throat. Fortified, he clicked the message open with a grimace.

Hey u!
Don't forget we're due at docs at 6.15. Don't be late, receptionist is a jobsworth and don't want to miss appt!
Luv Em xx

Yeah, he knew what a jobsworth the receptionist was. He also knew what a drama-queen Emily could be, and that she didn't trust him to remember their appointment without reminding him at least ten times. He was starting to feel more and more backed into a corner with every passing day, and he didn't like it one bit.

He nodded at the landlord for another whisky.

Emily sat in the darkening lounge and listened for long seconds to Tom fumbling to get his key in the lock. His inaccuracy and muttered curses spoke volumes of his lack of sobriety. *So that was where he'd been.* Drowning his sorrows or Dutch courage, she wasn't sure which and she was beyond the point of caring.

She watched his face as he came into the room on unsteady legs, his hand on the wall for a second as he reached out and flicked the lamp on. Being bathed in light did little to enhance his cause. His dishevelled hair looked as if he'd spent the last half an hour scrubbing his hands through it and his loosened tie was off centre.

'Emily,' he smiled and opened his eyes wide in the style of a drunk person attempting to appear sober. 'I'm late,' he muttered. 'Fucking boss called a meeting.'

His words rolled together as he dropped on the sofa opposite her.

'In the pub?' she asked, her heart beating too hard in her chest. She needed him to talk to her. To really talk, like they used to, talk like lovers rather than strangers on a train platform.

'I haven't been to the pub,' Tom tried.

'You reek of whisky, Tom.'

He shook his head. 'Just to toast the deal. Had to do it. Fucking boss.'

'So you said.' Emily forced her voice to stay calm. 'And did your fucking awful boss make you have another one? And then another? Because you've had so much you can barely stand up.'

Tom looked affronted, the kind of indignant that only a skinful of alcohol can induce.

'Or maybe, just maybe it was your fucking awful wife that made you turn to whisky, Tom.'

He shook his head and scrubbed his hands in his hair.

'I don't want to piss in a fucking bottle,' he mumbled. 'And I don't want to crack one off into a paper cup with . . . seventies porn.'

Emily stared at him. He sounded like a teenager who didn't want to do his homework, and she resented being cast as the nagging mother. 'So it was the quality of the pornography that bothered you? Well, you should have said, Tom, I'd have picked you up a copy of *Playboy* from Bob & Aud's.'

Tom half laughed, most probably because Bob & Aud's local shop was just about the most conspicuous place possible to buy top-shelf mags.

'Don't laugh at me, Tom. Don't you dare laugh at me for wanting your baby.'

The exaggerated smile fell from his face, to be replaced by something perilously close to pity. He'd gone from teenager to pantomime dame within seconds. Fury burned bright in Emily's heart, because it was the only thing she had besides tears.

'Keep your pity, Tom. Save it up along with your precious semen for someone who's interested, because as of right now, that person isn't me!'

He reached out for her and missed as she stood from the chair and stalked from the room, and she heard him curse as he slipped from the sofa to the floor. Served him right. She'd never felt less loved or understood by the man she'd married, and it hurt even more than not being able to conceive his child.

The following afternoon, Emily stepped out into the sunshine and locked the chapel doors. She lifted a hand to shield her eyes and squinted towards the funeral parlour. Going by the amount of banging she could hear, there was still someone at work over there. Maybe she could try and speak with Gabe one to one, plead Marla's case whilst she was safely away at that tricky meeting with the local bakery. They had a *Star Trek* wedding in a few weeks' time and the bride had her heart set on a four-foot-wide Starship Enterprise cake.

The front door of the funeral parlour was locked, so Emily made her way around the back and clicked open the gate. She stopped short at the sight of a huge, vintage black hearse with its bonnet popped and a pair of navy overall-clad legs poking out from beneath it.

'Hello . . .' she called out hesitantly, bending down a little to make sure Gabe heard her.

'Just a sec, darlin',' a deep voice rumbled up, and a moment or two later the owner rolled smoothly out from beneath the jacked-up chassis. Emily looked away quickly. His overalls were un-popped right down the front, affording her a prime view of his conker-brown chest and a six-pack that would make Jonny whimper.

It wasn't Gabe. This guy had none of Gabe's brooding Heathcliff qualities, but he had his own charms. He made Emily think of sunshine and freedom and surfers with lips that tasted of sea salt. He jumped up when he saw her and wiped his oily hands on the front of his overalls.

'I was looking for Gabe?'

He shook his head and shrugged his arms out of the sleeves of his overalls, turning slightly to reach for a T-shirt that hung on the car aerial. Emily swallowed as she glimpsed hard muscles and a large tattoo inked across the smooth skin of his back before the peach-soft pale blue cotton slipped over his head. It clung to him like a second skin.

He shoved the overalls off, and Emily thanked her lucky stars that he did at least have jeans on, although she couldn't help but notice how the faded, frayed material did precious little to disguise his attributes. He balled up his work gear and chucked it aside, then stuck out his hand with a wide grin.

'Nah, sorry, sweetheart. The main man isn't around. I'm Dan. Will I do?'

She took his big brown hand and shook it.

'I'm Emily, from the chapel.'

'Well hello, Emily from the chapel.'

Dan's blue eyes danced when he smiled again.

He leaned inside the kitchen and hooked a couple of bottles out of the fridge.

'Fancy a beer?'

If it had been a different day, and if Dan had been slightly less gorgeous and accommodating, Emily definitely would have said no.

But it wasn't a different day. It was the day after Tom had failed to turn up for their doctor's appointment. The day after they'd had the mother of all rows. The day after Tom had spent the night on the sofa, and she'd barely slept at all.

As it was, she didn't argue when Dan knocked the bottle tops off with a brick and handed her one, and she found herself sitting down alongside him on the back step to bask in the optimistic warmth of the spring afternoon sunshine.

'So, Emily from the chapel. What do you want with our Gabriel?'

She took a good slug of beer to embolden herself. 'To appeal to his better nature, I guess?'

Dan laughed. 'He'll be sorry he missed that. Want to try to appeal to mine instead?'

Emily eyed him. The beer made her brave. 'Depends. Have you got any sway around here? You look like the lackey to me.'

'Ouch.' He clutched at his heart. 'I'll have you know that I'm Gabe's wing man.'

He took a long drink, and Emily noticed a bead of sweat running down his neck as he swallowed.

'Goose to his Maverick.' Dan paused. 'Actually, no. He's Goose. I'm way cooler.'

'Okay then, Top Gun. Seeing as you two are so close, can you please persuade him to take his dead bodies some-place else?'

'Aaah.' Dan shook his head regretfully. 'No can do, pretty lady. See, he's dead set on this place.'

He laughed at his own wit.

'Dead set . . . Get it?'

'It's not funny.' Emily reproached him with a frown. 'I love my job at the chapel.'

Dan hitched himself up on the doorframe and grabbed a couple more beers, then dropped back down and stretched his long legs out in front of him again.

'So, Emily from the chapel . . . I'm guessing from that flashy sparkler on your finger that you're married.'

He nodded towards the diamond solitaire that Tom had maxed out his Visa card for as a birthday surprise six years ago. Theirs had been the most romantic of whirlwind romances, star-crossed lovers from the moment they'd both reached for the last coronation chicken sandwich in Marks & Spencer. 'No one else ever likes them,' she'd murmured, and he'd floored her with his wide smile and merry eyes. He left without his lunch, but with the telephone number of the girl of his dreams in his pocket.

It felt like a lifetime ago right at that moment, like they were two completely different people.

Emily stroked the diamond with the tip of her finger and nodded.

'Five years this summer.'

'Wow. You must have been a child bride.' Dan didn't attempt to hide the cheeky admiration from his eyes.

'Flatterer.' Emily flushed. It had been a long time since Tom had looked at her that way. She knew she really ought to leave, but accepted the fresh beer Dan held out instead.

'And you?' She glanced at his ring-free hands. 'No wife to declare?'

'Nope. Why? You fancy doing a Bonnie and Clyde and running away with me in that thing?'

He grinned and jerked his head towards the dusty hearse snoozing in the sunshine.

If only life were that simple, Emily thought, suddenly overwhelmed with the desire to jump in the hearse and run away from her problems. From Beckleberry. *From Tom*. A wave of desolation swept over her, bringing a sudden lump to her throat and tears to her eyes. When Dan slid closer and eased a strong, warm arm around her shoulders, it felt way too good to shrug off. It had been so long since Tom had comforted her and *really* meant it.

'God, I'm sorry,' Emily gulped, embarrassed by the tears welling up in her eyes. 'Ignore me. I'm being a total idiot.'

Dan gave her shoulders a gentle squeeze. 'Hey, it's cool. You gave me a bona fide reason to put my arm around you without risking a slap on the face.'

Emily was grateful that he chose to make light of things rather than pry.

'You hit a bit of a nerve, that's all. I'm okay, really.' She swiped at her cheeks with the back of her hand and stood up. 'I need to go. Thanks for . . . for this.'

She thrust her still-full bottle into his hands and backed away towards the gate. Dan set the beers down on the step and leaned against the doorframe.

'I'll tell Gabe you came by.'

Emily's guilty heart banged in her chest as she nodded and fled.

CHAPTER FOUR

'Standing room only, you said,' Marla hissed out of the side of her mouth at Jonny as he straightened the wine glasses on the table by the entrance for the third time. She glanced around at the sparse gathering in the chapel. Barely thirty people, even though Jonny had used the promise of free wine as a shameless lure on the flyers for the public meeting and had stocked up on cheap chardonnay in the expectation of a full house.

'Sshhh, chillax, flower. There's time yet. It's still early.'

Jonny slapped Emily's hand away as she sidled over and reached for a glass of wine.

'Did you see the hot reporter from *The Herald* over there?' she stage-whispered with an exaggerated tilt of her head towards a guy standing alone on the far side of the chapel. His starched shirt and tie set him apart from everyone else in the room, as did the camera slung nonchalantly around his neck.

Jonny grinned. 'Did I ever, sweet cheeks! He can take my

close-up, anytime.' He flexed his muscles and turned his chin so Emily could admire his best side.

'Put your guns away, Rambo. I think he has his eye on our Marla,' Emily said, laughing at Jonny's disappointed pout.

Marla shook her head at the pair of them, but shot a glance over at the reporter anyway. He caught her eye and smiled, and she looked away quickly. She was way too nervous to flirt. They all turned as the heavy door inched open, and slumped again as Dora and Ivan shuffled in, arm in arm.

'Evening all.' Ivan nodded jovially around before making a beeline for the drinks table.

'I'm only here for the wine, dear,' he confided loudly to Emily behind his hand. 'Are there sandwiches?'

Dora, resplendent in her Sunday-best coat and her sparkly brooch, frowned and batted him with her handbag. 'You said you were too full to eat much of my cabbage and sausage hotpot.'

Ivan pulled an exaggerated look of horror at Emily then smiled beatifically at his wife and patted her hand. 'You must have misheard me, my love. It was a triumph as always.'

Emily shook her head affectionately at them. She'd never known her own grandparents, but in her head Dora and Ivan were the perfect replacements. They were quite the double act, as in sync as any comedy duo, and yet every now and then she caught the odd look and private smile between them that melted her heart. She knew from snippets that Dora had revealed over the years that Ivan had been the love of her life from the very first day she'd met him as a starry-eyed teenager. Behind their banter and their light-hearted jokes lay solid gold love; theirs was a marriage to aspire to.

Emily sighed and glanced at her watch. Tom had promised

to try and make it, but given the shaky state of their relationship she'd have been more surprised by his presence than his
absence.

Half an hour later it was apparent that no one else was
going to turn up. The only people to come through the
door since Dora and Ivan had been Kevin, the village
plumber and occasional Elvis impersonator at the chapel,
and Ruth the florist, who needed to stay abreast of the
village gossip in order to keep her customers happy and
spending their pennies.

Jonny made his way up to the lectern with a resigned
look on his suntanned face.

'Right, then. Let's make a start, shall we?'

'Hang on! I think there's someone coming!' Ruth called
out, and an expectant hush fell over the small crowd as
they stared at the doors with bated breath.

It swung open, and a dramatic gasp rippled around the
room as Gabe and Dan strode in.

Marla shot to her feet in panic as Jonny's eyes popped
out on stalks. He had yet to meet either of the men in the
flesh, and his tongue was practically hanging out.

Gabe nodded in greeting towards Marla. 'Don't mind us.
We'll just sit at the back.'

He relaxed into a seat in the back row and smiled genially
around at everyone, as if he'd just entered his local pub
rather than a meeting held with the sole intention of running
him out of town.

'Yeah. And heckle loudly,' Dan muttered as he slid into
the seat next to Gabe with a mutinous expression on his
face. He couldn't stand the way Gabe was being treated by
the villagers, and he fully intended on letting the

small-minded nimbys have it with both barrels at some point this evening.

At the front of the chapel, Marla alerted Jonny in hushed tones to the fact that the two sex-gods on the back row were in fact the opposition party, crushing his hopes of dragging them into the vestry later on to drink the crate of left-over chardonnay.

Marla took her seat and nodded in encouragement as Jonny moved to the lectern and cleared his throat, though she privately felt this was almost certainly a wasted evening that could have been better spent treating Emily to dinner at the pub.

'Right then . . .' Jonny held up his hands to shut down the low-level chatter around the room, then wiped them on his thighs as if they were sweaty. 'We're here tonight to discuss the effect that the proposed funeral home next door will have on our local community.'

Marla's toes curled and her eyes hit the floor. Gabe infuriated the hell out of her. Why on earth had he come here tonight? She wished with all of her heart that he'd stayed away, because his presence in the room changed everything. Even Jonny had been rendered polite by uncharacteristic nerves. Gabe raised his hand.

'Just for the sake of clarity, I should say at this point that it's *approved*, not proposed.'

Dan snickered next to him, but fell silent again as Emily turned around and caught his eye. Ruth the florist, who'd once again been press-ganged into the role of reluctant minute taker, struck out 'proposed' and wrote 'approved' above it in dark letters instead.

Jonny's lip curled at Gabe's direct attempt to undermine

him. Marla saw his confidence click back into place as he threw his chin up and rolled his broad shoulders. She held her breath for the onslaught.

'Ladies and gentlemen, you all know why we're here.' Jonny planted his hands on his hips as his cat-like eyes flashed. 'If we don't do something sharpish to stop the Addams Family from opening up their frickin' freak show next door, then this village will be going to hell in a hand-cart. *Capisce*?'

He looked out at his wide-eyed audience. 'Brides and bodies are a bad combination, you hear me people? This stops now, before Lord Voldemort over there casts his dark mark above our village!' He thrust his arm skywards and looked towards the rafters, and every neck in the place craned back as if they fully expected him to have cast an actual spell with an invisible wand.

Gabe laughed out loud and threw his hands up in the air, whilst Dan's chair scraped loudly against the flagstones as he shot to his feet in temper. 'What the fuck is going on here, people? A witch hunt?'

Gabe stood and laid a hand on Dan's arm. 'Let the people speak, Dan. I want to hear what they have to say.'

Jonny faltered as they both sat down again. Such a blatant display of rampant testosterone was something he'd normally pay good money to see.

'I'll tell you what *they* have to say,' Jonny said, swishing his arm over the crowd to indicate their collusion in his speech. '*They* say that you have no place here. *They* say that they don't need you.'

'And do you agree with them?' Gabe said softly, his eyes fixed on Jonny. Marla glanced between the two men in the few silent seconds that followed and saw straight away what Gabriel Ryan was up to, and, judging by Jonny's pink cheeks, he'd succeeded. He was melting in front of her eyes.

'Because it strikes me that you're a respected man here in the community. Your opinion matters to these people,' Gabe went on, and Marla watched her campaign leader preen like a lion getting his mane stroked. *His ego, more like*. She cleared her throat and caught his eye with a deep frown.

'I most certainly do agree with them,' Jonny blustered, flapping his arm half-heartedly rather than swishing it this time. He licked his lips and pushed his hand through his hair. 'You, Gabriel, are a very, very, bad man . . .' He sounded as breathless as a heroine about to pass out. Marla groaned as someone at the back heckled 'get a room', and Jonny fanned himself with his speech, clearly at a loss for what to say next other than *'yes, let's get a room.'*

'Marla, would, er, you like to say something?' he croaked eventually, and stepped down from the lectern without waiting for her reply.

She shot him daggers as she walked past him. This hadn't been part of their carefully worked-out plan. He was supposed to be the front man of the operation. She was thrown even further off her stride when the reporter stood up and flashed his camera in her face.

'First of all, thank you everyone for coming tonight, we really do appreciate your support.'

She ignored Dan's loud snort, but even from the other end of the chapel she didn't miss the swift dig in the ribs that it earned him from Gabe.

'As you all know, the "proposed" funeral parlour,' she

paused to shoot Gabe a 'don't you dare interrupt me' look, 'creates a huge problem for us here at the chapel.'

Gabe lifted a warning brow but let her continue without interruption.

'If they are allowed to open, there is every likelihood that we will be put out of business within twelve months.'

She looked around at the people in the room, and was gratified to see the troubled expression that crossed their faces.

'We bring a considerable amount of business to this area. The florist is busier than ever, the B&Bs are full most weekends, and a new one has just opened its doors to meet the demand for rooms from our wedding guests.'

Marla glanced over at Helen and Robert Jones, the owners of the latest boutique B&B. She was encouraged by their nods of agreement.

'The tea shops are packed, the art gallery sells out, and the pubs and restaurants enjoy full houses. In short, ladies and gentlemen – as long as this chapel thrives, then the community does too. Just yesterday we lost out on a booking directly because of the funeral parlour's presence. The first of many, no doubt.'

A frisson of shock reverberated around the room and Gabe's head snapped up. Marla flinched with guilt. It wasn't a lie, exactly, but in truth, the bride-to-be had probably already decided that the chapel was way too kitsch for her sensible accountant fiancé. The funeral parlour next door had been the last on a long list of issues, and Marla strongly suspected she'd used it as a convenient excuse to make a quick getaway. She brushed off any lingering guilt and threw back her shoulders to deliver her killer punchline:

'I'm not here tonight to beg for favours. I'm here to spell out the hard facts. If we go under, then I'm sorry to say that the rest of the village will go down with us.'

She let her eyes travel slowly over the faces of her friends and acquaintances in the room, until finally, she settled on Gabe. She was glad to see that she'd managed to wipe that smile off his face.

She'd served and, even if she said so herself, she'd very nearly aced it.

Fifteen: love.

The atmosphere in the room had changed as she spoke. Brows had furrowed, and accusatory eyes had turned towards Gabe. He got to his feet with a sigh, and laid a restraining hand on Dan's shoulder as he went to stand too.

'May I speak now, please?'

He looked only at Marla. To refuse would be to play into his hands, so with the tiniest of shrugs she moved aside to offer him the floor.

Every eye in the place was on him as he made his way along the aisle. When he reached the front he stood silently for a couple of seconds, scrubbing a slow hand over his stubble while he searched for the right words.

'Thank you.' Again, his eyes lingered on Marla, who looked down and studied her burnt-orange shoes as if she'd never seen them before, to avoid holding his gaze.

'Most of you know who I am, but for those who don't, I'm Gabriel Ryan.' He paused for a second and looked around. 'Gabe to my friends, which I sincerely hope one day you will all be.'

His small smile didn't penetrate the stony looks on their

faces. 'Contrary to popular belief,' he looked pointedly at Jonny, 'I *haven't* come here to cause trouble. I happen to believe that this community really needs me, and that I *can* be here without threatening the chapel – or anyone else's business, for that matter.'

He glanced towards Dan at the back of the room. 'I'm sure many of you knew Dan's grandmother, Lizzie Robertson.' Gabe cast a sad smile of solidarity towards his friend.

'I was there on the day she died, and I saw firsthand how hard it was on her family to wait for the undertakers to get there from almost forty miles away. It made a terrible situation even harder than it needed to be. That won't happen to other families now that I'm here.'

Lizzie had been a much-loved and respected member of the community and her death had come as a terrible shock to many. The mention of her name instantly softened the hard edges of the atmosphere in the room. 'I'm passionate about what I do.'

Marla swallowed hard at his choice of words and stamped down the image that popped into her head of Gabe in the throes of passion.

'I've grown up in the funeral business, and I'm damn good at it. My father was an undertaker, as are my brothers back in Dublin. It's in my blood.'

He had an unfair advantage with that musical voice. Marla could feel her own defensive walls shaking under the assault, so God only knew how everyone else in the room was holding up.

'Being accepted by all of you is vitally important to me. Believe me, I *can* be here without being a threat to the chapel.'

He zeroed in on Marla.

'I'm sorry if you've lost a booking, Marla, but I've already offered to sit down and iron out a compromise. I'm ready and waiting whenever you are.'

She frowned. He'd batted it right back at her, and somehow he'd managed to make her sound churlish and uncooperative.

Fifteen all.

She stood tall next to him and lifted her chin.

'Nice words, Gabriel. But nice words can't change the fact that no bride wants to risk being confronted on her wedding day by a hearse and sobbing families. They'll choose another venue just as soon as they see your sombre shop front, because they won't want that as the backdrop to their picture-perfect day.'

Thirty: fifteen. He didn't answer straight away and she pressed home her advantage.

'We aren't just a little bit incompatible, Gabriel. We are polar opposites, and we simply cannot exist as neighbours.'

Forty: fifteen.

It was pin-drop silent in the room as everyone awaited Gabe's comeback.

'You're wrong, you know.'

Marla's stomach flipped as his voice softened to a velvet boxing glove. 'We're not so different. I guess you could say that we're both in the business of helping people move on to the next stage of their lives.'

Oh, oh. Danger. He was clever. She grudgingly conceded a point.

Forty: thirty.

'"Till death do us part", Marla . . . isn't that what you're so fond of saying over here? Well, when that sad day eventually comes, trust me, it won't be you these people will turn to. It'll be me.'

Deuce. And rather unsportingly, he didn't give Marla a chance to get back into the game.

'I'm not asking you to like me. But I *am* asking that you pay me the common courtesy of being civil.'

Advantage Gabriel Ryan. Marla felt like she was five years old. She could feel him limbering up for match point and she couldn't think of a damn thing to say to stop him.

The reporter, who had been madly scribbling notes, stood up and flashed his camera in Gabe's direction. Jonny, clearly less enamoured of the reporter now that the meeting had gone awry, reached over and ripped the nearest page out of the journalist's pad, balled it up and shoved it into his own mouth with a sarcastic smirk.

'You know, it would have been so much simpler to have just allowed us to open here without the fanfare,' Gabe said from the front. 'As it is, you've created a media story that's nothing but free advertising for me and bad publicity for you. Way to go, Marla. Way to go.'

Game, set and match, Mr Gabriel Ryan.

Jonny slumped back and stared with satisfaction at his computer screen. The brainwave had hit him last night as they'd sat picking through the bones of the disastrous meeting over too warm chardonnay.

They should use the chapel's website to take their petition nationwide.

Up until now they'd only targeted the locals for support,

but what of their actual customers? After all, the majority of the weddings they held at the chapel were for outsiders. Maybe *they* were the people who could swell the petition numbers enough to make the local council sit up and take notice.

Cherry-red 'Save our Chapel!' and 'Vote for Love!' banners now covered the homepage. His next job was to drum up support on every wedding forum and celebrity wedding blog in the land. He'd set up an online petition for people to add their names to, and whilst he was on a roll he'd emailed several high-profile couples who'd been married at the chapel, hoping to rope them in.

After much deliberation, he'd decided not to mention his plan to Marla just yet. He felt shoddy about the way the meeting had ended last night; he'd let Gabe and Dan's arrival throw him right off-kilter and he badly wanted to make amends. If he could pull this off and present it as a *fait accompli*, then Marla would know for certain that she still had his unwavering support.

Besides . . . much as he adored her, Marla could be terribly straight sometimes, whereas he was more of a 'whatever gets the job done' type of person. If that meant delivering the occasional low blow, then so be it. She was too classy to resort to underhand tactics, but as her self-appointed big brother and protector, he certainly wasn't.

He clicked his computer to sleep and headed for his leopardskin-covered bed, safe in the knowledge that by hook or by crook, he intended to claw back the upper hand from Gabriel Ryan.

CHAPTER FIVE

Gabe shuffled through the disappointingly thin pile of CVs on the reception desk with a heavy sigh. The job advert he'd placed in *The Herald* had yielded eleven applications for the receptionist post, but on closer inspection only a clutch of them were even remotely suitable for interview. He'd briefly considered the interesting but wildly unsuitable Ms Scarlet Ribbons, a part-time stripper who'd handily enclosed an eye-catching photograph of herself rather than a CV. He could think of many things Ms Ribbons would no doubt excel at, but handling bereaved relatives wasn't one of them.

In the end he'd whittled it down to the three most decent-sounding applicants and arranged the interviews over the course of this afternoon. A knot of pressure formed in his gut. He needed to get this right. Hiring and firing was yet another aspect of business that was a first for him, but he knew from experience that a great receptionist could be the lynchpin of such an organisation.

He glanced up as Dora appeared with a tray of tea and biscuits.

'You're an angel, Dora,' he smiled and glanced at the clock. 'Time for a quick one?' He nodded towards the teapot and two cups, knowing that she'd banked on him asking exactly that. She made a show of looking at her duster for a second before pushing it into her apron pocket and sitting down at reception.

'You look grand sitting there. I don't suppose you're any good at reception work?' He grinned as he poured Dora a cup of tea and added two sugars, knowing her preference because they shared a cuppa most mornings these days.

'Not me, Gabriel,' she said. 'All that sitting about. You know me, I like to be up and about.' She was right there. Dora was one of life's bustlers, a behind-the-scenes person who oiled life's wheels for the front men. Not that it made her any less important. She was already proving herself indispensable, both in her professional capacity and as a warm and funny listening ear to his problems. Gabe had grown up in the bosom of a large Irish family where the women ruled the roost, and here in Beckleberry, Dora had slipped seamlessly into that role.

'I'll keep an eye on these three that are coming in this morning,' she said. 'Tell you what I make of them.'

Gabe nodded, mildly concerned for the job applicants. Dora's approval had proved to be a hard-won commodity. 'Thanks Dora. I've not done this before. I need to get it right.'

'You will, Gabriel. I've faith in you.'

He glanced down for a second, fiercely reminded of home by Dora's kindness. Reaching out, he picked up the plate of biscuits, grinning when she shook her head and patted her stout tummy the way she did every day.

'Ah go on with you, you're gorgeous. Have a biscuit.'

He glanced up at the clock ten minutes later as Dora left reception and then squinted through the driving rain outside. A whippet-thin woman in a long flasher mac was on her way over, hunched beneath a black umbrella. Gabe checked the appointment sheet. Five minutes early. Punctual. A good first sign.

He opened the door for her, and then pretended not to hear the choice collection of swear words she rattled off as she battled with her umbrella in the high wind. Droplets of rain bounced off her lacquered helmet of short, peroxide-blonde hair, and when she'd finally beaten the brolly into submission she turned to him with a cigarette-stained smile. She pumped his hand with surprising strength for such a slight woman.

'Valerie McDonald,' she barked, and declined his offer of a drink unless it was a neat double vodka. Gabe smiled, and dismissed her oddness as nerves. 'So, Valerie. Maybe you could start by telling me what it is about the job that appeals to you.'

Valerie snorted and shot off at a pace.

'I've spent my entire life flogging one thing or another, Mr Ryan. Houses. Photocopiers. Cars. You name it, I've sold it.' She smiled, and Gabe decided it was a safe bet that she'd never sold toothpaste.

'Coffins will be a damn sight easier to sell than sports cars, let me tell you. Not so many optional extras.'

Her nasal laugh had the same effect on Gabe as fingernails down a chalkboard. He ran a nervous hand over his stubble.

This wasn't going quite as he'd hoped. Valerie leaned towards him across the desk and lowered her voice, even though there was no one else in the room to keep her secrets from.

'I'll make sure the punters buy the expensive mahogany boxes rather than the plywood, if you get my drift.' She tapped the side of her nose twice with an arch wink. 'Bit of a captive audience around here. Plenty of old coffin dodgers in these villages. A shrewd move, if I may say so, Mr Ryan.'

Gabe decided he really wasn't keen on Valerie McDonald. 'That's not why I . . .'

She drew her hand across her throat to shut him up. 'It wasn't a criticism. Au contraire. I've already developed a sales strategy for you, actually.'

'You have?'

Valerie nodded. 'I'll need to move this desk closer to the window first though.' She slapped the beechwood surface of the brand-new and carefully positioned reception desk. Gabe was almost afraid to ask why, but his silence was encouragement enough for Valerie.

'If I'm by the windows, I can check out the family's wheels when they pull up, see? Then when they come in, I'll be able to pitch my sales patter at the right level. Merc equals solid oak casket. BMW more modern, maybe something in birch with Shaker handles? Dented Fiat Panda equals bargain-basement pine.' She laughed, and nodded at her own wit. 'It's clever, isn't it?'

Gabe had heard enough. Valerie McDonald might have a glittering career ahead of her in kitchen sales, but she certainly was not going to be his new receptionist.

'Umm . . . actually, no. No, Valerie, it's not clever. It's

rude, and it's grossly insensitive, and it's not going to happen to my customers.'

He walked over to the front door and held it open.

Valerie, for her part, looked genuinely shocked by his failure to be impressed, and it took her a moment to recover herself before she got up to leave. She turned back on the step, pointing her umbrella at him with a bitter sneer across her hard face.

'I'll give you six months. Twelve, at most. Business is business, no matter if it's coffins or cars.'

Gabe closed the door behind her and leaned his back against it. She'd been truly hideous. But was there any truth in Valerie McDonald's parting shot? *Did* he have enough of a business head to make a success of this? He knew he was bloody good at the nuts and bolts of his work, but he would be the first to admit he was no accountant. He didn't have time to dwell on it though – a tap on the door behind him heralded the arrival of his second interview of the day. *Please let Genevieve Lawrence be better than Valerie McDonald,* he prayed, even though he didn't especially believe in God. That was another fact that he preferred to keep to himself. People mostly assumed that undertakers have a direct line to the Almighty.

He turned around and found two huge, watery eyes staring back at him. He opened the door, allowing the woman on the step to float in on a cloud of ethereal under-skirts. She promptly sparked up a joss stick on the reception desk to create 'the right vibe'.

Gabe's heart sank into his boots as she flicked her long black wig over her bony shoulders and heaved a large framed picture of a Red Indian chief out of a Lidl carrier bag that had, up until now, been concealed amongst her skirts.

'My only request' – she fixed him with her disconcertingly direct gaze – 'is that I can hang Big Chief Running Water behind my desk. He must be given due prominence at all times, you see.'

Gabe didn't see, and he had absolutely no desire to.

'And does Big Chief expect to be on the payroll, too?'

Genevieve's eyelids fluttered down for a few moments to hide her pained expression. When she opened them again, she licked her finger and thumb and snuffed out the joss stick.

'Big Chief does not appreciate your poor wit, Mr Ryan, and neither do I. I'm afraid that we must withdraw the offer of our services.'

She slid Big Chief back into the safety of his Lidl carrier bag and flounced out into the rain.

Gabe thumped his head against the doorjamb a few times. Maybe it wasn't too late to call in Ms Scarlet Ribbons after all. He needed a beer, but he needed a receptionist even more. Please let it be third time lucky. In the back office he caught Dora's eye as she ripped Valerie and Genevieve's CVs in half and dropped them in the wastepaper bin with a shake of her head.

Melanie Spencer turned up just before four o'clock, reassuringly normal with her sensible clothes and her shiny dark hair wound into an efficient chignon. She laid her references out on the table before him, and gazed at him hopefully.

'So, Melanie. Tell me what it is about this role that appeals to you.'

Her small, delicate hand smoothed over her hair as she fixed him with a small, serene smile. 'I like to help people,

Mr Ryan. I've held reception posts before, but this one is different. I mean, it isn't just admin, is it? It's a chance to help people who need me.'

Her answer was music to Gabe's ears. She was quite right. The administrative aspect of the role was important, but not as important as being the sympathetic, warm, front-of-house presence that his business demanded.

'This can be quite a sombre place to work at times. Does that worry you at all?' he asked, almost holding his breath with hope that she wouldn't suddenly baulk at the prospect of working in a funeral parlour. But no. There was that small, reassuring smile again, coupled this time with a gentle shake of her head.

'On the contrary, Mr Ryan. That's actually part of the reason why I'd love this job so much. It's a chance to make a difference for your customers.' She hesitated and lifted her shy gaze to his. 'And a difference to you too, I hope. I know you're new here and some people aren't so keen, but I see what you're trying to do and I admire you for it. I'd like to help you, Mr Ryan.'

Twin spots of colour appeared in her pale cheeks, and she seemed almost breathless by the end of her speech. She left Gabe with no doubt at all about her sincerity.

'Please, call me Gabe.'

She smiled again then, a wider, more relaxed smile. 'Gabe.'

Melanie Spencer ticked all of Gabe's boxes. She'd said the right things, had experience with people, and there was a calm efficiency about her that Gabe warmed to straight away. Best of all, she didn't insist on bringing her spirit guide to work, or display any apparent desire to fleece grieving relatives.

Hallelujah. He offered her the job on the spot.

CHAPTER SIX

Emily looked at her watch. Ten to eight. In a little over four hours, she'd be thirty. There were no balloons or banners, just a small clutch of cards arranged in a sad little line on the fireplace. She got up and scraped her barely touched ready meal into the recycling bin and reached down for the bottle of Shiraz she'd stashed in the wine rack earlier on in the week. It was gone. Crap! Bloody Tom, he'd probably stuck it in his bag for his business trip. Pity he couldn't have given as much thought to being here for her birthday, rather than at a conference somewhere up in the wilds of Scotland. But then, he was away more than he was at home these days so she shouldn't really have been surprised. She glanced down at her pyjama bottoms and Uggs, and made a snap decision. They'd have to do for a run around to the corner shop, because there was no way she was leaving her twenties stone-cold sober.

She grabbed her purse and keys and let herself out, breaking into a desperate half-jog to get there before Bob and Audrey closed up for the evening. They were famously erratic, prone to shutting up shop early to watch the soaps.

Bugger.

The lights were off. The door was locked. Horror of all horrors, the sodding bloody shop was shut, and Emily could just hear the strains of the *EastEnders* duffers floating down from the open upstairs window. She rested her forehead against the cool glass, defeated and stupidly close to tears. She didn't hear the car come to a standstill next to her, but suddenly she felt a warm hand on her shoulder.

'Hey, Emily from the chapel.'

She turned around and found herself looking right into Dan's crystal-clear blue eyes. Several thoughts flashed through her head at once. *Christ, he's gorgeous. Shit, I'm wearing PJs. I'm going to cry if he's nice to me.* 'You're out of luck if you wanted beer. They're shut.'

Dan didn't want beer. He'd been on his way to drop the hearse back at the funeral parlour when he'd spotted Emily and hit the brakes.

'Pity. You look like a girl who really needs a drink.'

Emily sighed and leaned her back against the glass. 'Is it that obvious?'

'The pyjamas kind of give you away.'

She looked at the floor and half shrugged, half laughed. He must think she was a total flake. First she'd cried on his shoulder, and now he'd caught her running around the street in her nightwear like a desperate alcoholic.

'Listen . . . I could run you out to the supermarket if you like?'

She cast an apprehensive glance towards the hearse. 'In that?'

'It's just a car, Emily.' He laughed, opening the passenger door in invitation.

'Your chariot awaits.' He performed a low bow.

Emily knew full well in the back of her mind it *wasn't* just a car, and this wasn't just a mercy mission to the supermarket. But faced with the lonely alternative of an empty house, an empty wine glass and an empty bed, she willingly climbed into the passenger seat. Dan got in and clunked his door shut, and Emily noticed that he wasn't in oil-splattered jeans tonight. Jeans, yes, but clean, and there was a woody, warm hint of masculine shower gel about him.

'Were you going out?'

'Nowhere special.' Dan grinned. Gabe was a big boy; he'd be fine on his own in the pub for a while. This was a far more interesting option.

Emily fell silent as Dan turned out of the village towards the supermarket.

'So, Emily from the chapel. What makes you desperate enough to cry over wine?'

Emily sighed and twizzled her rings around on her fingers as she debated how to answer. *Because I'm thirty in a few hours?*

Because I just felt like throwing myself an almighty pity party?

Because I can't get pregnant?

Because my marriage is dead in the water?

'Can we just not talk about it?' she eventually managed.

'Not talk about the serious stuff?' Dan grinned. 'You're talking my language, lady.' He turned INXS up loud on the stereo and drummed his fingers on the steering wheel. 'I can go in for you, if you like.' He cast a pointed look at her pyjamas as he manoeuvred the hearse into a parking space. Emily grimaced. She really didn't want to cruise the aisles of Sainsbury's in pale pink fluffy trousers with love hearts on them, but then she didn't especially want to be on her own in the hearse either.

'What will I do?'

'Stay here and creep out the locals.' Dan jumped out and jogged across the car park without giving Emily a moment to protest. She sat for a few seconds and tried to be rational. *It was just a car.* An estate car, maybe, with lots of room in the back for shopping. She screwed up her courage and glanced over her shoulder, half expecting to see a coffin, even though she'd double-checked it was empty before she got in.

Still empty.

When she looked forward again she spotted Kev, the chapel's part-time Elvis impersonator, heading out of the supermarket, stuffing biscuits into his face. Did the man not know *anything* about tempting fate? He'd be keeling over on the toilet next if he wasn't careful. She ducked as he passed her window so he wouldn't spot her fraternising with the enemy and mention it to Marla.

Or, God forbid, to Tom.

She breathed a sigh of relief when Dan slid back into the driving seat and passed her a bag clinking with bottles. 'Red, white and sparkling. My treat.'

Emily laughed. 'Now you're talking *my* language.'

Dan winked and gunned the engine. 'Do you want me to take you home?'

His directness caught her off guard and the smile slipped

from her face. He might have kept his tone deliberately light, but the subtext behind his question was clear. 'I don't know.' She looked down at her lap. 'No.'

He nodded and turned out of the car park in the opposite direction to the village.

They drove out into the countryside for a little while before Dan finally eased the hearse up a battered dirt track and came to rest in a sheltered copse. Beyond the trees Emily had a clear view of the full moon as it glittered over the placid waters of the River Severn.

'This place is beautiful,' she said softly, and wound down her window to drink in the night sounds and smells.

Dan nodded, his eyes on her profile instead of the view. 'Beautiful.'

Emily fidgeted in her seat and the carrier bag tumbled over with a clink that reminded her of her need for wine.

'I don't suppose you happen to carry wine glasses in this thing, do you?' she asked, glancing hopefully around the surprisingly plush interior of the hearse.

'Sorry, Princess.' Dan shook his head. 'Although, hang on . . .' He stretched an arm back between the two seats, and fished around for a few seconds before coming up with a battered red KitKat mug.

'I was working in the back this morning. Left this in there.' Dan wiped the mug clean on the edge of his dark T-shirt.

Emily unscrewed the cap from the red wine and sloshed the mug half-full, then saluted him with it before taking a good long swig. It was a little cold, but she welcomed it all the same.

'Better?'

'A bit.' She had another glug. 'A lot.' She grinned.

Dan laughed and refilled her mug.

Emily sighed heavily. 'It's my birthday tomorrow.'

'No way! Let me guess . . .' He turned her chin slightly towards him to study her face. 'Twenty-four?'

'I wish.' Emily looked at her watch and groaned. 'I've got exactly two hours left of my twenties.'

Dan whistled under his breath. 'Well, here's to you, Mrs Robinson.'

'Don't. You make me feel even older.' She sipped her wine and idly wondered exactly how much younger than her he was. Couldn't be much. A year. Two, maybe?

'So . . . Is there anything you've always wanted to do before you hit the big 3-0?'

Emily shook her head, unwilling to allow herself to even think about the obvious baby-related answer to his question.

'Skydive, maybe?' he suggested. 'Bungee jump?'

Emily wrinkled her nose with distaste at his daredevil suggestions. She preferred to get her kicks on terra firma; even domestic flights had her swigging Rescue Remedy in the airport loos.

'How about wild sex in the back of a hearse?' he added.

A charged silence crackled between them as his question hung in the air.

Emily had known where this was headed from the moment she'd got into the hearse back in the village. She hadn't planned it, but then again, she hadn't resisted it either.

And she didn't resist now as Dan reached out to cradle her jaw, tracing her cheekbone with his thumb. She didn't resist him, because she *couldn't*. She turned her face into his hand and pressed her lips against his warm palm. A shiver of pleasure rocked through her at the intimacy of his unknown taste against her mouth, and she knew from the way his breath quickened that he'd felt the heat kick up a notch too. He took the mug from Emily's fingers, slung it out of the open window, then promptly pulled her across onto his lap, leaving her in no doubt of exactly how much he wanted her.

He was different, he was exciting, and he made her feel like someone else. His kiss left her breathless, and Emily opened her mouth to let his tongue slide in.

Michael Hutchence had nothing on Dan when it came to sexy moans. Any last vestige of common sense followed the KitKat mug out of the window when his hands moved underneath her T-shirt to stroke her breasts through the lace of her bra.

She was lost in him. In how new and adored his hands made her feel. In how his ragged breathing gave away the extent of his arousal. In the erotic power of being wanted again.

Emily needed more. Right there and then she needed all of him, and she reached down to where he strained against the confines of the buttons of his jeans. He swore into her mouth, and in one swift move, he dropped the seat and hauled her over into the back of the hearse.

'Dan! We can't . . . not in here!' she squeaked, and somewhere in her head, Emily actually meant it. It was scandalous on just about every level to steam up the windows of a hearse, but on the other hand, it *was* kind of perfectly proportioned for stretching out.

'Oh yes we fucking can,' he muttered, pulling her T-shirt over her head without breaking their kiss, like a magician pulling out the tablecloth without upsetting any teacups. He unfastened her bra with the ease of a practised man, and Emily's protests dissolved as his warm hands and wet mouth roamed over her body. He licked and sucked until she gasped and begged. Somehow, he managed to wriggle off both her trousers and his own in one go and settle back over her, warm skin against warm skin. He was hard and heavy between her legs, but it was Dan's kiss that tipped Emily's world upside down.

Slow, sweet and exquisite over her mouth.

Feather gentle over her squeezed-shut eyelids when he pushed himself all the way inside her. Outside, the hearse creaked to the rhythm of INXS and Emily and Dan's efforts.

Inside, she buried her tear-damp face in his neck and clung to his broad shoulders for safe harbour while he rocked her to the moon and back.

Sometime later, Emily opened her eyes as Dan's mouth traced a lazy pattern on the sensitive hollow below her ear. She gazed out at the moonlit river, still and serene despite the fact that three lives had just changed forever on her banks.

CHAPTER SEVEN

'Gerroffme . . .'

Marla grumbled at Bluey as he tried to nudge her awake with his huge head. She turned over and snuggled deeper into the crisp, white, cotton duvet, desperately trying to hang on to the coat tails of her delicious dream. She stuck her head under the pillow as the ever-patient Bluey thumped his way around the bed to poke her again from the other side. She shot up with a guilty flush. She'd been dreaming about Gabe, who for some fathomless reason had been shirtless and fixing her wonky shower when it suddenly sprayed all over him. Jeez, he'd been very, very wet. She shook her head in an attempt to dislodge the disconcertingly sexy image.

Bluey stood by the door whining low in his throat with his head cocked to one side, and it finally dawned on Marla that there was someone knocking on the door. She scowled at the clock. It was just after eight on her first morning off for quite some time, so whoever the hell had decided to interrupt her much-cherished lie-in had better have something vitally important to say.

She shrugged her white waffle dressing gown on over the top of her cotton slip and belted it tight. A peep through the white voile blind didn't help, because whoever was at the door was too close to the cottage for her to see. She straightened the blind and pushed her toes into her white terry-towelling flip-flops. A gift from Dora – she'd snipped the little pink ribbons off the front before she'd worn them. Jonny had been appalled, and insisted that her obsession with white was a direct reflection of her uptight personality. Marla eschewed his attempts at pop psychology; her mother had analysed her to death over the years. You didn't get to be the child of a sex therapist and not have your every thought and word examined. Marla had learned pretty early on not to share her inner feelings with her mother unless she had at least an hour to spare and the inclination to spill her guts. She was self-aware enough to know that this was part of the reason behind her reserved nature as an adult. She'd watched her effusive, colourful parents run constantly at life head first and wanted something different for herself. Something less complicated. More relaxed. *More white*. White just made her feel clean, that was all. It helped her to breathe more deeply, to relax more easily. She shook her head at Bluey to warn him against climbing into her recently vacated, warm bed, and ran her hand along the handrail as she picked her way down the steep cottage stairs to the front door.

Her attempts to peer through the bevelled glass pane in the old oak door proved fruitless; she couldn't recognise the warped silhouette on the other side. It looked male though. She slid back the bolt and inched the door open. She was right in her assessment. Male. Very definitely male. Very definitely attractive, too. And naggingly familiar somehow, but without its first hit of caffeine her brain had some way to go to catch up with her feet.

His smile sailed through the Marla Jacobs teeth test, and his sparkling blue eyes melted her last vestiges of annoyance at being woken up. To his further credit, he rather heroically didn't let his eyes wander down over her state of undress.

Belatedly, she noticed the newspaper in his hand.

'Are you the oldest paperboy in the world?'

He laughed and ran a hand through his floppy hair. It was so Hugh Grant that she wondered if he'd actually cut a photo out of a magazine and taken it to the hairdressers. If he said the words crikey and gosh in the same sentence in the next few minutes she'd know for sure.

'Marla, hi. You probably don't remember me from the other night . . .'

He looked at her as if he fully expected that she might well recall his face. She shrugged, and shook her head with an apologetic smile to soften the blow. He was going to have to help her out a little more than that.

'I'm Rupert Dean. I was at the public meeting last week. From *The Shropshire Herald*?'

She took the newspaper he held out as her brain fog lifted.

That was where she'd seen him. All her memories of that evening revolved around Gabriel Ryan turning up and completely derailing everything.

'Yes, I remember now,' Marla murmured, thoroughly

distracted by the 'Village Under Threat!' headline splashed across the front of the newspaper next to a large colour image of the chapel. A smaller, grainy, black-and-white image of a scowling Gabe also accompanied the piece – he looked positively demonic. Served him right. But then, a second, private image of him snuck back into her head too, of him half-naked and soaked through in her bathroom . . .

She looked up as she suddenly remembered that Rupert Dean was still standing on her doorstep. He nodded towards the paper with a grin.

'Thought you might like to see it hot off the press, so to speak.'

Much as Marla was heartened that the paper had taken up their cause, she remained perplexed as to why Rupert had gone to the trouble of providing a personal delivery service.

'Do you hand-deliver copies to all your front-page stars?'

Rupert scuffed his toe on the path like a bashful schoolboy.

'Only the beautiful ones.'

Marla laughed and gathered her dressing gown a little tighter.

'I was just about to put some coffee on. Would you like one?' She opened the door wider and stepped aside.

'I'd like that very much, actually.'

She left him in her cosy sitting room whilst she flew upstairs to fling some clothes on, and returned to find the coffee already made and Rupert leafing through her book collection. He had a classical profile, good bone structure and an aquiline nose. His hair flopped in that artful way that oozed Head Boy, but his eyes hinted at the wicked thoughts going on inside his head.

'For a woman who runs a wedding chapel, your collection seems remarkably light on romance novels.' He slid the latest John Grisham back into its place on the shelf.

'Oh, I have a special room upstairs just to house my Mills & Boon collection,' she joked, unwilling to share her own very private views on romance with a stranger. She was used to people making the assumption that she must be a romance junkie to run a wedding chapel, and she was savvy enough not to disillusion them.

'Interesting, Ms Jacobs. Are you trying to lure me upstairs to see your smut collection?' He waggled his eyebrows at her suggestively as she plunged the coffee with a laugh.

'Would I make the front page again for seducing the paperboy?' she laughed.

'No publicity's bad publicity, as they say.'

His words reminded her of Gabe's parting shot at the meeting, dampening the flirty atmosphere in the room.

Rupert's eyes lifted at the sound of movement upstairs.

'Have you got a husband up there who's about to come down here and lynch me?'

'It's just the dog,' Marla said, as Bluey thumped down the stairs and pushed the sitting-room door open with his huge head.

'Fucking hell.' Rupert gasped, his eyes like saucers at the sight of Marla's gentle giant. 'It's a donkey. I'd have stood a better chance against a bloody husband.'

Bluey took position in front of their visitor, and cocked his head to one side to study the suddenly sweating man who had invaded his home.

'Is he going to kill me?' Rupert managed to speak without moving his mouth.

'I don't know. Probably.'

Marla bit her lip to stop herself from laughing. Bluey was the daftest dog in the world. He had never killed so much as a spider, but the opportunity for sport was too pleasurable to pass up.

'Call him off, Marla. *Please.*'

'I can't. He's still sizing you up.'

She took a leisurely sip of her coffee and inspected her fingernails.

'Same as me, really. We're both trying to decide if we like you enough to let you live.'

Apart from the slight clink of Rupert's white Jamie Oliver coffee cup as it trembled against its saucer in his hand, silence reigned in the room.

'Bluey. Come here, baby.'

Marla spoke softly, and the huge hound loped across to sit sentry next to her with his head plonked on the arm of her chair.

'Good boy.'

He closed his eyes and grumbled with contentment as she fussed his soft ears.

'Should I take that as a good sign?' Rupert breathed out, his confidence returning now that he wasn't staring death in the hound-dog eye.

'I think so. Just don't try any funny stuff.'

He eyed Bluey with suspicion and reached out to catch the newspaper just after the dog swiped it off the coffee table with his tail.

'Listen, Marla. About your problem. I can help. This,' he indicated the front-page article. 'This is just the beginning.'

Marla sipped her coffee and regarded him with interest.

'I'm thinking along the lines of a series of features on the chapel, maybe cover a couple of the weddings; you know, really get the locals behind it. I could run interviews with the different local businesses that benefit from your presence, even print the petition in the paper. What do you think?'

Marla was beyond grateful. They needed all the help they could get.

'I'd greatly appreciate it, thank you. But I have to ask . . . why? Don't tell me you're a die-hard romantic with an equally impressive collection of girly books?'

He snorted on his coffee. 'Girly mags maybe, but bodice rippers? No.' He leaned forward, an intent look on his face. 'I just recognise a good story when I see it, Marla, and I happen to believe that you're right about the knock-on effect for the local community.'

Marla sat upright in her chair. Maybe there was a glimmer of hope, after all. A press campaign would certainly up the ante, in any case. 'I don't know how to thank you, Rupert.'

When he smiled, that naughty twinkle was back in evidence in his vivid blue eyes.

'I do. Have dinner with me.'

CHAPTER EIGHT

A few Mondays later, Gabe flipped the front door key over in his hand and looked at the clock. 8.55 a.m. He was officially opening for business in five minutes' time.

Melanie perched behind the reception desk. The sunshine-yellow tulips Gabe had given her this morning had been awarded pride of place beside her books. In actual fact he'd bought them to make the reception area more welcoming, rather than for Melanie in particular, but it would have been embarrassing for both of them if he'd corrected her innocent assumption. She'd blushed pink with pleasure when she'd found them on the desk earlier, and fluttered off to make coffee.

'Ready?' He turned and smiled at her, key poised by the lock.

She nodded.

'You?'

'I sure am. Let's do this thing.'

He winked at her and turned the key, then swung the door back on its hinges once or twice to make sure it was definitely unlocked. He turned the little black and silver sign on the door over to declare them open, and almost felt the warm hand of encouragement from his Da on his shoulder.

'Time to grow up, Gabe.'

It was all quiet on the street outside, still sleepy apart from the odd pensioner pulling a trolley and a young mum pushing a pram. Not that he'd expected a stampede. It wasn't the kind of business that attracted a queue.

He glanced at the chapel. Earlier, Marla had dashed by as usual, robbed of her opportunity to snarl at his bike because he'd parked it out of sight around the back. It was hardly a suitable advert for the funeral parlour. Just as he was an unsuitable advert for the wedding chapel, he acknowledged with a flicker of a frown.

He hadn't had a chance to speak to her since the public meeting. Just thinking about that evening made him wince. He'd never actually intended to stand up and speak, but he'd been so incensed by the injustice of it all that he'd found himself on his feet before he'd had a chance to think it through.

The Shropshire Herald had ripped him to shreds as a result, and the battle lines between the chapel and the funeral parlour were now marked out as clearly as if they'd been painted in bold white lines across the pavement.

From behind the blind of her office window, Marla watched Gabe swing his freshly painted black door open, then stand still and cast his eyes skywards for a few seconds. Was he weather watching, or praying, even? If he needed a sign, he should have said. She would have hurled a bucket of cold water over him.

It was the first time she'd seen him out of jeans and

leathers, and, although if quizzed she would have hotly denied the thought had even entered her head, the sight of him in a close-fitting suit did something strange to her insides. Of course it could be the ill effects of the omelette that Rupert had attempted to cook for breakfast. Marla grimaced at the memory. Cooking certainly wasn't one of Rupert's strong points, but she was willing to overlook it because he'd turned out to be pretty hot at other things, not least laughing her into bed. Marla appreciated his humour and his candour, and had found herself happy to accept his offer to stay over after their dinner date. He was her ideal man of the moment; easy on the eye, accomplished in bed, and with no expectations of a messy, complicated love affair.

Whichever. Rupert's omelette or Gabe's hotness in a suit, it was immaterial. The grim fact was that the funeral parlour was now officially open for business, which meant that the chapel was officially a step closer to closing down.

Marla huffed, and kicked the desk leg with frustration. Jonny had assured her that the petition was going great guns, and that in no time they'd have enough signatures to present to the council. He'd better hurry up about it, because every day with the funeral parlour as a neighbour was a day closer to bankruptcy.

Her mobile buzzed as she flicked her shoe off to massage away the ache in her foot from kicking the desk too violently. Rupert's name flashed up when she reached over and swiped the screen.

Hey beautiful. Missing you already. Chinese take-out tonight? My treat.

Marla sighed, both glad of Rupert's support and concerned at the romantic slant to his words. She sagged down into the chair and opened the desk diary. Much as she hated the idea, she needed to pull on her big-girl pants and take Gabe up on his offer of a civilised discussion, because damage limitation was about as good as it was going to get for the foreseeable future. She twisted her hair into a bun, pushed a pencil through the knot, then grabbed the diary and headed to the door.

Nerves made her hesitate as she approached the funeral parlour door. She gave herself a mental shake and pushed the door open, to find herself pleasantly surprised by the tasteful, welcoming decor. Not that she was sure what she'd been expecting. Cobwebs? A rattling skeleton in the corner, maybe? The reception desk looked empty apart from a bright jug of tulips, but then a slender, dark-haired girl straightened up from behind it and smiled.

'Hi there, come on in.'

Marla smiled back. Her fight wasn't with Gabe's pretty young receptionist.

'Hi. Is Gabriel around, please?'

The girl's smile dimmed from mega-watt to energy saver at Marla's use of Gabe's first name. She glanced quickly over her shoulder. 'I can certainly check if he's free. Who should I say is here?'

Her eyes flicked up and down Marla's red spotted dress and high heels.

'Marla Jacobs. From the chapel.' Marla noticed the flash of recognition in the receptionist's eyes and the energy saver smile disappeared altogether.

'Ah. I see.' She shook her head. 'Well, I'm sorry. No. I'm afraid Gabe isn't here right now.'

The obvious way she shortened his name to stamp her position of authority infuriated Marla. 'But you just said you'd check if he was free.'

The girl shrugged. 'I can tell him you called by, if you like?'

That smile was back, this time simpering with saccharine instead of sugar.

They stared at each other for a few long seconds. Short of yelling for him, there was nothing Marla could do.

'Make sure you do that,' Marla shot back through gritted teeth and turned on her heel.

Gabe stuck his head through into reception. 'Did I hear the door?'

He looked up just in time to recognise Marla's familiar red hair through the window as she stomped away.

'That woman from the chapel, yeah.' Melanie rolled incredulous eyes. 'Some nerve, coming over here to cause trouble on our first day, eh?'

'What did you say to her?'

'Just that you were busy.'

Gabe shook his head and tried not to sound as irritated as he was. 'Ask me. Always ask me, okay?' He opened the door and broke into a jog to catch up with Marla before she disappeared into the chapel.

She stopped and slowly turned when he called her name.

'Well, well, well. Did your receptionist give you permission to talk to me after all?'

'Sorry, crossed wires. Did you, er . . . did you need something?'

He glanced down at the diary clutched against her chest, and noticed the pale gold freckles on her throat as his eyes made their way back up to her face.

She nodded. 'We need to talk.'

Gabe's heart tripped a beat. *You're telling me lady, you're telling me.* 'I'm a bit tied-up over there right now.' He jerked his head back towards the funeral parlour, where he'd been in the middle of a practice session with his new pallbearers. 'How about tonight?'

Marla shook her head so hard that the pencil fell out of her hair and rolled along the pavement towards Gabe. 'Tonight? God, no. I can't. I'm, erm, I'm busy.'

Gabe retrieved the pencil and handed it back to her, thinking how gorgeous she looked with her red waves released around her face. *Why, Ms Jacobs, you're beautiful!* He thought it, but somehow managed to keep the cheesy line inside his head.

'Tomorrow maybe?'

'No, I'm busy tomorrow night too. In fact, I'm busy every night. *With my boyfriend.*'

Boyfriend. The word made Marla's tongue feel too big in her mouth.

'Your boyfriend?'

'Yes, Gabriel, my boyfriend. You know – a man I actually enjoy spending time with, as opposed to one who is trying to ruin me?'

Okay. So perhaps that had come out a little more caustic than was strictly necessary, but Jesus, Gabe riled her something rotten. Why had he instructed his jumped-up secretary to lie to her? And God knew he had no business looking so effortlessly cool in a suit, with his barely tamed curls kissing his collar like a flirty Sunday morning lover.

'I meant tomorrow afternoon, Marla. Your personal life is none of my business.'

His markedly clipped tone told her that she'd scored a direct hit. Good, he deserved it.

'Fine.' She looked at her watch. 'Come over after lunch tomorrow.'

He nodded. 'As long as your *boyfriend* can spare you.'

Marla narrowed her eyes at his sarcasm, and had to clamp her teeth together to stop herself from sticking her tongue out.

'You know what? I'm not so sure he can, actually. I guess I'll just have to think of a really special way to make it up to him afterwards, won't I?'

Jonny was torn between pride and unease at quite how effective his online campaign was turning out to be. He'd posted strategic links all over the net on wedding forums, and people had responded to his battle cry with aplomb.

Over two thousand people had signed the petition since he'd posted it on the chapel website last week, and their web stats had shot through the roof. Not to mention the messages of support that were flooding into his in-box on a daily basis – everything from well-wishers to a couple of much darker, sinister offers to 'eliminate the threat' for them.

He'd struck a match, and he'd started an inferno.

And amidst all of this, he still hadn't found time to mention it to Marla.

CHAPTER NINE

Tom stared at the artisan chocolate stand in the busy department store. Shoppers bustled around him, but he stood oblivious and racked his brain to remember Emily's favourites.

Because this wasn't just a box of chocolates.

It was an olive branch.

Over the last week or so, something had changed. He couldn't put his finger on it, but he'd sensed a profound difference in Emily.

A subtle detachment, and it scared him witless.

She wasn't waiting for him any more.

He felt like a prize fool, because he knew with the crystal clarity of the damned that he was just a few steps away from the most colossal fuck-up of his life. Emily's change of attitude had stripped the scales from his eyes and he'd finally, *finally* realised that he didn't want to fuck up.

So many things he hadn't made the time to say.

So many occasions when he'd made the coward's choice

and run when he should have stayed with Emily and been her rock.

He'd let himself blame her, cast her as the villain of the piece for forcing them through the barrage of tests and check-ups.

He'd allowed himself the luxury of behaving like the victim, and he was deeply, deeply ashamed.

'Emily?'

Clammy fear settled over his heart at the sight of the suitcase propped against the radiator in the hallway.

He'd left it too late.

Emily came through from the lounge and stood in the doorway, car keys in hand and an expression on her face that went so far beyond sadness that Tom felt his own heart crack open too. Fear paralysed him. He didn't know whether to pull her into his arms, or if he should just step aside and let her pass.

'I wrote you a letter,' she said.

No. No way was this all going to end with a 'Dear John'.

'I don't want to read it. Talk to me instead. Tell me.'

Tears spilled down her cheeks, and he closed the distance between them in two paces and grabbed her hands. 'In fact, don't. Don't say anything. Listen to me first. Please Em, just listen, and then go if you still want to.'

His eyes searched her face as his thumbs rubbed back and forth over her knuckles.

'I'm so sorry. I've been such a prick. I'm never here when you need me. I've deliberately missed appointments. Truth is, I'm scared.'

'Tom . . .'

'I can't make it without you.' His voice cracked. 'A family, kids . . . all that stuff would be great, Em. But if we never get lucky enough, then it just means that I can be selfish and keep you to myself forever.'

He hauled her into his arms, not sure where her tears ended and his own began.

'We aren't defined by whether or not we have children, Emily. We are so much better than that. Aren't we?' He held her at arm's length and studied her face. 'We've let this . . . this *thing* push its way between us. It's in our bedroom like an unwelcome mistress. I hate it.'

He touched his fingers against her wedding ring. 'This means everything to me. Do you still love me?'

Emily nodded. She loved him with all of her being, but that hadn't stopped her from finding solace in the arms of another man. Guilt ate at her heart as surely as loneliness had eaten away at her fidelity. 'Of course I do. But I barely see you anymore *to* love you, Tom. You'd rather be at work, or away. Anywhere but here. And when you *are* here, it's worse. I'm so lonely, even when we're in the same room.'

Tom reached out and cradled her face in his hands, unsure how to pull their relationship back from the cliff edge it teetered on. 'I don't know what the future holds, Em. I just know I want to hold you in mine.'

He moulded her against him as she cried, the familiarity of her curves feeling like home under his hands. Comfort slid sideways into raw desire, as instinctive as breathing.

He unbuttoned her blouse, desperate for the warmth of her skin against his own.

Clinging.

Remembering.

Longing.

Reawakening.

Soothing away the bruises from each other's heart.

Sometime after midnight, Tom dropped a kiss on Emily's warm shoulder and slipped out of bed, careful not to wake her. He stepped out onto their front step, cigarette lighter in one hand, and Emily's unopened letter from the mantelpiece in the other.

Should he read it? He could rip open the envelope right now and read the words she'd written, know for certain why she'd stopped waiting for him.

Or should he flick the flame of his lighter against the unopened corner, let what had passed between them over the last few hours be all the truth they needed? His thumb pushed against the cold metal, wanting to burn the unread words, unsure which of the choices was braver or best.

CHAPTER TEN

Marla used both hands to push Bluey's huge backside out from underneath her desk in order to make more room for her knees, then scowled at her watch. She'd told Gabe to come over after lunch. What time did the man eat? No doubt he was playing mind games, keeping her waiting as a casual demonstration of the fact that he held all the cards.

As if she wasn't painfully aware of that already.

She could, of course, just storm over there and steal his thunder, but the idea of a rematch with Gabe's guard dog of a receptionist didn't hold much appeal. Anyway, what would it show him, besides the fact that he'd got under her skin? The home turf advantage was worth waiting for. She reached into her bottom drawer and pulled out a doggy treat for Bluey to apologise for banishing him to the other side of the room.

Her head snapped up as her office door creaked open, then shot down again to hide her disappointment as Dora came in, a can of polish in her hand.

'You look as if you've found a penny and lost a pound,' she said as she tipped the contents of the wastepaper basket into a black bin liner, produced from the pocket of her pinny.

Marla conjured up a smile. Or bared her teeth, in any case.

'I'm fine, Dora. Or else I would be, if that man over there could tell the time. He's late.'

She jerked her head towards the street. Dora's eyes followed and settled mistily on the funeral parlour.

'Gabriel? Oh, but he's ever so busy, chicken.' The dreamy smile fell off her face. 'Is he coming over here? You really should have said, I'd have bought some Jammie Dodgers. They're his favourites, you know.'

Thoroughly distracted, she dropped the polish into the rubbish bag by mistake, and didn't even notice when Marla crossed the room and fished it out again.

'Maybe I should slip over to the shop to get some?'

Marla was irritated to hear the same proprietorial tone in Dora's voice that she'd detected in Gabe's snotty receptionist's the day before. What was it about him that turned women around him into territorial tigresses?

'Only if you'll lace them with cyanide when you get back. He's not coming for a tea party, Dora, he's . . .'

'He's outside the door and can hear every word you're saying.'

Dora ruffled up her feathers like a peahen. 'Gabriel, sit down. I'll just pop downstairs and put the kettle on.'

'I'll take mine without the cyanide, if you don't mind.' He winked at Dora, who laughed girlishly as she left the room.

92

'She's a one-off, isn't she?' Gabe said, sitting down across the desk from Marla. 'Reminds me of my gran.'

Bluey unfurled himself from beneath the window and looked Gabe square in the eye, and Marla crossed her fingers underneath the desk, hoping he'd be terrified of dogs.

'Hey there, big guy. Aren't you just the most beautiful thing?'

Bluey padded across and rested his huge chin on Gabe's knee, his half-eaten dog chew still wedged in his jowls. Gabe laughed and fussed the dog's velvet head with both hands.

Great. Another traitor. That was the last treat Bluey was going to get out of her this week.

She frowned at Gabe across the expanse of her walnut desk.

'Just so you're clear, all this blarney won't work on me. You can't charm your way around me the way you have every other man, woman and dog in Beckleberry.' On cue, Bluey fell to the floor at Gabe's feet.

'I wouldn't insult you by thinking that I could, Marla.'

'And there you go, you're doing it again.'

'For Christ's sake, I didn't do anything.'

Marla dismissed his protestation of innocence with an acid laugh and pushed a sheet of paper across the desk.

'This is a list of all of the weddings we have booked in for the next two months.'

His eyes scanned down the list. 'And you're telling me this because?'

'Are you being deliberately obtuse?'

'Are you?'

The challenge in his dark eyes scorched her throat sandpaper dry.

'You sat downstairs in the kitchen a couple of weeks ago and promised to at least cooperate with us, Gabe.'

'Yeah. That would have been before you called a public meeting to make our neighbours hate me.'

'Our neighbours? *Our* neighbours? Oh, please. You don't know these people from Adam. They're *my* neighbours, and *my* friends, and they would support me over you any day.'

A tiny tap on the door disturbed them, and a second or so later Dora appeared with a tray laden with teacups and a plate stacked with Jammie Dodgers.

Gabe grinned and cast a look of lazy triumph across the desk at Marla. Hot fury bubbled in her stomach, and as soon as Dora left the room she reached for the plate and upended it into the wastepaper basket. She regretted it the instant he laughed at her.

'Now that wasn't very nice, was it?'

Bluey loped over to recover a stray biscuit that had rolled towards the skirting board and disappeared after Dora in search of more. Marla got up to close the door behind him, sucking in a deep breath to calm herself down. She hated the fact that Gabe had her on the ropes already. She forced a placid smile onto her face as she sat back down behind the desk; she badly needed to get this meeting back on track.

'Look. Let's just both say what we need to, and then you can leave.'

As placatory statements went, that one wasn't going to win any awards, but it was as close to civil as she could muster.

'Go on then, you first. This should be good.'

Marla was struggling. He'd discarded the jacket she'd

spotted him in earlier and turned up for their meeting in rolled-back shirtsleeves, his tie loosened a little to accommodate his undone top button. It was incredibly difficult to stay professional, given the fact that she wanted to rip both his head and his shirt off at the same time.

He looks like a gigolo, Marla thought sourly.

It pained her greatly that she understood his catnip effect on women. She didn't want to acknowledge it, and she certainly wasn't going to let her head be turned by it, but Gabriel was on a scale all of his own when it came to beauty. No doubt he was accustomed to using it to get his own way, but he was about to get a lesson from a woman who well and truly had his number.

'I'd appreciate it if you could schedule those dates into your diary.'

'Why? Do you need a date?'

Gah! He was seriously pissing her off.

'It's no joke, Gabe. Just make sure that filthy great hearse is out of sight and try not to wheel any dead bodies across the pavement when the bride's outside, okay?'

He picked up the list again and whistled. 'Business seems good. Maybe you could think about calling off your hate campaign after all.'

'Those weddings were booked long before you arrived here. It's next year's bookings that will suffer. And the year after that. Assuming we're still here by then, which I very much doubt.'

She couldn't be sure, but he looked less comfortable than he had a moment ago. Maybe a drop of compassion lurked somewhere underneath all that hair and charm.

'And for your information, there is no hate campaign.'

His words had hit a raw nerve. 'You make it sound petty and personal, and it's neither of those things. It's business, pure and simple.'

Gabe studied her in silence and then slowly folded the list of wedding dates in half.

'Sure. Leave it with me. I'll take care of it.'

His abrupt gear change from teasing to deadly serious left her flailing for a suitable response.

'Gabe . . .' They were distracted by a sudden, loud smash in the street below and sprang out of their seats. The front window of the funeral parlour lay shattered in a thousand pieces across the pavement, and as they watched, a visibly shaken Melanie emerged onto the street with what looked horribly like a house brick clutched in her hand.

'What the . . .' Gabe muttered as he flung Marla's office window open. 'Hang on, Mel! I'm coming,' he yelled.

He turned to Marla. The incensed look of accusation in his eyes stole her breath away.

'Not a hate campaign, eh? Well it fucking looks like one from where I'm standing.'

Marla gasped at the conclusion he'd leapt to.

'Gabe, please! I swear, this has *nothing* to do with us. I would never . . .' Marla couldn't articulate past his automatic assumption of her guilt. Surely he could see that mindless vandalism wasn't her style? He had to understand that she'd never stoop so low.

He held a hand up to silence her, his usually Jagger-esque mouth twisted into a thin line of distaste. 'Methinks the lady doth protest too much.'

Gabe ripped up the list she'd given him earlier and hurled the pieces across the office floor.

'You've just picked yourself a fight with the wrong man, Marla Jacobs.'

He stalked out of the office.

Marla stood rooted to the spot in shock, both by the thuggish vandalism and Gabe's instant assumption. Quite why Gabe's opinion of her mattered so much wasn't something she was prepared to give any headspace to. Sour fear unfurled slowly in her belly. *Did* this have anything to do with their campaign? *Had* she been the indirect cause of this? Jesus, she hoped not.

She watched Gabe run across the pavement to Melanie; unable to drag her eyes away as he eased the brick from her fingers and wrapped his arms around her slender body. Heavy footsteps echoed up the old wooden staircase towards the office. Marla shivered, and turned away from the window. Jonny appeared, his face a sickly shade of green, beneath his usual tan.

'Er, Marla? There's something I really need to talk to you about.'

Marla's horror spiralled as she listened to Jonny's heartfelt explanation of how his well-intentioned online petition had grown to leviathan proportions. It had gone viral, and it now appeared that he'd lost any kind of control over it. His over-zealous pleas had been taken as a call to arms, and he'd been troubled over the last week by emails landing in their in-box threatening to 'make sure that Gabriel Ryan never opened for business'. It was pretty obvious that the incident on the street this afternoon was linked, but what the hell were they going to do about it? And worse, what might come next? Sure, she wanted the funeral parlour gone.

But not like this. Not because of a dirty hate campaign in her name. If this got out, her professional reputation would be in tatters, but it was the possibility that someone might get hurt that filled her with shame.

She wasn't even aware that she was crying until Jonny put his mug down and handed her a tissue.

Half an hour later, Marla picked her way over the broken glass on the pavement, feeling gaudy and mildly ridiculous in her sky-blue vintage tea-dress and patent red heels. The Dorothy-esque qualities of her outfit had appealed when she'd dressed that sunny morning, but right now she felt more akin to the cowardly lion. Jonny's revelations had robbed her of any rights to indignation or the moral high ground, leaving her with apologies to make and humble pie to eat.

She sucked down a deep breath and pushed the funeral parlour door open.

Unsurprisingly, Gabe's receptionist didn't throw down the red carpet to herald her arrival. In fact, given the outraged look in her pink-rimmed eyes when she looked up, Marla could only count herself lucky that Melanie didn't throw the jug of flowers from the reception desk at her instead. As it was, the younger woman pulled herself up to her full height and stared Marla down across the desk.

'I need to speak to Gabe,' Marla said quietly.

A sound somewhere between a laugh and a cry of outrage twisted from the other girl's throat as she folded her arms across her chest. 'I don't think so, somehow.'

'Look . . . I really am sorry about all of this . . .' Marla cast an uncertain glance behind her at the shattered window. She really wanted to tell this to Gabe himself, not his hostile receptionist.

'Please. Ask him if he'll see me?'

'He won't. Just get out.'

Irritation prickled hot beneath Marla's skin. Despite the other woman's tearful face and her right to her anger, she detected an element of self-satisfaction in Melanie's over-bright eyes. However shaken up she was, she was drawing an element of pleasure from Marla's fall from grace.

'I've asked real nicely,' Marla said, stepping closer and laying her shaking palms on the desk. 'If Gabe won't listen to me, he needs to send me away himself.'

A flash of pure hatred lit Melanie's eyes as she mirrored Marla's stance and leaned in.

'And I've asked you *real nice* to get the hell out of here.' She mimicked Marla's American accent with a sneer.

'What's going on here, ladies?'

They both flinched and looked towards the door behind reception, where Gabe leaned against the doorframe with a deep frown over his unhappy eyes.

'She threatened me, Gabe,' Melanie said, traces of panic in her plaintive voice.

'I did no such thing!' Anger made Marla's voice louder than she'd intended. Gabe crossed to stand shoulder to shoulder with Melanie. 'What do you want, Marla?'

Marla looked from Gabe to Melanie. From pure misery to crocodile tears. She really didn't want to have to explain Jonny's actions in front of Miss Snark.

'Can I please speak to you?' she said, keeping her gaze only on Gabe.

He looked at her in silence.

'*Please*?' she said softly.

'I already told her you wouldn't see her, Gabe,' Melanie

almost whispered, laying a hand on Gabe's forearm. 'That's when she got aggressive.'

The urge to get truly aggressive right there and then burned in Marla's gut, but she held her silence and Gabe's gaze, hoping he'd be reasonable.

'You've got five minutes,' he said eventually.

Melanie pursed her lips and looked at her watch as if about to start the stop clock.

'Can we at least speak in private?' Marla asked, hating how small her voice sounded.

Melanie shook her head. 'I don't think so.'

Mild surprise registered in Gabe's eyes before they slid from Marla to his receptionist.

'Give us five, please Mel? I'm sure you could do with a cuppa anyway.'

She shook her dark head, resolute. 'I'm fine.'

Gabe touched her shoulder. 'Take a break, Melanie.'

His voice held a quiet authority that brooked no argument, and Marla watched as Melanie struggled hard to hold on to her professional veneer.

'Fine.' She smiled through gritted teeth. 'I'll be in the kitchen if you need me.' She flicked a last accusatory glance at Marla as she turned away, and then down at her watch again, leaving Marla in no doubt that she'd be back from that tea break in exactly five minutes and not a second more. She better start talking.

Gabe clicked the door closed behind Melanie and then turned back around.

'Well?'

Marla glanced at her ruby shoes, wishing again for that elusive courage.

'I'd like to pay for the damage to the window.'

'Even though it's not even your fault?' Gabe said, and his cool eyes told her that he was in no doubt that she was the guilty party.

'Gabe, I would never behave like that. Not intentionally, anyway.'

'Oh, hang on. No, don't tell me. You did it unintentionally,' he said, with a humourless laugh. 'Why didn't I think of that?'

'I didn't do it at all, Gabe,' she said. 'But I know now that it might have been connected to the chapel, somehow, and if it was, I'm truly very sorry.'

Faced down by Gabe's impenetrable expression, she haltingly explained about Jonny's online campaign, ever aware that Melanie would be back soon.

'So, what do you expect of me, Marla?' He assessed her coolly. 'A pat on the back for telling the truth? You pay for the damage and we forget all about it? It's criminal bloody damage.'

Marla sighed heavily. He would be well within his rights to call the police.

'Just get the hell out of here,' he sighed with a resigned air of disappointment. 'I don't want your money, and I won't be calling the police.' Marla closed her eyes and breathed out. 'And don't kid yourself that I'm doing it for you, or Jonny. I'm doing it for me, and for my business. The last fucking thing I need is to turn this into a sideshow in the paper.'

They both looked out towards the street as Dora, who had started to sweep up the glass, suddenly began squawking.

'Get out of it! You should be ashamed of yourself!'

They stepped nearer to the window at the exact moment

the photographer from *The Herald* pointed his camera towards them and flashed it in their eyes. Melanie burst through from the back at the sound of raised voices, as outside Dora started poking the broom at the hastily retreating backside of the photographer.

Gabe rounded on Marla, his eyes blazing. 'Everything is a fucking opportunity to further your petty campaign, isn't it? You come over here with your pretty apology, knowing all the time that that lowlife was on his way to splash this all over the front page. Bravo, Marla. You really are a piece of fucking work.'

Words failed her. For the second time that day, Gabe had been all too quick to automatically assume the worst of her, and it wounded her more deeply than she could have expected. Melanie strutted to the door and yanked it open, jerking her head, her venomous eyes making her message clear in no uncertain terms. *Get out before I throw you out.* In the absence of the necessary magic to tap her ruby heels together and disappear, Marla dipped her head and left the parlour. Even Dora emanated disapproval, shaking her head slowly as she stoutly swept the glass from the pavement without meeting Marla's eye.

By the time Marla reached the relative safety of the chapel, she needed another good cry and a large gin.

CHAPTER ELEVEN

'Two glasses of Shiraz please, Bill. Large as you can.'

'I'll bring them over for you, ladies.'

Emily smiled gratefully at the landlord and steered Marla across to a table in the corner of The Mermaid's busy bar.

Bill followed with their glasses and a big smile, but made a hasty retreat after one look at Marla's stricken face.

Marla picked up her glass, grateful for the wine's warmth and spice after the strangeness of the day.

'You can't keep blaming yourself, Marla. You had no idea what was going on.' They had talked of nothing else but the window incident since this afternoon, and despite searching relentlessly through the emails for clues, they were no closer to finding out who was behind it. Whoever had thrown that brick made sure they covered their tracks well.

'What am I going to do, Em? This has all got badly out of hand.'

Emily nudged Marla's glass closer. 'Drink your medicine. It helps.'

Uncharacteristically, Marla did as she was told. She was tired. Exhausted, in fact. Going over to the funeral parlour this afternoon with her tail between her legs ranked up there amongst the most toe-curling moments of her life.

'Jonny's pretty cut up you know,' Emily offered, swirling her wine around in her glass.

Marla shook her head and sighed. She and Jonny were chalk and cheese in so many ways, yet somehow it worked and they'd become close friends as well as colleagues. Up until this afternoon, anyway. She hadn't been able to hide her disgust when he'd showed her what was going on online, and though it was clear he realised with horror exactly how much jeopardy he'd placed the chapel in, it had been all she could do not to fire him on the spot. As it was, she'd sent him home to pull their website offline completely, and to retrace his steps, wiping absolutely every hint of the campaign from the net.

'I'll talk to him in the morning. If I ring him now I'll say something I regret.' Marla still couldn't believe that Jonny had been so monumentally stupid. However well intended, he should never have started the campaign without consulting her, and to have kept the spiralling problems to himself like a child afraid of getting into trouble had placed them all at risk. It had been by far the biggest disagreement between them, and Marla had been too humiliated and horrified to offer an olive branch yet.

Emily nodded.

'How did you leave it with Gabe?'

Marla's shoulders slumped even more.

'I'm officially the Wicked Witch of the West over there.' Marla couldn't bear the fact that she'd lost her moral high ground. The village would turn against her pretty quickly if they believed that she would resort to mob tactics.

'He definitely didn't believe you?'

Marla shook her head. 'Can you blame him? *I* wouldn't believe me.'

Emily squeezed her friend's hand.

'It'll be okay – honestly, it will. People around here know you a lot better than he does.'

Marla nodded and clung to Emily's pragmatic common sense. 'God, I hope so, Em. I really hope so.'

'What time is the gorgeous Rupert coming?'

Marla glanced at the big brass clock behind the bar.

'Anytime now.'

The sooner the better as far as Marla was concerned. She was badly in need of a little TLC after the bashing she'd received from Gabe this afternoon.

They both looked up as the door swung open on cue, but it was Tom, not Rupert, who came in. He ruffled Marla's hair as he squeezed behind her seat, beer in his hand.

'Bad day at the office I hear, sweetheart.'

'Yeah. Just a bit.'

His easy affection brought a lump to Marla's throat. Tom was just about the nicest man in the world, and Emily was a lucky girl to have him. He obviously adored her, given the way he leaned in to kiss her lingeringly on the mouth as he pulled his chair in close.

Such a fleeting gesture, yet so laden with love that Marla had to look away.

The door swung again, and this time she wasn't disappointed. Rupert shot her a cheeky grin as he sauntered over to their table and pulled up a chair.

'Marla Jacobs, I didn't know you had it in you. I am seriously impressed.'

He laughed and held his hand in the air to high-five her. He dropped it again quick smart at Marla's stony glare and Emily's exaggerated headshake.

'Hey, I was only kidding. You know that, right?' He slid an arm around Marla's shoulders and pulled her against his side, any trace of humour wiped from his face.

She forgave him instantly, leaning into his hug, grateful for his warmth and affection after the afternoon from hell. His smell was becoming familiar and she breathed deeply, looking for comfort.

'Yeah, I know. Sorry. It's just a bit raw, that's all.'

'Well, let me tell you something that might cheer you up again then.'

He released her from the hug to pick up the pint Bill put down in front of him and savoured the creamy top on his beer slowly, keeping them in suspense.

Emily cracked first.

'Come on then. Spill.'

'Okay,' he grinned. 'I've arranged for a big wedding pull-out next week in the paper, and guess what's going to be our star feature?'

Marla smiled, easily able to see where this was headed. At least Rupert was trying to help in a conventional way, unlike Jonny. All she wanted was a good clean fight.

'The chapel?' Emily supplied.

'The chapel,' Rupert repeated with a flourish. 'We'll photograph whichever wedding you've got on this weekend and do a nice big double-page splash.'

Marla mentally rolodexed through the bookings to the

wedding they had that Saturday. If her memory served her well it was a gothic affair, which should make for eye-catching pictures, if nothing else.

'Where would I be without you?' She smiled gratefully. Rupert slid his arm around her waist and planted a warm kiss on the side of her mouth.

'Heading for bankruptcy, I reckon. Good job you've got me then, eh?'

Marla laughed for the first time since lunch.

'I guess it is, yeah.'

She truly was glad of Rupert in her life. He seemed to genuinely want to do anything he could to help with the campaign, and he looked like he enjoyed her company without needing to deepen their liaison into relationship territory. They'd slipped into a pattern of seeing each other every few evenings, and a couple of times he'd stayed over at Marla's cottage. She didn't like the phrase *friends with benefits*, but if pushed she'd have deemed it an appropriate way to summarise the situation developing between them.

The pub was filling up nicely, but a western movie-style hush fell over it a second or two later when Gabe and Dan came in, a study of perfection in biker's leathers and oily denim.

Marla sucked in a sharp breath and Rupert stiffened next to her, his fingers digging into her waist. Emily looked equally stricken by Gabe's appearance, and Tom, the only one who hadn't yet had the pleasure of meeting Gabe, glanced quizzically around the table . . .

Behind the bar, Bill slid his glasses off and put down his newspaper. He pulled two pints of Guinness and placed them on the bar.

'On the house, lads.'

Gabe studied the glasses for a long moment and the pub held its collective breath.

'Thank you, Bill. I appreciate it.'

The noise level returned to normal as if someone had turned the volume dial, and Marla released the breath she didn't realise she'd been holding.

'I take it that's yer man then,' Tom said. He nodded towards the newcomers as he took a swig of beer.

Emily followed his gaze and saw only Dan, even though there was a throng of people at the bar. She felt as if someone had dropped a concrete block on her chest and she couldn't get her breath. The rational part of her brain knew that Tom was referring to Gabe, but his words still sliced through like an axe. She knocked her almost-full glass of wine back in one go.

'Can we go now, Tom?' She was already on her feet and had her arms halfway into her jacket. 'Please?'

Tom laughed.

'Hang about, Em. I haven't finished my beer . . .' but Emily was already away across the pub. He pushed his chair back and stood up with a resigned grin.

'Can't wait to get me home.' He shrugged. 'Sex maniac. She's killing me, man.'

He drained his glass and picked up his car keys.

'Have fun, kids.'

He winked at an amused Marla and Rupert. As he picked his way through the busy tables, Tom couldn't help noticing the way Gabe's friend turned to look at Emily as she passed. He felt a fierce stab of pride that she was his wife. He couldn't blame other men for looking at her. Then Emily turned and held the guy's gaze for a few seconds and, even in profile, he knew her well enough to recognise the look of ill-concealed panic on her face. Each second felt like a lifetime, until she whipped her head around and ran out of the door.

Two thoughts swam around in his head.

What was that all about? And, *Not a chance pal. She's mine.*

'What was that all about?' Gabe asked as the door swung shut behind Tom.

'Not a clue. Probably fancied me.' Dan shrugged. 'Most women do, my friend.'

'Did you not notice her husband was three steps behind her, man?'

'Yeah, I noticed. But did *she*?' Dan muttered darkly and waved to Bill for more beers.

Gabe was well aware that Marla was sitting across the room with the reporter from the meeting. That figured. They were probably hatching phase two of their hate campaign. He could see them reflected in the mirror behind the bar, and he flinched as the guy smoothed a stray lock of Marla's hair back behind her ear.

This was the boyfriend she'd mentioned? The tosser from *The Herald*? Christ, he'd credited her with better taste. But then, in light of events this afternoon, maybe he shouldn't be so surprised.

He had to hand it to her. It had taken some balls to come over to the funeral parlour with her chequebook in hand, ready to pay for a new window. He still couldn't make up his mind whether he believed her pleas of innocence or not, but either way she'd proved that she had a brave streak a mile wide. Thinking back, he knew that he'd come down hard on her, but disappointment could do that to a man. Petty thuggery didn't match up with the woman she'd become in his head, and she'd fallen off her pedestal with an even louder crash than the window.

He excused himself to the gents and found himself shoulder to shoulder at the urinal with Rupert, who'd followed him in.

'Stay away from her,' Rupert muttered, midstream.

'I *beg* your pardon?'

'You heard me. Leave Marla alone, or I'll smear your fucking name in so much shit that you'll be hounded out of the country, let alone the village.'

Gabe zipped his fly and turned to Rupert, who did the same.

'Are you actually trying to *threaten* me?' Gabe couldn't decide whether to laugh at him or knock him out.

Rupert shrugged, and turned to the mirror over the washbasin to fiddle with his artfully arranged hair. 'Call it what you like.'

Gabe was having a bad day, and Rupert's glib smugness made his fists itch. He stepped in close behind him and met his eye in the mirror. 'You've got that much right. I will call it whatever the hell I like, and I will *do* whatever the hell I want, *with* whoever the hell I want. Have you got that?'

'Tosser.'

Gabe sensed the scared posh boy lurking behind Rupert's glib, Boden-poster-boy confidence. 'What is it that *really* bugs you, paperboy? Don't you trust me with her? Or is it that you don't trust Marla around me?'

* * *

Back in the bar, Gabe glanced over at Marla as he sat back down and found her watching him. Her expression gave him little clue of what was going through her head. Something serious though, going by her frown. She was probably wondering if he'd just killed her fop of a boyfriend in the loos. Even from across the other side of the room, he could make out the dark circles underneath her eyes and, despite the events of the day, he still wished he could smooth them away.

Crazy.

CHAPTER TWELVE

'This has to be one of the weirdest weddings we've ever done.'

Emily glanced over at Jonny as she arranged the huge displays of dyed black and purple roses around the altar, glad that he and Marla had made up again after their falling out. He'd been bereft after the smashed window incident, sending her all manner of oddball gifts, from subscriptions to cakes in the mail, to an oversized handmade card complete with glitter and lipstick kisses. In the end Marla had forgiven him on the understanding that he stopped putting her in such an untenable position with her postman.

'I love it. So dramatic . . .' Jonny sighed as he wobbled around on the stepladders to adjust the fake cobwebs that shrouded the rafters.

'Of course you do. It involves dressing up,' Emily rolled her eyes and shuddered. 'I'm not struck. It's like a scene from *Night of the Living Dead*.'

It wasn't Emily's idea of romance, but then who was she

to define love? She'd lost any authority on the subject the moment she'd allowed Dan anywhere near her. She admonished Bluey with a stern tut as he delicately pulled one of the black roses out of her artful display with his teeth.

Marla came through from the storeroom with her arms full of heavy purple velvet to create the gothic aisle. Alaric and Gelvira weren't your run-of-the-mill couple, but despite their ghoulish make-up and dark sense of fantasy, Marla had warmed to them straight away. They wanted a full-blown gothic extravaganza for their special day, and that was exactly what she intended to give them. The chapel looked resplendent in forbidding regalia, and Jonny was all too happy to conduct the ceremony decked out as the Grim Reaper.

'How long have we got left?' she yelled. It was tricky to make herself heard above the creepy organ music Jonny had stuck on the sound system.

Emily glanced at her watch. 'Three hours or so? We're on track.'

Marla joined Emily by the doors and together they surveyed the transformed chapel with a laugh.

'It's hideous.'

Emily nodded. 'I know. Perfect, huh?'

'Absolutely.'

'At least there's no danger of the funeral parlour upsetting these guests,' Emily said, leaning back to glance out of the shrouded chapel window at their neighbours. 'Looks like it's all quiet over there, anyway.'

'Let's just hope it stays that way,' Marla muttered.

She'd mailed a second copy of their bookings list to Gabe in the hope that he'd honour his original promise to do his best not to disrupt them, but after the fiasco with the window last week there could be no guarantees.

'Jonny, you better get your gear on soon. The photographer from *The Herald*'s coming by early to take some atmospheric shots.'

Jonny all but curled his lip. 'Will super-toff be coming too?'

Marla shook her head and shot him a glare. 'Stop being such a bitch, will you? Rupert is doing his best.'

'His best at what though, my love? Prancing around like Little Lord Fauntleroy? Tell me he has some knee breeches and I'll think about forgiving him.'

Jonny hadn't warmed to Rupert at all, and when pressed for an explanation he could come up with nothing more tangible than an ominous feeling in his famously sensitive waters.

For his part, Rupert had been as good as his word and had arranged for the wedding to be covered by the paper. He really was a powerful ally to have on side, as well as a skilful lover to have in her bed.

Jonny batted his lashes at Emily. 'Will you help me with my make-up?'

'Like you need it. You've got more eyeliner on than I do.'

'Guyliner,' he corrected cattily, even though there was no way his eyeliner erred on the discreet side. 'I need more than my usual day look for this. I'm thinking heavy kohl,' he painted around his eyes with his fingers to demonstrate. 'And white pan-stick.' He dragged his hands down his cheeks, ghoulish.

Marla laughed and headed up to the office, glad of its plain white walls and stark cleanliness after the lurid scenes downstairs. The only thing that stood out in the bleached room was her black lace dress hanging behind the door and her blood-red skyscraper heels ready for the ceremony.

She hadn't been able to stay mad at Jonny for long. Although he'd overstepped the mark by a long way with the campaign, she knew that his actions had come from a place of loyalty and affection. The way it had spiralled out of control had terrified the living daylights out of him. Over the last week she'd helped him to conduct a huge clean-up operation online, which was rather like trying to unpick the stitches of a very long scarf one by one. Finally they'd re-launched the chapel website with a huge banner thanking people for their support and officially closing the campaign. She could only cross her fingers and hope like hell that it was enough to put the whole affair to bed.

Marla might want the funeral parlour closed down, but she wasn't prepared to play dirty to make it happen.

'I now pronounce you husband and wife,' Jonny declared. 'You may now snog her face off!' He threw back his sackcloth hood and hurled his fake scythe to the floor to join in the thunderous applause.

The ghoulish congregation were packing the chapel almost to its spooky rafters, and from her standpoint at the side of the room, Marla had a clear view of the pure love in Alaric's heavily made-up eyes as he pulled his new wife into his arms. *The Herald* photographer whizzed from position to position in the background, keen to capture the wedding from every angle. She could see why: it would certainly make an eye-catching splash. The whole

115

production had been like *Gone with the Wind* crossed with *The Addams Family* – it throbbed with a vein of true love that challenged Marla's mistrust of marriage in a way that few of the more conventional weddings she had organised ever had.

Much as she loved the chapel, she'd fallen out of love with the institution of marriage a long time ago. Her parents had provided her with a close-up view of the reality of marriage throughout her childhood. It seemed to Marla that at its best, it was a soap opera with an ever-changing cast of principal players. If she'd taken one lesson away from her parents' example, it was that marriage was only ever to be regarded as a temporary arrangement. 'Till death us do part' was nothing more than a fairytale, and she wasn't a little girl anymore.

Outside on the chapel lawns, ghoul-faced guests posed by the fake rusty railings and blood-splattered mock head-stones that Jonny had organised to create the perfect 'fright night' backdrop for the photos. Jonny himself flitted around the lawn, his scythe raised aloft behind people as a macabre photo-bomber. Marla caught Emily's eye and laughed, relieved that yet another wedding had gone by without incident. And that was precisely when the incident happened.

'You haven't got a coffin, have you?'

Marla shook her head at the guy who lay on top of one of the fake graves. 'Sorry, no.'

'I bet *they* would.' Alaric's eyes slipped towards the funeral parlour.

A whoop went up around the crowd.

'I'll ask them! They can't turn a bride down on her wedding day.' Gelvira hitched up her scarlet velvet skirts and ran out across the pavement, hotly followed by her new husband and a motley trail of ghouls and ghosts.

Marla watched in horror, well aware that she didn't stand a hope in hell of halting the stampede. She could only cross her fingers and pray that Gabe wouldn't be there at this hour on a Saturday afternoon. He shouldn't be. She knew that much, because she'd surreptitiously checked the sign on the door earlier. It was well after four, so God willing he'd be off in the pub with his jack-the-lad mate. Or sleeping in one of his coffins to avoid the sunlight. Or whatever else it was he did for kicks in his spare time.

The small flicker of hope died as Gelvira and Alaric disappeared through the black and silver doorway. *Damn it!* Why was he still open? Marla leaned back against the porch and groaned. *Just when it had all been going so well.*

Several minutes later the wedding party spilled back out onto the pavement. Gelvira's boobs frothed over the top of her corset as she laughed and led her gothic troupe back over to the chapel.

'Man, this is the best day of my life!' Gelvira flung her arms around Marla in delight.

'He's bringing over a couple of coffins in a minute. Can you fetch loads of those black rose petals, please? I want to lie down inside one in my wedding dress.'

Inside the chapel, Marla could have screamed with frustration as she grabbed one of Emily's huge rose displays from the altar. She took her temper and embarrassment out on the dyed flowers as she yanked the petals off, managing to prick her finger on a thorn in the process.

Bloody Gabriel Ryan. Why couldn't he have just said no?

She sucked the blood from her finger and watched through the window as Gabe, assisted by one of the bridal party, deposited the first coffin onto the grass and strode back over to his lair to fetch a second one. He'd fit right in with this crowd, she thought, not quite able to take her eyes off the sight of his retreating denim-clad backside.

Once they'd set the second coffin down on the grass, Gabe shook Alaric's hand. His eyes flicked over the groom's shoulder to Marla as she struggled through the doorway with a huge cardboard box in her arms. Even amongst the impressive display of gothic cleavage that surrounded him, her relatively demure black lace dress clung to her curves in a way that rendered it indecent. Gelvira jiggled up and down with excitement next to him and waved her arms at Marla.

'Over here!'

Gabe clocked Marla's gritted teeth through her smile as she headed their way. He grinned, happy in the knowledge of how much it would grieve her that her guests had chosen to call on his help.

'Marla. This is an unexpected pleasure.'

Her eyes flashed with ill-concealed fury. 'Thank you, Gabriel. For your help, I mean.'

He could see that the outwardly cordial words had cost her dearly. He leaned over to lift the box from her arms and took the opportunity to whisper in her ear.

'See? I told you. Good things *can* happen when we work together.' His eyes lingered on the fresh bloom of blood on her fingertip. 'You might want to suck that.'

He heard her sharp intake of breath and winked imperceptibly as he pulled back and upended the petals all over a laughing Gelvira, who had climbed into the coffin.

'Bluey, no!' Emily's frantic shout rang out across the grass as the over-enthusiastic Great Dane bounded past her out of the side doorway of the chapel to join in the festivities. He made a beeline for the coffins and jumped straight into the empty one next to Gelvira on the grass.

'Here, boy!' Marla called out, aware that the sheer size of the dog was enough to spook most people. Even spooks. But Alaric, thankfully, fell instantly for the big hound with his droopy jaws and comic sense of timing. He stole a lace-trimmed top hat from one of the guests and placed it on Bluey's huge head, as someone else unwound their black tie and placed it around the dog's neck. To everyone's amusement, Bluey posed solemnly between the happy couple laid out in their coffins.

'One for the album,' Gabe murmured to Jonny, who grinned and turned pink beneath his theatrical make-up. He couldn't help it. It might be fraternising with the enemy, but he was high on the success of the wedding and Gabe was too hot to freeze out.

Emily leaned against the porch and laughed, right up to the moment when Dan pulled up in the hearse, at which point she promptly threw up behind the nearest mock headstone.

As proceedings wound down Alaric and Gelvira finally roared off into the sunset on a Harley, whilst their guests splintered off to scare the locals and boost the pub's coffers and Jonny vanished with a transvestite Bride of Dracula.

Marla turned to Emily inside the chapel and found her still slightly green around the gills.

'Cup of tea?'

Emily shook her head and glanced out of the window at the sound of a car engine.

'I couldn't stomach it.'

'Still feeling rough?'

Emily nodded. 'With lots of things.'

Marla looked at her quizzically. 'Is everything okay?'

Emily half shrugged. 'Yes. No . . .' She leaned back again to glance out of the window at the sound of another car engine outside the chapel. This time it slowed to a halt. 'There's Tom.'

Marla laid her hand on Emily's arm, sensing that her friend had been about to say more. 'Em, if you ever need an ear, choose mine, okay?'

Emily leaned in and kissed Marla's cheek. 'I'm fine. Honestly, I am.' With a squeeze of her hand and a small, tight smile, she was gone.

Which left Marla alone for a couple of moments, until Gabe shouldered open the front door and stepped inside.

CHAPTER THIRTEEN

'I guess I should say thank you again.'

Gabe followed her along the aisle into the kitchen. 'Go on then. I'm all ears.'

Marla reached for the coffee jar, but then thought better of it and grabbed a bottle of wine down out of the cupboard instead. 'You're enjoying this, aren't you?'

Why did saying thank you have to feel like such a huge admission of defeat?

She knew she owed him that much: he hadn't called the police about the window last week, and now he'd gone undeniably out of his way to make Alaric and Gelvira's wedding day perfect.

'You're welcome, Marla.' His soft laugh excused her reluctance to verbalise the apology, but somehow it made it worse too. Did he have to keep displaying that vein of decency and making her feel like a fool?

She reached down a glass from the top shelf, sighed and reached for a second.

'I believe you, by the way,' he said, as he leaned back in his chair. 'About the window, I mean.'

'Thank you. I may want your business closed down, Gabe, but I'd never stoop that low.'

She turned from the counter and held out a glass towards him.

'What's this, an olive branch?'

Marla sank down into the chair opposite him and kicked off her heels with a heavy sigh. The cool stone of the kitchen floor felt fabulous against her tired feet. It had been a long, long day and she was done in.

'Nothing's changed, Gabe, but we don't have to be arch-enemies either, do we? We can be grown up about our differences.'

He clinked his glass against hers. 'I like the sound of being grown up.'

Marla suddenly felt bolt awake. She wound her fingers around her glass to stop them from shaking, and took a swig of wine for good measure. Gabe's accent was enough to make a nun's knicker elastic twang, so she could easily justify her own physical reaction to him. It didn't *mean* anything. Besides, she hadn't eaten since breakfast. The butterflies in her stomach had more to do with lack of calories than Gabe's edibleness.

'Have you lived in the UK for long?'

Marla cast her mind back, glad that he'd steered the conversation into more serene waters.

'Fifteen years or so, I guess? My mother married a doctor and followed him here under the delusion of becoming lady of her very own English manor.'

'I take it it didn't work out then?'

'It was never going to. My mother is Floridian through to her very bones,' Marla answered. 'Robert was husband number five. He's lovely actually, I still meet up with him every now and then for coffee. He's a specialist over at the General.'

She sighed. 'It's a shame Mom couldn't settle here. She grew sick of the British weather and decamped back home to the States within four years.'

'But you stayed?'

She nodded. 'I was studying by then. And . . . other stuff.' She shrugged. 'You know how it is.'

He didn't actually, but he'd very much like to.

'Do you miss it? The States?'

'Sometimes. On the holidays, mostly. Halloween, Thanksgiving, that sort of thing.'

She swallowed a mouthful of wine and stared out of the window. 'It'll always feel like my home, but I'm pretty settled here now. The climate suits my skin. Unlike my mother's.'

He looked at the luxurious red waves that fell around her shoulders and had to hold down the urge to wind them around his fingers.

'I take it the red comes from your father's side then?'

Marla smiled. 'And the freckles.'

Gabe took her comment as an invitation to study her face, and this time he couldn't hold back. He reached out and traced his fingertip lightly down the dusting of freckles on her nose. 'I like your freckles.' Marla swallowed, her throat suddenly parched as his gaze held hers. His touch had been so fleeting and yet so intimate. He glanced away, breaking the moment, and refilled their glasses to cover the loaded silence that followed. 'Do you see much of your dad?'

Marla laughed, slightly hysterical with misplaced lust. 'You're kidding. He's always off on another exotic honeymoon.'

'I'm starting to see why you opened a wedding chapel.'

'He's in Bermuda with wife number six at the moment. Or it could be Hawaii with number seven . . . I've lost track.'

Gabe whistled. 'That must have made for interesting Christmases.'

Marla rolled her eyes. 'You have no idea.'

She picked at the edge of the wooden kitchen table and winced as a rough splinter caught the tender cut on her finger from the rose thorn. 'And are you upholding the family tradition with a string of ex-husbands littering your past, too?'

She flinched. 'No. I'm breaking the pattern and staying single.' He nodded slowly and dropped his gaze to their hands on the table. 'You're bleeding again.'

They both stared at the little bloom of blood on her fingertip and knew what was supposed to happen next. There wasn't a convenient box of tissues on hand to blot it, and no one interrupted them with a well-timed knock on the door. Gabe's warm hand closed over hers, and Marla's breath hitched in her throat. He lifted it to his lips and sucked her fingertip gently. He didn't take his eyes off hers and for a few seconds Marla felt as if he could see right inside her head, see just how much she wanted him to carry on. She'd been right all along. He *was* a vampire, and he'd glamoured her into submission. This was not her fault.

Jesus, his mouth was hot. And wet. And way, way too sexy to pull away. Up until that moment in her life, Marla had no idea about the secret vein that ran directly from her fingertip to her clitoris. But as Gabe circled his tongue slowly around her to seal the wound, each little suck on her finger fired off an answering volt of electricity between her legs. She closed her eyes, afraid he'd be able to see it there. *Or did he know already?* Marla squirmed in her seat, too turned on to get her breath properly. Or to care. On an erotic scale of one to ten, it was an eleven. Twenty. To infinity and beyond. The knuckles of her hand bumped against his jaw, rough stubble against soft skin. She suddenly wanted to know exactly how good that stubble would feel against her skin in much more private places. Her inner thighs, for instance. She almost cried out in protest when he slid her finger from his mouth and placed a whisper kiss on her palm, a barely there trail of his tongue against the vulnerable pulse point inside her wrist. She never wanted to open her eyes again.

But if she *had*, she'd have seen a very dejected Rupert turn and slope away from the window, where he'd just spent the most crushing five minutes of his life.

CHAPTER FOURTEEN

It was just after nine in the morning on the first Tuesday in May, and Emily lay curled in the crook of Tom's shoulder, relishing the decadent pleasure of a long and lazy extended bank holiday. Around them everyone else had gone back to work this morning, but they'd planned otherwise and closed the curtains against the world. She fuzzily contemplated getting up to make coffee as the hairs on Tom's chest tickled her closer to wakefulness. He traced sleepy circles low on the hollow of her back with his thumb, halfway towards soothing her to sleep and halfway towards turning her on.

She wriggled closer, and he slid his hand between her legs to settle the question.

This was who they were.

Emily and Tom. Tom and Emily.

The coffee could wait.

Half an hour later and fully awake, Emily slipped out of the warm circle of Tom's arms and padded downstairs to make coffee. She scooped up the newspaper and letters from the mat as she passed and dropped them on the kitchen table. The last couple of weeks had been amazing, like a second honeymoon. Except for one thing. One painfully huge, enormous elephant in the room.

Dan.

What had happened on her birthday had been a long time coming, an inevitable consequence of the Chinese water torture-style erosion of their marriage. She had hit rock bottom, and Dan had been her soft landing. A soft landing that she'd paid a daily penance for ever since with the ever-present weight of guilt on her shoulders. She could, of course, tell Tom. But who would she really be doing it for? Did he have a right to know, or was it better to shoulder the guilt and spare him the pain? She'd turned the question over in her mind all day, every day, and each night she'd tussled with it in her dreams.

She skim-read the doom and gloom headlines as she waited for the kettle to boil, and her eyes were pulled back again to the date. May 2nd. *May 2nd?* How had her head become so full of other stuff that she'd managed to stop watching the calendar more closely than a death row inmate? She grabbed her trying-to-conceive diary from the kitchen shelf and fumbled through the pages with shaky fingers. April 2nd, day one of cycle. April 16th, ovulation due. And there, with a bold red ring around it, was April 30th. The day her regular-as-clockwork period was due. Two days ago. She sank down onto the nearest chair. Elation soared through her heart like a songbird, followed by a great crashing tsunami of fear. Three minutes later, a trip to the bathroom delivered the life-changing news she'd

127

previously longed for. A precociously bright line popped up with indecent haste in the window that up to now had remained so stubbornly empty month on month.

She was pregnant.

CHAPTER FIFTEEN

'Champagne, please. Your best.' Marla cringed a little at Rupert's dismissive tone, and smiled at the unimpressed waitress.

'Are we celebrating?' She shuffled along the bench seat in the booth to give herself some breathing space from Rupert, who'd shunted himself in right next to her.

'Ta-da!' He whipped the freshly printed wedding supplement for the upcoming Sunday edition out of his briefcase and slapped it down on the table in front of them. 'Look. Go on, centre spread.'

She smoothed it out on the restaurant table and studied the splash of wedding pictures from Alaric and Gelvira's big day. *The Herald* photographer had managed to perfectly capture the essence of the day with his lens, the pictures bubbled over with fun and love. The accompanying piece on the chapel was undeniably fabulous PR, and would hopefully encourage the villagers to feel proud of the unique chapel in their midst.

She laughed at the shot of Bluey in the top hat, and then found herself unable to look away from Gabe in the background of the frame. It had been just over two weeks since the finger-sucking incident, and she'd gone to considerable lengths to avoid him. She could only thank her lucky stars that on that memorable day, Rupert had texted to let her know that he'd be there in five minutes, or else who knows what he might have walked in on. She badly needed to cool her engines as far as Gabe was concerned. She was old enough to have learned the hard way that a physical reaction to someone meant next to nothing; being turned on by a hot body was never to be confused with real feelings. She couldn't deny that the chemical reaction between herself and Gabriel fizzed like popping candy, but she also knew that too much candy would make a girl sick.

Marla accepted a glass of champagne from Rupert with a grateful smile, and clinked obediently when he held his own glass out with an expectant look.

'It's brilliant. Thank you, Rupert.'

'Should piss on Gabriel Ryan's bonfire, anyway,' he smirked. Marla's smile faltered. As much as she appreciated Rupert's help, sometimes she wondered if he was more interested in saving the chapel or bringing Gabe down. He was right though; the article would be a strong piece of supportive evidence to include in the dossier she was preparing to submit to the council on the matter. The petition might have been sidelined, but she was still intent on lobbying the council to make them see sense about the situation.

The feel of Rupert's hand massaging her knee under the table brought her swiftly back to the present.

'So, am I the best boyfriend you've ever had, or what?'

She laughed and rolled her eyes. 'And so modest, too.'

'Should I take that as a yes, then?' Marla coughed on her champagne. *Jeez, it wasn't a rhetorical question.* He actually wanted an answer. But then, it was one of those questions with only one possible answer anyway, wasn't it?

'Um . . . let me think.' She smiled and played for time. *Was* he the best boyfriend she'd ever had? Was he even her boyfriend? It seemed such an arbitrary title. She hadn't planned on their relationship status progressing beyond friends with benefits, yet they'd somehow slipped into the more official roles of boyfriend and girlfriend regardless. He knew how she took her coffee. She knew his shoe size from a recent shopping trip. He rubbed her aching shoulders at the end of a busy day. She'd mastered the art of Welsh rarebit because he'd mentioned in passing that it had been his childhood favourite. If these familiarities and kindnesses could be considered markers of a relationship, then yes, Rupert was indeed her boyfriend, and given how bad her other boyfriends had been, he, bizarrely, stood every chance of being the best one she'd had to date. He wasn't married to anyone else, for a start, which gave him a big advantage over the other two men who'd made up her significant romantic history to date. She enjoyed his company, and he could make her squirm with pleasure in bed – or at least he *had* been able to, before a certain dark-eyed Irishman had set up his X-rated camp temporarily in her head. Rupert was entertaining. He made her laugh, and behind closed doors he could be kind and thoughtful. But the most important thing about Rupert was that her heart was safe. He would never break it, because it would never be his to break.

'You know what, Rupert? I can hand on heart say that, yes, you are the best boyfriend I've ever had.'

He leaned in and kissed her for longer than she was entirely comfortable with in a restaurant, even if they were tucked away in a booth.

'Happy?' he whispered, when he finally allowed her up for air. She nodded with an affectionate smile. He looked like a schoolboy, eager to please. 'I am. Thank you.'

His fingers slipped under the hemline of her skirt. Okay, maybe not so schoolboy, after all. 'You're welcome, Marla.' He leaned back in and kissed her again, taking the chance to inch his fingers further up her thigh.

'Rupert,' she warned, and slid away from him a little more until she was wedged against the wooden wall of the booth. He scooted closer in response, his fingers scandalously near to her knickers. 'Rupert, stop it,' she hissed out of the side of her mouth with a surreptitious glance at the neighbouring booths.

'Chill out. No one can see.' Lust had thickened his voice to a growl as he tried to work a finger under the cotton of her underwear. Marla clamped her thighs together hard in an effort to cut off his blood supply and prove that she really meant it.

'Tease,' he laughed and tickled her ribs, which had the unfortunate effect of forcing her to release her death grip on his hand.

Marla cringed. God, he thought she was enjoying this, and the worst thing was that she couldn't even blame him for the assumption. She'd found herself over-compensating ever since that night in the chapel kitchen with Gabe, and had been all but hanging from the chandeliers during sex in order to tip the scales back in Rupert's favour. It didn't help that it took all of her concentration not to imagine that it was Gabe rather than Rupert who reached for her in bed; so much so that she'd started to insist on sex with the lights on and her eyes open. As a consequence, Rupert now had her pegged as something of a sex maniac, and no doubt imagined that a spot of public groping would get her all steamed up. He couldn't have been more wrong.

'Rupert . . .' She twisted her fingers into the back of his floppy hair and yanked it. Hard. 'If you don't get your hand out of my skirt right now, I'll stab you with my steak knife.'

She felt him still momentarily as he glanced at her taut fingers curled around the silver handle of the knife on the table.

'You are a naughty, naughty little minx,' he croaked. 'I'm going to have to punish you severely for this when we get home.' He sank his teeth into her earlobe, but removed his hand from her skirt all the same. Marla breathed out and eased her grip on the knife, not even sure herself how much she'd been joking.

CHAPTER SIXTEEN

Dan straightened his black tie and winked at his reflection in the rear window of the hearse.

Not too shabby, Danny boy. Not too shabby at all.

It was just a shame that Emily from the chapel didn't seem to agree with him. He'd only caught one fleeting glimpse of her since her birthday and she'd looked scared witless. What did she think he was going to do? Fall on his knees in front of her in the street and declare his undying love? She needn't fear that of him.

He knew the score. She was a married woman. He wasn't going to broadcast her infidelity to anyone else, but something about her melancholy beauty had got under his skin in a way that didn't sit easily with his usual 'love 'em and leave 'em' attitude. He'd actually *liked* her, as well as wanting to get in her knickers. He knew he couldn't expect anything to come of it, but all the same, he couldn't quite shake her.

'Dan, you almost ready?'

Gabe appeared at the back door dressed in equally sombre attire, his dark hair marginally more tamed than usual out of respect for Charlie Gibbons, a local veteran of both world wars. Come one o'clock, Beckleberry High Street would be filled with mourners ready to walk the five-minute journey behind the hearse to the local church, a fitting tribute to a man who deserved only the very best of send-offs.

'What's up, bud?' Dan asked, tipping his head to one side.

Gabe sighed. He looked to Dan like a man who could do with a cigarette, but as a non-smoker Gabe would have to shoulder his stress without that convenient crutch to lean on.

'I just need today to go without a hitch, you know? It's our biggest funeral so far. I didn't know Charlie for long, but long enough to know that he was one of the good guys.'

Dan nodded. Charlie had been a part of his childhood; the local hero who'd always laid the village poppy wreath on Remembrance Sunday. He'd spent much of the last decade propping up the bar in the pub, reminiscing about the past with his personalised Jameson glass in his hand.

'He was that,' Dan said. 'His will be one heck of a bar stool to fill.'

Gabe ran through the order of events in his head for the hundredth time. 'You've fuelled the hearse up?'

Dan nodded. 'Fuelled and immaculate. We're good to go.' He put a hand on Gabe's shoulder. 'Relax, bud. I've got your back.'

Gabe appreciated his best friend's support. Dan wasn't the most likely of hearse drivers with his ever-present big smile and a joke always hovering on his lips, but he'd bent himself into shape for the job to help Gabe out. He swallowed hard. Half an hour until Charlie's family were due to arrive.

'Come on then, Dan. We'd better get Charlie into the hearse.'

Over at the chapel, Marla searched around by the CD player in confusion.

'Emily, where's the CD gone with today's music?'

She'd almost completed her third and final set of checks, her ritual safety net half an hour before any wedding was due to start. The CD had been there on the two previous passes, but it was now nowhere to be seen.

Emily came through from the kitchen with the disc balanced between her fingers.

'Don't panic, it's here. I was just giving it a last polish.' She glanced outside as she slid it back into the machine. 'It's gorgeous out there today. Perfect wedding weather.'

Marla nodded. Everything was in place, even the sunshine, so why did she feel an uneasy sense of foreboding? She checked her watch and chewed her bottom lip. Half past midday. The guests would be arriving soon.

'Dora definitely, *definitely* let them know next door that we have a wedding on today?'

Due to Marla's reluctance to go within spitting distance of Gabe, they had ungraciously settled on a system of using Dora as a neutral go-between to ward off potential problems. It was far from ideal yet so far it had worked, just about; but this wedding had been a last-minute booking from a couple who'd decided at the eleventh hour that they wanted to start married life in a more exciting way than the registry office they'd had planned.

Emily nodded.

'All covered. I asked her twice. Stop worrying, Marla, we're ready to go.'

Dora wasn't on duty at either the chapel or the funeral parlour that morning.

At precisely half past eleven, Ivan held the door open to the little Italian restaurant further down the High Street for his wife to walk in ahead of him. It was their wedding anniversary, and come hell or high water, he always made a point of taking Dora out to celebrate. It used to be dinner, but had slowly crept forward to a lunchtime date because it was easier on their ageing digestive systems. Their bodies might have aged, but their love and affection for each other burned as bright as the day they'd married.

Alfonso, the effervescent Italian chef and owner appeared, and ushered them across the restaurant to a candlelit alcove he'd prepared especially for them.

'Dora, my darling, bellissima as always,' he said, and kissed her cheek as he pulled a chair out for her to take a seat. His heavily accented English added to his charm as he greeted the couple like old friends, shaking hands with Ivan and wishing them both a happy anniversary as he handed them their menus.

Dora settled into her chair and smiled around at the smattering of other diners, knowing most of them by name, or face at least. Beckleberry was small enough for few people to be strangers, and Dora and Ivan were well respected as quite possibly the eldest and most established residents of them all.

Ivan opened his menu, dazzled by the delights of a lunch

cooked by someone other than Dora. Much as he loved his wife, he hadn't married her for her culinary skills.

Dora flicked a cursory eye over the menu and then closed it.

'Lasagne, my love?' Ivan said, knowing she was a creature of habit.

Dora nodded. The lasagne was not only delicious, it provided no challenge to her false teeth.

'I think I might have the T-bone,' Ivan mused, adjusting his tweed dickie-bow.

'Don't be an old goat, Ivan,' Dora chided, knowing that however much his rheumy eyes might still have their same blue twinkle, his gut didn't have the same cast-iron constitution it had enjoyed thirty years back.

Alfonso reappeared in short order and threw a knowing look towards Dora.

'Lasagne for you, bella?'

Dora preened, hoping that the other customers had overheard and realised that she was a regular customer. Or once yearly, in any case.

Alfonso scribbled on his pad and then looked up and tipped a wink at Ivan. 'For you, I have something special, my friend.' He pocketed his pen without further comment and left them alone again, feeling thoroughly special and spoiled.

Ivan reached across and patted Dora's hand. 'Sixty-nine years. Thank you, a-Dora-ble.'

She smiled at the use of the nickname he'd given to her, looking down at their old hands, his wedding ring and hers. Neither had been taken off so much as once since the day they were slid in place. It had been a day full of joy, and loaded with the anticipation of many happy years ahead and children on their knees. The years had indeed been happy ones, but the much-longed-for children had never come to pass.

'No regrets?' she asked.

'Not one.' Ivan squeezed her hand, knowing that she was thinking of the babies she'd never been able to carry to term. 'I've even grown to love your cooking.'

Dora laughed softly, aware that he was joking to lighten her heart and she loved him all the more for it. These days there was all sorts of medical help available for women, but back in her day, her miscarriages had been put down to Mother Nature decreeing that she just wasn't destined to be a mother. She'd settled instead for mothering everyone around her.

She glanced up as Alfonso approached the table with two plates.

'Lasagne for the lady,' he said, presenting it with a flourish.

'And for you, Ivan, my special roast beef.' He placed Ivan's lunch down; meltingly soft beef, baby rosemary and garlic roast potatoes and seasonal vegetables. Leaning in to imply confidentially, he said 'better than any T-bone,' and kissed his fingertips expressively. 'Delizioso. Enjoy!'

And they did. They enjoyed each other's company, and the perfectly sized portions that Alfonso had carefully prepared. It was a rare treat, and an injection of old-fashioned romance into their old-fashioned love affair. At their time of life romance wasn't high on either of their priority lists. They were just happy to have a warm hand to hold in bed, daily episodes of *Countdown*, and a nightly nip of whisky in their tea.

'Dessert, a-Dora-ble?' Ivan said, eyeing up the tiramisu that had just arrived at a nearby table.

Dora frowned and patted her stomach. 'I really shouldn't.'

Ivan played the game. He was well used to it after almost seventy years together. 'You're as lovely now as you were on our wedding day. Have some pudding.'

'Oh go on then,' Dora grumbled. 'Just to keep you company.' She opened her sweet menu gleefully, blissfully unaware that further on down the High Street, Gabriel's receptionist Melanie had deliberately chosen not to pass on the message she'd asked her to give him about the wedding that was due to take place at the chapel at one p.m.

'Come on Charlie old boy, your public awaits you.'

Dan opened the funeral parlour gates and drove sedately around into the street, his precious cargo behind him. Charlie's many friends and family fell silent as the hearse eased its way amongst them, and several veteran soldiers, their medals glinting in the warm sunshine, removed their hats and saluted their brother-in-arms. Gabe emerged out onto the street with Eleanor, Charlie's widow, on his arm. She'd chosen to say a private farewell to her husband, and had just accepted a nip of Jameson as Dutch courage to help her through the ordeal of burying him.

Gabe took a respectful step away and the crowd bowed their heads as Eleanor placed her wedding hand flat against the glass, a final moment to draw strength from the man who'd shared her life for the last sixty years.

Just up the road in the pub, a posse of bright and raucous wedding guests drank up and streamed outside, in fine

140

voice as they belted out the chorus of 'Chapel of Love'.

Seconds earlier, Marla had caught sight of the funeral procession in the street and flung herself out of the chapel doors, just in time to see the wedding party tottering towards her in a flurry of rainbow-coloured feather fascinators and mini-skirts.

Inside, Emily and Jonny escorted the groom away from the windows in the nick of time with the promise of a fortifying brandy. A Mexican wave of silence rippled through the wedding guests as they came to a halt outside the chapel and caught sight of the sombre gathering amassed further along the pavement. Each party looked dazed by the presence of the other – a gaggle of effervescent peacocks faced down by an austere flock of ravens. They turned in unison at the sound of a car's engine, and watched in fascinated horror as the bride's Rolls-Royce arrived to complete the tableau. Its white ribbons fluttered in the breeze as it came to rest nose-to-nose with the hearse.

Marla was going to literally kill Gabriel Ryan for this.

She met his eyes across the crowd, and even from this distance she could see her own fury reflected at her.

The man had some nerve.

The bride's chauffeur opened her door and helped her out onto the pavement, a celebratory confection in white. Marla could hardly bear to watch as her expression slipped from joy, to confusion, to shock, before finally settling on horror as she stared at the floral 'husband' tribute that lay in the hearse next to Charlie's coffin.

For a few seconds, everyone stood motionless, as if someone had turned off the music in a game of musical statues.

The sunbeams that bounced off the crystals on the bodice of the bride's dress were reflected by the tears that shimmered on her cheeks as she met Eleanor's eyes.

Charlie's widow was the first to recover herself enough to make a move. She braced her bird-slender shoulders in her neat black suit and walked slowly to stand in front of the bride. She unsnapped her handbag and pulled out a starched white handkerchief.

'Dry your eyes, pet. You don't want to greet your new husband like that.'

The bride took the handkerchief and dabbed her cheeks.

'Thank you. I'm so sorry about . . . about your husband.'

Eleanor nodded, and reached out to touch the bride's bouquet of blood-red roses.

'Roses were Charlie's favourite. He was never much of a gardener mind, but he loved roses.'

The bride eased a stem from the bouquet and held it out to Eleanor, who accepted it with faraway eyes.

'It rained on our wedding day, you know. Absolutely poured down. Charlie's mother said it was a bad omen, but then she always was a sour old crow.'

The bride laughed gently through her tears.

'She was wrong, though,' Eleanor said. 'The day I married Charlie he held an umbrella over my head to keep me safe, and he carried on doing that for sixty-two years.'

She reached out and placed her hands over the bride's clasped ones.

'Go on now pet, you've kept that young man of yours waiting long enough.'

*   *   *

142

Inside the chapel a little while later, the bride's eyes shone with happy tears as she surprised her new husband with a new line in their chosen wedding vows.

'I'll always be your umbrella.'

CHAPTER SEVENTEEN

Later that afternoon, Marla hoovered the aisle, aware that they'd avoided disaster only by the very thinnest skin of their teeth. It could very easily have gone differently, and ruined both the bride's and the widow's most important days. Gabe had obviously played it fast and loose on purpose to ram home his point. He held the cards. He could play God and rain havoc down on her head any time he chose, so if she had any sense she would shut up and put up.

The already-spotless carpet bordered on baldness as she ruminated on what she *should* have done, what she *should* have said. Marla was an expert at creating the perfect put-down with the benefit of hindsight; she wished she could wind back the clock and deliver the punchlines at the time. Her chest flamed with anger as she leaned on the vacuum cleaner and glared at the funeral parlour. Something inside her snapped, and she shoved the vacuum aside loudly enough to make Bluey open one eye and check on the situation. Maybe she couldn't turn back time, but she *could* do the next best thing – she could go over there right now and deliver her thoughts in person.

Marla glanced through the window to check the funeral parlour was empty of customers and then flung the door open, heartened immeasurably by the look of undisguised horror on the receptionist's face.

'Gabriel. Now. And don't try telling me he isn't here, because I know damn well that he is.'

She stared pointedly at Melanie, who flushed a dull shade of puce and was clearly in the grip of a desperate desire to come up with an equally pithy reply. She was saved the bother by Gabe, who stalked into reception with a face like thunder.

'I take it you've come to apologise.' Icicles dripped from his every word. A tiny smug smile crept over Melanie's lips, and Marla's hand itched to wipe it off.

'*Excuse me?*'

Was he seriously going to attempt to foist the blame for today's fiasco onto her? Marla's hands found their way onto her hips of their own accord as her blood cooked in her veins.

'Not that I'm interested in an apology from you, anyway,' Gabe muttered, almost as an afterthought.

'Good. Because you're not going to get one.'

Gabe snorted. 'That figures. So why *are* you here?'

'To tell you that your sordid little scheme was a low blow. To deliberately set out to ruin someone's wedding day was . . . it was beyond cruel, Gabriel. Not to mention the mess you made of that funeral.' She paused to draw breath and shook her head. 'God knows why, but I actually thought better of you.'

She stood firm on her moral high ground and watched

a sequence of expressions filter across his face like a silent movie. *Did he flinch?* She saw confusion, definitely, uncertainty, maybe, before he settled on cold disbelief.

'You can stop right there, lady. Don't storm in here and try to shove the blame onto *my* shoulders.' He turned to Melanie with an incredulous shrug. 'Can you believe you're hearing this?'

Melanie gave a nervous little laugh as she shook her head and inched closer to Gabe, subtly staking her claim.

'Too right I'm blaming you, Mister,' Marla blazed. 'I know full well that Dora told you about the wedding today, and you never said a damn word about a funeral.'

'Dora did no such bloody thing,' he half yelled, and turned towards his receptionist with that brief flicker of uncertainty again. 'Did she?'

Melanie shook her head with wide regretful eyes.

'No. I told her about Charlie's funeral at *least* twice, Gabe, honestly. She *definitely* never mentioned a wedding or I'd have realised there was a problem,' Melanie replied, her voice cracking and her fingertips dabbing at her eyes.

Gabe put his arm around Melanie's shoulders and favoured her with a supportive smile. 'Hey, it's fine, Mel. No one's blaming you.' He shot a look of disgust at Marla. 'Happy? Is your day complete now that you've managed to make another innocent person cry?' He guided Melanie down into her chair and handed her a tissue from the customer box on the desk. 'You've been baying for blood all day, you must have been gutted when there weren't any fireworks at lunchtime.'

Marla's fists balled up in frustration.

How had Gabe managed to cast her as Cruella de Vil?

Staring at his hostile face, she realised she would gain nothing by staying any longer. He'd wiped the floor with her argument and made her feel a fool. He obviously had no interest in hearing her side of the story.

She'd lost this particular battle, but she was going to win this bloody war, or die trying. And the first and most satisfying bullet of all was going to be wiping that smug look right off Melanie's pretty face.

Gabe thumped his fist down onto the desk, torn between fury and frustration as he watched Marla stomp back to the chapel. On the one hand he wanted to believe the best of her, because the idea that she had engineered today's events cast her in a distinctly unflattering light.

But if she hadn't been behind it, then how the hell *had* things gone so wrong? Surely Dora wouldn't have made such a disastrous mistake? She might be well into her eighties but she was as sharp as a pin.

Which left just one other person who could have influenced the day's events.

Melanie.

He turned to look at her, with her pale mascara-streaked cheeks as she picked at the hem of her cardigan. She was on his side. Why on earth would she sabotage things? It didn't make any sense, and the last thing he wanted to do was upset her more by expressing any doubts. He sighed heavily. None of the possible scenarios added up. Awarding the benefit of the doubt to Melanie and wanting to believe the best of Marla left him having to make uneasy peace with the idea that it must have just slipped Dora's mind.

*   *   *

147

Emily flushed the loo and sat down on the seat to get her breath back. Was it possible to actually die of morning sickness? She certainly felt like it at least five times a day. And it wasn't just mornings either. It was morning, noon and night sickness. Was she being punished? If she wasn't, she felt as if she should be. Tom had slipped straight into overprotective husband gear as soon as she'd told him about the baby. The kitchen cupboard brimmed with ginger biscuits, and he ran her a warm bath each evening with the lavender-scented oil he'd picked out especially to help her sleep. His thoughtfulness only added to Emily's burden of guilt as her salty tears slid into the lavender bath water each night. Theoretically, there was a slim chance that the baby could be Tom's, but her mind wouldn't permit that thought in amongst the self-flagellation and recriminations. She'd slept with another man. How dare she try and comfort herself with maybes?

She deserved to suffer daily for what she'd done, and what the hell was going to happen when Dan found out that she was pregnant? It wouldn't take a genius to work out that it might be his. Would he tell Tom, come over all paternal and insist on blood tests and such like? Fresh waves of horror washed over her every time she thought about it. God, it would make perfect fodder for the *Jeremy Kyle Show*.

How could she have been so stupid? She could see it now, Jeremy sitting on his top step and pouring scorn on her pitiful excuses as the entire audience bayed for her tainted, slattern blood.

God, she could kill for a glass of wine.

* * *

Marla lay in bed just after midnight, Rupert spooned around her, warm and deeply asleep less than ten minutes since he'd orgasmed. He'd taken good care of her tonight, bringing her an unasked-for takeaway from the Chinese restaurant on the High Street, and rubbing her shoulders as he listened to the whole sorry tale of her disastrous day. She knew that he had his faults and that Jonny couldn't stand the sight of him, but she appreciated the pressure-free nature of their relationship. He was a warm body against hers, and he had a sharp sense of humour that made her laugh. He wasn't her soul mate, but then she wasn't searching for that. Hell, she didn't even believe in all that. They enjoyed each other's company both in and out of the bedroom, and for Marla at least, that was enough.

CHAPTER EIGHTEEN

Melanie held the small envelope over the kettle and winced as the steam scalded her fingertips. It always looked easier than this in the movies, she thought, as she finally managed to open the damn thing and extract the note.

She stopped and sighed at the sight of Gabe's bold, slanted handwriting, even though she already knew perfectly well that it was from him. But the dreamy smile slid from her face as she scanned the missive.

Dear Marla,
Something to help make your July 4th go with a bang, and to say I hope we can enjoy a less explosive friendship from here on in.
Yours,

Gabe
X

Melanie read it twice more. Her heart thumped with adrenalin from her own audacious detective work, as well as annoyance at Gabe's blind determination to smooth things over with that woman.

Why couldn't he just let it be? Dora had unknowingly become the fall guy for last weekend's debacle, and Melanie had learned a valuable lesson. She needed to be less obvious with her meddling.

Gabe had gone off to some undertaking convention for the day and left her in charge, making her all glowy inside with the knowledge that he trusted her. She'd even managed a mechanical smile earlier when Gabe had asked her to run a package over to the chapel at some point during the day. She sat down again at reception and poked the offensive parcel with her toe, hard enough to put a little rip in the pretty paper Gabe had used to wrap it. Bad luck if Marla's gift looked a little shabby and hastily put together by the time it arrived. A surreptitious glance under the ripped corner of paper revealed the contents of the box. Fireworks. Melanie all but growled with anger as she slid the little note back into its envelope, but didn't re-attach it to the parcel. Instead she placed it on the desk in front of her, tapping it with one finger and trying to decide if she had the guts to bin it.

A tiny scream of temper escaped as she recalled his sign-off again.

Yours, Gabe. X

He wasn't Marla's.

He was *hers*. Or at least, he should be.

Bugger. She *really* didn't want to deliver the parcel, which was why it was still sitting under her desk at gone half past four.

Hope we can enjoy a less explosive friendship.

Pah. He wasn't that witty with the notes he left for Melanie.

Do this please, Melanie, or *Ring so and so please, Melanie,* was about the sum of it. Although actually, a couple of weeks back he had left one note where he'd signed-off with an x under his name, a much-handled Post-it note that now resided in her bedside table for nightly stroking purposes.

She scowled at the fireworks. It was a great big box to lug about. What did Gabe think she was, a packhorse? She wanted to be the one who received his thoughtful gifts and notes, not just the delivery girl to someone else who clearly didn't want or deserve his attention.

Much as she'd like to go and fling the box in the nearest canal, there was no way out of the fact that she had to take them to the chapel. Gabe was sure to mention them to Marla, and then where would she be? She'd just have to tough it out, because, well, love was just like that sometimes.

Outside the window, the owner of a small open-top sports car revved his engine as he made a meal of parking. She recognised the driver and huffed again. Great. Another man hanging on to Marla's irresistible coat tails. Melanie had originally been thrilled that the feckless guy from the newspaper had arrived on the scene. Surely he would stamp on any buds of friendship between Marla and Gabe? She was doing everything she could at this end to subtly nurture the 'us and them' mentality between the funeral parlour and the chapel, but Rupert had so far proved himself too much of a fop to be much use as an accomplice.

She watched him unfurl his gangly limbs out of the car with a sour taste in her mouth. The man oozed wealth and self-satisfaction in his Ray-Bans and white Ralph Lauren jeans.

A zing of irritation flashed through her as he reached down into the back of the car and emerged with a bunch of flowers. Marla bloody Jacobs should just be done with it and erect a sign outside the chapel telling lovesick gift-givers to form an orderly queue. And then the brilliant idea struck her.

Quick as a flash, she hopped around the desk and flung the front door open just as Rupert rounded the bonnet of his car.

'Excuse me!'

She called out, and added a loud cough for extra security. She didn't want to risk him not hearing her now that she'd spotted her big chance.

Oh good, he was turning around. Melanie felt the heat flood her cheeks.

'Could I, er, have a word please?'

Rupert slid his glasses down his nose and glanced over his shoulder as if he expected her to be talking to someone behind him. Finding no one, he shrugged and sauntered back across the road.

Melanie faltered. Close up he really was a rather attractive man, in a clean cut and useless sort of way.

'I have something . . . a parcel. It's to be delivered to the chapel.'

'Have you mistaken me for the postman?'

His smug smile did nothing to lessen the pompousness of his joke, but Melanie decided to play along with a nervous laugh.

'Hang on there a sec please . . .' She ducked back inside the funeral parlour, and emerged again a few seconds later, dumping the big box awkwardly into Rupert's arms.

He stared at it with a furrowed brow. He'd obviously been expecting something redirected from the regular mail, not a brightly covered gift box. He looked at Melanie blankly.

'It's fireworks. From Gabe.'

His jaw tightened, giving away his annoyance.

'Fireworks? What the hell for?'

'It's July 4th. Americans have fireworks. Independence Day, and all that.'

A look of pure hatred turned Rupert's handsome face momentarily ugly. Melanie took the limp flowers dangling from his fingertips and laid them on top of the gift box as an idea formed in her head.

'The card has fallen off. It's on my desk. I could get it, if you think . . .'

Melanie held her breath as she waited for him to connect the dots, and breathed out as the light of understanding clicked on.

'No, no need for that. I'll see that Marla gets them.'

Melanie nodded and rewarded Rupert with a small smile for taking the bait.

''Kay then. Thanks.'

She watched him swagger away towards the chapel, struggling to get his sunnies back in place before he opened the door.

Melanie brushed her clammy hands down her skirt as she went back inside. Rupert had just gone up a notch in her estimation. Perhaps now he would be the ally she'd hoped he would be. She slumped into her chair, exhausted. All this duplicity was turning out to be hard work, but also strangely enjoyable. Hell, she might even let herself eat the Mars bar she'd been saving up for the last three months as a celebration.

'Rupert, that is so thoughtful!' Marla flung her arms around Rupert's neck and hugged him tight. His gift touched her deeply. She hadn't expected him to even realise the significance of the date, let alone go out of his way to find fireworks in the middle of summer.

'Will you help me with them tonight?'

She pulled the lid off the box as she spoke and laughed with delight at the sight of the multicoloured rockets.

'We'll have to do it here though, your garden is way too small for this kind of thing.'

Rupert eyed the large firework in Marla's hand. She nodded. He was right. Her garden was tiny with overhanging trees, and Rupert's communal apartment garden was out of the question. No, the chapel garden out back would be perfect.

She placed the rocket back in the box and turned to Rupert. His skin was warm and smelled of expensive aftershave; she wound her arms around him and nestled into his neck.

'Thank you.'

His hands moved straight down to massage her bottom as he sought out her lips with his own.

'You can show me the full extent of your appreciation later.' He waggled his eyebrows, whilst privately thinking that he looked forward to personally thanking Gabriel Ryan later, in private, for his thoughtful and well-received gift.

Marla kissed him and leaned back in the circle of his arms.

'Oh, go on then. I'll let you light the first rocket.'

Rupert laughed low and dirty.

'You've just lit my rocket.' He rocked against her and pinched her bum hard to prove his claim. Marla jumped away and slapped his hand.

'Rupert, I'm at work. Come back later.'

He rolled his eyes.

'You're the boss. I'll be back at eight. Be ready for action.'

Marla watched him leave, not entirely sure if he'd been talking about the fireworks or not. Probably not. She bit her lip, and tried to summon enthusiastic thoughts, not prepared to give headspace to the fact that the thought of sex with Rupert didn't excite her as much as it really ought to.

She knelt down and scrubbed Bluey behind the ears.

'Don't worry darling, I've got some lovely furry earmuffs and a big bone to distract you from the fireworks.'

Bluey was impractically large for her office, but her neighbours complained if she left him at home because he wailed like a baby. As long as he was with Marla he was happy, a feeling that went both ways. Bluey's constant presence at her side was something she'd come to love and rely on. On previous bonfire nights he'd proven himself to be mostly unfussed by fireworks, which was just as well if he was going to be here for their little display later.

Melanie took the Mars bar out of the fridge and sliced it into tiny slivers, before arranging it on the plate in a perfect spiral.

'I'm going to my room.'

She wasn't sure why she bothered to tell her father. It wasn't like he could care less whether she was in her room, or in the house at all for that matter. As long as his dinner hit the table at six o'clock and she left betting money on the side each morning, he didn't give a damn what happened in between. He must have been thrilled that her mother had given him a daughter rather than a son before she so thoughtlessly passed away, someone to take over the mantle of caring for his every need. She'd been the only kid at her primary school who understood the washing machine cycles better than her seven times table. Her senior school days had been governed by the need to get home to cook her father's dinner, ruling out the after-school clubs and discos that the other kids took for granted. Her only solace came from her excellent grades and the fact that they allowed her to find a decent job. A place to escape to, somewhere where no one knew her drinking, gambling father or had been inside their dark, shabby home.

Up in her room, Melanie perched on the edge of her bed and slid open the bedside drawer. Gabe's Post-it note from a few weeks back was the only thing in there, and she held it for a few seconds to help to calm down. Gabe. Just thinking of him warmed her cool skin. He was so lovely. No one had ever given her flowers before, or made her a cup of tea, or given her little notes. She placed it reverentially back in the drawer and reached out for a piece of chocolate, when the most terrible thought struck her.

The other *note.*

The note from the fireworks box was still on her desk.

Shit, shit, shit.

157

Cold panic iced her heart. There was no way she could leave it until the morning. Gabe might get there early and spot it; she couldn't bear him to question her on what had happened.

She'd have to go back and get it right now. Thank God Gabe had trusted her enough to give her a set of keys. He'd never know that she'd been back there this evening.

She tipped the Mars bar into the dustbin in disgust and dashed outside, grabbing the keys to her Mini as she went.

CHAPTER NINETEEN

'Happy Independence Day, gorgeous.'

Marla clinked her glass against Rupert's outstretched one with a smile. She was all warm inside and out from two glasses of champagne and the last rays of the evening sunshine.

'Thank you,' she smiled and sipped her fizz. 'Do you know what Independence Day actually celebrates?'

His eyes sparked with amusement. 'I rather fear it's when the Americans liberated themselves from the British.'

'That's right,' Marla laughed and nodded. 'Watch your step, mister. Your days are numbered.'

'I don't think so, lady,' Rupert arched his eyebrows and topped up her glass. 'Although I'm fired-up and ready if you'd like a skirmish.' He ran an experimental hand down her backside and she admonished him with a playful frown.

'Fireworks first. I think it's dark enough now,' she declared as she fished around in the box for the lighting rod. As a child back home in the States they'd have rowed out on the lake near her mother's Florida holiday house to watch the July 4th fireworks with blankets around their shoulders, but in its own unexpected way, this was just as exciting.

She banged the stake into the lawn and nodded towards the box.

'Choose one.'

Rupert studied the contents and picked out a small fountain.

'A rather reserved choice, sir.' Marla laughed as the swish of flame shot along the fuse, sending a spray of gold shimmers up into the dwindling light.

'What shall we have next?'

She rummaged in the box like a kid in a sweetshop and came out with a huge rocket in her outstretched hands.

Rupert took it from her with a look of barely disguised alarm on his face and pranced around with stiff arms as if she'd given him a live grenade with the pin pulled out.

'It's not even lit yet, you idiot!' Marla giggled.

He somehow managed to get it onto the spike, still as skittish as a pony as he flicked the lighter ineffectively towards it.

'Move over, Guy Fawkes. Let me.'

Marla took the lighter, igniting the fuse like a pro, and they stepped back hand in hand to watch the rocket fizz into life. It hissed and sizzled for an uncertain second, before whooshing up into the darkening sky in a glittering cascade of scarlet stars.

Marla clapped with delight and set up the next one straight afterwards, this time a spangle of blue stars. A ball of homesickness lodged in her throat as she imagined the beautiful rainbow skies over America tonight. In that moment she forgave Rupert for his reticence to light the fireworks. He'd given her this wonderful surprise; she should cherish his kindness far more than she did.

She wrapped her arms around him and tilted her chin up with a smile.

'Rupert, thank you. I love that you did this for me.'

He smiled and lowered his mouth to hers, thanking his lucky stars that he'd been the one to give her the fireworks. 'I love you too, Marla.'

Despite the fact that he'd read far too much into her remark, she didn't correct him because his arms felt a lot like those warm July 4th blankets from her childhood.

She let herself melt against him as he kissed her long and slow, and for the first time in a while, he was the only man on her mind.

Less than a mile away, an increasingly desperate Melanie stamped her foot down on the accelerator, desperation clouding her usual careful judgment. The lanes were thankfully quiet as she hurtled towards the village centre, her heart banging out of her chest. She'd never so much as broken the speed limit before, let alone pushed the Mini as hard as it could go, but needs must. She had to get that note. *Was that fireworks?* Her concentration thoroughly broken, she took her eyes off the road and raised them to the skies.

Gabe heard the bang in the sky as he searched for the key to the front door of the funeral parlour in his pockets. Being the boss meant that he was never off duty, even on days like today when he'd already put in fifteen hours at the convention. He'd just called by to make sure all was well, and that Melanie had remembered to deliver the parcel to Marla. Not that he really needed to go inside for confirmation, given the blaze of tiny blue stars in the sky. He grinned, glad that she'd obviously accepted the fireworks in the spirit they were given.

The sound of her laughter drifted across to him from the back garden of the chapel. Was she having a party? Her laughter pulled him across the space between their properties like a shard of metal to the Hadron Collider. He was powerless to resist. He didn't actually try all that hard, to be honest. He hoped he would be a welcome visitor at her door tonight.

He pushed the side gate open a little and stopped short. If it was a party, it was a damn exclusive one. A party for two. Just Marla and Rupert, wrapped in each other's arms, the glow of a couple of candles on the table casting a gold gleam over Marla's hair.

She looked more relaxed than he could ever remember seeing her. Her laughter carried towards him on the breeze, along with her words as she thanked Rupert for bringing her fireworks.

Rupert?

And then she kissed him. How the hell had that sly gobshite managed to pass off Gabe's gift as his own? He wanted to march right on in there and set the record straight so much that his feet hurt with the effort of keeping them rooted to the spot. How dare he? But as much as he wanted to steam in and show Rupert up for the liar he was, he couldn't bring himself to smash Marla's fragile happiness for his own gratification. She looked incredible. So beautiful and content, he couldn't do it. What the hell did she see in

Rupert frackin' Dean? In his head he'd managed to convince himself that the thing going on between Marla and Rupert wasn't serious. How had he got it so wrong? Got *Marla* so wrong? He backed out of the gate, his ears ringing with the sentimental exchange he'd overheard. *Love*. How could the woman he loved love someone else? It didn't make any sense.

Utterly dejected, he made his way around the front of the chapel and back towards the funeral parlour, just as an ear-splittingly loud rocket exploded in the skies above them and a familiar green Mini came hurtling down the road towards him at breakneck speed.

Rupert caught sight of Gabe's receding back over Marla's shoulder. He wanted to laugh out loud with triumph and punch the air. Marla had said she loved him, and all in clear earshot of Ryan. He couldn't have planned it better if he'd tried. Jesus. Marla was setting up yet another bloody rocket. Would she never get bored? He hated fireworks with a passion, and fond as he was of Marla, Rupert was dangerously close to his limit of fake *oohs* and *aaahs*. This called for something stronger than champagne. He let himself into the side door of the chapel in search of Dora's whisky.

From that moment on, things seemed to happen in slow motion, and yet at breakneck speed too. Marla's earlier instruction not to open the kitchen door because of Bluey had gone in one ear and out the other. As he opened the door the loud crack of the rocket rendered through the quiet night like a gunshot and startled the slumbering dog into wide-eyed panic.

163

The big hound almost mowed Rupert down as he bolted straight across the lawn, not even registering his mistress desperately lunging for his collar, who ended up instead holding the ridiculous fluffy headphones she'd slid over Bluey's ears as he slept. He cleared the side fence in one easy leap, and escaped out onto the High Street beyond. The squeal of tyres and the sickening thud of metal preceded Marla's scream by mere seconds.

About to call it a night, Gabe sat astride his bike and saw it all happen, so fast that there wasn't a damn thing he could do to stop it.

The racing-green Mini was hurtling down the road at some pace; Marla's big furry dog hadn't really stood a chance. Not that the driver could have expected a Great Dane to come barrelling into its path, but all the same Gabe was pretty sure that they had been a considerable way over the speed limit.

He was already off his bike and running as Marla came flying out onto the pavement, her red hair streaming behind her like a danger flag. Tears coursed down her cheeks as she fell to her knees in the pool of blood at the dog's side and cradled his big, still head in her lap, unable to look at the mangled mess the car had made of his side.

Marla didn't register Rupert's arrival at her side, nor the driver's door on the green Mini as it creaked open. All she could see was her big beautiful boy. She knew he'd gone. The light had left his gentle eyes.

Gabe looked over in confusion as Melanie staggered, ashen-faced, from the vehicle.

'Melanie . . . what are you doing here at this time of night?'

His dazed receptionist was shaking from head to toe. He placed a steadying hand on her shoulder.

'Are you hurt?'

'I don't think so.' Her lip wobbled. 'I didn't see him, Gabe, I swear I didn't. He came out of nowhere. One minute the road was empty and the next . . .' She waved an arm towards Bluey and tears spilled down her cheeks. Gabe guided her down onto the pavement and grabbed a blanket from the back seat of the Mini to wrap around her shoulders.

'Sit there for a few minutes and get your breath. I'll be back soon, okay?'

He rubbed her back for a second to comfort her, then headed over to where Marla still knelt beside Bluey.

Marla ran a hand over Bluey's matted coat. She felt Rupert pat her shoulder, and accepted the pristine hankie he shoved into her hands.

'Come on Marla, get up.'

His fingers were firm on her shoulder but she didn't budge.

'Sweetheart, please.' He reached down and attempted to manhandle her onto her feet.

'Leave her be.' Gabe's voice cut through the fog around her as Rupert tried again to haul her up, and once again she resisted his hands.

'On your feet, Marla, come on. I'm going to call the vet to come and fetch the dog.'

What had started out as a genuine gesture turned into

an awkward tussle as Rupert jockeyed for control of the situation.

Gabe stepped forward and placed a hand on Rupert's arm. 'I said leave her be.'

'Fuck off, Ryan.'

'Have some decency, man. She needs a few minutes.'

A sneer twisted Rupert's mouth. 'You think you know everything, don't you, Ryan?'

Gabe stared at him, disgusted that he'd rather argue over the top of Marla's head than hold his silence for her sake.

Rupert mistook his silence for acquiescence, and looked back at Marla.

'Come on now, darling. Stand up. It was only a dog.'

His words had a gunshot effect. Everyone's head snapped towards him in shock. Even Melanie's.

Marla hauled herself onto her feet. 'Go home, Rupert.'

Rupert flinched under her hostile gaze. 'I'll go and call a vet for you.'

'You'll do no such thing. Just go. And take *her* with you.'

She jerked her head towards Melanie. It was the first time that she'd even acknowledged the girl was there at all.

'But . . .'

'Rupert, please. If you truly want to help, then just get her out of my sight.' Marla laid a hand on his chest. She knew him well enough to know that he'd die rather than lose face in front of Gabe, and that alone was her guarantee that he wouldn't make a scene. She allowed him to pull her into his arms for a second, but his lips landed on her cold cheek as she turned away from his kiss.

'I'll call you in the morning,' he muttered, and with that

166

he swept Melanie into his sports car and away into the night.

An eerie silence settled over the street as the sound of Rupert's engine faded into the darkness.

'I'm so sorry about Bluey, Marla. He was a gorgeous guy.'

Her face crumpled with pain, and Gabe did what he knew she needed most at that moment. He held her in his arms and let her cry. Great big sobs that racked through her frame. He absorbed them all, wishing her pain away. He shrugged out of his jacket, wrapped it around her cold shoulders, and stroked her hair like a child until the tears subsided.

'What do I have to do about him now, Gabe?' Her voice was small and broken, so unlike the strong vibrant woman she was. He was glad that this was something that he could take care of for her.

'What would you like to happen?'

Marla sighed and leaned her head on his shoulder. 'I'd wind the clock back and save him.'

Her voice cracked with raw emotion, and he squeezed her gently and rested his chin on the top of her head. He'd heard similar responses many times over the years from grieving relatives and it never failed to make his throat tighten.

'I could see how much you loved him.'

'It was my fault. I should have taken him home, but he cries if I leave him. He was always with me. Always.'

Gabe stroked the red waves beneath his fingers.

'Let me bring him inside for tonight. I can talk you

through things in the morning.' Experience had taught him that people appreciated solid guidance at times like these. It was hard to think straight when your world was skewed. He felt the tension slump from her shoulders; saw the relief in her eyes when she looked up.

'Thank you.'

She was so close he could see the tears that still clung to her lashes. Grief had rendered her soft and vulnerable, and it would be the easiest thing in the world to lean down and kiss her. His gaze dropped to her swollen mouth. Fuck. He tipped his face up and stared at the stars for a couple of silent moments, pulled himself back from the feelings she stirred in him. This wasn't the time.

'You're welcome, Marla. You're welcome.'

He stepped away from her and held out his hand. 'Come and sit inside. It's cold out here.' He settled her at the reception desk and produced a crystal tumbler and a bottle of brandy. 'Drink some of this. I'll be back soon.'

The brandy seared the back of her throat, but it had the desired effect. Her fingers stopped shaking, and warmth chased the shivers from her body. She could see Gabe outside steering Melanie's Mini towards the kerb, and then moments later crouching down next to Bluey's body.

She looked down, unable to watch, and noticed the small white envelope that had stuck itself to the base of the bottle. Peeling it off, she tipped her head to one side and read the name written across the front of it in confusion. Marla. Her own name. It was unusual enough to safely assume the note was intended for her, but she was certain that Gabe hadn't put it there just now.

She glanced out at the street again, where Gabe had

rolled Bluey onto a gurney and covered his still form with a blanket.

'Sleep well, my fur-boy,' she whispered into the silence as Gabe wheeled him past the window to the back gates.

She looked at the little envelope again. Turned it over. Sealed. Bugger. Should she open it? Was it technically hers because it bore her name? Or was it still Gabe's until such time as he chose to give it to her? She was too exhausted to compute it, and noises behind her told her that Gabe was in the mortuary with Bluey. She placed the envelope back on the desk and pushed it away. But then, after a heartbeat, she grabbed it again and shoved it into her pocket to think about later.

Gabe had done as much as he could for Bluey tonight, so he headed back to reception where he found Marla sitting stiff-backed, his jacket still wrapped around her. She swivelled to face him as he laid a light hand on her shoulder.

'Okay?'

'Not really. You know.' She shrugged.

'Yeah, I guess I do.'

Marla glanced up, struck by the melancholy note in Gabe's voice, and she glimpsed the pain in his gaze before it slid from hers.

'Need a ride home?'

She nodded, grateful not to have to face the walk home without Bluey.

'If you're sure it's not out of your way?'

She realised as she said it that she had no clue where Gabe lived.

He dismissed her comment with a shake of his head,

zipped back through to the kitchen and returned a moment later with a spare motorcycle helmet and his keys.

'Come on. Let's go.'

Marla made to slip out of his jacket as she stood up.

'Keep it on.'

'But . . .'

'No buts. Keep it on.' His tone brokered no argument, and she didn't feel much urge to fight. The jacket was bringing her more than warmth. It smelled of leather, and spice, and lemons, and Gabe. It was a comfort, and a shield.

Outside, he tucked her hair behind her ears like a child and slid the helmet down over her face.

'Have you been on a bike before?' He lifted her visor as he spoke.

She shook her head.

'Okay. Just hold on and trust me. I'll keep you safe.'

In that precise moment, Marla had absolutely no doubt that he would.

She did exactly as she was told and wrapped her arms around Gabe as he gunned the engine into life. He glanced over his shoulder and closed her visor before giving her the thumbs up. She nodded, and they were off.

On another evening the adrenalin of the ride would probably have thrilled her inner speed demon, but tonight she was more moved by the comfort of Gabe's warm body against her own. Arms wrapped around his waist, the intimacy of him nestled between her spread thighs as the bike throbbed beneath them sent her senses reeling. It knocked her sideways how very turned-on she was. Disloyalty clashed against desire. Grief battled with visceral need. She was powerless to do anything more than let the sensations wash over her like a tidal wave and hope to still be breathing at the end of it.

She was just about the most mixed-up she'd ever been in her entire life. Her canine best friend had just died, her boyfriend had gone from hero to zero in a crisis, and the man between her thighs was fast becoming the most enigmatic, frustrating person she'd ever known. He was turning her into a veritable Jekyll and Hyde. One day she wanted to kill him and tonight, right now, she wanted to take him to bed.

Gabe pulled into the country lane and eased the bike to a stop outside Marla's cottage, but she made no move to let go of him. Her arms still gripped tight around his middle, her fingers were still searing his skin through the cotton of his T-shirt. He hadn't ridden a bike without leathers for years, not since way back when he'd been a teenager taking Cheryl Brady home from their first, and last, date to the cinema. One look at the wild-haired boy on the motorbike was enough for her mum to ban him from ever setting foot near Cheryl again.

He touched Marla's hand, a gentle nudge to remind her that she needed to dismount before he could, and he felt colder the instant she peeled her body away from his. He climbed off after her, helped her with her helmet and laid it down next to his on the bike.

'You okay?'

As she stood there and shook out her hair by the front door, she reminded him all over again of long-gone teenage dates. This would have been about the time when he'd have been trying to work up the guts to kiss the girl in question

171

goodnight, and now he found himself with the opposite problem. It was all kinds of inappropriate, but right at that moment he wanted to kiss Marla so badly that it physically hurt.

Frankly, Marla wasn't helping the situation, either. Was it his imagination, or had she stepped closer? One second there was space between them, the next she'd dragged him against her. The world shrank to the size of Marla's doorstep as she tipped her head up. Yes, she was definitely closer. She was so close that he could feel the warmth of her breath dancing on his lips, and the heat of her body pressed against his own. *Hot.* Gabe dropped his eyes to her mouth as she drew her bottom lip between her teeth and released it. When he lifted his eyes back to hers and found them sensual and wanton, he lost the battle. Marla was irresistible. She was a woman who needed to be kissed, and he was the man who badly needed to kiss her. Any lingering thoughts of resisting her took flight when she closed the space between them and found his mouth with her own. Her kiss stripped away his good intentions in a heartbeat as lust roared through his veins, a lit match dropped on tinder-dry brushland. Somewhere in the recesses of his mind he knew he should stop her, but Jesus, she was all over him. Her tongue insistent in his mouth. Her magic fingers already learning his skin beneath his shirt. His hands wound their own way into the gilt waves of her hair as he surrendered himself to her siren call. When he moved them lower, her bottom moulded itself perfectly into his palms, and that appreciative little moan she made when he bit down on her lip made him burn to know how she'd sound when he thrust himself inside her. Her heart banged against his. Jesus, if she didn't stop grinding against him like that he was going to screw her right here against her own front door.

'Come inside,' she gasped, and slid one hand down between them towards his crotch as she fumbled behind her with the other to put the key in the latch.

It would have been the easiest thing in the world to just go inside, and it was the hardest thing he'd ever had to do to put the brakes on.

'Marla, stop. We can't.' He pulled his head up and grasped her gently by the shoulders. Her eyes dragged open.

'You don't mean that,' she whispered, even as he reached down and stilled her fingers against the strained buttons of his jeans.

'Yes, I do. You don't want this. Not really.'

The desire in her eyes spluttered to a halt and died, replaced by despair and the glitter of unshed tears.

'God, I'm so sorry Gabe. What the hell am I doing?' He hauled her back into his arms as the tears spilled down her cheeks.

'Sshhh, sshhh, it's okay. It's the shock, Marla. It does strange things.'

He counted to ten, trying to force his mind away from how good she felt as she buried her face in his neck.

'It's a natural reaction. Kind of life-affirming, if you like. Sometimes, when we stare death in the eye it can tap into our basic survival instinct and makes us . . . well, horny. It's procreation. All that circle of life stuff.'

He knew his words sounded dry and textbook, but that's exactly what they were. It was part of the funeral directors' unwritten handbook to be prepared for relatives who could mistake their heightened emotions of grief for sexual attraction, but up until now he'd never actually experienced it firsthand. He wanted Marla to feel those emotions for him more than anything else in the world, but not like this.

'But you stare death in the eye all the time,' she mumbled with a shaky laugh, her breath warm against his skin. 'So what does that make you?'

He laughed softly.

'Frustrated, in your case. Go inside, Marla. You need some sleep.'

CHAPTER TWENTY

A bright shard of dawn sunlight slanted through the blind and half-woke Melanie from her slumber. As she flipped over away from the window in protest she registered the unexpected smoothness of Egyptian cotton against her cheek. Her eyes snapped open as memories of the night before pieced themselves together like a macabre jigsaw in her head.

Oh God, oh God, oh God.

She'd killed Marla's dog.

She winced in horror at the memory of that sickening thud. It was a miracle she hadn't been injured herself; the dog had bounced hard enough against the front of the car to send him flying clear over the roof.

She shivered. It had all seemed like such a simple plan. Slip back to work, grab the note from her desk, and then hotfoot it out of there again. Nowhere in the plan had she accounted for the possibility of Gabe being at the funeral parlour, or even worse, of him being outside on his motorbike. He couldn't see her there, he just couldn't. She'd panicked and stamped down too hard on the accelerator. In her desperation to get away she hadn't noticed the huge dog until he'd bolted out into the road right in front of her. He hadn't stood a chance.

Oh God.

Would they call the police?

Would she lose her job?

It was all way too much to consider so early in the morning. Melanie picked up the metaphorical broom in her head and swept all the horrible thoughts into a dark, unvisited corner to revisit later. Or not at all, if she could get away with it. Decision made, she closed her eyes, turned over again, and settled back into the warm crook of Rupert's naked shoulder.

Marla closed her eyes as her mobile trilled yet again. She'd avoided Rupert's numerous calls and texts so far, because she couldn't bear to hash over the events of the previous night or listen to his apologies for Bluey's escape. It wasn't that she was mad with him, exactly. She knew in her heart that it had been a horrible accident. Rupert hadn't meant to be so utterly useless in a crisis, and his badly chosen words hadn't been malicious or intended to hurt her.

She just felt incredibly let down. He hadn't been the rock that she'd desperately needed last night. Which led her thoughts to Gabe, who had.

But then again, in Rupert's defence, last night's situation *had* played to Gabe's strengths, so hadn't it been all too easy for him to jump in and be her knight in shining armour? Her head ached with the pressure of trying to be judge and jury, of juggling the facts to make them fit the evidence.

She wasn't stupid. She was well aware that there was no

love lost between Gabe and Rupert. It was entirely possible that last night had been an exercise in posturing and one-upmanship that had nothing much to do with her at all. She cringed at the memory of how she'd thrown herself at Gabe, and was only too glad of the pop-psychology cover story he'd handily provided her with, even if she didn't entirely buy it. She'd compromised her position badly last night, and she had no clue how to recover lost ground.

But now she had guilt and betrayal to add to the ever more confusing list of emotions she felt towards Rupert. What had started out as fun had turned into something far more intense than she'd bargained for, definitely on Rupert's part at least. He'd muttered the 'L' word last night, albeit in a lighthearted manner, and she'd felt a shiver of fear run down her backbone. Throwing herself at Gabe within a couple of hours of the declaration left her feeling distinctly shabby and disloyal, not to mention incredibly foolish. One moment she was running him out of town, the next trying to rip his clothes off on her doorstep. Jeez, he must think her a prize idiot, because she certainly felt like one. She was in over her head with both Rupert and Gabe.

She pushed it all to the back of her mind as she glanced out of the window to the private shady spot at the back of the chapel gardens beneath the oak tree. It had been one of Bluey's favourite flop spots, and Gabe had already been across early this morning to prepare a permanent resting place there.

Once again she'd found herself glad of Gabe's guidance to lead her in the right direction. He'd made a horrible situation bearable with his subtle strength, and she was aware that she owed him a debt of gratitude for the way he'd taken care of all the behind-the-scenes practicalities.

It comforted her to know that her fur-boy couldn't be in safer hands. Bluey had been so much more than a pet to Marla. People had come and gone in her life over the years; her gentle giant had been her only constant, her faithful friend, guardian of her secrets.

She glanced up at the clock. Almost five. Gabe would soon be closing up for the day and heading over to bury her best friend.

At the funeral parlour, Gabe laid Bluey's blanket over the huge dog and tucked a packet of Jammie Dodgers inside the casket with him. 'A snack for the journey, buddy,' he said softly, taking a few seconds to give the big old boy a final scratch behind the ears before he closed the lid with a sigh. This was going to be a difficult afternoon for Marla; he knew how much she'd adored Bluey. He'd handled one other animal funeral in the past, and the elderly owner of the cat in question had broken her heart far more than she had at the funeral of her husband which Gabe had arranged six months previously. He didn't expect Marla to fall to pieces. Her outburst on her front step had obviously been very out of character for her, and he still half regretted not letting himself go inside her home, inside her bed, because Lord knew that he'd wanted to.

He sealed the coffin and slid it onto the blue-ribboned gurney, then picked up his screwdriver to fix the nameplate he'd spent the morning making onto the lid.

Bluey. A woman's best friend.

Gabe and Jonny lowered Bluey's simple pine casket into the sun-warmed earth, then stepped back for a few seconds of reverential silence. Jonny had dressed for the occasion in blue, all the way from his sapphire eyeliner down to his blue suede shoes. Pale blue ribbons fluttered around Marla and Emily's wrists as they stood arm in arm next to the grave. Rupert had offered to attend too, but Marla had found herself reluctant to accept. Much as she knew he was trying to be supportive, her emotions were too raw for her to be able to be anything but truthful. He'd sounded like a crestfallen child when she'd insisted she'd rather he didn't come, but as she stood at the graveside she was relieved that he wasn't there. Both Emily and Jonny had adored Bluey, and it felt fitting to surround him only with those whose hearts he'd genuinely touched.

Silent tears tracked down Marla's cheeks as she bent to place Bluey's favourite, dog-eared chew toy on top of his casket.

'Bye, Bluey,' she whispered, her palm flat against the wood. 'I'll miss you every day.'

Words deserted her. She wanted to say something perfect, but her heart felt too heavy, her throat too constricted.

Emily held out a hand to help her back up again, and kept a tight hold of it as Gabe stepped forward. His dark, knowing eyes were sombre as he watched Marla for signs, giving her time to speak if she needed to. When she glanced up and met his eyes, he saw there all of the words that she couldn't bring herself to say. He coughed lightly and Emily and Jonny looked towards him.

'A man far more eloquent than I am wrote a few special words about his dog. Maybe now would be a good time to hear them?'

Marla nodded at him with gratitude, her shoulders ramrod straight with tension. She couldn't find the words to express how losing Bluey so cruelly had shattered her heart. He'd been such a huge physical presence in any room, utterly unwieldy and impractical in her small cottage with his gangly legs and huge head. He'd been forever knocking things over with his eagerly wagging tail, but if it had come down to a straight choice between moving house or losing Bluey, she'd have called the estate agents without a moment's hesitation. And now he'd gone, and Marla had never felt so alone in her life.

Gabe couldn't bear the look of desolation on Marla's face. He moved to stand at her other side and folded her smaller, cool hand into his, rubbing his thumb over the taut, paper fine skin of her knuckles. He waited in silence as the nearby church bell rang out six solemn times, then cleared his throat.

Near this Spot are deposited the
Remains of one who possessed beauty without vanity,
Strength without insolence,
Courage without ferocity,
And all the virtues of Man without his Vices.

Fresh tears ran down Marla's cheeks. In a million years, she couldn't have found more appropriate words. She leaned her head against his shoulder, an instinctive search for comfort.

'Thank you, Gabe,' she murmured. 'That was perfect.'

Gabe nodded and lowered his lips against her hair and breathed her in deep, his eyes closed. 'Byron was obviously a dog lover.' He squeezed her fingers and then gently let her go as he opened his eyes and reached for the spade that rested against a nearby tree trunk. 'Go inside with Emily, Marla. You don't need to see this.'

180

CHAPTER TWENTY-ONE

'Marla, honey?'

Marla's heart plummeted at the sound of the familiar nasal twang. Why, oh why had she answered the phone? Mondays were her Sundays. They were the only day of the week that could be relied upon to be wedding-free and calm, the only day that she ever took off for herself.

She plopped down into her armchair and resigned herself to a good hour of listening to her mother's latest forays with men and mayhem Stateside. Much as she loved her mother, hearing about her exploits as a sex therapist ageing disgracefully in Florida always gave Marla the makings of a headache. At least it wasn't hard work. Her mother never gave her a chance to get a word in edgeways. She reached for her coffee mug and curled her feet up underneath her bum, glad to be on the opposite side of the pond to her mother for the majority of the time. She cursed silently as she wriggled and slopped coffee on her knee, before tuning back in to try to make sense of the tail end of her mother's monologue.

'It'll only be a flying visit for Brynn though, hon, he has to give a speech at a taxidermy conference. He's flying out again after the weekend, but I thought I'd stay on and spend some time with my little girl. Whaddya reckon?'

Marla's mind played hectic catch-up. Brynn? *Who the hell was Brynn?* And a *taxidermy* conference? Jeez, her mother had been with some odd men in her time but this one ranked up there alongside Herman the snake-wrangler.

She was so thrown by Brynn's profession that it took her a couple of seconds to compute the fact that her mother had mentioned a visit.

Her mother's uncharacteristic silence lengthened, and Marla cast around for a response that wouldn't convey her horror.

'When would this be, again?' she squeaked.

Please don't say tomorrow or something ridiculous, Mom, or I may well lie down on the floor and die right now.

She heard her mother's dramatic sigh on the other end of the line.

'Marla, are you even listening to me? End of the month. Clear your diary. We can hit Harrods.'

'Mom, you know I'm miles from London.'

'Yadda yadda yadda. You can't be far from anywhere on that tiny godforsaken island. I lived there so I know, remember?'

Marla was glad her mother wasn't in the room to catch the way her eyes flicked up to the heavens. At least it was a few weeks away. Given her mother's track record, there was every possibility that Brynn the taxidermist would have exited the scene well before then with an otter under his arm, or whatever the hell he happened to be stuffing at the time.

* * *

'You know what you need, my friend?'

Gabe watched Dan over the rim of his pint glass as he waited for the pearl of wisdom. It was his third beer, and it had him well on the way to being more relaxed than he'd felt in weeks.

'What's that then?'

'To lighten up. You've had that same long face on for weeks now.'

'Undertakers need long faces. It's part of our job description.'

'I know that's a lie, Gabriel, because your dad had the biggest smile in Ireland.'

Gabe couldn't argue with that one. Dan had spent several summers in Ireland in and out of Gabe's family's funeral parlour when they were students. He'd grown close to all of the family, his warm, goodhearted father in particular, owing to a shared love of bar-room jokes and thick, creamy-headed Guinness. Gabe took a swig of beer to help loosen the sudden tightening in his throat.

'Let's go into town, man.' Dan shoved his chair back with a pointed glance around the quiet pub. 'It's crawling with bars full of birds. You need to touch some flesh that isn't stone cold.'

Gabe sighed loudly, but drained his glass anyway. This thing with Marla was doing his head in. Maybe some distance from the village and its headaches would be welcome. He craved the boozy forgotten nights, to be twenty-two again and not give a damn about tomorrow, or work, or about the red-headed girl who was driving him slowly crazy with need. Marla was thoroughly infuriating, not to mention someone else's girlfriend.

Which left him with, to coin one of Dan's choice phrases, 'two-fifths of fuck all' and the guarantee of a headache in the morning. He grabbed his jacket and ducked outside towards the taxi Dan had flagged down.

Gabe looked around the busy town square. It was thronged with brightly lit bars and glossy-haired girls in heels they couldn't walk in.

'Where we headed?'

Dan managed to drag his eyes away from an impressive lycra-encased cleavage of a passing girl to glance down at the flyer she had thrust into his hand. He stuffed it into his pocket and clapped Gabe on the back with a grin.

'I've just had a fuckin' stormin' idea, mate.'

Gabe grimaced. He knew that tone of old, and it usually meant Dan was a few hours away from his next walk of shame. He had no time to consider his options though, because Dan yanked him sideways into a black doorway and up some narrow wooden stairs.

Five minutes later, he found himself installed in a red, velvet booth with a cold bottle of Budweiser and a half-naked blonde thrusting her G-string-clad bottom at him from a nearby pole.

'A strip joint. Really?'

Dan winked and chinked his bottle against Gabe's, clearly pleased with himself. 'So. What's your poison tonight, my friend?' He inclined his head towards the woman wrapped around the pole. 'Blonde?'

Gabe took a slug of beer and looked away.

'Not blonde. Okaaay . . . how about a classic brunette?'

Gabe followed Dan's gaze across to the main stage, where men were shoving bank notes of encouragement into the silver thong of an exotic-looking girl as she peeled down the straps of her bra. He took it all in, feeling detached and grubby. He'd been in strip joints several times over the years; enough times to know it wasn't his scene.

'A nice little redhead, then? You seem to have developed quite a soft spot for them lately.'

Dan slid his sly eyes from Gabe's with a grin and nodded towards a girl at the bar with wild red curls and barely there black lace underwear.

Gabe drained his bottle and reached behind him for his jacket.

'I'm gonna shoot through. This isn't for me tonight, mate.'

Dan pouted and punched him on the shoulder. 'Lighten up, man. It's just a bit of fun.'

He winked at the blonde, who licked her lips and held a hand out to him in reply. Dan shrugged his shoulders with a helpless laugh at Gabe.

'Wait for me, yeah? I'll be back in five.'

Gabe sighed in resignation as he watched Dan trail off behind the glistening blonde like an excited puppy with a juicy bone. He traded his empty bottle for a full one from a passing waitress and settled in to wait, trying to avoid the parade of girls vying for his attention.

'Feelin' lonely, cowboy?'

Gabe glanced up from the depths of his beer to find the redhead from the bar had slid into the booth alongside him. Her riotous red curls sent a vicious kick of longing into his stomach.

Yeah. He was feeling lonely.

She scooted closer and trailed long, emerald-green nails along his thigh.

'I can make you feel a whole lot better.' She batted her false eyelashes and wiggled her cleavage closer to his chest.

He couldn't help himself.

He looked down.

He had to hand it to her; she jiggled in all the right places. She dipped her head for a second, her hair tumbling over her face, and with the benefit of a few too many beers she might have been Marla. When she threw her head back and grinned, a ridiculous shiver of disappointment ran through him.

The girl was wrong. She couldn't make him feel better. In fact, with one flick of her red curls she'd managed to make him feel a hundred times worse.

'I'm not a cowboy,' he muttered.

'That's alright, darlin'. You can be anything you like in here.'

'I'm an undertaker.'

To her credit, she faltered for only the briefest of nano-seconds before she was right back on her game.

'Kinky.' She swung a leg over him and straddled his thighs. 'Then I'll be Buffy the Vampire Slayer.' She flashed her eyes and leaned close to whisper in his ear. 'Here, or somewhere a little more private?'

Out of the corner of his eye Gabe spied Dan as he saun-tered back across the bar. *Thank God.* 'I'll pass, thanks.'

'Come on, goth boy . . .' The girl started gyrating to the music.

'Get off me. Now.'

She could obviously tell from his tone that he meant

business, because she stood up and tipped his drink into his lap.

'Get a life, weirdo. You're in a strip joint, remember?'

'Nice taste, man,' Dan murmured as he slid into the booth, swivelling his head to check out the redhead's bum as she strutted away.

'Did you just put her up to that?'

'Fuck off. You must have given her the glad eye yourself.'

Gabe brushed the beer from his crotch and Dan's face creased up with laughter. 'For fuck's sake, Gabriel, I did you a favour. That girl was smokin'.'

'I don't need fixing up.'

Dan shook his head without malice. 'I hate to say it, Gabe, but from where I'm standing, it kind of looks like you do.'

As they grabbed their jackets, neither of them noticed the floppy-haired guy alone in the corner, phone in hand.

CHAPTER TWENTY-TWO

'I need to make another appointment with the midwife for three weeks' time please,' Emily said to the doctor's receptionist.

She was distracted as she rooted around in the bottom of her handbag for her mobile. The damn thing was ringing, and her handbag had unhelpfully chosen this moment to do its best Tardis impression.

Half-eaten KitKat? Check. Hairbrush? Check. TV licence fee she should have posted three days ago? Check. She shoved the licence fee envelope into the front pocket in a vain attempt to remind her to post it, but still she couldn't find the phone.

It didn't help that Tom had pulled his favourite trick; changing her ringtone to some entirely inappropriate bump and grind porn theme for his own amusement.

Yeah, okay everyone, you can all stop staring at the pregnant lady with the slutty ringtone now. Show's over.

Her cheeks flamed as disapproving mothers gathered

their children onto their knees, and the receptionist tutted and waved a little cream card in her face.

'Your next appointment.' She handed it over with a haughty glance over the top of her crescent moon glasses.

Stuck-up cow.

Emily dumped the detritus of her bag onto the desk, including the minty green spare pair of granny knickers she carried around at all times these days because some pregnancy know-it-all on TV told her she needed to.

'And this has been sitting in your file, too. Should have been given to you a while back. Not sure what happened there.' The receptionist dangled a brown envelope from her shell-pink fingertips, not willing to risk direct contact with anything connected to such a blatant jezebel. She shrugged and turned away to tap on her computer keyboard. 'Sorry.'

Emily glowered at her. She didn't look very sorry. She tucked the extra paperwork underneath her chin as she gave up on the phone and swept her belongings back into the Tardis. It was probably only some shonky salesman on the flip side of the globe trying to sell her something she didn't need, anyway.

Outside, she made a dash for her Micra, barely noticing as she passed beneath a window cleaner's ladder. She flung the offensive bag into the passenger side and hurled the brown envelope down on top of it. Back in the relative safety of her seat, she placed her hands in the ten to two position on the wheel and breathed out slowly. Back in again. Out again nice and easy, eyes closed as she tried to connect with her inner peace, or whatever it was the smug TV pregnancy guru insisted on at least twice a day for the baby's wellbeing. Her eyes snapped open in surprise as someone rapped hard on the window. The whistling window cleaner, his chamois in one hand and something pale green in the other.

Oh, God. No. Just, no.

Emily inched the window down a fraction and squinted at him, her cheeks already fiery with humiliation.

'You dropped yer knickers, darlin'.'

Evil git-bag. He was having a good old laugh at her expense.

'Thank you,' Emily squeaked. 'They *are* clean.'

Ground, swallow me up.

She yanked them through the gap and whizzed the window up again as he sauntered away, shoulders still shaking with laughter.

The accuracy of his words, however, wasn't wasted on her. How she wished she hadn't dropped her knickers. She wouldn't be in this mess now. The smug TV guru wouldn't have been impressed by the way Emily thumped her forehead against the steering wheel and cursed like a navvy as she pulled out of the car park in tears.

Marla placed the outrageously large arrangement of crimson roses on the windowsill in her office, then changed her mind and moved them over onto the desk. Two seconds later she got up again and took them out of the office altogether, balancing them on the landing shelf. They'd be better off out there anyway; it was cooler, and she wouldn't have to look at them all the time. She had to award Rupert a ten out of ten for effort over the last few weeks. He'd sent flowers. Three times. He'd rung and apologised. Daily. And just five minutes ago he'd emailed to let her know that he'd reserved a table at her favourite restaurant that evening. She grimaced and bit down so hard on the end of her pencil that shards of wood splintered into her mouth.

Try as she might, she just couldn't untangle Rupert from Bluey's death in her mind. Whenever she thought about him she got an uncomfortable sensation of dread in the pit of her stomach and had to think about something else. It would pass, she was sure. She'd go to dinner with him and get things back on track.

Gabe, on the other hand, had made himself conspicuous by his absence since the funeral, and boy was she glad. Shame made her hide her face in her hands whenever she thought about the way she'd flung herself at him on her doorstep.

She spat the shards of wooden pencil into the wastepaper bin and tried to will her way back into the easy groove she'd worn for herself before Gabriel had turned up and rucked his way through it rough-shod.

Cupcakes.

It would have all been *so* perfect if it had only been a cupcake bakery.

Okay, so maybe they'd all have been letting out their belts a little by now, but her business would have been safe and her sanity would still be intact. Her rock-solid world seemed to have tipped on its axis, sand slipped under her feet whenever she tried to get a grip.

She rubbed the pale blue ribbon from Bluey's funeral that she kept on her desk. Dora was continually tidying it away into the drawer, but Marla kept pulling it back out again like a child with their comfort blanket.

Darling Bluey. Her mind tracked back over the same

painful loop every time she thought of him. If only she'd taken him home. If only she'd stopped Rupert from opening the chapel door in time. If only she'd managed to catch hold of his collar.

If only.

Sometimes, in the darkness of the middle of the night, she even managed to hang the blame on Gabe's shoulders. Without him there would have been no need for a campaign, no public meetings, and she'd never have met Rupert. She didn't dwell on the fact that the idea of life without Rupert stirred a distinct lack of emotion in her.

She focused instead on the fact that no Rupert would have meant no fireworks, and no fireworks would have meant that her beloved Bluey would still be here. And there she was again, full circle, Rupert and Bluey tied together in her head.

She wound the blue ribbon around her fingers, her eyes on the funeral parlour.

If it had been a cupcake bakery, she'd never have met Gabe. She didn't dwell, either, on the fact that this was a much more disconcerting thought than having never met Rupert.

Much to her own annoyance, her mind insisted on road testing the idea of Gabe as a cupcake baker rather than an undertaker, and however hard she tried, she couldn't get the image of Gabe, naked except for a cooking apron, out of her head for the rest of the afternoon.

Rupert did his best at dinner, he really did, and Marla was grateful, she really was.

He pulled out her chair, and he poured wine, and he

switched plates with her when she wasn't as keen on pigeon as he'd insisted that she would be.

In between their main course and dessert, he reached into his jacket pocket and handed her a gift-wrapped package.

'What's this?' she smiled, caught off guard.

'Open it,' he said, nodding towards it without his usual flourishes and drama.

Marla picked at the blue tissue paper carefully, flicking her eyes up to Rupert's and finding him pensive. She folded back the tissue paper and revealed a beautiful silver photograph frame engraved with Bluey's name across the bottom. Tears prickled behind her eyes at the memory of him, and also at the unexpected thoughtfulness from Rupert. She looked up when he touched her hand.

'I thought it might look nice on your fireplace with your family photographs. I really am truly sorry, Marla,' he said. 'I feel so guilty.'

Any lingering unease about Rupert's part in Bluey's demise melted away as she looked into his sorrowful eyes. 'It was an accident, Rupert. An awful, horrible accident. Please don't feel guilty, there's no need.' She twisted her fingers to hold his and gave them an encouraging squeeze as the waiter arrived with their puddings.

Back at her cottage a couple of hours later, she slid her favourite shot of Bluey into the frame and placed it carefully alongside her other photographs.

'He looks good there.' Rupert appeared from the kitchen, two glasses of brandy in his hands. 'I'll take these upstairs.'

Marla nodded, slowly turning off the lamps and crossing to draw the curtains. The lane outside was silent and still, and she could hear the sound of moving around upstairs in her bedroom. Her heart leapt for a second, thinking it was Bluey until her mind played catch-up and reminded her of the cruel truth. She didn't let herself think about the fact that she really wished it was her dog and not her lover waiting for her upstairs.

CHAPTER TWENTY-THREE

Over at the funeral parlour the following day, Gabe shook the hand of Gladys Macintyre's son-in-law and gently handed her daughter a third tissue. Much as he was accustomed to dealing with bereaved relatives, he never grew immune to their grief and suffering. 'Don't worry about a thing,' he assured them. 'I'll take care of absolutely everything for you on the day, and I'll care for your mother as if she were my own while she's here with me.'

Gladys' daughter sniffed loudly and pulled him into a hug. 'You've been so lovely, Mr Ryan,' she squeaked, and her husband patted her back and took her arm as she stepped away.

'Call me if there's anything at all. Day or night. You have my numbers,' Gabe said, opening the door for them to shuffle out onto the pavement. He raised a hand to them as they drove slowly away, and then turned to Melanie at reception.

'Are you sure you're alright?'

He cast a doubtful look at the neck brace Melanie had

worn on and off since the accident had happened several weeks ago.

'It's fine Gabe, honestly. It looks worse than it is.'

It was a small miracle that she hadn't been badly injured, or worse. A big dog and a small car was a bad combination. He'd been concerned enough to call at her home the day afterwards to check on her, and although he was sure that he'd seen the net curtains twitch, no one had answered the door. Odd really, but just as he'd been on the verge of starting to wonder if she was inside and too ill to make it to the door, a text had blipped in from the lady herself.

Hi Gabe,

Thxs 4 ur help yday. Am fine, just at A&E to get neck strain double checked.

C U on Monday

M x

How fortunate that she'd chosen to text him at that precise moment. A less trusting man might have found it too convenient, but Gabe was determined to think the best of her. Melanie was a good worker, and she was loyal to the hilt. Too loyal sometimes maybe, but could that really be considered a fault?

Anyway, her explanation for being at the funeral parlour at that late hour had turned out to be perfectly watertight. After all, it was the first time she'd ever locked up for him. It was only logical that she might have had a little panic and nipped back to check she'd shut the door properly. She was conscientious, that was all.

The dog had come from nowhere, she'd said.

Impossible to stop in time, she'd said.

It was patently clear that she felt wretched about it, and as far as he knew Marla didn't wish there to be any further investigations. Why stir the already-muddy waters with the suggestion that she may have been going a smidge over the speed limit? Truth be told, he hadn't been able to look Marla in the eye either, given that he was the one who had sent the damn fireworks.

His father would no doubt have muttered 'least said, soonest mended, son' and in this case, he would have been one hundred per cent right. The harsh reality was that no amount of recriminations and arguments would bring Bluey back.

The other inescapable truth was that the whole sorry incident had made the fractious situation between the chapel and the funeral parlour even worse. He'd sent the fireworks, and then Melanie, the receptionist he'd hired, had killed Bluey.

Not to mention the fact that he'd knocked back Marla's advances on her doorstep. He'd suffered for it every night since – memories of how she'd felt in his hands had been the only thing on his mind. She'd robbed him of sleep, turned him into a teenage boy. The old dear in the village shop had glared at him with unconcealed disapproval when he'd been in for the second box of man-size tissues last week.

Something had to give, and unfortunately, it was probably going to be his wrist.

Melanie stuck her head around the mortuary doorway a couple of hours later.

'Fancy a coffee?'

Gabe glanced up with a distracted smile that warmed Melanie's skin, despite the coolness of the room and the presence of the village's most recently deceased resident, Gladys Macintyre.

'You're an angel.'

Melanie melted and retired to the kitchen, where she unsnapped the neck brace and rubbed her sore skin. The bloody thing was a pain. She'd dug it out of her dad's wardrobe where he'd stashed it after his dubious whiplash injury claim a few years back. Once she'd lied to Gabe about going to A&E, she figured she better have some kind of treatment to show for it. She'd had to think of something to text Gabe to get him to leave. She was twenty-four years old and still living at home with her dad – that's bound to be a turn-off.

In truth she'd been remarkably lucky to not be injured at all apart from shock, but she could hardly parade that around, could she?

Besides, she was enjoying the extra fuss from Gabe.

Much to her relief, he'd been wonderful about the whole episode. Her fears that he might sack her had proved totally unfounded. If anything, the accident had solidified her place at the funeral parlour, rather than threatened it. She felt genuinely awful about Bluey, but then Marla really ought to have been more careful. She should have been more careful with her boyfriend too, for that matter. Rupert had been simply lovely to Melanie. He'd insisted that she go back to his apartment for a brandy to steady her shredded nerves. He'd joined her in a large one, then another, and then she'd joined him in his large bed. It had felt like an inevitable chain of events, one of those serendipitous things that it's pointless to fight or question.

She snapped the neck brace hastily back in place a couple of seconds before Gabe wandered into the kitchen and rinsed his hands at the sink. He shot her a grateful smile as he picked up his mug.

'Thanks, love,' he smiled and his black hair flopped over his brow in a way that made Melanie's fingers itch to stroke it.

Love. He called me his Love.

She watched his backside retreat from the room as he left and cast a glance out of the window towards the chapel.

It seemed the mighty were falling, after all.

A few short weeks ago, Marla had had them all. Gabe, Rupert and Bluey.

Since then, Melanie had managed to take them all away, one by one. Not on purpose of course, it had just happened that way. Poor little Yank girl. Melanie pouted her lip. Life was hard sometimes, eh?

'Any chance of a cuppa?'

Dan appeared in the doorway.

Melanie couldn't make her mind up about him – he unsettled her. He was too cocky, and she wasn't sure if he'd guessed how she felt about Gabe. But then two could play at that game, because she'd noticed him making doe eyes at Marla's sidekick over the road.

The way his gaze automatically lingered on Melanie's breasts annoyed her as she splashed a minuscule drop of milk in his hastily thrown-together coffee.

'Does working in such a gloomy place never get to you?' she asked with an innocent smile as she handed it over.

'Not really.' He shrugged. 'Gabe's a mate. Anyway, I don't spend as much time here as you do. Maybe you should be more worried about your own happiness levels rather than mine.'

Privately, Dan harboured no doubts at all about Melanie's happiness at the funeral parlour. There was a coldness about the girl that gave him the creeps. He winced as the coffee burnt his tongue.

'Yeah. Maybe I should apply for the job vacancy over at the chapel.' Melanie flashed her eyes at him in direct challenge.

Confusion clouded his handsome expression. He really was an easy target to reel in, like a little goldfish flapping on the end of a very large hook. Melanie licked her lips in anticipation. This going in for the kill thing was addictive.

'Job vacancy?'

'Yeah, Marla's assistant's bound to be leaving soon. At least I'm guessing so, anyway.' She paused, leaning back against the kitchen counter. 'Seeing as how she's having a baby, and all.'

Dan placed his almost-untouched coffee onto the kitchen table.

'Emily's pregnant?'

'Well, I don't mean Dora, do I?'

Melanie laughed with the pleasure of the big reveal.

It was almost painful to watch. Dan's expression went from self-satisfied to bewildered, and then to something else, something she didn't quite understand. It wasn't surprise, and it definitely wasn't the face of a man casually lamenting the loss of his favourite piece of eye-candy. She leaned in a little, keen to know what was going on behind his baby blues.

'You okay, Dan? You've gone a bit pale.'

'What? No. I mean yes, course I am. 'Scuse me, love.'

Dan hightailed it out of the kitchen, leaving Melanie alone with just her coffee and her thoughts.

'Curiouser and curiouser,' she murmured, as her mind took the hop, skip and a jump towards the obvious conclusion.

Gabe looked up from Gladys Macintyre's peaceful form just in time to see Dan kick the tyre of the hearse and then spark up a cigarette. By the time he made it outside a minute or two later, the cigarette had mostly gone and Dan was perched moodily against the bonnet of the old black car.

'You okay, bud?'

Dan looked up sharply, obviously jolted from deep thought. The frown lines across his brow looked out of place on a face more given to laughter. It took a few seconds and considerable effort for him to rearrange his features into a tight smile.

'Fine. Just grabbing a smoke.'

Gabe nodded and went to perch alongside his friend.

'You thinking of taking up the habit?' Dan said, offering Gabe a cigarette even though he knew perfectly well he wouldn't take it.

'What's the old car done to deserve a kicking?' Gabe patted the bonnet affectionately, knowing that the hearse was an innocent party.

Dan took a long last drag on the cigarette and then screwed it into the gravel with his foot. 'It's not the car.'

'No shit,' Gabe murmured. 'If it's not cars it has to be a woman.'

Dan reached for a second cigarette and lit it slowly. 'I've fucked up.'

'With who?' Gabe couldn't keep the surprise out of his voice. Dan had told him about pretty much every girl he'd been involved with over the years, but lately he hadn't mentioned anyone at all. Thinking on that now, Gabe saw how that in itself should have rung a warning bell.

'It doesn't matter who.' Dan huffed and blew out a plume of smoke. 'She's someone else's.'

'Oh.' A second warning bell rang out for Gabe. However much of a Romeo Dan liked to be, he had his own unique code of moral conduct that ruled married women out of his remit. He'd always maintained it was because he wanted an uncomplicated life, but Gabe knew him well enough to know that it was more likely because he'd been raised with old-fashioned values, within a rock-solid family. He wasn't someone who'd hurt someone else on purpose; if he'd gotten himself involved with someone else's woman, he hadn't done it lightly.

'Is she happy being with her other half?' Gabe asked.

'I think she is, yeah.'

'Sounds complicated.' Gabe laid his hand on Dan's shoulder. 'I'm sorry, man.'

'It's complicated alright,' Dan muttered. 'A right royal fucking mess, to be honest.'

'Can you untangle yourself? Sounds like you need to.' Gabe didn't ask who the woman in question was. Partly because he didn't need to know, but mostly because he knew Dan wouldn't tell him anyway.

'I need to. I just don't know if I want to, or even if I should.'

He dropped the second cigarette onto the gravel and ground it under his foot. 'It's cool, Gabe, honestly.' He reached into his pocket for his mobile. 'I'll be in in five. I just need to make a call.'

As much as Emily knew that avoiding Dan wasn't going to magic the problem away, she was still desperate not to have *the* conversation in the next few minutes. The park basked in the late afternoon sun, all dappled and lush. Glossy trees hid her from prying eyes. She'd suggested meeting here because it wasn't her natural habitat and she hoped they wouldn't run into anyone who knew them. Yet, give her a few months and no doubt it would become one of her regular stomping grounds.

She was just glad that she'd been alone when she'd answered the office telephone earlier. How the hell would she have explained her reaction to Marla or Jonny, or even worse, to Dora? She'd grown accustomed to carrying this secret around inside her, and every day it seemed to grow along with the baby. There was no denying her pregnancy now. She was, if the smug TV guru was to be listened to, 'in her bloom'. Although, to be honest, she'd lost faith in the TV pregnancy guru some time back, right about the time that she'd started to bang on about the importance of involving 'Daddy' in the pregnancy.

Oh God. What was she going to say? What was Dan going to think? He had every right to demand she at least talk to him. Should she lie? Maybe he'd secretly *want* her to say the baby was nothing to do with him so that he could wriggle off the hook. But then, any fool can add up, and though she didn't know him well, he didn't seem like a village idiot. Christ, it was hot. She stripped her flimsy cardigan off from over her sundress and closed her eyes as she leaned back and fanned herself with her hand.

It was only when she realised that her inefficient cooling system had dramatically improved that she opened her eyes to find Dan wafting her with a rolled-up copy of *The Sun*.

'Lookin' swell, darlin'.'

He sat down next to her and looked at her little bump, his blue eyes far more serious than his words.

Emily scooted herself upright and automatically draped a protective arm over her middle. At least he didn't seem angry – that had to be a start, right?

'Why did you call, Dan?'

He shrugged and looked away for a few silent seconds, his eyes on an after-school kick-about in the distance.

'I don't know. I heard about the baby today from the queen of the undead.'

Emily looked at him quizzically.

'Melanie,' he muttered, with something that might have been a shiver.

She nodded with a heavy sigh. It had been inevitable that she'd find herself here, and she'd agonised over how she should play it. Now the moment had arrived she knew that the only option open to her was the absolute truth, but actually saying the words turned out to be really, really hard.

'Is it mine?'

Wow. He wasn't pulling any punches. Straight in with the million-dollar question; the question that kept her awake into the small hours and haunted her restless dreams when she finally fell asleep. She'd answered it a hundred different ways in her head and none of them had felt right.

'I don't know. Probably.' She knotted her shaky fingers in her lap. 'Yes, I think it is.'

'Fuck.' Dan watched the footballers again and rubbed his stubble with one hand.

'Look, Dan . . .' She wasn't sure how to say that there was no need for him to feel obliged to play any part in his child's life.

'Does your husband know?'

'No. I've tried to tell him, but the words won't come out.'

'I see.' Dan nodded, and turned to search her eyes with his own. 'So . . . what am I supposed to say now, Emily?'

This was her one chance to make the best of this for all of them. She couldn't blow it. 'I *think* you're supposed to say that it's best Tom never knows.'

'Right . . . right.' He stared at the ground. 'And what if I don't say that?'

Terror held Emily's breath captive in her chest.

'What if I said that I need to know for certain if it's my baby?'

'I'd say that you were within your rights. It'll probably destroy my marriage and make me a single mother, but you're within your rights.'

'And what about the *baby's* rights, Emily? To know its real dad?'

And there it was. The other question that worried her daily.

'I don't have all the answers, Dan.' Her shoulders slumped in desolation. 'Do you want to be a father right now?'

He put his head in his hands and groaned. He didn't. Much as he liked to paint himself as the local lothario, he wanted the same thing as everyone else really. To fall in love, settle down, and then maybe think about babies. Knocking up someone else's wife had never figured in his plans.

'Because Tom does. Desperately. And I know he'll be brilliant at it.'

'So you're saying, what? I should just walk away?'

'Can you?'

'I don't know, Emily. I honestly don't know.'

'Of course you don't.' She bit her lip. 'Sorry.'

They stared in silence at the footballers playing five-a-side across the park.

'I don't want to smash your marriage up.'

'No. Thank you. Me neither.'

'I need to get out of here.' He pushed his hands through his hair and stood up. 'I'll call you sometime. Maybe we can talk again, when I've got my head around it.'

Emily nodded, and the sincerity in his blue eyes reminded her why he'd been the one she'd turned to when the chips were down. His gaze dropped to her bump.

'It suits you.' A tiny, sad smile glanced across his mouth. 'This pregnancy thing. It really suits you.'

Emily watched him walk away. His usual swagger was nowhere to be seen. In fact, he looked like a man with the weight of the world on his shoulders.

CHAPTER TWENTY-FOUR

'Yoohoo! Marla, honey!'

The distinctive squawk assaulted Marla's ears across the crowded arrivals hall. She held her arms out and her mother tumbled into them, all suntanned wrinkles and expensive jewellery that jangled every time she moved.

'Let me look at you.' She gripped Marla hard by the upper arms and leaned backwards.

'Still too pale.' She clucked her tongue then reached up and pinched a cheek. 'Are you using that juicer I sent you?'

Marla laughed. It had taken all of forty seconds for her mother to find fault. She just couldn't help herself. Moments later she noticed the short man a few steps behind her mother, locked in a battle with two trolleys piled high with coordinated luggage.

'Honey, this is my fiancé, Brynn. Brynn, meet Marla. Isn't she every bit as gorgeous as I said she was?'

Brynn shuffled forward, a vision in crumpled cream linen and an ivory fedora. Marla shook his outstretched hand

and tried not to wonder where a taxidermist's hand might spend the majority of its time.

And fiancé? Was it her mother's life mission to reach double figures?

'Good to meet you, Marla. Cecilia has told me so much about you.'

He had a thin voice, and when he fixed her with his gimlet eyes, Marla got the alarming feeling that she was being sized up for a glass display case.

She forced a smile, but her heart had well and truly sunk at the thought of her serene cottage being invaded by her mother, the lover and their luggage. She eyed the trolleys to double-check Brynn hadn't smuggled any dead foxes or such-like through customs, before leading them outside to her car.

Neither of her passengers offered to help as Marla loaded the cases into the boot. Nor when she took them all out again because they wouldn't fit. She heaved the largest case onto the back seat next to Brynn, and then shoehorned the rest into the boot space.

'Have you been to the UK before, Brynn?'

'Only on a one-night stopover a couple of years back en route to the Austrian taxidermy championships.'

'Oh.' Great. He was a conversation killer as well as an animal stuffer.

Marla steered the car through the busy airport traffic onto the motorway and attempted to get the conversation with Brynn back on track.

'So. How long are you visiting for?'

'Oh, not long for me I'm afraid. I'm a keynote speaker at the London taxidermy exhibition, and then it's on to Russia.'

'Another lecture?'

'No. I'm collecting a dead zebra from Moscow Zoo.'

Marla met his gaze in the rearview mirror and couldn't decide whether or not he was joking. Terrific. Trust her mother to bring Hannibal bloody Lecter to visit.

'Please Jonny! You owe me.'

Jonny pouted as Marla clutched his checked shirtsleeve in desperation.

'How many more times are you going to use that line before we're done?'

'Oh, a lot more yet. You nearly closed us down. It's a big debt.' She gestured with her hands to demonstrate the size. 'Huge.'

'What do you want from me, little lady? Blood?' He held his upturned wrists out to her, and she shook her head.

'Cane?' He turned around and presented her with his jeans-clad backside with an exaggerated sigh.

'Not even close. Say you'll come to dinner with my mother.'

Jonny put his head on one side, considering. 'Will Prince-not-very-Charming be there too?'

'Actually, Rupert can be very charming if you'd just give him a chance,' Marla said.

'I'll have to take your word for it, toots, because I'm not seeing it. From where I'm standing he's a long streak of hair, teeth and . . . and not much else.' He drew his forked fingers sideways across his eyes. 'Dead behind the eyes,' he whispered, calling on his best am-dram skills.

'That's incredibly rude,' Marla chided, not rising to his bait. 'Come to dinner. He might just surprise you.'

'Oh, go on then,' Jonny grumbled. 'But *only* because I don't happen to have made other plans.'

He hummed 'Achy Breaky Heart' as he spun on his block-heeled cowboy boots and line-danced off down the aisle. They were preparing the chapel for a country and western themed wedding, and short of live horses to lasso, they were more or less on track.

Marla grinned at his retreating back. He was a true friend, and would have come on Saturday evening just because she needed him there, but she knew he was dying to meet her mother. Actually Brynn, to be precise. He'd howled with laughter when she'd relayed the conversation from the car, but all the same he couldn't possibly have accepted her invitation outright. That would have been far too straightforward for Jonny.

Marla counted up the dinner guests in her head. Jonny, Emily and Tom, Rupert and herself, and of course her mother and Brynn. Seven ought to be enough to dilute the effect her mother had. Cecilia had insisted on a swish dinner at Franco's, but the last thing Marla felt like was a cosy double date with her mother, Brynn and Rupert. The two men would have absolutely no common ground, and Lord knows Brynn could be relied on to stop a conversation in its tracks with a random comment about a female hippopotamus' enormous lady bits. He appeared to specialise in huge animals, and after two days under the same roof, Marla knew far more than she ever wanted to about the anatomical complexities of lions and tigers and bears.

What was her mother thinking? There was every possibility that she would end her days stuffed, mounted and on display in Brynn's travelling freak show, probably wedged somewhere between a giant panda and a Palomino.

Maybe he was rich. But then that wasn't something that usually turned her mother's head; Cecilia had enough independent wealth to not need to lean on anyone else.

Oh, God. A hideous thought crept into her mind.

Maybe he was awesome in the sack.

Marla fought to keep her lunch down at the idea and tried to banish it from her head. There had to be something though, and she was going to make it her business to find out what it was.

The chapel doors creaked open and Emily appeared, her arms loaded with red and white gingham. Marla started to laugh as she noticed what her friend was wearing.

'Yeah, well. You try finding a country outfit for pregnant women,' Emily grouched, dumping the gingham on the nearest bale of hay that had been delivered that morning from a local farm. They'd also contributed an old-fashioned wooden cart for the day, which now stood decorated in pride of place on the chapel lawns, ready for photographs after the ceremony.

Emily's floor-sweeping scarlet dress fell in deep, lace-trimmed tiers, and she wore red ribbons in her short pig-tails.

'I like it,' Marla ventured. 'It's kinda cowgirl-boho.'

Emily rolled her eyes. 'I'd rather be Daisy Duke.'

Jonny reappeared carrying two huge buckets of sunflowers and huge daisies. 'Ruth dropped these off.' He eyed Emily's dress with sartorial alarm. 'Whoa! Does Dora know you stole her curtains?'

Emily planted her hands on her hips and looked him up and down slowly as he placed the buckets down. Checked shirt shot through with threads of glitter. Chaps over his snug-fitting Levi's. A huge gold and rhinestone-studded belt buckle bearing an American eagle. Stack-heeled cowboy boots. And crowning it all, a huge Stetson.

'You come dressed as Howard Keel and you dare to criticise me?'

Jonny whistled. 'Showing your age there, Sue-Ellen,' he murmured, and then leaned into Marla and muttered, 'hide the whisky,' behind his hand. Both women rolled their eyes as Jonny cackled and rocked back on his heels to look out of the window at the funeral parlour. 'And we needn't look far for the poison dwarf,' he said, then coughed, 'Melanie,' under his breath. 'Ooh! Let's cast Gabriel as Bobby!' he said, rubbing his hands together. 'I always had a thing for those dark curls.'

Emily sorted through the flowers as Jonny warmed to his theme. 'Who shall we cast as JR?'

They all looked up as the door creaked open, and Rupert walked in. Jonny cracked up instantly and Marla swallowed hard and painted a newsreader's smile on her face.

'Rupert, you're just in time.'

'If rather underdressed,' he murmured, taking in their various outfits. Marla had opted for a denim and lace dress that somehow still looked classy, probably because of the woman wearing it. 'Not to worry,' he said, looking relieved. 'I can't stay, I'm just dropping Stuart over to shoot the wedding for the paper.'

Marla smiled warmly. Rupert really was doing his best to promote the chapel in the press, playing to his strengths to help their campaign. She was thankful for his help, and told him as much as she led him from the chapel and away from prying ears.

'I'll see you at the restaurant later,' he murmured, running his hand possessively down her backside. 'I might just have a surprise for you.' The look in his eyes should have served as a warning, but she was too wrapped up in the wedding to let it permeate. She pecked him on the cheek and wriggled out of his reach.

'Don't be late. And don't believe a word my mother tells you.'

She stood on the pavement to wave him off, and just as she went to turn back inside the chapel, Gabe appeared from his doorway with a box in his arms. Marla swallowed the usual knot of apprehension that accompanied an encounter with Gabe and raised a casual hand in greeting. Bluey's funeral had proved to be something of a turning point; it was hard not to be civil to him after he'd been so kind and gentle with her fur-boy. She tried not to dwell on the fact that her heartbeat had picked up for the wrong man in the last two minutes.

'These came for you just after you left yesterday,' he said, drawing near enough for Marla to be able to see the collection of horseshoes inside the cardboard box.

'Ah, thanks. I wondered where they'd got to.' Emily had sourced them from a local farrier to wrap with ribbons and give to the wedding guests as keepsakes. She held her arms out to take the box from him.

'I'll bring them in,' Gabe said. 'It weighs a ton.'

Marla bit back the urge to refuse. 'Thank you.'

She led him up the chapel path and paused by the door. 'Just there'll be fine,' she said casually, not wanting him inside the chapel because Jonny and Emily would prolong his visit. The only way she could maintain their tenuous truce was to keep contact between them as brief as possible. As it was, she could already smell the scent of him as he straightened up beside her after depositing the box by the door.

She smiled brightly. Too brightly, and felt his soft laugh all the way to her bones.

'You make a cute cowgirl,' he said, and then touched his fingertips to his forehead and left her there sniffing the air to catch the last traces of him before she went back inside.

A couple of hours later and the country and western saloon bar wedding had turned into a full-scale hoedown. The guests sat on hay bales and upturned barrels, and Jonny stood proud and central at the lectern, the bride before him in white lace hotpants and the groom in a black velvet tux and silver wingtips. The chapel lent itself perfectly to the theme, transformed for the day into a hayloft dressed in rustic gingham and Ruth's sunflowers and giant daisies.

Marla and Emily stood together at the back, arm in arm, best friends watching all of their hard work come to beautiful, unique fruition before their eyes. It might not be conventional romance, but the bride and groom's love ran clear and beautiful through the proceedings and informed the whole wedding with its own uniquely intrinsic, magical element that made the wedding flow and work.

It was a thread common with the vast majority of the weddings that they organised at the chapel; they brought to life a vision that wouldn't sit easily in your average church or wedding venue, but that was no less heartfelt or honest, in fact, in many cases it was more so.

'Joey junior, do you take this little lady to be your wife?' Jonny cried, his faux-Texan drawl bang on.

'I do.' Tears coursed down Joey junior's cheeks. 'I sure do, my darlin',' he said, his over-bright eyes fixed on his bride.

'And you, sugar-buns?' Jonny twirled his fake gun like a pro. 'Do you take this sharp shootin' outlaw to be your lawfully wedded husband?'

'Aw, Joey, ma big daft cowboy,' Joey junior's bride said, her Liverpudlian accent clear behind her terrible deep-south drawl. 'I most certainly do.'

The crowd yee-hawed as the bride and groom kissed, and Jonny threw his arms to the skies and praised the good Lord until silence reigned. All eyes on him, he broke into a full-bellowed rendition of 'Stand by your Man' to thunderous applause as Joey junior and his bride clung to each other for their first impromptu dance as husband and wife. Little by little the congregation moved into the aisle to dance; the jeans and leather vest-clad bridesmaid and the bandana'ed best man, the mother of the bride with the leather-trousered grandpa of the groom.

Marla clapped, happy tears on her cheeks. The chapel had woven its magic once again. For a little while she let herself forget all of her worries and enjoyed the moment of celebration. There would be plenty of time later to dwell on her problems. Her effervescent mother, her macabre new stepfather to be, her overcrowded cottage, her tangled emotions. Not to mention the small matter of dinner at Franco's that evening, fraught with the potential for disaster.

CHAPTER TWENTY-FIVE

Gabe ran the iron over his black shirt, his mobile phone cradled in the crook of his shoulder as he tried to call a cab at the same time. He wished he'd never mentioned the fact that they'd now been open for three months. Melanie had pounced on it like a vulture and insisted that the whole team should go out and celebrate. He'd humoured her, and left her in charge of organising something, and now here he was, heading into town to meet Melanie, Dan and the pall-bearers for dinner at some fancy restaurant. She'd made the arrangements and invited everyone before he'd even got wind of it. He'd tried hard to hide his surprise; all he'd had in mind was a swift half down the pub, not a full-scale dinner. On the flip side, he was glad that Melanie enjoyed work enough to go to such trouble.

He put the iron down as the switchboard operator muttered an unintelligible greeting against his ear.

'Hi. Taxi to Franco's please. Soon as possible.'

* * *

Franco's was one of those *chichi* restaurants with glitzy chandeliers and mushroom suede banquettes, and on a different day in different company Marla would probably have loved it. But sitting around the table that evening, she felt uneasy. Their party had swollen to nine with the late addition of Dora and Ivan (Emily and Tom had threatened to drop out and Marla had become desperate). In the end they made it anyway, but hey ho: the more the merrier.

Brynn sidled up to Marla as they walked through the double glass front doors at Franco's.

'What a fabulous smell,' he murmured, his mouth far too close to her ear for comfort. *God, please let him mean the food and not me,* Marla prayed silently.

And please don't let him order a nice Chianti, either, or I'll insist he sleeps somewhere other than my house tonight.

'Jonny!'

Marla waved as she spotted her saviour lounging in the bar area, looking particularly splendid in a leopardskin shirt, a lurid blue cocktail in his hand.

'Well don't *you* look lovely, darling.'

He smiled and kissed her cheek with a discreet nod of approval towards her close-fitting aubergine silk dress, which was held up on one shoulder with a glittering brooch. She'd opted for all-out vintage glamour tonight in an effort to prove to her mother how sorted her life was. She was sophisticated, and successful, and she had an attractive, *normal* man on her arm. Although, to be honest, Rupert's behaviour since the accident with Bluey had been anything but normal. He'd been on edge and overly attentive, but maybe she was reading too much into it. She just wanted things to settle back to the no-strings-attached relationship they'd had at the beginning. Back then he'd been fun and sociable, and she'd enjoyed his company.

Why did it always have to become more complicated?

He seemed happy enough tonight, thankfully, and she had to confess she was glad to have him there. He was by both nature and breeding a 'social animal'. Between him and Jonny, conversation was guaranteed to flow easily.

Marla felt conspicuously on show as they took their seats around a circular table in the centre of the room, as if they were the after-dinner cabaret act. Given that their party included a sex therapist, a taxidermist and a gay wedding celebrant, the other patrons of the restaurant would be well within their rights to expect something of a performance. *Please don't let them get one*, Marla prayed as she sat down.

Her daily quota of prayers had risen significantly since her mother's arrival – impressive for someone who didn't really have faith. It just made her feel better to ask someone, *anyone*, to intervene and come to her rescue if the going got too tough. Her mother had only been around a few days, and already Marla's arms ached from the effort of juggling balls, trying to maintain the illusion that she was sorted. It wasn't that Cecilia was judgmental. It was more of a personal battle to prove that she wasn't going to reverse up the same emotional cul-de-sacs as her mother.

She shot a glance across at Brynn, the latest case in point.

He'd found himself perched between Dora and Rupert. She wasn't sure who she felt most sorry for. Possibly Brynn, which spoke volumes.

The group had already started to yack between themselves and not so much as glanced at their menus. At this rate, it would be a long, long evening.

'Shall we order?' Marla attempted to steer the group in the right direction.

Cecilia took this as her cue and cleared her throat with a dramatic cough as she stood up.

'Could I just take a moment to thank you all for being here this evening.'

Marla smiled. Her mother was in her element when she was the centre of attention.

'I feel truly blessed to be here with my daughter's special people. You've all made me feel very welcome,' she gushed, and fluttered her ringed fingers at her throat. 'At this rate I won't want to go home!'

She squeezed Marla's shoulder to a flurry of 'aaah' from around the table, and Marla arranged her face into what she hoped looked like a smile to mask her inner horror at the thought of her mother staying forever.

'And can I also just add a huge good luck to my darling Brynn before his speech at the taxidermy expo tomorrow. You go, honey!'

She raised her glass down the table towards her fiancé.

A mildly bewildered silence fell across the table until Jonny leapt into the breach feet first.

'So, Brynn. Taxidermy. Tell me, what's the biggest cock you've ever stuffed?'

Everyone around the table gasped in unison and stared from Jonny to Brynn like tennis spectators. Brynn, for his part, appeared completely unperturbed by the question as he paused for a moment's thought and chewed on his bread roll.

'Well, Jonny, I guess that would have to be a bull. Boy oh boy, was he a cracking specimen. Well over two foot long.'

Brynn held out his hands to demonstrate and Jonny's eyes boggled with excitement. 'Why do I suddenly feel so inadequate?' He cackled and crossed his legs.

'No need at all, Jonny my love,' Cecilia squawked from down the table. Marla groaned, shut her eyes, and wished for death. Her mother was always eager to don her sex therapist hat. She cast a longing look towards the door. Could she get away with a loo break yet?

Cecilia pointed a long, red nail at Brynn.

'Brynn honey, be honest. Don't I always tell you that girth is more important than length?'

Brynn turned beetroot, casting a glance down at his own trouser department.

'I mean,' Cecilia leaned forward and dropped her voice to a stage whisper and they all leant in a little, 'I, for instance, am terribly small –' she glanced at her lap with an exaggerated grimace, '– down there.'

Marla, who had heard this spiel many times before, waited for the requested earthquake or alternative divine act to strike her mother and shut her up.

'Anything more than a few inches would just hang around outside in the cold.' She threw her hands up and nodded sagely at her stunned-into-silence audience. 'Girth wins every time. A man can never be too wide.'

Dora smiled fondly across the table at her husband. 'My Ivan's hung like a donkey.'

Ivan stuck his thumb up at his wife and patted his groin absently as he reached for the butter.

Marla glanced at Tom, who had tears of laughter coursing down his cheeks. He raised his glass in salute. 'This is hands down the best dinner I've ever been to in my life.'

Jonny whistled under his breath and shot an excited look at Emily. 'Don't look now, but Gomez and Morticia just walked in.'

Marla followed his gaze to the doors. Crap. That was it. She was done with praying. She cowered behind her over-sized menu and hoped desperately that Gabe wouldn't spot her. She flicked a glance at Rupert. Things had only just settled back into an uneasy truce between them. She was well aware of the simmering animosity between Gabe and Rupert, and she wasn't sure that their relationship was back on an even enough keel to handle them all being in the same room together.

She risked a quick look around the menu to see who Gabe was with.

Oh. My. God.

Was that his *receptionist*?

Marla scrutinised the woman in the clinging black dress with her hair piled up and too much make-up on. *It was! It was Melanie. Surely Gabe wasn't seriously dating that hideous, dog-murdering girl?* But then, why would they be out for dinner à deux at Franco's, if he wasn't?

Crap. Melanie was looking their way.

Look away, look away, look away. But of course, Melanie didn't look away. She tipped her head to the side and met Marla's gaze with raised eyebrows and a tiny smile. What *was* that look in her overly made-up eyes? Was it smugness, or triumph maybe? A horrible mix of both, Marla decided, burning up with hatred.

She murdered Bluey. She's a horrible manipulative little cowbag, and she murdered my dog. *What the fuck was Gabe thinking?* And did he not think it was unethical to

221

wine and dine his receptionist? He ought to watch his back. Melanie was the sort of woman who would cry sexual assault the minute he stepped out of line. Marla sniffed and tried to concentrate on the menu, although the idea of food was beginning to make her queasy.

Meanwhile, realising that she'd lost her audience, Cecilia turned to see who Jonny and Emily were craning their necks to get a look at.

'Who are they, honey?'

She elbowed Marla and nodded over at Gabe and Melanie. Marla feigned ignorance.

'Er . . . I'm not sure.' She glanced pointedly at her mother's menu. 'Have you decided? I think I'm going to have the salmon.'

Cecilia wasn't fooled. 'Marla, who *are they*?' she hissed. 'Ooh, they're coming over. Introduce me.'

Marla sank lower in her chair and chanced a look at Rupert, whose thunderous expression confirmed that he had also clocked Melanie hauling Gabe across the restaurant.

Jonny leapt to his feet – ever the genial host, despite the fact that it wasn't even his party. The gentle way that Gabe had handled Bluey's death had left Jonny with a newfound respect for Marla's adversary. He reached out and shook Gabe's hand. 'Gabe.'

Marla was at least heartened by the way he dismissed Melanie with a curt nod.

Cecilia was out of her seat and bobbing like an excited child as she waited to be introduced.

Gabe glanced around the table like a watchful lion sizing up the enemy. His gaze came to rest on Marla just as her mother delivered a sharp kick to her shins to make her stand up.

'Gabe. This is a surprise.' She placed her menu down slowly and stood begrudgingly next to her mother. 'This is my mother, Cecilia.'

Her ingrained good manners demanded that she make introductions at the very least.

'Mom, this is Gabriel Ryan. He runs the funeral parlour. You know, the one *right next door* to the chapel.'

She shot her mother a warning look and Cecilia frowned for a second. She'd heard enough about the High Street battle to be aware that Gabe and Marla were not the best of friends.

Please don't say anything ridiculous, Mom. Just say hi and let them return to their table.

'Oooh. I've heard a lot about you, and all bad, you naughty young man!' Cecilia's eyes danced as they always did in the presence of an attractive man. Marla should have known better than to hope family loyalty would trump good looks.

'Come on over here and let me fraternise with the enemy!' Cecilia's laughter tinkled as she threw out her arms to beckon him closer.

Naughty young man? Fraternise with the enemy? Marla was instantly transported back twenty years to schoolyard fights. Her mother had never fought her corner then either, especially if the kid in question had a good-looking dad. But Marla was all grown up these days, and she was going to kill her mother for this. She'd let Brynn stuff her too, for good measure.

Gabe's smile couldn't have been more awkward as he made his way around the table and kissed Cecilia's overly powdered cheek.

Marla watched in horrified fascination as her mother fluttered her false lashes and swooned under Gabe's attention. The fact that this particular good-looking man was trying to wreck her daughter's life was clearly not reason enough to refrain from flirting.

'Good to meet you, Cecilia. Marla tells me you're to be married?'

Marla's toes curled as she peeped at Rupert through her fringe. She hadn't talked about her mom with Rupert before this visit, so her obvious confidence in Gabe was not likely to go down well. Oh dear. He was purple-in-the-face kind of angry. *Please don't make a scene, Rupert.*

But then, he's never asked you about your family either, has he? the little devil on her shoulder prompted.

'Please, come join us. We're having a bit of a party,' Cecilia asked.

'We'd love to, thank you,' Melanie piped up and beamed at Marla's mother.

'We would?' Gabe shot her a quizzical look.

Melanie leaned in and cupped her hand around Gabe's ear for privacy.

'There's been a bit of a hitch with the others, they went to the wrong restaurant,' she whispered.

It was a toss-up for who looked more mortified, Marla or Gabe. Shock robbed them both of the power of speech for a crucial moment, and Cecilia jumped in and beckoned the waiter over to organise two extra chairs next to her own.

'And who is this delightful creature?' Cecilia enquired, her eyes on Melanie.

Delightful? Marla reached the end of her tether. 'This is Melanie, Mom. She's the one who killed Bluey.'

Melanie blanched beneath her make-up and Rupert coughed nervously.

'Marla, darling, that's umm, not . . .' he flicked a glance between Marla and Melanie. 'Well, not strictly fair.'

Why. Thank. You. Rupert. His lack of public support stung like a slap.

Tom raised his glass again, merry as a mad monk on too much wine and not enough food. 'A toast.' He paused until everyone had quietened down to listen. 'To Bluey.'

'Who's Bluey?' Brynn hissed to no one in particular as everyone reached for their glass.

'Marla's Great Dane. Melanie ran him over,' Emily supplied quietly, as she topped up her wine glass with more water.

'Lovely big boy he was,' Dora said, her lip quivering so much that Brynn was moved to upend the wine bottle into her glass and push it towards her.

Ivan nodded and pointed a crooked index finger at Brynn. 'I'll tell you something for nothing. He'd have given your bull a run for his money. Huge todger. Spotted it when he piddled on my roses.'

Brynn clapped his hands in delight and looked over at Gabe with hopeful eyes.

'You don't still have him in the deep freeze do you, Gabriel?'

'No, he bloody well hasn't!' Marla banged her glass down on the table. With as much control as she could muster, she shot out of her chair to make a break for the sanctuary of the little girls' room. She would have made it, had she not barrelled headlong into a strong pair of arms instead, just a few feet from the table.

'Marla, I thought it was you.'

She looked up, and one glimpse of the familiar, craggy face of her ex-stepfather Dr Robert Black was enough to make her crumple against his crisp white shirt.

He was an unexpected and comforting lifejacket in a stormy sea, and she clung on tight.

'Robert?' Cecilia's voice quivered from behind them, stripped bare of her trademark confidence.

Robert smiled warmly at his ex-wife. 'Cecilia. Long time no see.'

When Marla returned to the table some minutes later, her main course was cold and her seat was occupied by Robert, head to head in quiet conversation with her mother. Marla couldn't help but notice the way her mother leaned her body in towards him, or how her face had softened in his presence, in a way that had nothing to do with the candles flickering on the table.

On Cecilia's other side, Melanie looked up from her salad, giving Marla a sly wink over Gabe's dipped head.

Marla comforted herself with a split-second fantasy of gouging out Melanie's eyes with one of the dainty, silver fish knives that lay close at hand.

Perhaps Brynn would like to pop them into his pocket to dissect later. On second thoughts, maybe not. No doubt they'd be full of putrid, evil stuff that would splatter the walls if he sliced into them, because Melanie's smug look was laced with pure bromide.

Robert spotted Marla behind him and jumped up to fold her into another quick hug. He held her at arm's length and looked her over with a concerned frown.

'Alright now, sweetheart?'

She blinked quickly as a fresh platoon of tears marched eagerly up her tear ducts. *Left, right, left, right! Fall back! Fall back!* His kind, fatherly tone threatened to unpick the good the five minutes she'd just spent deep breathing with Emily in the ladies' had done. She smiled, her eyes overly bright.

'It's so lovely to see you,' she answered. Robert had been more of a fatherly presence in his few short years as Cecilia's husband, than her own dad had been in a lifetime.

'You too, honey. Call me soon, yes?'

Marla squeezed his hands and nodded.

'Who are you here with?' she asked, keen to steer the conversation into less emotional waters. Behind her Cecilia leaned forward to catch the answer to the question she probably hadn't dared to ask herself.

'It's a work thing,' Robert said. 'Bit dry, to be honest. Was a relief to spot my favourite girls over here . . . my favourite girl.'

He tailed off and corrected himself with an awkward smile. 'My favourite girls' had always been his term of endearment for Marla *and* Cecilia, and it was clearly inappropriate now. Hearing it then was almost enough to summon the tears legion back to duty.

Brynn shot around the table and screeched to a halt behind Cecilia's chair. It was a tactical error. Standing close to Robert only served to highlight the fact that Brynn was a head shorter and a darn sight less attractive.

'Brynn Holt. Taxidermist. And, Cecilia's intended.'

He slicked hair back into place and held out his hand towards Robert.

227

'Intended for what?' Jonny called. 'A glass display case in the cellar?'

He earned himself a high-five from a rather drunk Tom and a sharp elbow in the ribs from Emily.

Robert suppressed a smile.

'Dr Robert Black. Gynaecologist. And ex-husband number five.'

'Oooh, excellent,' Tom said, brightly. 'You should be able to verify Cecilia's tiny fanny claim, then.'

Gabe spluttered on the large glass of wine that Cecilia had pressed on him. Brynn looked askance, Robert looked amused, and Cecilia, who loved nothing more than discussing sexual anatomy around the dinner table, nodded in excitement.

'In my professional capacity, I most certainly cannot.' Robert frowned at Tom, and then grinned at Cecilia, well aware that unlike most women, she'd want him to broadcast her anatomical information at the dinner table. 'However, in my capacity as ex-husband, I can indeed confirm that Cecilia is delightfully snug.'

Parting shot delivered, he turned on his heels and headed back to join his own party. Marla realised with a jolt that most of *their* own party had been too interested in Robert to carry on conversations between themselves, and now he'd gone they were all gazing at her like attentive students in a classroom. All except Jonny, who leaned back on his chair legs to watch Dr Robert's retreating backside.

'What an amusing man,' Brynn ground out through gritted teeth as he made his way back to his seat.

'Amazing,' Cecilia corrected, too quietly for anyone but Gabe to catch.

Marla sat down on her mother's other side, mortified that Gabe had had to witness the spectacle that was her mother in full flight. She picked at her dinner for a few seconds longer before placing her knife and fork down – her food was significantly messier but barely eaten. She had no appetite for anything except the mercifully large glass of Shiraz in front of her. Tonight had turned into a fiasco of unprecedented levels, and the only constructive thing she could think of to do was to get too drunk to remember it.

Gabe picked up the wine bottle to refill Cecilia's glass, and then Marla's, but a big tanned hand stretched across the table and covered it.

Rupert.

God, with all of the shenanigans, Marla had almost forgotten he was there.

He looked a little odd, actually. Fidgety and awkward. Maybe he'd spotted that she was at the end of her tether and was about to sweep her right out of there? A violent longing to be curled up at home on the sofa with Bluey pierced her, and her heart cracked afresh. Her head hurt, and she smiled gratefully as Rupert got to his feet.

Phew. They *were* leaving.

Hang on, why was he clinking his glass with his knife? There was no need to make a drama of it, much better to slink out . . . Why did he always have to be so formal? She sank back down into her chair and picked up her wine glass in resignation as a hush fell around the table.

Rupert let the table settle into silenced anticipation, and then carefully placed the knife and glass back down on the table.

'I have something important that I need to say . . . or should I say, I need to ask.'

He flashed a wide smile. 'And there could be no better time than here, in the presence of our friends and family,' he continued, in the style of a vicar about to deliver a sermon to his flock. Beside her, Marla heard a tiny gasp from her mother – and a much more audible one from Melanie.

'Marla,' Rupert turned to face her. She nodded encouragingly back.

Just wrap it up, Rupert. Say thanks for coming and goodnight, then let's get the hell out of here. Please.

But it was another prayer to no one that fell on deaf ears.

'Marla, we've been together now for some months, and I can honestly say that I've never felt so happy, and I think you feel the same way.' He paused for dramatic effect and laid a hand over his heart. '*You complete me.*'

'Plagiarism! Get yer own lines!' Jonny heckled. Rupert shot Jonny a murderous look whilst he started a slow walk around the table towards Marla. She knew he was still speaking because his lips were moving, but the roar of blood in her ears made it impossible to hear his voice.

Sweet baby Jesus, no! Please don't let him get down on one knee, or I'm done for. I take back all I said about being a non-believer, I'll change my ways if you help me just this once.

Please, he's coming . . .

Rupert picked up her limp hand and sank down on one knee.

Alone in his luxurious marble bathroom the next morning, Rupert angled his chin from side to side to better admire himself in the mirror. Last night couldn't have gone better if he'd planned it. He'd only intended to ask Marla to go on holiday with him, but given the company around the table he'd hastily revised his plan. He threw a celebratory wink at his reflection.

Keeeer-ching! Hoist by your own petard, Melanie.

In one fell swoop he'd managed to propose to Marla, piss on Gabriel Ryan, and spell it out to Melanie that he wasn't a man to mess with. Jesus, he'd only slept with the woman once out of sympathy; *well, three times,* if you wanted to split hairs. Rupert glanced ruefully down at his flaccid cock. *He couldn't help it if his little tiger had a big stride when it was let out, could he?*

And now she was trying to cling on, making unreasonable demands as if she had some right to his time. Tiresome. She probably thought she'd been terribly clever last night; he hadn't missed the sly glint of triumph in her eyes when she'd wangled herself a place at his table. What sweet revenge it had been to watch fury twist her thin face when he'd proposed to Marla; almost as pleasurable as the tears of joy Marla had cried. Poor girl had been completely overcome, couldn't get a coherent word out. She'd seemed jumpy of late. Probably in need of a good seeing-to, it was frustrating for them both with her mother hogging all of her time.

His little tiger stirred against his thigh at the thought of Marla in flagrante on her white cotton sheets, and he stepped into the shower to let the beast roar.

Marla lay on her back and stared at the smooth, white bedroom ceiling. Pointless anger surged through her as her mother and Brynn banged around in the kitchen downstairs. She craved the solitude of an empty cottage and her own counsel rather than being forced into the sanctuary of her bedroom like a skulking teenager. The idea of going downstairs to rake over the coals of last night's events turned her stomach. She dragged the quilt over her head and closed her eyes, but still the memories played behind her eyelids. Everyone around their table last night had fallen silent the moment that Rupert dropped down on one knee. Actually, a Mexican wave of silence had fallen over the entire restaurant. She'd even spotted the chef pop out from the kitchens to lean against the doorframe with a spatula in his hand.

No pressure, then.

Time had seemed to slow down, *Matrix*-style, as Marla glanced around at the faces of her nearest and dearest.

Her mother, fascinated.

Emily, shocked.

Tom, grinning like a drunken loon.

Melanie, outraged. *Outraged?* What *was* that woman's problem?

Jonny, surreptitiously shaking his head from side to side and mouthing 'say no'.

And finally Gabe, whose expression she'd been unable to read at all. Her eyes had moved from his to Rupert's, who had sprung onto to his feet to stare expectantly at her.

Had she actually said the word yes? Had she? Surely she hadn't.

She'd cried, certainly, which Rupert had presumed to be tears of joy and popped the cork on a celebratory champagne bottle he'd produced out of thin air.

Could she love Rupert? She lay still and tried the idea on for size. It was too big. It swamped her. She was fond of him, but fond wasn't the same thing at all, was it? Love was bigger than her feelings for Rupert. More painful, more blinding, more destructive. Rupert was good company. He'd looked out for her since the campaign against the funeral parlour had started, and God knew he'd made sure she had an unfair amount of coverage in the newspaper. He could make her laugh and he could make her come, but that was really all she wanted from him. Up until last night she'd assumed he felt the same way.

Strictly between Marla and her coffee cup, the fact that she could never emotionally invest in him was one of his main attractions. *Poor Rupert.* Had she led him on? She'd tried hard to define the boundaries, but he wasn't to know that the local wedding guru had an acute case of love-phobia, was he?

Marla flipped face down into the mattress and decided to stay in bed, because, for better or worse, she had an engagement to break off when she got up.

Gabe hit the accelerator, breaking the speed limit by a long way in an attempt to blow away his anger and frustration from the night before. What a fucking fiasco. Melanie had managed to royally screw up the arrangements for the work dinner to the extent that the rest of the staff had ended up in a completely different restaurant ten miles away. He'd been almost grateful for Marla's pushy mother's insistence that they gatecrash their party, right up to the point when Rupert-fuckwit-Dean had dropped down on one knee. Gabe stamped down hard on the accelerator and wished wholeheartedly that it was actually Rupert's throat under his foot.

Why the hell had Marla agreed to marry that spineless excuse for a man?

The possibility that she might truly love Rupert bled into his consciousness and refused to go away, even at breakneck speed.

CHAPTER TWENTY-SIX

Marla left the cottage before her mother and Brynn had a chance to surface on Monday morning. If she'd had to stomach any more wedding talk she'd have thrown up her muesli all over the kitchen table.

She stirred sugar into her coffee in the quiet chapel kitchen and wondered why Cecilia seemed to have completely forgotten about Marla's profession as a wedding coordinator and insisted on taking over. But then, her mother did have far more personal experience in the matter than most women, Marla mused uncharitably as she made her way upstairs to her office.

Dresses. Bridesmaids. Cupcake tower or traditional wedding cake?

Marla couldn't handle any more questions. She had ended up drinking too much red wine and lurking in her room like a teenager ignoring the numerous calls and texts from Rupert.

Not the most auspicious start to an engagement, she admitted to Jonny when he arrived half an hour later and listened to her grumble over tea and Hobnobs.

'Marla, darling.' He crossed his legs gracefully and screwed up his nose. 'It sounds to me as if you don't actually want to marry Henry.'

'Rupert,' Marla corrected with a frown.

'Sorry. He's Hooray Henry in my head.' Jonny was completely unabashed by his mistake and fixed her with a beady glare. 'I'm right, aren't I? You don't want to marry him. I know you Marla Jacobs, and that is not the face of a happy bride-to-be.'

Marla rubbed her temples, half glad that Jonny knew her well enough to see the truth and half wishing that he wasn't so perceptive.

'Do you love him?' he asked baldly, his eyebrows raised over eyes that told her he already knew her answer. 'And don't even bother trying to lie, because I already know the answer.'

Oh jeez, not the love question. She felt her muesli make a break for freedom.

'Jonny, it's way too early for a heart to heart. We'll talk later, okay?'

'Why? To give you a chance to work on your evasive answers some more?' He arched his eyebrows and smirked as he headed out. 'Pub after work. And no "buts",' he shouted ominously as he took the stairs two at a time.

Marla shook her head.

She had plenty of buts.

But I don't want a big meringue dress.

But I don't care whether the napkins match the seat covers.

But I've always hated red roses.

But I don't want to get married.

Not to Rupert, nor to anyone else. Not now, not next month, not next year. Not ever.

Jonny would regret dragging her to the pub when she got started on that little lot.

She placed her empty mug down and spotted the corner of a little envelope hidden beneath her mouse mat. A little tug and a quick rack of her brains, and it came back to her. It was the note she'd taken from the funeral parlour the night that Bluey died, the one with her own name scrawled across the front. She'd stashed it beneath her mouse mat, unsure if it was right to open it or not, but as she turned it over in her fingers, she reached a decision.

It was her name written across the front of it. It was intended for her.

What harm could it do, really? She ripped the envelope across the top and eased the little card out.

Dear Marla,

Something to help make your July 4th go with a bang, and to say I hope we can enjoy a less explosive friendship from here on in.

Yours,

Gabe
X

She frowned and read it twice over, still none the wiser. What did he mean, July 4th? Bang? She gasped out loud and clamped her fingers over her mouth, as the tinkling penny stopped spinning in the air and began to drop, flipping

237

over several times in slow motion before it landed with a dull thud of realisation.

The fireworks.

But how could they have been from Gabe? Rupert had brought them over; she'd seen him with her own eyes. She tapped her nose as she mentally rewound back to when Rupert walked into the chapel on July 4th. It was a day she'd prefer to never think of again.

Yes. She was one hundred per cent certain that Rupert had expressly said that the fireworks were his gift to her.

Hadn't he?

And if he hadn't *said* it, he'd definitely encouraged her to *think* it.

How could she ever know for sure?

She could hardly come right out and ask Rupert, because the mere mention of Gabe's name was enough to give him a coronary. And she couldn't ask Gabe either because a) they weren't on speaking terms, and b) even if they were, she'd sound a deranged fool.

'Hey, Gabe. *I stole this note from your desk, and now I need to know if my boyfriend-slash-unexpected-intended passed your gift off as his own.*'

It sounded absurd, but what else could 'something to help make your July 4th go with a bang' possibly mean? Unless he'd sent a bomb, which would be more in keeping given the general state of affairs between them.

She frowned out of the window at the funeral parlour. The constant 'push me, pull me' nature of her relationship with Gabe was draining. Their basic chemical reaction to each other made everything more complicated than it needed to be. If only he were pig ugly, it would make it so much easier to hate him.

'A bottle of red and three glasses, please, whenever you're ready, Bill.'

Jonny winked at the landlord before gesturing Marla and Emily to a quiet table in the pub.

'Make that two glasses. I'll stick to OJ,' Emily added, standing on tiptoes to lift her growing bump over the back of a chair.

They flopped down on the low sofas with a collective groan. It'd been a hectic day of preparations for a mid-week Las Vegas-style wedding, and the Elvis impersonator had dropped out at the eleventh hour, causing pandemonium. It was all sorted now, thanks to a desperate runner-up from *Stars In Their Eyes* who still craved his five minutes in the spotlight. He was prepared to make the two-hundred-mile round trip in order to don his star-spangled spandex again.

'Emily, do you think Marla should marry Henry?' Jonny poured the wine and got stuck straight into his intended topic of conversation, no doubt deliberately using the wrong name to make his antipathy clear.

Marla spluttered as she unwound her Missoni scarf and placed it on the table. 'Excuse me?'

Emily shifted cagily in her seat and turned anxious eyes on Marla. 'Do you want to?'

'I . .' Marla flailed around for the right words. Her sense of loyalty and fair play insisted that Rupert really ought to be first to hear that there wasn't going to be a wedding.

'See? Told you! She didn't jump straight in there with a big fat "yes", did she?'

Jonny wagged his finger, clearly something else he'd learned from his many hours watching *Oprah*. He stopped just short of adding 'girrlfreeend' on the end of his sentence, but then he *was* still warming up.

Marla fixed him with a measured stare.

'Just quit it with the inquisition, will you? I'm fine.'

Jonny took a leisurely sip of his wine and ignored her plea. 'I asked you a question this morning.'

Emily looked at Jonny, nonplussed, as Marla shrugged noncommittally.

'Did you?' Marla said, deliberately evasive.

'I asked you if you loved Rupert.'

Emily's head swivelled back to Marla, agog.

'So?' Marla folded her arms across her chest and glared at Jonny squarely across the table.

'So, do you?'

The weight of both of their expectant stares proved too heavy. Marla slumped, elbows on the table and her face buried in her hands.

'No. I'm fond of him, but I don't love him. And no, I don't want to marry him, either.'

Jonny rubbed her back, immediately contrite.

'Poor baby, I knew it.' He shot a pained look of horror over her head at Emily and mouthed 'Help me!'

'You have to tell him it's off, darling, and sooner rather than later,' Jonny advised, making Marla howl behind her fingers.

'But why did you say yes?' Emily whispered, fishing a tissue out of her massive tote bag and pushing it into Marla's hands.

Marla lifted her head and ripped the tissue slowly into ribbons.

'*Did* I? You were there. Did I *actually* say yes?'

Jonny and Emily exchanged troubled glances.

'It sort of looked like you did, yeah. You nodded, and then you burst into tears,' Emily said.

'*I nodded*. You're sure?'

''Fraid you did, sugar,' Jonny confirmed.

'And to think I thought it was all so romantic,' Emily marvelled with wide eyes.

'Are you sure? That you don't love him, I mean?'

Marla took a good slug of wine and nodded.

'He's fun company and he makes me laugh. We have a good time together.'

She balled the shredded tissue up.

Emily's face said all Marla needed to know.

'He doesn't make your heart miss a beat when he looks at you?' Emily asked. 'He doesn't make you melt, make your stomach flip?'

Marla smiled sadly and patted Emily's hand. 'We can't all be as lucky as you, Em.'

She registered the shadow that passed across her friend's eyes.

'Well, that's that then. You can't marry him if you don't love him.' Emily placed her other hand over Marla's. 'Marriage is hard enough when you *do* love each other, so it'd be a complete disaster if you don't.'

'Is everything okay with you and Tom?' Marla asked, partly out of concern and partly because she badly wanted to change the subject.

Emily batted the question away with a wave of her hand. 'We're fine. Ignore me. It's just hormones.'

Marla debated for a second before reaching for her handbag. She pulled out her diary, and extricated the note she'd found on Gabe's desk from between its pages. Jonny and Emily stared at the innocuous little envelope in silence as Marla slid it towards the centre of the table.

'There's this, too.'

'What is it?' Emily asked.

'It's a note I never received.'

Marla took the card out of its envelope and passed it to Emily who, clearly confused, read it with a frown then handed it on to Jonny.

'I found it by accident on Gabe's desk the night that Bluey died,' Marla said quietly. 'I put it in my pocket and forgot about it until this morning.'

'I don't understand . . .' Emily shrugged, her face a picture of frustration.

'No? Well I bloody do!' Jonny burst out, slamming the card down on the table a few seconds later. Marla chewed her lip and waited in silence to see if Jonny's conclusion tallied with her own.

'I knew that jumped-up twatface couldn't have come up with anything so thoughtful on his own!'

'Tell me what's going on!' Emily hissed at them.

Marla placed a hand on Jonny's arm to stop him from shouting again, then turned to Emily.

'I think the note should have been attached to the fireworks.'

'But Rupert gave you the firewo— Oh my God!'

Emily's mouth dropped into a perfect 'O' as realisation dawned.

Jonny drummed his fingers on the tabletop in an attempt to control his temper. 'Have you said anything to Rupert about this yet?'

Marla shook her head. 'I only read it today.'

'Good. Let me tell him. Or, better yet, let me smack his teeth down his throat for you.'

Marla covered Jonny's tightly balled fist with her own hand, grateful to have him in her corner, even if he had temporarily morphed into Bruce Willis from the *Die Hard* years.

'I still don't get it though . . .' Emily muttered.

'I don't either, really,' Marla said. 'Rupert definitely gave me those fireworks himself. How did he get hold of them, if they were actually from Gabe?'

Emily shook her head with a perplexed look at Jonny. 'Well, I know one thing for sure. Gabe wouldn't have given them to Rupert to pass on, since they can't stand the sight of each other.'

Marla nodded. She'd arrived at that same stumbling block herself.

Jonny, however, was streets ahead of both of them.

'You're right. *Gabe* wouldn't give them to Rupert. But you can bet your sweet ass that *Melanie* would,' he said, slowly. They lapsed into silence and stared at each other.

'Bitch,' Jonny spat eventually. 'I've told you all along that she was fucking venomous.'

'But why would she take Gabe's note off first?'

Jonny looked at Emily as if she were the village idiot.

'Durr! Because she's got the hots for him herself of course! Haven't you noticed the way she moons over him?'

'But why would Rupert not mention that they weren't from him?' Emily asked, her eyes flicking between Marla and Jonny.

Marla was silent – still turning the idea over in her head.

'Because he's a thieving opportunist shitbag. Why else?'

Marla cringed at Jonny's typically harsh words. 'Go easy,

Jonny. Maybe he intended to tell me they were from Gabe, but then felt awkward when I was so thrilled.'

'Yeah, right.' Jonny laughed sourly. 'Why are you determined to see the best in him?'

Marla shrugged. 'I just know him better than you do. And anyway, since when did you become a fully paid-up member of the Gabriel Ryan fan club?'

'I'm not. I just don't like people lying to you.'

'What are you going to do?' Emily asked, her chocolate eyes soft with sympathy.

Marla rubbed a hand across her forehead, then knocked what was left in her wine glass back in one go.

'I don't know yet. But one thing's for sure. I'm not marrying Rupert.'

Marriage was number one on her 'things not to do before I die' list, so how the hell had she ended up with a bona fide fiancé? Let alone one who was already lying through his teeth before he'd even got a ring on her finger?

Over at Emily's cottage, Tom poured Dora a second sherry.

'Thank you Dora,' he said, relieved beyond measure to have someone to talk to. Dora had turned up unexpectedly in her usual forthright manner, no doubt more than aware that Emily was in the pub with Marla and Jonny. She'd bustled in, asked for sherry instead of tea, and sat him down for a good talking-to. He hadn't realised how much he needed to get things off his chest until he'd started to speak and had been unable to stop.

'So, the baby,' she said, sipping her sherry and watching him closely. 'You're happy about it?'

He lifted both shoulders and sipped the scotch he'd poured for himself. 'We'd been trying for a while.'

Dora nodded slowly. She still remembered how painful those days and months had been for her, and formed the basis of her visit tonight. Age had bestowed wisdom upon her shoulders, enough to see that Emily and Tom had been given a chance at the family she'd never been blessed with herself. She didn't want them to miss it. 'Thomas, is this baby yours?'

Tom took a second good slug of whisky, momentarily blindsided by the baldness of Dora's opening question. Emotions warred for supremacy in his head. Anger, whether at Emily or himself; he wasn't even sure anymore. Love, for Emily and for the tiny life growing inside her, regardless of whether it shared his DNA. Confusion, and fear. Fear of losing everything, fear so big that he took a third glug of his drink. 'I don't think it is, no.'

Dora looked at him beadily over the rim of her wine glass. 'I thought not.'

'You did?'

'Emily has the weight of the world on her shoulders. She should be happy as a pig in muck, but she isn't, and I don't think she has been for a while.'

Tom's heart hurt. His wife had been struggling, and everyone had been able to see it. He was a fucking moron.

'Love's a funny thing, Tom,' Dora said. 'It's easy to take for granted.'

He nodded. Guilty as charged. He'd prioritised just about everything in front of Emily, work especially.

'Ivan and me wanted children when we were your age,' Dora said, her eyes wistful.

Tom watched Dora and saw the same pain amplified

there that he'd seen on Emily's face month on month. 'It's the only thing I'd change, Thomas. If I could go back, it's the one thing I'd do differently. The chance to have a family is a blessing.'

Tom reached for the whisky bottle. 'What are you saying, Dora?'

'You love each other, Thomas. Let that be enough.' Dora looked him straight in the eye. 'Let this baby come. Love your wife.' She sipped her sherry. 'Love them both.'

Tom looked at Dora with new, appreciative eyes. He hadn't asked her to come to the cottage. She'd come because she could see they were in trouble and wanted to help. He owed it to her to listen, and he owed it to Emily to take her advice. He hugged Dora warmly as she left, knowing that something inside him had changed a little; that the fear and anger he'd harboured had subsided to let hope in.

Alone again a little while later, he unzipped the suit carrier that hung on the back of the spare bedroom door and felt around inside the jacket pocket of his linen wedding suit. It was still there, folded in half, just as it had been that night on the mantelpiece.

He clutched the pale green note and stared at it as if it might explode in his fingers.

The night he'd found it, he'd so wanted to destroy it, but something had held him back. Was today the day he would actually read it?

Was *any* day the right day to find out the real reason your wife planned to leave you?

His fingers touched the cool cotton of his jacket. If he reached into the pocket of the trousers, he knew he'd find powder-soft Antiguan sand from the beach they'd married on. He'd never got around to having the suit dry-cleaned, for fear that it would wash away some of the magical memories of that day.

Emily, barefoot and beautiful, an exotic flower tucked behind her ear. Of how she'd laughed at the way the wedding celebrant pronounced his surname, and how thrilled she'd been to finally share that name with him.

Of the love they'd made on that very same beach to consummate their marriage, beneath a blanket of stars so bright you could almost reach up to take one home as a souvenir.

He flipped the letter over again. He'd told Emily that he'd thrown it in the fire that night without reading it. He wished he had.

Did he really want to know what had driven Emily to the point of leaving him?

Did he want to rake it all up again, now that she was finally having a baby and they'd stepped back from the brink of disaster?

The baby.

He closed his eyes and sighed hard, the letter suddenly as lead-heavy as his heart. Inevitability swamped him. He already knew.

He traced his own name with his fingertip, scrawled across the front of the paper in Emily's familiar looping handwriting.

Today was as good a day as any, because whatever lay in that letter didn't have the power to destroy him any longer. Dora was right. They loved each other. They would weather this storm, no matter how rough the seas got.

He sat down on the edge of the bed, and opened the letter.

Dear Tom,

I'm so sorry that I'm not brave enough to do this face to face, but we seem to have lost the ability to talk to each other these days anyway, so maybe it's for the best. I miss that so much. Talking, I mean. I miss <u>you</u> so much – even when you're home, it's like we're strangers living under the same roof.

I've done something terrible, Tom, and it's ripping me apart. I don't even want to write it down because I know how much reading it will hurt you, but I have to because you deserve to know the truth.

I've slept with someone else. It was just once, and he means nothing to me, honestly, he doesn't. I won't try to make excuses, and I'm not asking for your forgiveness because I can't forgive myself. I was just so desperately lonely, and he was kind to me. God, I wish I could wind the clock back and not do it, but life isn't like that, is it?

I'm so sorry – for this, and for wanting a baby so much that I've let it rip our marriage apart. Jesus, Tom, how did it come to this?

You are the love of my life, it wasn't supposed to end like this. I'm so ashamed of myself, and I won't blame you if you decide that you can't be with me anymore.

I've broken my own heart as well as yours, I'm sorry to the ends of the earth and back.

Love always,
Emily
x

CHAPTER TWENTY-SEVEN

'Rupert, we need to talk.'

Hmmm. Too clichéd.

'Rupert, did you lie to me about the fireworks on July 4th?'

Bad idea. Too confrontational.

'Rupert. I don't want to marry you.'

Too honest. Too true.

As she waited for Rupert to arrive at the chapel to take her to lunch, Marla ran through several other possible ways to open the conversation. Her stomach had been churning with nerves and questions had been buzzing around inside her head since she'd left Emily and Jonny in the pub last night.

The crunch of tyres on the gravel ratcheted her nerves up another notch, and she peeped out of the window just in time to see Rupert climb out of his sports car and cast a furtive look over towards the funeral parlour. As she watched, Melanie opened the door and gave Rupert a smug little wiggly finger-wave, and Marla felt her temper rocket from a low simmer to totally furious in two seconds flat.

By the time Rupert waltzed through the chapel doors, she'd backtracked on her plan for a civilised discussion over lunch and decided to just get things over with, here and now in the chapel.

'Hey gorgeous.' Rupert breezed in and flicked his hair back in that way that was really starting to get on her nerves.

'Hey yourself,' Marla said.

Something in her flat tone must have alerted him to incoming thunder clouds, because he dropped his keys on the nearest chair and pulled her into his arms.

'You okay?'

He frowned as she ended his kiss a nano-second after it started and squirmed out of his embrace.

'Not really.'

Marla watched his jaw work furiously as he tried to decide how to play things.

'Bad morning at work?' he tried.

She shook her head and sighed.

'It's not work, Rupert, it's us.'

His Adam's apple bobbed as he swallowed hard. He ran a finger around his neckline to loosen his collar.

'It's lunch, isn't it? You're too busy. I'll call and cancel, we can just walk down to the café and grab a sandwich if you like?'

'It isn't the lunch arrangements, Rupert. It's *us*.'

Marla repeated the 'us' more firmly this time to stop him from attempting to side-step the issue again.

'Okaaaaay.' He dragged the word out as if he were trying to reason with a five-year-old. 'What about us?'

She detected a note of irritation in his voice and tried not to rise to it.

'I . . . I feel as if we're rushing into things. You know, the wedding and all.'

He nodded slowly.

'Riiiiight.'

He dragged that word out too, and Marla fought back the urge to slap him.

'So we'll slow it down then. Get married later on. No big deal,' he said brightly. 'Grab your jacket, we'll miss our table.'

Marla sucked in air and looked out of the window for a second before meeting his eyes again.

'That's the thing though, Rupert. I don't want to get married – sooner *or* later.'

The spoilt schoolboy in him surfaced instantly.

'But you said yes!'

'No. I didn't. You assumed it.'

'Marla, we had a whole audience who would beg to differ! You can hardly back out now.'

His outrage would have been funny in any other situation.

'Can't I?'

'No you bloody well can't. You'll make me look a total fool.'

'And that's your main concern, is it?'

'Don't be stupid, I love you,' he protested, and then for good measure, he added, 'and you love me.'

'I do?'

'Well . . . don't you?'

Marla bit her lip and frowned. She didn't want to hurt

him any more than was necessary, but this wasn't the moment to pull any punches.

'I'm sorry, but I don't think I do,' she whispered.

Disbelief hit his face first, followed hot on the heels by self-righteous anger.

'So you've been stringing me along then?' He was like a petulant child.

'No! I was fine with dating, but then you got all heavy out of nowhere and proposed.' Marla knew her voice was rising but she couldn't control it. 'And for the record, I did *not* say yes!'

He glared at her, shaking his head slowly, and Marla wondered how she'd never noticed the coldness in his eyes before.

'There's a name for women like you,' he said with a nasty laugh. He took a few steps closer.

'What are you talking about?' Marla whispered in shock, taking a few small steps away from him.

'Women who lead men on.'

He moved closer still.

'I didn't lead you on, Rupert, I never . . .'

She backed up again, now halfway up the aisle.

'Prick tease.'

He made a lunge for her and she stumbled on her high heels.

'Get your hands off me!' she yelled, as his fingers gouged into her upper arms.

He made a noise in his throat that sounded horribly like a snarl as he yanked her hard against him. Panic kicked in hard when she felt his excitement bulge against her thigh, and she sent a chair flying as she tried to scrabble out of his grasp. The thud of footsteps echoed through the chapel as Jonny flew down the stairs and dragged Rupert off her.

He floored him with a hard left hook.

'You've broken my nose!' Rupert wailed as he struggled to stand up, blood all over the turned-up collar of his pristine shirt.

'And I'll break your fucking neck if you come within fifty foot of Marla again!' Jonny roared, dragging Rupert along the aisle by the scruff of the neck.

He karate-kicked the front doors open and flung him unceremoniously out onto the path.

'I'll sue you for assault,' Rupert squawked from his lowly position on his backside.

Jonny loomed over him menacingly. 'Do you *want* me to kill you?'

'And you can add threatening behaviour to the list!' Rupert tried to get up but Jonny pushed him back down again with a size ten crocodile-skin cowboy boot to the chest.

'Just try it, twatbag, and the police will be knocking on your door for sexual assault,' Jonny glowered, aiming a sharp kick at Rupert's ribs.

He turned his back on Rupert to take care of a visibly shaken Marla. 'You okay, sweets?' He shepherded her back inside the doors and put his hands on her shoulders as he scrutinised her with concerned eyes.

'God, I'm so glad you were here, Jonny,' she said, her voice shaky with relief. 'You are officially the most macho gay man in the world.'

He pulled her against his chest and laughed softly. 'And you thought these guns were just for show.'

'You're my hero.'

'Well, he certainly wasn't, was he?' Jonny said with a grim nod towards the door.

Marla shuddered in revulsion. She hadn't expected Rupert to take it on the chin and shake hands, but she'd never have imagined he would turn on her like that. She'd glimpsed a darkness in him that he'd never let her see before, and she felt completely relieved to be free of him. A shaft of sunlight bounced through the window, and the glint of metal caught her eye. His keys. He'd left them on the chair. A quick double-check outside confirmed that he was too scared of Jonny to come back in and retrieve them. He had scarpered without his car.

'Leave it to me, sugar, I know the perfect place for that little beauty.'

Jonny grinned as he pocketed the keys, already thinking about the hot guy who worked at the local scrap yard. It was a warm, sunny day. With any luck he'd be shirtless and oily.

Over at the funeral parlour, Melanie sat at her desk, watching the events unfold with interest. A knife had twisted in her gut when Rupert ignored her on the doorstep earlier, so to see him upended on his backside a few minutes later brought a certain karmic pleasure. She'd been stewing over what to do about him for a while now. Hats off to him, it had been a bold move to propose to Marla right in front of her when she could so easily have spilled her guts about their affair. His physical ejection from the chapel just now, however, indicated that things were no longer rosy between Marla and Rupert, affording Melanie pleasure and pain in equal measure.

On the one hand, it served him right. May the pain of rejection hurt even more than his nose, which rather looked like it was broken. But on the other hand, Marla had better not look towards Gabe for a shoulder to cry on. Melanie stabbed her pencil repeatedly into the mouse mat until the nib snapped, leaving a latticework of holes across the sponge surface.

She'd seen Marla Jacobs off once, and she'd do it again in a New York minute.

CHAPTER TWENTY-EIGHT

Dora opened Ivan's wardrobe, determined to fill the charity bag with clothes. His cupboard was stuffed to the gunnels with clothes than hadn't seen the light of day for at least ten years. He wouldn't even realise that she'd thinned it out.

Ivan's distinct and comforting smell floated out as her fingers skimmed several immaculate suits from times long gone. She lingered as she recalled happy memories of carefree days. Of weddings and tea dances. She couldn't toss those out.

Daunted, she moved on to the shelves. She could always come back to the suits again afterwards.

Up on the top shelf, she moved aside his gardening pullovers and threadbare checked shirts to feel around in the back. Belts and braces. A shaving brush. A chipped shoehorn.

Dora tutted. It was no wonder Ivan could barely close his cupboard doors. The ridiculous man hoarded everything.

A square edge bumped against her fingers, and she dragged the package forwards to get a better look. The sight of the yellowing bundle of envelopes held together with a frayed blue ribbon made her sigh. It had been a good many years since she'd last looked at these, and many more again since she'd written them.

She sank down on the edge of their neatly made bed and stroked the ribbon with her arthritis-riddled fingers. The liver spots and wrinkles that covered the back of her hands hadn't been there when she'd penned the letters. She'd been young, and strong, and madly in love with her handsome soldier.

A faraway smile curved her lips as she touched the top envelope, date stamped 1943. She could still picture her younger self so clearly, full of excitement about the dress her mum had given her as a seventeenth birthday gift. Sunshine yellow, a deft alteration of one of her mother's favourite evening dresses. Dora had loved it with a passion, and had waited impatiently for Ivan to come back on leave to see her twirl in it. She'd worn it the evening he proposed.

She still owned that dress. It was wrapped carefully in tissue paper in a box at the back of her own wardrobe, along with a very similar bundle of letters.

Her replies from Ivan, tied with an equally frayed yellow ribbon.

It had always been her favourite colour, and even now Ivan grew only yellow flowers in their front garden as an unspoken expression of his love. Daffodils in spring, and glorious, huge, double-headed roses throughout the summer months. Even in wintertime, the garden blossomed with the heavy scent of lemon wintersweet and fragile, yellow helle-bores. He wasn't a man for overblown speeches or big romantic gestures, but from the moment they'd met, Dora had felt cherished and loved beyond measure.

He'd never wavered an inch.

She hauled herself onto her feet and tucked the letters back into their place at the back of the shelf without reading them. She knew them well enough anyway. Just holding them in her hands had been sufficient for today.

She closed the doors of Ivan's wardrobe without throwing out a single thing.

He could keep every last moth-eaten shirt if it made him happy.

CHAPTER TWENTY-NINE

'Gabriel, hello again!'

Cecilia sparkled at him as they collided in the flower shop doorway a couple of weeks since *that* dinner. He'd popped in to settle his monthly bill, and Ruth had been only too eager to fill him in on the scrap between Jonny and Rupert on the chapel lawns. She'd obviously hoped for further embellishments of the story from him, but as far as he was concerned it was all fresh news. Worrying on one hand in case Marla was upset, but welcome, too, if it meant that Rupert was off the scene.

'Cecilia, good to see you again.'

He smiled and dropped a kiss on the cheek she proffered, and then the other as she turned her head expectantly. He nodded at the huge armful of flowers she'd chosen from the buckets outside the door.

'It's a bad rap when a woman has to buy her own flowers. Where's Brynn?'

'Aw, he had to fly on to Hamburg.' She rolled her eyes

back in her head. 'Don't ask what for, darling, it's too grisly to repeat.'

Gabe laughed at her pained expression.

'These are for Marla actually.' She waved her spare hand towards the flowers. 'It's her birthday tomorrow.'

'Her birthday? Wow.'

'I know!' Cecilia gasped. 'Can you believe I have a daughter who's turning twenty-eight?'

'You could be sisters,' Gabe smiled, turning over the nugget of information in his head. 'So are you two painting the town red to celebrate?'

'Gawd, no! Gabriel, the girl drives me nuts! She's ditched that boyfriend of hers and won't even let her friends take her out for her birthday. Just wants a quiet night in, apparently. Whoever heard of that at her age?'

Cecilia gawped and placed a conspiratorial hand on his arm.

'I mean, when I was that age, I'd already got a wedding, a baby and a divorce under my belt!'

Gabe hadn't heard a word Cecilia had said since her confirmation that Marla had kicked Rupert to the kerb. He laughed vaguely and shook his head.

'Tell her to have a drink for me, yeah?'

'Hmmm. You could always tell her yourself.'

Cecilia twinkled up at him. 'I've got plans this weekend so she'll be home alone, probably eating pints of ice-cream and feeling sorry for herself.'

She tapped the side of her nose and waggled her eyebrows at him as if she'd just passed him a secret code, leaving Gabe perplexed that she'd made other plans on her only daughter's special day. It was probably the first time they'd been in the same country for her birthday in a number of years; surely it would have been a good chance to celebrate? But from the scraps of information that Marla had shared, he knew Cecilia was a woman who put her own happiness in front of everyone else's. Including, it would seem, her own daughter. It was hard not to warm to Cecilia's infectiously loud personality, but he could see the threads of steel that held her backbone ramrod-straight, enabling her to glide through life – and husbands – unencumbered by baggage.

Out on the street, he hesitated for a moment or two and then reached for his mobile.

'Melanie, hi. Can you hold the fort this afternoon? Something's come up that won't wait.'

CHAPTER THIRTY

After waving her mother off from the step the following morning, Marla closed the door with a sigh of relief. She'd have indulged in a little jig around the living room if she hadn't been concerned her mother might nip back and catch her in the act.

Admittedly, it had been easier to have Cecilia around since Brynn had gone off in search of his dead zebra, but, for Marla, having her home completely to herself for a couple of weeks was a birthday gift in itself. Cecilia had gone to stay with a friend in London, leaving Marla gloriously free to kick her heels up – or, more accurately, to enjoy the haven of having her home to herself again. She didn't let herself dwell on the fact that her mother had chosen to go away on her birthday. It wasn't as if her mother was going home to the States anytime soon – a couple of days ago she'd even mooted the idea of staying on for Christmas.

Marla turfed the scary prospect out of her head. Nothing

was going to spoil her plans for a totally decadent weekend. It was a shame Emily had family commitments and Jonny a hot date, but Marla didn't mind. Spending time alone had never been a problem for her. And this weekend, even the chapel's bookings had fallen neatly into place at the last moment, though not on an entirely positive note. A tearful bride had called two days ago to cancel their big day because she'd found her husband-to-be in bed with her best friend. Marla had winced with shock in all the right places, but couldn't help the shiver of fear that it would be the first of a landslide of cancellations.

She banished that thought hastily.

If she let her mind wander down that path she'd spend the weekend curled up in a ball of panic.

Invigorated by the quietness of her cottage, she headed straight for the fridge. Smoked salmon and scrambled eggs beckoned, followed by a long soak in the bath with the new Jo Malone bath oil she'd treated herself to. She hummed a jaunty rendition of 'Happy Birthday to me' under her breath as she cracked the eggs, and savoured the prospect of a whole weekend dedicated to Ben & Jerry's, girly movies and bubble baths.

Bliss.

'I could kiss you, Eve, this looks perfect,' Gabe grinned as he strapped the wicker basket onto the back of his motorbike.

Eve Jones stood on the pavement outside her store and turned beetroot with pleasure. She found herself very much wishing that he *would* kiss her, but just managed to stop short of saying so.

'Just try and keep it upright, okay?' she flustered, eyeing the huge bike apprehensively.

Gabe winked and threw his leg over the saddle. 'Don't worry, I'll drive carefully. Precious cargo and all that.'

He slid his helmet down over his head and blew her a kiss.

'You're a diamond, Eve, I owe you big time for this.'

He snapped his visor shut and the bike growled into life under his hands.

Eve watched him roar away with her arms folded across her chest. What was there not to love about a gorgeous man on a dirty, great motorbike? Romantic too, if his gift choice was anything to judge him by.

There was one very lucky lady out there somewhere.

Marla combed her damp hair through with water-crinkled fingers. She'd soaked for far too long in the bath, but the heavenly scent of nectarine and honey had been too sublime for her to tear herself away.

Besides, there was no hurry. The day stretched out ahead of her like a sheet of silk, to be slowly luxuriated in and enjoyed.

She slid out of her robe and into the brand-new La Perla white lace underwear she'd laid out on the bed. A birthday gift from her mother, although picked out by Marla, of course. Cecilia had never been one to give much thought to gifts. She preferred to wave her credit card around and for the magic to just happen. Not that Marla begrudged her on this occasion; one glance in her knicker drawer was enough to confirm her status as a class-A lingerie junkie, and these babies were a very welcome addition to her collection.

She turned, pausing to study her reflection in the dressing table mirror, appreciating the cleavage-enhancing effect of the balconette bra. In a perfect world she'd like to have woken up that morning to find that her 34B boobs had gone up a cup size for her birthday, but in the absence of magic wishes, couture wizardry would do nicely.

The September sunshine warmed her skin through the window, and she bypassed the jeans she'd planned to wear, reaching instead for a white cotton sundress. With any luck she'd be in the garden drinking Bellinis this afternoon and the dress would be perfect for catching a few rays.

Spending your birthday alone might not be everyone's idea of a barrel of laughs, but long spells alone as a child had equipped Marla with self-reliance by the bucketload. It was a feeling that went way deeper than being content with her own company; it was a visceral need for solitude that she had been denied since her mom and Brynn's arrival, leaving her distinctly frayed around the edges.

Throw the debacle with Rupert into the mix and stir well, and it was hardly surprising that the prospect of a little peace and quiet held such allure.

A couple of sun-warmed and languid hours later, Marla's book slipped from her fingertips as she dozed, an empty champagne flute on the grass beside her lounger. Half awake and half asleep, she thought she heard someone call her name and struggled up through the hazy layers.

Had she dreamt it?

Nope, there was definitely someone calling her. A deep, male voice, with an unmistakable lilt and a delicious roll of the R in the middle of her name.

Jeez, what was Gabe doing here?

Marla scrabbled to her feet, her cheeks pink from the sun and two peach Bellinis.

She tiptoed through the back door into the kitchen and jumped as he rapped on the front door.

'Come on Marla, I know you're in there.'

How the frig did he know? She could be out. She could be shopping, or ice-skating, or even out with an actual real live man! How dare he assume that she would be home just because he'd deigned to visit?

She fell onto her knees commando-style and crawled around the edge of the living room, staying out of sight in case he looked through the window. Her dress snagged on the floorboards, and laughter at her own absurdity bubbled in her throat.

He'd gone quiet at last. *Oh God.* Was he listening out for her?

She stopped dead by the hall doorway and eyeballed the front door. Crap, he was still there, she could see his silhouette through the glass. And double crap, he could probably see hers, at least enough to know she was skulking around on the floor like a burglar in her own home. She held her breath and debated her next move. The mature thing would be to stand up and answer the door. Could she make up some excuse about not having heard it? He would be too polite to point out that he'd spotted her doing her best canine impression, and she could get rid of him.

She squinted at his outline through the glass. He seemed to be messing around in his pockets, and she was just about to get up off all fours and bluff it out when he bent down too.

Shit! Oh God! Please don't look through the letterbox!

Marla stayed glued to the spot in horror, but instead of peeping at her, he pushed a small folded piece of paper through. It skittered across the polished floor towards her, and she inched her arm forward to grab it. She stared at it in confusion. Why was he giving her his old petrol receipt? Was he trying to claim that she owed him reimbursement for fuel? She racked her woozy brain to no avail, until finally she noticed there were words scrawled across the back. She flipped it over.

'I can see you. Open the damn door.'

Oh, the shame. Marla let her head drop onto the wooden floor for a second and wished it would open up and swallow her. Then inspiration struck.

She opened the letterbox and tilted her head to the side next to it, which was no mean feat given that it was less than three inches off the floor.

'I'm looking for my earring, if you must know,' she yelled, and threw her arms around under the table in an exaggerated fashion to search for the non-existent missing jewellery. She heard him laugh, a rumble that shuddered through the door and all the way into her bones.

She hauled herself onto her feet and glanced in the hall mirror. Christ, her hair was a sight. It had dried naturally in the garden as she'd snoozed and turned into a holy red mess. She pushed it behind her ears and threw back her shoulders. If he would be so impertinent as to turn up on her doorstep uninvited, then he'd just have to take her as he found her. She swallowed hard and opened the door, braced for the inevitable chemical reaction.

Dark waves. Merry eyes. A dirty laugh. And whoops, there went her stomach.

'You aren't wearing any earrings. Rookie mistake.'

He laughed again as she guiltily touched her naked earlobes. Marla flicked her hair over her tell-tale ears and stared at him, wishing she hadn't had a drink because it seemed to have amplified his beauty even more.

'Did you want something?'

He nodded, completely unperturbed, that big, annoyingly gorgeous smile still plastered all over his face.

'To say happy birthday.'

How the hell did he know it was her birthday?

'Well, thank you. You've said it now, so you can leave.'

He raised his eyebrows in mock shock. 'Aren't you going to be polite and offer me a coffee?'

'Let me think about that . . .' Marla tapped the tip of her nose. 'Nope.'

'Shame. I brought you a gift too.'

'Why would you do that?'

He studied her for a second with inscrutable eyes. 'Because, despite our professional differences, Marla, I like you, and I want you to like me too.'

His honesty wrong-footed her, making her feel ungracious in the face of his charm offensive.

'Fine. You can have coffee,' she grumped. 'But I have to go out soon, so . . .' She tailed off in the hope that she'd said enough for him to make his visit a short one.

'Really? That's weird, because your mum said you were hiding out in here all day and pretending it wasn't your birthday.'

She gasped. 'I'm doing no such thing!'

Her mother. She might have guessed. That woman had some serious questions to answer when she came back.

She leaned sideways and glanced around him at the empty lane. 'Where's your bike?'

'Not here. I hitched a lift with Dan.'

Marla tried not to visualise Dan and Gabe cruising down her lane in the hearse. She nodded for him to follow her through to the kitchen, where she reached for the coffee beans and swung open the fridge to grab the milk. Her eyes landed longingly on the open bottle of champagne, lurking next to the milk carton. Her fingers lingered on the neck of the bottle. Offering Gabe anything more serious than coffee was a risk, and drinking anything other than coffee around him was riskier still. 'Unless you'd rather have champagne?' *Jesus. The treacherous words actually came out aloud.*

'It would be rude to refuse you on your birthday.' He grinned.

Marla reached down for an extra champagne flute and grabbed the bottle. 'Come on, let's go outside.'

Gabe glanced back towards the front door. 'You go on out. I'll just grab your present.'

Marla dragged a second sun lounger from the shed and set it up a safe distance from her own, then pushed the table between the two chairs for extra protection. She heard Gabe close the front door as she poured the champagne, and a second or two later he appeared in the garden carrying a wicker basket tied with ivory ribbons.

'Oh God! It's not alive is it?' It reminded her of puppy baskets from schmaltzy American movies.

'Relax.' He laughed easily. 'It's not alive.' He set it down on the grass and accepted the glass she held out. 'To you. Happy birthday.' He clinked the rim of his glass against hers and watched her over the top.

She smiled. What else could she do in the circumstances? He'd rumbled her cover story right away, so she could hardly knock the champagne back and run out the door. Besides, where would she go? She was slightly squiffy, with wild hair and a crumpled sundress. The pub garden would be her only viable option, and there was something unbearably grim about drinking in the pub alone on your birthday. In your own garden, fine, but in public? No.

Besides, she wanted to stay in.

It had been her fabulous plan. She'd *loved* that plan.

But right now, curiosity was getting the better of her. She wanted to know what was in that basket. Gabe nudged it towards her as they perched on their respective loungers.

'Open it then.' His dark eyes flashed, as he took a long swig of his champagne.

Marla wrinkled her nose and placed her glass down carefully on the table. Sparkles of undeniable excitement bubbled in her belly. Her life hadn't been big on presents up to now. As a child her parents had always encouraged her to pick out her own birthday gifts, more for their own convenience than her pleasure, she now realised. Hell, she'd even chosen her own card most years.

The ivory ribbons fell away with the gentlest of tugs, and she wound them around her fingers and placed them on the table beside her drink.

Gabe sipped his champagne. 'You're one of those annoying people that opens their presents ridiculously slowly and folds the paper up, aren't you?'

She shook her head. 'I've no idea. I don't usually get presents.'

His brow furrowed, and she scolded herself. She didn't like the idea that she'd let her guard down. Bloody champagne.

She unbuckled the leather straps on the basket and lifted the lid.

Inside lay a folded-up blanket, its pattern so distinctive that a wide grin of appreciation spread instantly across her face. The stars and stripes.

'Wow! Thank you!' She hopped to her feet and spread it out over the short, dry grass to admire it properly.

Large and soft enough to snuggle under on a wintry evening, it moved her that he would put such thought into his gift. But then she already knew he was thoughtful when it came to presents, didn't she?

'I love it.' She beamed at him as she dropped down in the middle of the blanket. He topped up her glass and handed it to her.

'Hungry?'

He nodded towards the basket again, and she realised that the blanket had hidden further gifts from view.

She crawled towards the basket and stared at the contents in surprise.

Food. Lots of it. See-through containers with little American flags attached to them announcing their contents.

Chicken salad with ranch dressing. Florida coleslaw. BBQ ribs. Peanut butter and jelly sandwiches. Pumpkin pie. Smores. Frosted cookies. The list went on and on, all American favourites – right down to the bottles of Budweiser to wash it all down.

Marla's heart raced as she touched the lids one by one with reverential care, her lips moving as she silently read the labels.

This was, without exception, the loveliest thing anyone had ever done for her in her entire life. She cracked open the lid on the PBJ sandwich container and inhaled deeply. Their scent evoked an emotion so powerful that it whooshed out of nowhere and almost winded her, and tears prickled behind her eyes. Tears of longing for a home long gone, and tears of gratitude to Gabe, who was chewing his lip as he awaited her verdict on his gift.

She set the sandwich container down and sighed. Gabe was turning himself into a problem, and she didn't quite know how to handle him.

On one level, the real threat he posed to her business made him the Freddie Krueger of her nightmares. She'd spent the majority of last week studying the books and trying to think of new ways to generate business, because their bookings for next year were worryingly scant compared to the previous year. The enquiries were rolling in just fine, but the visual effect of having a funeral director right next door was definitely putting people off when they came to look around. One glance of a coffin or a hearse cruising by and they hightailed it out of there, never to be seen again, and she couldn't really say she blamed them.

But then on a whole different level, Gabe had developed an uncanny knack of being there when she needed him. He'd been her rock the night that Bluey died, and now here he was again, unceremoniously interrupting her lonesome birthday, knocking her sideways with his thoughtful gifts and ridiculously sexy backside. She'd noticed its peach-tasticness earlier and hadn't been able to get it out of her mind since.

Which brought her on to the real problem.

Chemistry. The laws of attraction. Call it whatever you like.

The fact was she was overwhelmingly, outrageously attracted to him, and not in a little, manageable way.

That would have been okay.

Awkward, but okay.

No, this thing was way bigger.

The sight of him made her skin prickle, and the sound of him made her want to move to Ireland so she never had to hear anything but that beautiful brogue again. Being near him turned her into a human stick of dynamite, and he the flame she daren't stand too close to. It was an entirely involuntary physical reaction, and as far as Marla was concerned, it was the biggest, brightest red flag in the world.

She'd watched her mother succumb time after time, but she was smarter. The way she saw it, she could either repeat her mother's mistakes or she could learn from them. With a couple of near-misses already blotting her copybook, Marla knew she was on decidedly dodgy ground.

She glanced up at Gabe again through her lashes.

'I don't know what to say. This is . . .' She touched the basket and shaded her eyes with her hand. 'I love it. Thank you. You didn't make all this stuff yourself, did you?'

He nodded just for a second, and then cracked into laughter. 'Did you really think I might have?'

She shrugged. 'I honestly never know what to expect with you.'

Gabe grinned, glad that at least she didn't find him dull. 'Okay, well, it was my idea, but someone much cleverer put it together for me after I bumped into your mum yesterday.'

'Yesterday? Someone made this overnight?'

He nodded, and she mulled over his reply for a couple of seconds.

'What if I'd refused to let you in?'

'Then I'd have had one hell of an interesting dinner.'

She laughed. Gabe had a way of making everything sound so uncomplicated, and right now, uncomplicated was good. She drained the last of her champagne and her stomach growled in noisy protest at the lack of food and overload of fizz.

She scooted back on the blanket and pulled the basket with her. 'I'm starving. Let's eat.'

'You're sure? You don't need to rush out? Only, earlier you said . . .' He trailed off with a knowing gleam in his eye.

She leaned back on her hands with her chin jutting out and eyed him beadily.

'If you've spoken to my mother, then you know perfectly well that I don't have plans.'

He shrugged noncommittally. 'She might have said something along those lines, yeah.'

He was practically laughing, but she could hardly blame him.

'Right. So now that's sorted, get down here and eat.'

He emptied the last of the champagne into their glasses with a mock salute, then joined her as she unpacked the basket on the stars and stripes. She stole a glance at him, long legs stretched out, his face tipped up to bask in the warmth of the sun. Thoughts of Helios, the hot and handsome sun god ran through her mind, and heat gathered between her thighs that had nothing at all to do with the afternoon sun that shimmered above them.

A couple of minutes later Gabe slid the pale blue china plates and cutlery from their straps inside the wicker lid, and Marla spooned generous servings of chicken salad onto them.

He tweaked the little flag on the container.

'Tell me then. What's ranch dressing?'

'Heavenly. Kind of like garlic mayo, but better. Try it, you'll see.'

Marla ate her first mouthful with closed eyes, an involuntary smile on her face as the familiar flavours reacquainted themselves with her taste buds. She was transported straight back to Saturday afternoon BBQs in the back yard – or in her friends' yards, as was most often the case. Her own folks didn't really go in for family dinners back then. They were never really inclined to spend their spare time together. Gabe handed her the open rib carton and licked sticky sauce from the end of his fingers.

'These are seriously good.'

Marla could feel the food soaking up the alcohol in her belly, rescuing her from the brink of being far too tipsy for Gabe's company.

'Why were you so intent on spending your birthday alone?' he asked.

Marla placed her rib bone down on her plate and looked at him levelly. 'I like to be alone sometimes.'

'I get that. But on your birthday?'

She sighed and reached for her glass. 'It's no big mystery, Gabe . . . it's been a tiring few weeks, that's all. Mom going to London, this was too good an opportunity to pass up.'

He nodded and seemed to accept her explanation. 'Your mum's pretty full on.'

Marla laughed. 'And there's the understatement of the year. Joan Rivers wouldn't get a word in edgeways with her.'

'Has she always been that way?'

'Pretty much. She goes at everything full-throttle. We moved house a lot when I was a kid because she was always searching for something or someone new.' Marla shrugged. 'Bit exhausting, really.'

Gabe's eyes were troubled as she reached for the PBJ sandwiches and handed him one.

'Brynn seems . . . interesting?'

Marla snorted. 'That's one way to describe him. He's okay I guess, in a freaky, homicidal kind of way.' She laughed shakily and bit into her sandwich.

He eyed the one she'd slid onto his plate with trepidation. 'I'm not so sure I'm going to like this.'

'Be brave. Trust me. It's the best sandwich in the world.'

After a couple of bites, he set it down with a frown. 'I guess now would be a bad time to mention my peanut allergy.'

'Holy shit! Gabe!'

He burst into laughter. 'Just kidding, no need to dial 999.' He looked at the PBJ sandwich again. 'No, it's . . . it's interesting. Kind of salty but sweet at the same time.'

Marla nodded enthusiastically. 'That's the whole genius of PBJ.'

He leaned back on his elbows and stared at her. 'In fact, Marla Jacobs, if you were a sandwich, I'd say you were a PBJ.'

The look in his eyes made her stomach flip. 'Because?'

'Well, for one, you're American.' He counted on his fingers and she nodded acceptance of the tag.

'Secondly, you have strawberry hair.'

She screwed her face up, well aware that she was having what could definitely be classed as a bad hair day. 'I'm not sure that's really such a compliment . . .'

'Thirdly, you have prickly, salty edges that make you unpredictable.'

'I'm darn *sure* that's not a compliment.'

'Wait. There's one more.'

She braced herself.

He lay on his side propped up on one elbow, the mirror image of her pose opposite him. His fingertips brushed hers on the blanket as he held her gaze.

'Number four. You're utterly delicious.'

CHAPTER THIRTY-ONE

Pow!

A nuclear lust bomb exploded behind her rib cage, sending slivers of awareness hurtling through her body in all directions. Her bare toes tingled, and goosebumps shot up all over her arms. It was too much of a sensory overload. Marla needed to put some space between them fast – or else she'd jump his bones right there and then.

She scrabbled to her feet and made a dash for the back door, not brave enough to look back. 'I, er, I need the loo. Back in a sec.'

In the cool, safe sanctuary behind the locked bathroom door, Marla stared at her reflection incredulously. 'What the hell are you playing at?' she hissed at her pink-cheeked, sparkly-eyed evil twin in the mirror.

'Having fun with a drop-dead gorgeous man. It *is* my birthday, after all,' her reflection wheedled right back. If reflections could stick their tongues out, Marla had no doubt that hers would have at that moment.

'You're drunk!'

'And you're boring!'

Ouch. The slur pierced right through to the heart of Marla's biggest hang-up. She was mostly content with her life choices, with her decision to turn her back on love in order to protect her heart and her business, but it came at a cost. Life could be incredibly dull, and occasionally she battled with the urge to cut loose of her self-imposed rules and run amok for a few hours.

Evil twin sensed a chink in Marla's resolve and pounced.

'Come on! Where's the harm? He's handsome, he's available, and he's gagging for it.'

Marla closed her eyes, but she could still hear evil twin's words just as clearly.

'Just tell him up front that it's a no-strings attached, one day only, never to be repeated or spoken about again, special birthday deal, and that it's back to daggers at dawn in the morning.'

Marla's eyes flew open and she gasped in shock at the flame-haired harlot's outrageous suggestion.

'Who's to know, Marla? And aren't you just dying to kiss him again?'

Marla all but whimpered.

'Wouldn't you love to feel him hard between your thighs? You would, wouldn't you?'

'Yes,' she whispered. 'God, yes. I really, really would.'

Her reflection winked at her. 'Why are you skulking around in the bathroom, then? Get out there!' Marla swallowed hard, then opened the bathroom cabinet and shook a condom out of the box.

*　*　*

She found Gabe flat out on the stars and stripes with a contrite look on his face and two freshly opened bottles of Bud on the grass beside him. He sat up as she skirted the edge of the blanket. 'Marla, look . . . I'm sorry about just now. It was a stupid thing to say.'

She appreciated his apology, and let his silence hang in the air for a second as she quickly hid the condom in the basket and settled down alongside him. She reached out for her beer and clinked the bottle against his, then took a long swig for Dutch courage and looked him square in the eyes.

'I've been thinking, Gabe. If *you* were a sandwich, I'd say you were Marmite.'

He did the tiniest of double takes at her abrupt shift in gear. 'Yeah?'

'Uh-uh.' Marla nodded gravely. 'People either love you or hate you.'

Gabe stepped up to the mark without missing a beat. 'I see. And you, Marla? What's your position on Marmite?'

'You know what? That's the funny thing.' She propped herself up on her elbow and gesticulated towards him with the neck of her beer bottle. 'Most days I can't stand the stuff, and then very occasionally, I have to have it.' She licked her lips. 'I crave it, in fact, and nothing else will do.'

Gabe leaned in just close enough for Marla to feel his breath on her cheek. 'And is today one of those days?'

'I'm not sure,' she said, breathless and powerful. 'I'd probably need a tiny taste to help me make my mind up.'

He laughed softly, closing the space between them. Marla glimpsed the sweep of his dark lashes against his cheekbone as his eyes closed a second before hers, another second before his lips found hers.

Gabe's warm fingers bumped along her jaw, their bodies aligning hip to hip as he kissed her, long, slow and easy. He tasted of beer and sunshine, and the touch of his tongue against her lips turned Marla's blood to liquid lust. She opened her mouth to welcome him in, but he nipped her bottom lip and pulled back. 'So? Did you make your mind up?' He soothed her lip with his thumb. '*Is* today a Marmite kind of day?'

Marla lifted her eyelids and looked into his eyes, which, interestingly enough, were the exact colour of Marmite. She saw raw desire that he made no effort to hide, and an erotic intensity that shrank the world down to a bubble, just for them. The bottom dropped out of her stomach with need as she snagged her leg over his thigh and rolled him on top of her, her hands already beneath the edge of his T-shirt. She felt his stomach muscles jump with shock at the touch of her fingers. He felt like hard, warm silk. 'This is one of those days when I want to eat the whole damn jar.'

Gabe's appreciative groan rumbled through both of their bodies, and this time when he kissed her he held nothing back. His hands held her face steady as he branded her with his mouth, a crazy, hot kiss that left Marla reeling. More intimate than any sex she'd ever known, Gabe's kiss laid him bare and vulnerable. His tongue stroked hers, learned her mouth inside and out until she dug her nails into his shoulders and murmured his name in shock. She'd waited forever to be kissed like that, and she hadn't even known it. His skin was sun-warm beneath her fingers, and he snaked an impatient hand down between them to yank his T-shirt over his head, giving her unfettered access to his body.

Marla feasted her hands and her eyes. He was exquisite, all movie-star shoulders and firm, golden skin, with a fine smattering of dark hair that trailed down his chest. She dragged her dress straps down, desperate for the glide of his naked skin against her own. His mouth followed her hands, hot against her neck, damp across her collarbones.

Gabe caught hold of her wrist when she twisted an arm beneath herself. 'I want to do that.' He licked the dip between her breasts and unclipped her bra with one assured flick.

'Jesus fucking Christ, Marla.' He slid his thumbs over her nipples as he held her in the palms of his hands. Marla lost her head, caught up in him completely as he teased her with his mouth and his hands. She wound his hair around her fingers and held him against her, but he caught hold of her wrist for a second time when she moved to reach for the buttons on his jeans.

Heat gathered between her legs as he glanced up with his lazy, lopsided smile and shook his head. 'Slow down. I've got one more birthday present for you first.'

She lifted her hips to help him as he tugged her rumpled white dress off and flung it aside, his tongue already on the curve of her stomach as he scooted down to kneel between her knees. He bent his head low, a silk ribbon of kisses along the edge of her knickers.

Marla sucked in a sharp breath as his fingers cupped her, lava hot and territorial. 'Take them off, Gabe. Please. Take them off.'

He didn't need to be asked twice, and what followed was hands down the most erotically intense few minutes of Marla's life.

Gabe was tender and filthy dirty all at the same time.

He explored her with his fingers and his tongue, building her up but never quite letting her fall over the edge. She felt rather than heard the incoherent sexy words he murmured as he licked her, magic vibrations, erotic electric shocks that lit her up from the inside out. Marla arched, greedy to get more of her into his mouth, and Gabe read her signs well. He didn't take his mouth away for a second as his fingers moved inside her, deeper each time until her only thought was now, now, now. He held her steady when she tensed and cried out, and soothed her with endless, barely there kisses until she unclenched her muscles and laughed low with spent appreciation.

'Happy birthday, Marla.' His stubble grazed her inner thigh as he grinned. Marla loosened her grip on his hair, as he nuzzled her skin.

'Thank you. I think that was my favourite present of the day.'

Gabe slid up the length of her body and kissed her, the taste of her sex in his mouth, his forearms either side of her head on the stars and stripes. Desire kicked in again hard as his weight settled over her, his back silk and steel beneath her fingers as she committed his contours to memory.

'Still hungry?' She could feel his smile as he grazed her earlobe with his teeth.

'Mmm. Starving.' Marla turned to look into his beautiful eyes. 'Take your jeans off.'

He stood and stepped out of his clothes, uninhibited by her bold appraisal. Not that he had any need to be shy. Marla bit her lip and stretched across to retrieve the condom she'd stashed in the basket.

'I'm pretty sure I didn't ask Eve to include this in the

picnic.' He raised his eyebrows as he took the foil packet from her and ripped it open.

'No. That's my own contribution.'

'Siren.'

He reached for her again, and surprised approval flashed in his dark eyes when she rolled him onto his back and straddled his thighs. Marla gazed down at him, struck by his louche perfection in the gilt, afternoon sun.

'Angel Gabriel,' she whispered, and trailed her fingernails down his chest as he rolled the condom on. It was Gabe's turn to strain for more as she moved over him, used him shamelessly to stoke her own pleasure back up to boiling point. His chest heaved, and his coal-dark eyes begged her to finish what she'd started.

He hadn't made her wait, and she repaid the favour with pleasure.

Marla had had sex with other men, but none of them had prepared her for her first time with Gabe. He filled her to the hilt and then some, and for a few seconds, it was all she could do to just hold still in the moment and remember to breathe. He was heartbreak-beautiful; his dark lashes on his cheek, his teeth sunk into his lower lip hard enough to draw blood. He opened his eyes and looked up at her through lust-heavy lids, and Marla had to close her own eyes against the raw emotions she saw there.

'Marla . . .' Her name was a caress on his lips as he levered himself up to kiss her. She hadn't anticipated his move, and she gasped with pleasure when he held her close and slipped a hand down between their bodies to draw slow circles on her clitoris with his thumb. His tongue traced the same slow circles in her mouth. He gave, and he kept on giving, slow, languorous strokes until her orgasm shimmered through her veins. Marla wrapped herself around him and clung on vice-tight as, thrust by beautiful thrust, Gabe let go of his grip on control too. He pumped harder, breathed faster, and kissed her with abandon as he emptied himself inside her.

Tremble-limbed, Marla laid her damp cheek against Gabe's chest, content in the cradle of his arms. He kissed her neck. Stroked her hair. Stilled inside her, his heart against hers.

Gabe kissed the top of Marla's hair, his eyes closed, letting his hands and his emotions take the lead. For the first time in his life he'd made love with a woman he loved. It was like tasting champagne after chardonnay, or driving a Lamborghini after a lifetime at the wheel of a Volvo. The adrenalin rush, the taste, the touch, the reverence that bordered on a holy experience. There was no going back. He wanted to spend the rest of his life making love to Marla Jacobs.

Marla glanced at the bedside clock for the tenth time in as many minutes.

There were thirty-three minutes of her birthday left.

Thirty-three guilt-free minutes with her Marmite man, and then he had to leave. She couldn't bring herself to regret it, because it had been the sexiest sex she'd ever had. In fact, it was probably the sexiest sex *anyone* had ever had.

Her tiny shower cubicle had neither seen nor heard the likes of it before. She flushed just thinking about the things he'd murmured in her ear as he'd pushed her towards a violent orgasm. His accent turned even the dirtiest of words into music, and wow, did Gabe know how to use it to devastating effect.

He'd shared his gentle side too, right here in her bed. Marla closed her eyes and sighed at the memory of his weight over hers, the way he'd moved inside her with infinite tenderness, his fingers meshed with hers, his mouth slow on her lips. He'd built her orgasm until it glittered through her fingertips and her toes, snaked along her limbs in an unstoppable wave that gathered momentum until it broke and threatened to drag her right under. He'd kissed away the unexpected tears that spilled from her eyes, and rested his forehead on hers as his own release shuddered through him like a freight train. Marla had clutched him to her, rocked core-deep by the protective urge that filled her as she tangled her fingers in his dark curls, as she held him until his breathing slowed from a desperate gasp to steady in her ear.

Twenty-one minutes. She'd allow herself just five more, and then she'd wake him.

CHAPTER THIRTY-TWO

Gabe sat on the bench in his postage-stamp back garden some eight hours later and watched the pink sun creep up over the fields beyond. He'd spent most of the night trying to make sense of Marla's warped logic, but so far he'd failed miserably.

For him, yesterday had only affirmed what he already knew.

He loved Marla.

Wholly, completely, with all of his heart.

He'd learned the difference between sex and making love last night, and despite what she'd said to the contrary, he knew she'd felt it too.

He'd tasted it in her tears. He'd heard it in her moans.

She was lying to herself, and to him.

He shook his head as her words clanged around in there. Their knife-sharp edges took chunks out of him, new cuts over old.

He'd been her birthday treat to herself. That was *exactly* how she'd put it.

He didn't know whether to feel flattered or used.

A one-off indulgence, she'd said.

Fun, and now over, she'd said.

She was wrong.

They might technically be at war, but yesterday hadn't been their Christmas Day truce, and one way or another, he was going to make her realise it.

Resolution made, he tipped his bitter black coffee onto the grass and grabbed his jacket to go and buy milk.

Marla dropped a bag of porridge oats into her basket as she trailed listlessly around the village store. Back at home her fridge was packed with delicious leftovers from yesterday's picnic, but she needed bland, boring fare to mark her return to reality.

Purgatory food.

If there had been sackcloth and ashes in her wardrobe, she'd have donned them this morning rather than her jeans and black angora sweater. She stretched up on tiptoes for raisins to sweeten the porridge, then snatched her hand away as a particularly lurid image of Gabe holding her hands stretched above her head last night swam in front of her eyes.

God, she'd been so brazen.

No. No raisins. Far too frivolous.

'Honey?' a male voice suggested right behind her. A beautiful, Irish male voice.

'No thank you,' she replied on autopilot, and then froze.

'Syrup, maybe?'

She could hear the smile in his voice, and turned to find her nose about six inches from Gabe's chest. He had a milk carton in his hand, and the stubble and dark circles around his eyes testified to a sleepless night. She'd had matching circles herself in the mirror this morning, along with similar kiss-swollen lips and sex hair. She'd looked like a satisfied slut, but right now he looked like a rock star after a night on the tiles.

'Let me pass please.'

She couldn't meet his eyes. She just wanted to pay and get the hell out of there.

'Marla, please. Can't we at least talk?'

'No! Please, just move out of my way.'

She glanced around him in desperation towards the teenager behind the counter at the far end of the shop, but the girl was too engrossed in her phone to notice.

'Marla, come on. You can't seriously expect . . .'

'Stop it!' she cut across him. 'That's *exactly* what I expect.'

She couldn't listen to this, wouldn't let him weaken her resolve. Daylight had brought with it the realisation that she'd just made the situation between the chapel and the funeral parlour a million times worse, and the only course of action available to her was to pretend it had never happened and stay as far away from Gabe as possible.

'Read my lips, Gabe,' she hissed. 'It was a one-night stand.'

She pushed past him to the counter and shoved her basket at the vacant teenager with white earphones plugged into her phone. The girl flicked heavily kohled eyes over Marla's shoulder towards Gabe, and then yanked the earphones out quick smart as a slow grin spread across her face.

Marla tapped her basket, desperate to get out of the store and back to the safety of the cottage. The teenager ignored her completely as she removed her gum and stuck it to the underside of the counter.

'Another late night, eh, sex god?' she smirked, and flicked her eyes between Gabe and the pile of newspapers on the counter in front of her. Both Marla and Gabe followed her cue and looked down at the front page of *The Shropshire Herald*.

There was Gabe practically nose to pneumatic breast with a scantily clad, red-haired lap dancer straddled across his lap.

Oh God, I straddled those same hips myself yesterday.

A second, grainier picture, a wedding of some sort. She squinted at the groom and gasped, winded.

He was married?

Marla scanned the headlines.

Murky past of local undertaker exposed!

Convicted drug offender! Sex addict! Ex-wife reveals all!

'What the fuck?' Gabe made a grab for the top copy as she whirled around to face him.

'It would seem that you have a thing for redheads,' Marla muttered, sick to her stomach. She threw some money on the counter as she picked up a paper and made a dash for the door.

'Marla!' Gabe caught up with her on the footpath outside and reached for her arm.

'Marla, wait, please . . .'

'Get your hands off me,' she ground out as she shook his hand off, furious at the tears that amassed behind her eyes.

'I can explain.'

Marla laughed, despite the bitter bile in her mouth. How

dare he have the audacity to stand in front of her with those beautiful eyes full of anguish?

'Yeah, I bet you can. Save your pathetic excuses for someone who's interested, Gabe.'

She turned on her heel and ran, glad that she couldn't hear footsteps behind her this time. If he'd have followed her, she may well have hit him and shattered one of his oh-so-perfect cheekbones.

Her heart leapt around in her chest as she hurled herself through her front door and threw the bolt across. Tears spilled unchecked down her cheeks as she leaned her back against the door and trembled with rage.

She wasn't sure who she was most angry at. Gabe for being so damn typical, or herself for being such a gullible fool. Again.

Her hands shook as she forced herself to read the article properly.

Sordid life of undertaker at centre of local feud. Sleaze, drugs and strippers . . .

Marla dismissed the drugs thing out of hand; she was smart enough to see that one unconfirmed teenage caution for possession of a spliff had been sensationalised for the sake of a good headline.

Even the stripper didn't faze her that much. The picture was unsavoury, but Gabe was a man, and she wasn't a prude. Sex addict? She wouldn't have had him down as someone who frequented strip bars, but what did she really know of him, anyway? Going on his performance yesterday, she could safely conclude that sex was something he was well-practised at.

But the wedding photograph? That really made her guts

churn, as if someone had stirred them with a big wooden spoon.

Gabe had been married – perhaps he still was.

How funny that he'd never thought to mention *that* particular gem when he'd chased her like a dog after a bone. Even after she'd shared her secrets with him, how her parents' flippant attitude towards marriage had scarred her, he'd not thought to mention that he'd already started his own collection of wedding rings on his bedside table.

But then if he had, he wouldn't have been able to add her as another notch on his bedpost, would he? If the sleazy pictures on the front of the newspaper were anything to go by, he ought to be careful that his damn bed didn't collapse altogether, Marla thought sourly.

Christ, she could have caught some hideous disease from him.

She started up the staircase towards the shower, every step too much trouble.

At least he'd taught her one valuable lesson. She'd been on the money with her initial instincts. She should never have let him under her guard.

It was ironic really, that in her desperation to not be like her mother, she was behaving more like her than ever.

CHAPTER THIRTY-THREE

'Em, dinner.'

Emily leaned her forehead against the newly decorated nursery window and sighed. The last thing on her mind was food. Tom was killing her with his kindness, and after months of soul searching, she'd finally reached her decision. Finally *faced up to* the decision her heart had made on the banks of the River Severn. Dan's toothbrush might not be on their bathroom shelf, and there might only be two settings at their dinner table, but he was there nonetheless, a cuckoo in their home and their marriage.

She needed to tell Tom.

The power should be in his hands, not hers. Besides, she couldn't bear the weight of her secret any longer. Tom deserved the truth, and the choice.

She placed an apologetic hand over the baby as it aimed a furious kick at her ribs, almost warning 'don't you dare'. She couldn't blame the baby for wanting to hang on to Tom; she wanted to herself, desperately.

293

But not like this.

Not without honesty.

Tom stirred the risotto on the stove and threw in an extra splash of stock to get the consistency spot on.

'Come on, Em, it's almost on the table!' he called out again as he pulled on Emily's pink oven gloves to take the plates from the oven.

Emily appeared in the doorway. Every day her bump seemed to grow more evident. She slid onto the dining chair with an anxious glance at Tom as he placed her dinner down in front of her.

He plonked down in his chair and watched her test his efforts as he picked up his fork.

'Is it okay?'

She nodded with a quick, grateful smile, although the way she pushed it around her plate with her fork suggested otherwise. It was his turn to cook, and he'd scoured the supermarkets on his way home from work for wild mushrooms to make Emily's favourite comfort dinner.

'It's heavenly, Tom. What's the occasion?'

Tom shrugged. 'Can't I treat my wife without a hidden agenda?'

He could have bitten out his own tongue as the clouds rolled across her eyes.

Any mention of hidden secrets made her jumpy these days, and having read her 'Dear John' letter, he could see why.

Yet he hadn't mentioned a word about it to Emily.

He had no need to.

Her letter had only confirmed what he knew. It had

forced him to face the unpalatable truth. He'd pushed her away, and his careless neglect had driven her to places she should never have needed to go.

Her infidelity didn't change a thing. He could only thank his lucky stars that, in the end, she'd chosen him.

'I don't deserve you, Tom.'

Emily placed her fork down next to her barely touched dinner.

'Don't be stupid, Em. I'm the lucky one.'

He reached for the water jug and filled their glasses. He hadn't drunk in the house for months out of solidarity.

'Come on. Eat your dinner before it gets cold.'

Emily tried a little more, lacklustre and troubled. Her fork clattered down again a few seconds later.

'Tom. I can't do this.' Her voice wavered. 'We need to talk.'

Shit. Back up Emily, please back up. I don't want to do this.

'Just eat your dinner, Em. I went halfway to Italy for those mushrooms.'

He joked to lighten her mood, his stomach full of foreboding.

'That's just it, Tom. You're so kind, and lovely, and thoughtful, and me . . . I'm . . .'

Her fingers shook around the stem of her glass as she floundered for words to describe herself.

'Don't do this, Emily.'

The bleak defeat in her eyes terrified him.

'Tom . . .'

He pushed his chair back. A scream of wood against stone.

'Don't say another word, Emily. Just wait one minute, okay?'

He took the stairs two at a time, high on adrenalin and fear.

Twenty seconds later he was back in the kitchen, her green letter in his hand.

Emily's face crumpled as he held it up for her to see, a magician flourishing his cards to his audience.

He crossed to the cooker and lit the nearest gas ring.

She stood, trembling, but he held up a warning hand to still her and shook his head.

The flames caught the corner of the note, licked up the page towards his fingers until he couldn't hold it any longer. He dropped it into the sink and turned the tap on full, then scooped out the mush of paper and hurled it on the floor.

Stamped on it.

Again. And again. And again.

He was unaware of the tears on his face until Emily's tentative fingers touched his cheek. He was unaware of his own roar of anguish until he registered her gentle shush.

'It's gone,' he said, finally. 'It's history.'

She nodded, her hand still on his cheek.

'There's nothing to gain by raking over the coals.' He covered her hand with his own larger one. 'We're still standing. It's all that matters.'

He laid his other hand on her belly. 'You, me, and the baby.'

He was careful not to say *our* baby.

CHAPTER THIRTY-FOUR

'Morning, my gorgeous girlfriends!'

Jonny shimmied back into the chapel after a last-minute weekend in Mykonos, freshly bronzed, with a bottle of ouzo in his hand and an undeniable glint in his eye. It died as soon as he caught sight of Marla and Emily's coordinated miserable expressions.

'Shall I go out and come back in again?'

He cast a wistful glance back towards the doorway.

'You can if you like, but it won't make any difference.' Emily shrugged. 'Coffee?'

Jonny put the ouzo down and stared from Marla to Emily. 'Who died?'

Emily pushed the Sunday *Herald* across the table, and his frown turned to a grin as he scanned the headlines.

'Well, well, well!' He let out a low whistle and laughed. 'Who's been a naughty undertaker, then?' He skim-read the rest and then looked up, nonplussed. 'Why the long faces? This is good news for us, surely?'

Emily placed a steaming mug down in front of him.

'Except that everyone is going to think it's part of our supposed hate campaign.'

'So what?' Jonny shrugged. 'We're completely innocent this time around, and by the looks of it, old Gabriel certainly isn't.' He winked and looked back at the paper with something akin to admiration. 'I didn't think he had it in him.'

Shame slapped Marla's cheeks scarlet as she turned away on the pretence of loading the dishwasher. Seconds before Jonny had walked in, she'd almost confided in Emily about her weekend with Gabe. Wow, she was glad now of the timely interruption. At least if no one else knew she'd been so weak, then she could try to forget it ever happened. Gabriel had better keep his mouth shut.

Oh God. Gabriel's mouth.

Marla knew she was in real trouble, because the thought of the things he'd done to her with his mouth on Saturday still made her shiver with lust. She just had to face it. He must have had a good old laugh at her show of resistance, at her protestations that it had to be a one-night stand. She'd played right into his hands. Gabe must have thought it was *his* birthday, not hers.

Of course, none of this should matter to her. She was the one who had insisted on a grown-up, civilised one-night stand, so why did this feel so much like a betrayal?

She slammed the dishwasher shut with a harder than necessary swish and threw her shoulders back. She needed to draw a line in the sand. Gabriel Ryan had turned her over once with his charm and flattery.

He wouldn't get the chance to do it again.

* * *

298

Gabe opened the biscuit cupboard in the funeral parlour kitchen and sighed with resignation. Empty. Not a Jammie Dodger in the building.

It wasn't his unsatisfied sweet tooth that bothered him, so much as tumbling so spectacularly from grace in Dora's eyes. She'd never failed to see to it that his addiction was satiated. Her opinion mattered to him, and the fact that she'd so readily believed the rubbish being peddled by the local rag cut deep. Not that she was alone in her conclusions; the majority of the locals had been failing to quite meet his eye over the last couple of days, too. Gabe had no doubt at all that it would have a knock-on effect on his business. Reputation was everything in his line of work. Who was going to put their trust in the services of a disreputable, womanising young undertaker?

Rupert's article had been a real hatchet job, a sensationalist exposé of a sleazy, sex-mad drug addict that Gabe would never recognise as himself.

Was that really what people around here saw when they looked at him?

He had no idea how the hell photos from the strip club had even come to exist, and they certainly didn't paint a true picture of what had happened that evening.

But then, who cared about truth in all of this?

What did it matter that innocent people had been dragged into this mess?

Gabe hadn't seen his ex-wife Simone since a rainy Friday morning on the steps of a Dublin divorce court more than ten years ago, and yet she'd ended up with her face splashed across a Sunday paper, right next to some stripper.

Bad news travelled fast.

He'd had *his* mother, *her* mother, and two of her older brothers on the phone from Dublin over the last few days. His mother had tried to insist he come home, and Simone's family had all warned him in no uncertain terms to stay the hell away.

Gabe banged the kitchen cupboard shut. Rupert had been out for his blood, and he'd managed to bury the axe right in the back of his head.

He heard the front door open and looked down the hall to see Melanie dash in from the rain, her sopping umbrella held out in front of her in distaste.

'Morning,' he called, and she glanced up with a frown on her face. Dark shadows ringed her eyes, but Gabe bit down on the urge to ask if she'd had a heavy weekend. He'd learned over the months that Melanie always side-stepped questions about her home life, and he respected her enough not to pry.

She peeled off her coat and hung it on the coat stand to dry, then headed through to the kitchen with a crammed carrier bag in her hand.

'Morning.' She finally favoured him with a smile, as she opened the biscuit cupboard.

'No point. The cupboards are bare,' Gabe muttered.

'Yeah, I noticed. I thought you could probably use these.'

She unloaded at least half a dozen packets of biscuits onto the shelf. Gabe noticed with a pang that she seemed to have brought every possible variety, apart from Jammie Dodgers. The sooner Dora decided to speak to him again the better.

'What would I do without you?' he said with a diplomatic smile.

Melanie was good at her job, and right now she was one of a handful of people in the village not treating him as if he were the Peter Stringfellow of the undertaking world. Dan had practically cried with laughter at the idea of Gabe as the village lothario and smacked him on the back with pride, but otherwise, only the people he actually paid to talk to him were bothering to be civil – with the notable exception of Dora. If she looked at him at all, it was with reproach.

'What time is Dora due in?'

Melanie glanced at the clock.

'About ten minutes.'

Gabe nodded.

'Ask her to come and see me when she gets in, will you?'

He picked up his coffee and headed through to the mortuary. At least dead people wouldn't shoot him daggers or mutter about him behind his back.

'You wanted to see me, Gabriel?'

Gabe looked up at Dora as she hovered in the office doorway half an hour later. Her arms were folded across her apron-covered chest, and her mouth was set in a thin, pursed line.

'Come and sit down for a minute, will you?'

Dora bristled with disapproval, but sat down opposite him all the same.

'Dora, I have a problem.'

'You'll be wantin' the doctor, Gabriel, not me.'

She used his full name in the same ominous way his mother had when he'd been in trouble as a kid. He opened the desk drawer.

'Here. Look at these.'

He pushed a thin, dog-eared photo wallet across the table towards her. She glanced at it and sniffed, but resisted the urge to pick it up. Gabe knew her well enough to know that her outward restraint would be costing her dearly.

'Please?'

Dora huffed and picked the packet up by one corner between her finger and thumb, as if she might be contaminated with Gabe's sleaze by association. She looked through the wedding pictures slowly then slid them back onto the desk in frosty silence.

'I was nineteen. Simone was seventeen. We were stupid and rebellious, and eloping on her eighteenth birthday seemed like the most romantic idea in the world.'

Dora nodded begrudgingly for him to carry on when he paused.

'It was a disaster, Dora. We were kids, and her da was up for killing me – and looking back now, I don't blame him.' He shook his head as he remembered the rage on Simone's father's face. 'We didn't love each other, it was just childish infatuation.'

Gabe glanced out of the window and sighed heavily. 'We divorced a year later. Broke her mother's heart to have a fallen daughter.'

Dora had given up on any pretence at nonchalance and stared at him, agog.

'So there I was, twenty, and already a divorcee. An undertaker, and a divorcee – a hard sell in any market, let me tell you. Simone and I decided back then that we wouldn't speak about it again, so having it splashed across the front of a newspaper was –' he grimaced as her brothers' unveiled threats rang in his ears '– awkward, you know?'

Dora pulled her 'you reap what you sow' face.

'Why are you telling me this, Gabriel?'

'Because I miss your Jammie Dodgers?'

Gabe smiled and shook his head at Dora's outraged face.

'Okay, okay. I'm telling you because your opinion happens to matter to me, Dora. And because I'm sick of being the local pariah. People listen to you.'

Dora preened a little under Gabe's flattery, but he'd meant it sincerely. She was one of the village stalwarts. A few supportive words in the local store would be enough to turn the tide of opinion his way.

'Those pictures, that woman in the strip club . . . it wasn't what it looked like, I promise you.' Dora looked sceptical, but he ploughed on regardless. 'I hate those places. Ten seconds after that shot was taken she tipped a drink in my lap.'

'No more than you deserved in a place like that, young man.'

She chastised him with her words, but the frost had melted from her tone, as if warmed by a sunbeam.

After a few seconds' thought, she rummaged in her shopping bag and slid a packet of Jammie Dodgers across the desk at him. He grinned as he ripped the packet open with his teeth, and put one in his mouth whole in acceptance of her unspoken apology.

'You should call the police about that Rupert. It's harassment, it is.' She helped herself to a biscuit.

Gabe shook his head and swallowed his biscuit.

'I'll sort it out myself soon enough, Dora, don't worry

about it. Besides, that wasn't really what I wanted to talk to you about . . .' He leaned in across the table and dropped his voice. 'I need your help with something a bit more . . . well, personal.'

Dora's nostrils flared with horror.

'What sort of personal, Gabriel? You don't want me to look at any of your weird bits, do you?'

'It's not a health thing.' Gabe laughed. 'Well, not unless you count matters of the heart, anyway.'

Dora relaxed back into her chair.

'Aaah. *That* sort of personal.'

She reached for another biscuit.

'Go on then.'

'It's . . . well . . .' Gabe faltered under Dora's bated-breath attention.

'It's about Marla, actually.'

He watched Dora closely for signs after his revelation; she was fond of Marla and he expected her to be shocked. Protective, even.

Dora, however, just nodded without even the slightest flicker of surprise.

'I've been around for a long time, lad, and I've got eyes in my head.'

Gabe grimaced.

'Jesus, I feel like a schoolboy. Is it that obvious?'

Dora shook her head.

'Only to a nosy old bat like me. So, how bad is it?'

'Oh, it's as bad as it gets. I love her.'

Dora went slack-faced with alarm.

'You love her? Steady on, lad. I mean . . .' Her eyes lingered on the wedding photos on the table.

Gabe couldn't really blame her for questioning his feelings, given his newly revealed track record.

'It's nothing like that.' He nodded towards the photos. 'I had no clue what love was back then.'

He glanced over towards the chapel.

'But I do now. Love is five foot six with wild red hair and crazy shoes, and I just want to look at her and never look away again.'

Dora sniffed and rooted around in her apron pocket for a tissue.

'It probably sounds stupid, but I knew it the moment I met her. BOOM. Just like that. She's it for me. Marla's the one.'

Gabe grinned. It was a heady relief to say it out loud.

'Then just get your backside over there and tell her, lad.'

Gabe shook his head with a snort of derision. She made it sound so simple.

'You know what she thinks of me, Dora. Especially after we . . .'

'After you what?' Dora leaned across the desk with narrowed eyes. She didn't miss a trick.

Gabe fished around for a delicate way to phrase 'after we had mind-blowing sex in her back garden for hours'.

'We kind of spent her birthday *together*, if you understand my meaning.'

Dora's eyebrows sprang up into her grey curls.

'I see.'

'But then, all that stuff in the paper came out, and now she won't even look at me.'

Dora shook her head regretfully. 'You did look rather sleazy, Gabriel.'

Gabe sighed. 'I know. So here's the thing. I've come up with a bit of a plan, but I can't do it without help.'

He reached out and held her hand.

'Without *your* help.'

He knew from the excitement that twinkled in Dora's elderly eyes that he'd just gained himself an accomplice.

Outside the office door, Melanie flattened herself against the wall, listening to each poisonous word with her eyes screwed shut. Her fingernails bit into her palms as she balled her hands into tight little fists at her side.

Why were all men such stupid fucking idiots?

Gabriel had seemed so different.

How dare he? He was just like the rest of them. He didn't see her either.

She'd been so sure, yet here he was confessing his undying love for Marla fucking Jacobs.

A couple of months back she'd had both Rupert and Gabriel eating out of her hand, and now both had tossed her out of their hearts as carelessly as yesterday's newspaper.

CHAPTER THIRTY-FIVE

Like most plans, Gabe's was fraught with the potential for disaster.

The main challenge with *this* particular plan was timing; he required a morning when Marla was going to be alone in the chapel.

He definitely didn't want an audience.

Dora had proved herself to be an excellent inside spy, if somewhat heavy on the espionage drama. Their first attempt last week had been aborted at the last minute when she'd called him to say Jonny had turned up unexpectedly at the chapel. It had taken Gabe a while to decipher her loudly whispered telephone message. 'The peacock has landed. I repeat, the peacock has landed. Operation Lovegood aborted. Abort mission and await instruction. Over and out.'

He'd stared at the telephone for several perplexed seconds until Dora herself had slunk out of the chapel and over to the funeral parlour, a long beige mac over her pinny and a headscarf over her iron-grey curls.

'"The peacock"?' he'd asked, ushering her inside.

Dora untied her scarf from beneath her chin. 'Jonny,' she'd said, still whispering and craning her neck to see out of the window. 'I don't think they saw me slip over here.'

Gabe had shaken his head and laughed, even though disappointment coursed through his veins. 'Dora, it's okay.'

She'd moved to stand with her back against the wall next to the window frame and bobbed her head around quickly to look through the window as a car pulled up.

'Oh for heaven's sake,' she'd muttered. 'It's the raven.'

'"The raven"?'

Dora flattened herself against the wall and rolled her eyes. 'Emily,' she hissed, as if he really ought to get with the programme, as Emily's glossy black hair appeared while she hauled herself out of the passenger side of the car.

'Do you have a name for me, Dora?' Gabe had asked, interested.

'Archangel,' she'd shot back, as if he really should have known.

'And Marla?' He'd tried to suppress his smile.

'Hollywood.'

He'd nodded in approval. 'Figures.' The chapel door opened. 'Well, looks like the mission is well and truly aborted. The peacock, the raven and Hollywood have just locked up and left the chapel.' He'd squinted at the driver's seat. 'Tom's driving.'

'The dove,' Dora had supplied, shrugging out of the mac. 'The dove' seemed an odd choice to Gabe, but Dora no doubt had her reasons.

It was two long weeks later that she called him again to confirm that Operation Lovegood was once more good to go. The peacock and the raven were safely squirrelled away across the other side of Shropshire at a wedding fayre, and Hollywood would be holding the fort on her own at the chapel.

The plan was set. Dora, or D, as she'd assigned herself in the style of Judi Dench's M, was to come up to the chapel bright and early to let him in before Marla arrived, giving him enough time to go inside and arrange a surprise breakfast for Marla – or Hollywood, as Dora insisted on calling her.

Gabe hovered inside the funeral parlour at just after 7 a.m. on the morning in question. Autumn had well and truly blown into Beckleberry over the last few weeks. A sepia wash of leaves swirled across the High Street as he kept watch for Dora.

He stuck his head outside again and scanned the deserted street.

Nothing.

Where was she?

A frown ploughed tramlines across his brow. There was no way Dora would have forgotten, he'd had to strain to catch her whispered instructions on the phone the previous day, even though there was only Ivan around to hear her, and he was half deaf at the best of times.

'Seven o'clock sharp,' she'd said.

He checked his watch again.

7.12 a.m.

She was cutting it fine; at this rate Marla would be here before she was. He huffed in exasperation. Where the hell was she? She wasn't the type to oversleep; he'd half expected her to be on his doorstep at 6 a.m. in her mac and trilby.

As the clock inched slowly towards half past, Gabe stopped looking out for her and started to worry about her instead. *Had something happened to her on the way here?* Dora and Ivan's cottage was barely a five-minute skip and hop away from the High Street, but still . . .

The more he thought about it, the faster his heart started to beat. It was easy to forget Dora's age because she was such a livewire, but he'd never forgive himself if she'd tumbled in the lane or something. Oh God. What if a car had been speeding, not expecting to find any walkers at that early hour, especially ones dressed for espionage? Unable to wait any longer, he locked the funeral parlour door and set off at a fast walk. As he reached the end of Dora's lane, his walk turned to a jog, and by the time he reached Ivan and Dora's cottage he'd broken into a full-scale run.

The lounge curtains of Dora's cottage were still closed when he arrived. Gabe sagged against the gate post with relief. She'd just overslept. Lord knew the woman was entitled to that luxury at her age. He stood for a few seconds to get his breath back before he walked back to the funeral parlour. This cloak and dagger approach wasn't working. Marla would be alone at the chapel that morning. He was going to walk right on in there and tell her once and for all that he loved her.

His mind set, he glanced once more at Dora's cottage, and it suddenly struck him that although the lounge curtains were closed, the bedroom ones had been opened. That was strange.

Maybe Dora had got up, after all.

He nipped up the path to double-check and let himself

in through the unlocked side gate. Dora would no doubt be in the kitchen in a flap because she was running late.

He'd pop in quickly to reassure her that there was no need to rush anymore.

A quick glance through the kitchen window showed it to be empty, but the kettle on the lit gas stove was screaming for attention. Gabe frowned as he tried the door. Finding it open, he stepped inside and flicked off the shrill noise.

'Dora?'

He called out just loud enough to be heard, but not so loud that he'd startle her.

Silence answered him, and the ball of unease returned tenfold to his gut.

'Dora?'

He tried again. A little louder, a little more urgent.

Still no answer.

He went through into the hallway, not certain of the unfamiliar layout of the quiet cottage. He stuck his head around the first of the two doorways, and found a small, neat-as-a-pin dining room, but no Dora.

He moved along the carpeted hallway and stepped just inside the opposite doorway to the little front room.

To the untrained eye, Dora might have been sleeping in her cheery yellow chintz armchair.

But Gabe knew differently the moment he saw her. His wasn't the untrained eye.

'Oh, Dora,' he whispered. 'No.'

He crossed the room and dropped down on his haunches in front of her, then reached out and held her cool hands for a few moments. He brushed his fingertips gently over her eyes to fully close them, a tight ball of pain in his chest.

Dora wasn't snoozing.

She'd passed away.

A couple of hours later, the ambulance bearing Dora's body rumbled off up the lane, and Ivan, still in his dressing gown, sat in his small living room with Marla and Gabe, and also Ruth, who lived two doors down.

They drank sweet tea, and Gabe found a bottle of whisky in the dining-room sideboard to help steady Ivan's nerves. Waking the old man with such devastating news had been heartbreakingly difficult, and all of the funeral director training in the world hadn't made it any easier to watch the shell-shocked pensioner cry like a child.

He'd called Marla without a second thought, because he wanted to tell her himself, and also to ask if she'd come and be with him and Ivan while they waited for the ambulance. She'd been there in a heartbeat, shaken and red-eyed, but also amazingly strong and beautiful as she spoke quietly to Ivan and gripped his shaking hand.

Gabe followed her into the kitchen when she excused herself to make a fresh pot of tea. She picked up the kettle to fill it, but just stood at the sink with the tap running, her mind on Dora.

'I can't believe she's gone, Gabe,' she said softly. Gabe turned off the tap and placed the kettle down on the side, the crack in her voice too much for him to take.

'Come here.' He gathered Marla against him, holding her close with his chin resting on the top of her head, as she cried in his arms. She hugged him hard, giving him solace as much as drawing it from him. Dora had been Gabe's true friend and ally, and he hated the thought that he'd added to her burden of stress by asking for her help with Marla.

Marla in turn hated the prospect of Beckleberry without Dora at its heart, or the unbearably sad thought of Ivan having to find a way to live without the love of his life.

They held each other like that for long, precious minutes, all of their usual barriers down in the face of their over-whelming sadness. Marla closed her eyes and breathed in the familiar scent of Gabe's skin, the smoothness of his neck treacherously close to her salty, damp lips.

Gabe wanted more than anything to kiss the woman in his arms. To kiss her endlessly, and tell her how much he loved her, that she filled his heart up so much that it hurt. His lips rested against her hair, and his emotions led him to stroke a hand down her back. She was real, and here, and his. He needed to tell her. Maybe it was entirely the wrong time, but then maybe it was the best time of all.

And then the back gate banged and Marla jolted away from him a second or two before Emily, Jonny and Tom appeared, stricken, at the kitchen door.

CHAPTER THIRTY-SIX

'Would you drop these over to the funeral parlour please, Em?'

Emily took the little blue jewel box and the garment bag that Marla held out and peered through the plastic at the primrose-yellow material.

'What is it?'

Marla smoothed back the plastic to show Emily the dress inside.

'It was Dora's. Ivan brought it down when I went to see him last night. Her mum made it for her in the war.'

Tears sprang into Emily's eyes as she touched the delicate silk of the skirt.

'Oh.'

Emily nodded sadly and smoothed the cover carefully back over the dress.

'I know what's in here,' Emily said, stroking her thumb over the worn velvet of the jewel box. 'It's her brooch, isn't it?'

Marla smiled gently. 'Of course. It seems strange to see it without her.'

Emily eased the lid open on the jewel box, and they both sighed as a little diamond lighthouse glinted up at them. It was such an integral part of their memories of Dora. She'd worn it every day, whether she was dressed in her Sunday best or in her pinny to scrub the chapel floor.

Marla squeezed her friend's arm. 'Ivan thought Dora would have liked to have these with her. In her . . . well, you know.'

Marla tried, but the word coffin wouldn't come out.

Emily nodded quickly. 'That's so sweet. Poor Ivan.'

Emily looked out of the window to watch Ivan as he weeded the chapel gardens and then, after a final sniff, gathered herself together. The idea of going over to the funeral parlour terrified her in case Dan was around, but delivering Dora's special things took precedence over her fears.

'Right. I'll be back in a few minutes.'

Marla laced two mugs of tea with liberal splashes of whisky and headed out to find Ivan. He'd insisted on coming to tend to the chapel gardens, despite the fact that Dora's funeral was less than twenty-four hours away. It had been little over a week since Gabe had discovered Dora's lifeless body, and her husband had handled it in the quiet, stoic way that only an old war hero could hope to.

'Tea, Ivan.'

Marla sat down on the low wall along the path and waited for Ivan to put down his shovel and make his way over the lawns towards her. He nodded his thanks and eased himself slowly down next to her.

'Thanks, lovey.'

He picked up his mug and held it in his gnarled, shaky hands. Marla noticed that his checked shirt had grown a little threadbare, a tiny hole at the elbow. Dora would have had her thread box out the second she saw that, Marla thought.

Who would take care of Ivan now? They hadn't had any children; he really was alone in the world now that Dora had gone.

'How have you been?' She laid a hand on his forearm.

He shook his head and stared into his mug for a while. 'She was my best pal.'

Marla held back the tears that threatened. 'I know she was. I know.'

'I'm no good on me own, love. Can't cook. Can't work that bloody washing machine.' Ivan pulled a big, slightly grubby handkerchief out of his trouser pocket and blew his nose.

'Not that Dora was much of a cook, either, mind.' He laughed, sadly. 'Bloody awful actually, but I was fond of it all the same.'

'We all miss her so much at the chapel. It's too quiet without her.'

They sat in companionable silence for a couple of minutes.

'I've written something down, for tomorrow like. I can't stand up there and say it myself, so young Gabriel is going to read it for me.' Ivan glanced up at Marla. 'If that's alright, course?'

Marla nodded. 'Of course it is. I'll let Jonny know.'

Jonny was to lead the ceremony, and it would seem that Gabe was to be a speaker too.

She'd never held a funeral service in the chapel before, but when Ivan had asked, she hadn't hesitated for a moment. Dora was one of their own, and it would be an absolute honour to give her the send-off she deserved.

Emily was relieved to find Melanie missing when she pushed open the heavy funeral parlour door. It was Gabe himself she found in reception, and he smiled widely when he saw her.

'I'll just be one tick, can you wait? Sorry, Melanie's down at the florists.'

Emily laid the yellow dress across the reception desk in its plastic cover and glanced around the tastefully decorated room. She'd thankfully never had cause to visit a funeral parlour, but it was obvious that Gabe had made this place as welcoming as he could, given the sombre nature of his business. It was such a shame that circumstance had set them all against each other. She had a hunch that he'd be a good friend to have in your corner, not to mention a perfect match for Marla, if she weren't so stubborn.

He was undeniably easy on the eye too, which even in her very pregnant state she couldn't help noticing as he came through the door and smiled at her again.

'Hey, Emily.' His eyes dropped to her bump. 'Wow, that's coming along nicely. I don't need to fetch hot towels and water, do I?'

Emily laughed. 'Don't panic, you're safe. There's still a few weeks to go yet.'

'So. What can I do for you?'

Gabe's eyes softened as Emily explained about the yellow silk dress and the jewel box.

'Of course.' He picked the dress up carefully by the hanger. 'Leave it with me, I'll see that Dora has them with her.'

'Thanks.' Their business was finished, yet Emily lingered. Something in Gabe's expression held her there, as if there was something more he wanted to say.

Eventually, he broke the silence. 'So, is Marla well?'

Gabe kept his voice deliberately casual, even though he was desperate for news. Marla had kept their interactions to a bare minimum over Dora's funeral arrangements, and she'd made damn sure that they never had a moment alone since the emotionally charged interlude in Dora's kitchen.

'She's fine, I think.' Emily nodded. 'The trouble with Rupert knocked her about a bit, but she seems okay again now.'

He wished he hadn't asked; the last thing he wanted to hear was how Marla missed Rupert. 'Break-ups are always rough.'

'Rough?' Emily said. 'Rough? He was lucky she didn't have him locked up. I bloody well would have if he'd done that to me.'

Gabe stilled, as if someone had pressed *pause*. 'What did he do?'

'He's such a low-life. Called her all sorts of names, and then he lunged at her in the chapel.' Emily shook her head in disgust. 'You should have seen the bruises on her arms.'

I'm going to kill him with my bare hands.

'Bastard.'

'You can say that again.' Emily turned as the door opened. Melanie came in, her neat kelly bag over one arm and an enquiring look on her face. Emily took it as her cue to leave.

'I'll leave that with you then.' She smiled at Gabe and nodded towards Dora's dress in his hands.

Gabe watched her leave. As soon as she'd disappeared inside the chapel, he strode through the funeral parlour and right out of the back door, pausing only to lay the dress down and grab his helmet on the way past.

Some things just couldn't wait.

CHAPTER THIRTY-SEVEN

Gabe ditched his motorbike outside the glass front of *The Herald*'s offices half an hour later and strode straight through reception, much to the annoyance of the middle-aged brunette who'd been surreptitiously reading her *Hello!* magazine behind the welcome desk.

Every head in the huge open-plan office turned to look at the leather-clad figure as he pulled off his helmet. Some of them probably recognised him as the man they'd attempted to ruin a couple of weeks back, for the sake of selling a few copies, and others were just struck dumb by the sight of a dark angel in their midst.

He turned to the nearest girl, who according to her name badge was a trainee reporter called Esther.

'Where will I find Rupert Dean?'

She swallowed and waved a vague arm towards the glass offices that ran across the length of the back of the room.

Gabe nodded curtly and headed through the desks at a pace, not bothering to knock as he flung Rupert's office door open.

Rupert automatically minimised the lunchtime pornography on his screen before he glanced up, and then turned pale as he realised exactly who had just barged into his office.

Gabe slammed his helmet down and braced his hands flat on Rupert's desk.

'I can tolerate you printing a crock of bullshit about me in your piss-poor excuse for a newspaper.'

The entire staff of the newsroom strained to hear every last word. They downed tools and watched agog as Rupert turned puce and fiddled with the knot of his old boys' tie.

'And I couldn't give a flying fuck about you following me around at night with a camera.'

Rupert licked his lips and glanced nervously out at his audience as Gabe advanced around the desk and towered over him.

'Stand up.'

'What for?'

'Because I'm going to hit you.'

A gasp of excitement rippled through the staff.

'Get out of my office right now!' Rupert blustered. 'Security!'

Gabe hauled Rupert roughly onto his feet and backed him against the wall of his office.

'Get your dirty hands off me! Help!' Rupert yelled, but no one moved a muscle.

'But the one thing I really can't stand is men who hurt women. This is for Marla.'

And with that, Gabe smacked his fist straight into Rupert's jaw.

Rupert howled and wiped his mouth with his arm. 'Fuck off, Ryan! The little bitch deserved it!'

'I doubt it, but you deserve this.'

Gabe hit him again, harder this time, causing blood to spring from Rupert's nose and splatter down the front of his pristine candy-stripe shirt as he stumbled back against the wall.

'You bastard! That's only just healed after that Freddie fucking Mercury wannabe broke it!'

Gabe made a mental note to shake Jonny's hand the next time he saw him.

Rupert spat out blood and breathed hard, a crazed glint in his eye.

'You really think you stand a chance with her now I'm not in the picture?' He sneered at Gabe. 'Good old Gabriel, patron saint of dead dogs.'

Gabe watched him, trying to decide where to hit him next.

'You're so dumb, Irish. Always trying to do the right thing. You didn't even realise that I was shagging both of them, right under your nose, did you?'

'Both of them?'

Rupert laughed, enjoying his big revelation. 'You want to watch that receptionist of yours, Gabriel.' Rupert pointed his finger in Gabe's face. 'You've got yourself a right little viper in the nest there. Right little viper in the sack too, actually.'

Melanie?

Gabe shook his head and backed away. 'You disgust me. Just stay the fuck away from Marla.'

He picked up his helmet, and the staff parted like the crowds of Galilee, clearing a path for him.

Jonny kicked open the funeral parlour door and eyed Melanie with distaste. 'Get Gabriel.'

Fake regret dripped from Melanie's every pore as she shook her head.

'Sorry. He's unavailable.'

'I don't believe you.'

Melanie looked momentarily disconcerted by Jonny's bald confrontational manner, before she recovered herself and lifted a nonchalant shoulder.

'Sorry. Do you want to leave a message?'

'With you?' Jonny laughed. 'Er, hello? I don't think so, honey. You have a nasty little habit of not passing messages on, don't you?'

Melanie stared at him with a bland expression, but Jonny noticed the agitated way she fidgeted with her pencil. 'I'm not sure what you mean.'

'Really?' Jonny spat back and shot her daggers across the desk. 'Only I think you know *exactly* what I'm talking about.' He didn't hear the door open behind him.

'If I said fireworks, July 4th and dead dogs, would that jog your memory, I wonder? And what about a certain wedding–funeral clash that Dora definitely mentioned to you?' He wagged his finger at her and gave her his Oprah-inspired neck wiggle. 'I'm onto you, lady.'

A hand landed on Jonny's shoulder, and he whipped around to find himself face to face with Gabe.

'What's going on here?' Gabe asked quietly.

'Nothing,' Melanie said with a smooth smile. 'Jonny was just leaving.'

'No, I wasn't.' Jonny turned to Gabe. 'Marla asked me to do a last run-through with you, make sure everything is clockwork for tomorrow.'

Gabe nodded. 'Sure. Come on through.'

323

'I can do it, Gabe,' Melanie jumped in. 'Really.' She picked up a grey folder and tapped it. 'I have all of the info right here . . .'

'Thank you.' Gabe took the file from her fingers. 'But I'd rather do this myself.'

'But . . .'

Gabe dismissed her protests with a curt shake of his head and waved for Jonny to follow him through. 'Come up to the office.'

Jonny couldn't resist a victory wink at Melanie, and she met his eyes with a look of malice that would have rattled a mass murderer.

Gabe sat alone in his office for some time after Jonny left.

The preparations for Dora's funeral were watertight; it was the knowledge of Melanie's duplicity that held him despondent in his seat. The smokescreen she'd cloaked herself in had blown away on the winds of truth, and the additional information Jonny had just revealed about the note from the fireworks had been the final nail in the coffin.

It came at a great cost to Gabe. He'd been determined to think the best of her, and it unnerved him that he could have got her so wrong.

When had his judgment become so skewed?

He dropped his head into his hands and pushed his palms into his eye sockets.

He was starting to wish he'd never set foot in this place.

This thing with Marla was going nowhere, and he missed Dora's unique brand of acerbic humour around the place more than he'd care to admit. The realisation that Melanie had played him for a fool felt like one blow too many, and for the first time he questioned the wisdom of doggedly sticking it out when everyone in the village was so obviously against him.

He'd had just about a gutful of Beckleberry.

What was the point?

Gabe shoved his chair back and headed downstairs.

Melanie buttoned her winter coat as Gabe walked into reception, and she met his eyes with the startled gaze of a fox staring down the double barrel of the farmer's shotgun.

He crossed to block the closed door.

'I trusted you,' he said softly.

'You can *still* trust me,' she whispered, as she stepped towards him.

'No.' Gabe laughed bitterly and shook his head. 'No, I can't. You slept with Rupert. You took the note from the fireworks and gave it to him.'

He drew no pleasure from the way she flinched at each new accusation.

'But worst of all, you deliberately let a defenceless old woman take the blame for something that you did.'

'I can explain, Gabe. Please, just listen . . .'

'I don't think so.'

He handed her a brown envelope. 'Just leave, and don't come back.'

He swung the door wide and stepped aside to let her pass.

A little later, Gabe nudged the door to the chapel of rest open with one foot and carried two mugs of tea into the quiet room. He sat down next to Dora's lifeless form and picked at the seal on a packet of Jammie Dodgers.

He knew perfectly well that it made no sense to bring

tea and biscuits for a dead person, but he felt that Dora would appreciate the gesture, nonetheless.

'Cheers, Dora.'

He clinked his mug gently against her full one and dunked a biscuit.

'It's been a bit of a day, to be honest, Dora. I've smacked Rupert, sacked Melanie, and Marla still can't stand the bloody sight of me. Two out of three ain't bad, huh?'

He smiled, certain that Dora would have had plenty to say about the day's events. He sat in companionable silence with her until he'd finished his tea.

'I'll take special care of you tomorrow. Only the best, I promise.'

He touched her cool fingers, adorned only with a single band of gold.

The symbol of Ivan's eternal love.

Gabe picked up both mugs, one full and one almost empty, and left the room with a heavy heart. Tomorrow was going to be a long day in more ways than one, not least because the funeral parlour and the chapel needed to work seamlessly together. Marla had conducted all of her negotiations through either Jonny or Emily thus far, but the luxury of avoidance wouldn't be available to her in the morning. They'd have to work shoulder to shoulder if they were to give Dora the send-off that she deserved, and by hook or by crook, Gabe intended to make Marla understand that he wasn't that man from the newspaper article.

CHAPTER THIRTY-EIGHT

The next morning dawned, sprinkling a fairytale glitter of frost across the village. Lights and kettles were flicked on, and early morning cuppas were raised in silent salute to Dora. Wife, neighbour and friend.

At the funeral parlour, Gabe lingered before closing Dora's casket for the last time. Death had stolen her beady vivaciousness and replaced it with a soft serenity; her precious yellow dress was tucked safely under her arm.

'Sleep well, old girl,' he murmured, as he carefully sealed the lid. He laid his hand against the polished yew for a few seconds of silence before heading outside to check on Dan.

At the florist, Ruth and her two teenage daughters had been at work since five o'clock that morning to finish all of the floral tributes on order. They barely noticed that their fingers were red with exertion and the pricks of thorns as they chewed their lips and concentrated on the flowers.

Down the lane, Ivan, who had been out with his secateurs since sunrise, laboured slowly up to the chapel with his arms full of delicately scented lemon wintersweet and fragile yellow hellebores to decorate the altar. Marla chastised him gently as she made him a sweet cup of tea, then drove him home again and ironed his good shirt. Whilst she was gone, Emily moved the vases of white lilies she'd artfully arranged and replaced them with Ivan's love tokens, her cheeks damp with tears.

Jonny unloaded beer and wine from Marla's car into the chapel kitchen, where quiches, cakes and plates of sandwiches were overflowing every available surface. It was a testimony to Dora's popularity that so many of the villagers had turned up at the back door that morning with food clutched in their hands. Cecilia, back from visiting her friend in London, had appointed herself chief food organiser, thanking every neighbour as she took their offerings and gave them a nip of sherry in return.

'Dora would have loved all this fuss, wouldn't she?' Emily said to Jonny as she came through to the kitchen with a newly delivered trifle in her arms. She balanced it on her bump as she hunted for space to set it down.

Jonny puffed out.

'She'd have had this lot organised in five minutes flat.' He glanced around the overloaded kitchen and started to line up glasses on a decorator's table that he'd unearthed in Ivan's shed.

'I'll tell you what else she'd have loved, as well.' He swivelled around with one hand on his hip and a sparkle in his eye. 'That little bitch over there, getting what was coming to her.'

He'd taken great delight in relaying to Emily earlier the gossip Gabe had confided in him, particularly the part about how he'd then seen Melanie leave the funeral parlour in floods of tears.

'I wonder how Gabe's going to cope without her now though,' Emily said, then frowned as Marla came through the open back door, rubbing her hands together for warmth.

'How who's going to cope without who?' Marla asked, unwinding her pale-blue merino scarf from around her neck and glancing from Jonny to Emily.

'Gabe. He's given Melanie the boot,' Jonny replied, practically shimmying with excitement.

Marla's hand stilled at her throat. 'Really? Why?'

Jonny revelled in the opportunity to tell his story all over again, and spared no details when describing how shocked Gabe had been when he'd found out about the note from the fireworks.

'And then she came out, sobbing! Practically on her knees, *begging* him for her job back,' he finished with a flourish. 'Good riddance, I say.'

'Well, I can't say that I'll miss her,' Marla said, careful to keep her surprise from her voice. Gabe's staffing issues were his own affair, but up until now he'd always seemed to be Melanie's number one fan. It wasn't that long since he'd given the girl flowers and taken her for a fancy dinner, for God's sake. But then, she didn't know why she was even remotely surprised. It was entirely consistent with Gabe's behaviour to turn his affections on and off like a tap.

She glanced up at the kitchen clock.

'Come on guys, we'd better get out front. People will start arriving soon.'

Jonny eyed Emily's bump with a frown, as they filed through the vestry and out into the cool winter sunshine.

'I wish you'd hurry up and have that bloody baby. I'm sick of lurking outside every time I want a fag.'

Emily smiled at him sweetly.

'I'm sorry to inconvenience your legs, but my child says thank you.'

She laughed as he shot her a sarcastic look as he wandered off towards the old graves at the back of the chapel gardens. Laying a hand over her bump, she allowed herself a moment to offer up a silent thank you for the way that things had worked out between herself and Tom. Her respect for him as a man had increased ten-fold because of his refusal to allow her to shoulder all of the blame, and standing there on that cold, bright morning, she finally allowed herself to look towards their future with excitement, without the guilt that had accompanied her around like an unwanted shadow. They were to be a family at last.

On cue, Tom sauntered up the High Street in his dark suit and joined their little huddle. He slid an arm around Emily's shoulders and dropped a kiss on her damp cheek, then lifted his head, surprised.

'Dora wouldn't want you to cry,' he murmured, rubbing the top of her arm.

Emily shook her head. 'Happy tears, not sad,' she whispered, sliding her arm around his middle. 'You're the best man in the world, Tom.'

'I know,' he grinned. 'Now behave yourself, sentimental old fool.'

He glanced across at Marla.

'All set?'

'I think so,' Marla nodded as Jonny reappeared at her

side. It struck her how sombre a tableau they made, a huddle of black against the stark white chapel.

They looked up in unison as Gabe appeared momentarily on the street outside the funeral parlour. He glanced their way with a tiny nod of acknowledgment, before disappearing again through the side gate.

'Is it terribly bad form to find the undertaker sexy?' Jonny murmured. 'Sorry, Dora.' He crossed himself as he cast his eyes to the skies in apology.

'You won't like him so much when he puts you out of a job next summer,' Marla muttered with unnecessary acidity, mainly because very similar thoughts had invaded her own head at the sight of Gabe. It frustrated the hell out of her that the mad chemist in her gut refused to listen to the cool voice of reason in her head.

Today was going to be a long, long day.

By midday, the chapel was packed to the rafters with mourners. Marla hovered outside the door and sent a discreet nod towards Tom, who stood sentry in the funeral parlour doorway.

He disappeared inside, and moments later Ivan stepped out onto the pavement to lead his wife on her final journey. Dora's casket followed, borne on the steadfast shoulders of Gabe, Tom, Jonny and Dan. A painful lump rose in Marla's throat as she watched them match their pace to Ivan's. They made a slow and dignified procession, and she had to acknowledge that they all looked magnificent, with a yellow hellebore pinned to the lapel of their black jackets. Marla glanced down at the matching flower corsage around her wrist, the only splash of colour against her simple Jackie 'O'-style black dress.

Who knew that Ivan had such a romantic soul? Only Dora.

She looked up as Ivan approached the chapel doorway and reached out for his hands.

'Are you alright?' she asked.

He squeezed her fingers for a few seconds, his eyes sorrowful.

'I don't know what I'll do without her,' he said shakily, then let go of Marla's hands with a heavy sigh and stepped inside the chapel. She swallowed hard and met Gabe's eyes without rancour as he drew alongside her. Today wasn't the time for discord, a fact brought home by the strains of the wartime love song, 'Goodnight Sweetheart', that floated from the chapel speakers.

Emily and Marla had both shed a tear yesterday as they listened to the simple love song Ivan had requested, made all the more sentimental by the crackle and hum from the stylus of the old record player Jonny had hunted down for the occasion.

The four men placed Dora's casket carefully in its place before the altar and then took their seats. All except Jonny, who stepped up to the lectern and stood silent with his head bowed, until the last strains of the music ebbed away.

He drew a deep breath, and on behalf of Ivan, thanked the congregation for coming. Everyone in the church had their own memories of Dora, and Jonny enriched them as he shared a little of Dora's early life. How she'd been the last surviving member of seven children, and of how devastated she'd been to lose her beloved eldest brother Billy when he went down with HMS *Courageous* during the Second World War. Many of the elderly congregation bowed their heads, their own wartime losses ever close to their hearts.

Jonny's affection for Dora shone star-bright in his every word. He made many of the congregation cry with his heartfelt anecdotes gathered from Dora's many friends, and gentle laughter rippled around the chapel as he recounted a memorable day last winter when she'd tumbled down the step into the local shoe shop. She'd knocked over every single rack as she gathered momentum like a bull in a china shop, completely trashing the place. He paused to allow people to settle again, and then wrapped up his speech with a simple acknowledgment of how large a hole Dora had left behind in the lives of all who loved her.

Ivan, most of all.

One by one, people stood, wishing to approach the lectern and share their anecdotes about how Dora had touched their lives.

Ruth, her eyes red-rimmed and her fingers sore, told of how Dora had often babysat her daughters when they were small and her husband had passed away suddenly, leaving her to run the florists alone.

Alfonso, blowing his nose into his silk handkerchief, spoke of how Dora had always ordered Ivan's birthday cakes from him, even though she could have made them just as well herself. Laughter rippled the audience, because many fêtes and charity bakes over the years had been graced with Dora's less-than-perfect baking.

Tom shared his own special memory of Dora too, as the person he'd turned to when he needed someone to talk to, as someone who'd given him the single best piece of advice he'd ever received. He didn't elaborate, but the tear on his cheek spoke volumes.

Emily and Marla stood arm in arm at the lectern and

shared memories of the countless times Dora had made them laugh and brightened their working days with her acerbic humour and huge heart.

There was no rush to the proceedings, no need to hurry Dora away to her final resting place, in the cemetery beside her brothers and sisters.

Finally, Jonny looked across at Gabriel, who straightened his tie and approached the lectern.

Marla couldn't take her eyes off him. She hadn't allowed herself to so much as glance in his direction over the last few weeks; having him here was torture. It seemed that she was destined for famine or feast where he was concerned, and neither option did anything to settle her stomach.

He glanced her way and held her gaze for a second that might have been an hour, and in that moment she felt sure that everyone in the building knew they'd shared a night together. She dropped her eyes to her patent black Mary Janes to minimise the number of people that would see her scarlet cheeks.

'Ivan has asked me to speak on his behalf this afternoon,' Gabe began, and his beautiful accent pulled her eyes like magnets back to his face.

'It's my honour and my pleasure, because Dora was one in a million. She made my move here so much easier with her simple kindnesses, her endless supplies of biscuits and her no-nonsense advice.'

He smiled sadly.

'She was funny, and she was kind. A true friend, and I will miss her immeasurably.'

He paused, and he reached inside his jacket for Ivan's speech.

'Okay, so over to Ivan.'

He bowed his head towards Ivan on the front row, and then began to read.

'*It was raining the day I met Dora. October 6th, 1939. She was just fifteen but already very beautiful, like a young Rita Hayworth, she was. All the other girls were huddled together under the eaves of the youth club, but my Dora just twirled and lifted her face up to the rain.*

That was it, she was the girl for me and I didn't waste any time in telling her so.

Then the war came along and everything changed – everything apart from Dora, that is. Her letters kept me alive through times when I could have easily lain down and died. I was determined to get home to my girl.'

Gabe paused as Ivan wiped his eyes with his white hand-kerchief and held up a shaky hand to still him. He turned to Marla and handed her an envelope.

'I reckon my Dora would have liked you to read this out now.'

Marla nodded and swallowed her nerves as she looked at the frail envelope with tear-filled eyes.

She joined Gabe at the lectern, and he stepped aside to allow her centre stage.

Marla drew strength from the sad smile of gratitude on Ivan's face.

'Ivan has asked me to read this letter to you all.'

She eased the notepaper from its envelope.

'It's dated August, 1944.'

Her throat burned as she scanned the letter quickly, and she took a moment to compose herself. She needed to do Dora justice. Both the elderly lady she'd known and loved, and the hopeful young newlywed with a full heart and a primrose dress.

'Dearest Ivan,
  It was such a wrench to leave you at the station last weekend, although by the time this letter finds you it will probably be more like three weeks ago. Maybe even more. How I wish that you were not so far away from me, my darling. I keep looking down at my hand to make sure that my wedding ring is still there and I haven't dreamt that I am actually your wife!
  Wasn't it just the most marvellous day?
  You looked terribly handsome in your uniform, I really thought I might actually die of happiness when I saw you waiting for me at the altar.
  I have to go now as I'm expected at the factory in an hour, but whenever you read this, remember that you are always my first and last thought each day.
  All my prayers are that you will come home safely to me.
  Your loving wife,
  Dora.'

Silence fell over the congregation as Marla folded the letter and returned it to its envelope with trembling fingers. Gabe stepped closer, and the warmth of his hand against the small of her back made her long to turn into the safety of his arms.

'Well done. You did Dora proud,' he murmured against her hair, then propelled her lightly back towards her seat between Ivan and her mother. The old man patted her hand and nodded as he tucked Dora's letter back inside his jacket.

At the lectern, Gabe cleared his throat and glanced down at the paper in his hand to complete Ivan's speech.

'*I was the proudest man alive the day Dora married me. We were never lucky enough to be blessed with children, so she's been my everything for more than sixty years. She is more than just my guiding light.*'

Gabe placed the speech down slowly and raised his eyes to Marla's.

'*She is the rock that this lighthouse stands on.*'

Marla's heart cracked wide open. It was the most beautiful, sentimental thing she'd ever heard, and she suddenly understood why Dora had worn her little diamond lighthouse brooch every single day. It must have been a love token from Ivan, as precious in its own way as her wedding ring.

The hauntingly familiar intro bars of Dame Vera Lynn's wartime anthem, 'We'll Meet Again', floated out across the chapel, and all around the room tissues were pulled from handbags as old and young hearts alike swelled with pride.

Gabe stepped down from the lectern and joined the pallbearers around the casket. Dora's elderly friends and fellow war survivors stood and joined their voices with Dame Vera's, their swelling song a beautiful tribute as Dora left the chapel for the final time.

Marla rubbed Emily's back as she sobbed quietly, and together they flanked Ivan until just the three of them remained. Almost everyone at the service had taken a few moments afterwards to offer him their condolences, their hugs, and their reassurances of casseroles and visits to keep him company over the difficult weeks and months ahead. The old man looked thoroughly overwhelmed.

'Take a few seconds, Ivan,' Marla said, guiding him down

into the nearest chair and sitting alongside him. Emily sat on his other side, and each of them held one of his frail hands in theirs.

'It was a beautiful send-off,' Emily said, and they all nodded.

'She was very loved,' Marla said. 'I think the whole village was here.'

'They were very kind,' Ivan said, shaking his head. 'You know what she said to me recently? She said she wanted me to go first, because she didn't like to think of me having to cope without her.'

Marla and Emily's eyes met over Ivan's head. They understood Dora's sentiments exactly. They didn't know how he'd go on either.

'But she was wrong,' he said, surprising them both. 'I'm glad it was this way. I never wanted to leave her on her own.' His wavering voice broke, and Marla rubbed his shoulder as Emily held tight to his hand.

'And you didn't,' Marla said. 'Not for one day. You did her proud, Ivan.'

Everyone stood silently to watch the funeral cortège leave slowly for the cemetery: Gabe travelled with Dan in the front of the hearse, Emily and Tom escorting Ivan in the car behind.

It was only as the hearse disappeared around the corner that someone in the lingering crowd glanced towards the funeral parlour.

'Fire!'

CHAPTER THIRTY-NINE

A collective shriek went up around the group assembled on the grass, and several of the younger men sprang into action and dashed to see what was happening.

Marla, who had been about to drive herself and her mother to the cemetery, stared in horror at the orange glow inside the front window of the parlour.

'I'll call the fire brigade,' she yelled over the racket and ducked back into the chapel to grab her mobile.

By the time she ran back outside again several minutes later, the glow had grown into a blaze, and the crowd had at least doubled, if not tripled.

The flames had really taken hold in the reception area, and as the wail of sirens came down the High Street, the front window of the funeral parlour exploded outwards with an ear-splitting crack.

Within minutes, firefighters spilled out of an engine from all sides. They set up a cordon to keep the crowds safe, as others unreeled hosepipes at lightning speed.

'Poor Gabriel,' Cecilia muttered, as she clutched on to Marla's arm.

All around her, Marla could hear snippets of conversation from the overexcited crowd.

'He'll be ruined,' said one.

'I'll bet it was arson!' speculated another.

'Insurance job. Funeral was the perfect cover,' a sly voice chimed in.

Marla's head swum with all of the theories.

Why was it human nature to automatically assume the worst of people?

'I can smell pork!' someone yelled, hysterically. 'It'll be the stiffs in there cooking!'

Marla swung around to face a gang of teenage boys that had gathered behind her.

'Don't be so bloody disrespectful!' she spat, but all the same, the words struck fear into her heart.

Were there bodies in there? It was too horrific to contemplate.

'I'm going back into the chapel,' she murmured to her mother. 'Someone should try to get hold of Gabe.'

Back inside the quiet confines of the chapel, the enormity of the situation hit her. All of those people outside were right. Gabe *would* be ruined, and people *would* jump to conclusions. Jesus, she'd wanted him gone, but not like this.

She sat down at her desk in the office. Thankfully it looked as if the fire service were winning their battle to tame the fire; it was less inferno-like now and more of a drenched, smoking mess.

She dialled Emily's mobile number as she stared out of

the window, but after a couple of rings it clicked through to answerphone. *Crap.*

'Emily, it's Marla. Listen. There's been a fire at the funeral parlour. The fire service is here now, but it's bad, Em. It's really bad. Tell Gabe to get back here straight . . .' She trailed off, dumbstruck, as one of the firemen stumbled from the funeral parlour with a burned and blackened form in his arms.

A very limp, female form. Long black hair trailed over the fireman's arm as he carried her to the ambulance that had joined the scene.

Melanie.

Sweet Jesus.

'Just tell him to get back here, Emily. Quickly.'

'That's about all for tonight, Mr Ryan. We'll be in touch in the morning.'

Gabe shook DCI Pearson's hand and watched him hurry away down the street towards his car. It was a little after 7 p.m. on what had turned out to be one of the longest days of his life.

Behind him the funeral parlour smouldered, still officially off-limits until the fire officer declared it safe.

He didn't have the stomach to go inside anyway.

Not tonight, anyhow. Nor tomorrow. Maybe never again.

It was a miracle that the morgue had been empty. Although actually, it wasn't divine intervention that had saved him. His empty mortuary had a lot more to do with the fall-out from Rupert's scathing attack in *The Herald*. How ironic that it should turn out to be Gabe's saving grace; not that he would rush to shake Rupert's hand any time soon. He dropped down and sat on the edge of the kerb with his head in his hands.

'Beer?'

Dan sauntered across from the chapel and handed him an already-open bottle. Gabe downed it in one, and Dan handed him his own.

'What did the dibble have to say?'

Dan glanced behind them at the shadowy funeral parlour and winced.

'Nothing they could say, really.' Gabe shrugged. 'Melanie's confessed to starting the fire, so it's an open and shut case for them.'

Dan puffed out hard and shook his head.

'I always thought she was a bit weird, but even I didn't have her pegged as a full-on Glenn Close. Psycho or what?'

Gabe tried and failed to find the words to articulate his shock at the extremities of Melanie's behaviour.

'She could have died,' he muttered, as much to himself as to Dan.

He couldn't get his head around how desperate Melanie must have been to do something like this.

'She picked the right place to do it then,' Dan quipped, but even he couldn't expect to raise a laugh out of Gabe tonight. He dropped a hand on his friend's shoulder.

'You were insured though, right, buddy?'

Gabe nodded with a heavy sigh.

'That's alright then.' Dan clapped him on the back. 'This is as straightforward as it gets. You'll be back in business in no time, mate.'

Gabe downed the last of the second beer and didn't answer.

Dan was right, but he wasn't sure he had the heart for it anymore.

It had been bedlam when he'd arrived back from the cemetery that afternoon, but he'd taken one look at his burned-out business and made it clear that Dora's wake was to remain top priority for everyone else. His world might have collapsed around his ears, but it was bricks and mortar. Ivan's loss was far greater. He nodded bleakly towards the chapel.

'How's it gone over there this afternoon?'

'Ah, the usual. Lots of golden oldies who've had a skinful of sherry. Most of them have gone home now with a plate of leftovers balanced on the handlebars of their mobility scooters.'

Gabe knew Dan well enough to know that wisecracks were part of his DNA. They were his coping mechanism; this was the closest he came to being serious.

'Is Marla still there?'

Dan nodded.

Gabe pulled himself up from the kerb, the two beer bottles in one hand.

'Get rid of these, bud.' He handed the empties to Dan. 'There's something I need to do.'

Marla kicked off her heels and poured herself a well-earned brandy from one of the many half-empty bottles in the kitchen. She'd just closed the door on the last of the mourners, and Emily and Tom had taken a rather worse-for-wear Ivan home with them for the evening. At times it had felt as if the day would never end, and the lure of a strong drink and a quiet five minutes was irresistible. She'd flopped down into a chair when she heard the chapel door open again.

'Marla?'

She closed her eyes and wished for strength as Gabe's voice echoed around the chapel. Being around him was always such hard work, and she was so tired.

'In the kitchen,' she called out, not bothering to get up.

He appeared around the doorway, and the weary look on his face mirrored her own feelings so closely that she couldn't be annoyed by his interruption anymore. She waved an arm towards the empty seats around her in invitation.

'Come on in.'

He collapsed into the chair next to her. One glance at his troubled expression was enough to make her reach for the brandy bottle and an extra glass.

She poured him a drinker's measure and slid it across the table towards him.

'You're the second person to think I need a drink today,' he said, as he wrapped his fingers around the glass.

Marla breathed in deeply, and a heady mix of smoke and Gabe assailed her nostrils.

'I'm not surprised. You have every right to get drunk after the day you've had.'

She touched her glass lightly against his then swallowed a good glug of brandy. The heat stung the back of her throat, and, feeling fortified, she met his eyes.

'Is it as bad as it looks over there?'

Gabe humphed.

'Worse.'

He knocked back half of his brandy.

Marla grimaced.

'Was there anybody in there? Any *bodies*, I mean?'

She had to ask. The macabre question had been on her

mind ever since the crass comments made by the crowds earlier. 'Sorry . . . it's just . . .' She tailed off, struggling to find the right words. What had happened was hideous on so many levels, both practically and emotionally for Gabe. Dora's funeral had been heart-wrenching, and the afternoon had been shocking beyond belief.

'No. Thanks to your ex-boyfriend, business had gone extremely quiet.'

Gabe's mouth twisted into a line of distaste and he drained his glass. The mention of Rupert frayed Marla's already-tattered nerves.

She handed Gabe the brandy bottle and watched him pour himself a refill.

She looked away, blindsided by the need to make it better for him.

It had been a day of high emotion and drama, and her feelings for Gabe were a jumbled mess. On the one hand, he was damaging her business, and she still harboured a hulking great iceberg of hurt and resentment over the exposé in the newspaper. There was no denying the evidence, and he'd certainly failed to mention that he had been married.

But then in the next breath he'd turn around and do something so intrinsically decent that he'd make her question her judgment all over again. How could anyone but a good man stand up and represent Ivan as movingly as Gabe had today?

He was good. He was bad. He was a threat.

He was a comfort. He was beautiful. He scared her stupid.

She reached for the bottle and poured herself another stiff drink.

'Did Melanie start the fire?'

Rumours had been thrown around wildly ever since the fireman had stumbled out with her in his arms. Jonny had practically opened a book to take bets this afternoon after a couple of tequilas, until Marla had put her stone-cold-sober foot down and stopped him.

Gabe nodded.

'I had no idea what was going on with her. I still don't.' He stared into the bottom of his brandy glass. 'The hospital is keeping her in tonight, and she'll be formally charged in the morning.'

Marla cast around for something charitable to say about the girl but found nothing. 'I'm sorry.'

'Not as sorry as I am. I must have missed so many warning signs.' He shook his head with a bewildered look. 'I take it you know that she'd been sleeping with Rupert?'

'Rupert?' Marla squeaked, wide-eyed with shock. 'When?'

Gabe shrugged. 'No idea. Same time as you, I think.' He drank deeply and then looked at her with an apologetic shrug. 'Sorry. I assumed that was why you'd split up.'

Marla shook her head, still trying to wrap her head around the idea of Rupert and Melanie. In many ways they made a perfect match. 'No. I just realised that I didn't want to marry him after all.'

'Sensible decision. He's a dick.'

Marla laughed shakily. 'Jonny broke his nose.'

'I know. I think I broke it again yesterday.'

'Did you really?'

'He hurt you. I hurt him. He deserved it.'

Marla couldn't disagree, and the fact that Gabe had defended her honour was yet another tick on that intrinsically decent list.

'So what will you do now?' she asked eventually, not even sure she wanted him to answer. There was a broken, melancholy air around Gabe tonight that filled her with a fear she didn't understand.

He ran a hand through his dusty hair.

'I've had a gutful of this place.' He shrugged. 'I'm done.'

Her palms went clammy as she stared at him.

'But you must have been insured? You can rebuild.'

There were dark circles under his eyes and smears of soot mingling with the five o'clock shadow along his jaw. 'Yeah, I could rebuild.' A cynical laugh rattled in his throat. 'But why would I? Nobody wants the funeral parlour here, Marla. It's been one fucking nightmare after another, since the day I arrived.'

Marla stared into the amber swirls of her brandy. She couldn't argue with him, and what's more, she knew that she'd been a big contributor to his difficulties. The knowledge that their campaign had been justified didn't make her feel any less shabby in the face of Gabe's despair.

'I tried, and I failed. I'm no coward, but this is one battle I'm just not destined to win. You can have your street back.'

Marla was stricken by his U-turn. She felt no glory in the victory. 'What will you do?' Her voice shook with the effort of holding herself together.

'I don't know. I have nothing to stay here for anymore.'

He locked eyes with her, and she swallowed hard.

'You don't?' She regretted the whispered words, as soon as they'd left her lips.

'Do I?'

She didn't want him to leave, but she couldn't ask him to stay. 'Gabe, don't.'

'Don't what, Marla? Don't tell you I love you?'

Marla's heart swooped around in her chest like a caged bird. 'Don't say that.'

'Why not? It's the truth and you know it, Marla. I love you. I've loved you since the very first day I saw you.'

Marla slid her glass onto the table, not trusting her hands to hold it any longer. 'You're being ridiculous, Gabe . . . you don't know what you're saying. It's been a long day.'

'I've never been more sure of anything in my life. I love you.'

'Stop it, Gabe. Please, just stop.'

He dragged his chair closer until his knees touched hers. 'Deny it all you like, but you feel it too. I see you, Marla.' He reached for her hands. 'Your mouth says one thing, but your eyes beg me not to listen.'

'No!' Marla could feel her well-organised world ripping apart at the seams, and hot tears splashed down her cheeks as she battled to yank the edges back together again. She stumbled to her feet and turned away to grip the cool steel edge of the sink.

Gabe was behind her in seconds, so close that his breath warmed the exposed skin on the back of her neck.

'Tell me you didn't feel it when we made love in your garden. In your shower.' He braced his hands either side of her on the counter. 'In your bed, for fuck's sake, Marla.'

The raw catch in his voice squeezed her heart, and she rounded on him in fury and frustration. 'I didn't feel it. There, is that what you want? It was sex, Gabe, not love. Grow up . . .'

He shook his head, and his eyes glittered with hurt, every bit as intense as hers.

'You're wrong, Marla, and you damn well know it.'

She shook her head. 'I'm not.'

'So prove it.'

He kissed her. Hard, the kiss of a warrior. Marla couldn't fight him; his nearness wiped away any last vestige of her willpower. His kiss was desperate and furious as he hauled her body against his own, and for a few treacherous seconds, she let herself hold him.

His mouth softened instantly over hers, achingly sweet as his tongue licked over hers – she could taste his love. Honey-coated promises of things that could never be, of roses around doorways and dark-eyed babies with gypsy curls.

Emotions battered her from all sides as his hands moved to cradle her face.

Lust so strong she wanted to rip her clothes off and drag him down onto the kitchen floor; frustration so jagged she wanted to smash every bottle on the drainer behind her; and a protective rush more powerful than any lioness as her fingers slid into his sooty hair and held him close.

Soothed him.

Loved him.

When he lifted his head, the look in his eyes told her that he knew.

He'd dragged the truth from her, in actions if not words. 'I'm not the enemy anymore, beautiful girl. You don't have to hate me.'

It was the worst thing he could have possibly said. His words mainlined right into the visceral vein of fear that ran through Marla's core.

She *needed* those barriers between them.

She *needed* a reason to hate him.

She swiped at her mouth with the back of her hand, as

she fought to get her breathing back under control, and pushed against his chest to put some space between them. He waited for her to speak, his whole body braced for impact, like a passenger on a jet free-falling out of the sky.

'You're right. I don't have to hate you anymore. But I don't love you, Gabe, and I never will.'

She stared him down across the chapel kitchen as his eyes scraped her face, looking for any chink in her armour. He found none. She was marble white and just as impenetrable.

'You're the most stubborn, fucking infuriating woman I've ever met in my life,' he said, frustration and ferocious hurt warring inside him. He wanted to shake the truth out of her, because there was no way he had this wrong.

'Go home, Gabe,' she said softly.

He raked his hand through his smoky hair. 'I don't even know where that is anymore.'

Marla paused, and Gabe found himself holding his breath. 'Maybe it's not here,' she said eventually, so quietly he had to strain to hear her.

He felt his strength ebb away. She was telling him to leave, to give up, to go home. He'd told her that he loved her, and she'd told him to take his love and disappear. He was a long way beyond weary. His tired bones ached, and his empty, broken heart ached.

'Winner takes all,' he said quietly. 'Congratulations, Marla.'

He stalked down the aisle and out into the cold, crisp night, knowing without a doubt that the woman he loved would never let herself love him back. He was done.

CHAPTER FORTY

Cecilia poured two glasses of wine and put them down on the kitchen table, along with the open bottle ready for the refills. She had a feeling they were going to need them.

She stood behind Marla's chair and stroked her hair for a few seconds. She'd listened to her daughter cry herself to sleep every night for at least two weeks, and she wasn't prepared to do it again.

Marla didn't want her hair stroked, and she didn't want to talk. She wanted to go to bed.

'What's wrong, honey?' her mother asked.

Marla fiddled with the belt of her dressing gown as Cecilia pulled up a chair beside her.

'Nothing,' she sniffed.

'Nothing doesn't make you cry as much as you have been these past few weeks.'

Marla's shoulders slumped, defeated. She didn't have enough fight left in her to deny the truth any longer. Gabe had laid his soul bare that day in the chapel, and she'd sent him away because she'd been too scared to be honest with him, or with herself.

'It's Gabe.'

Cecilia nodded and lifted her daughter's chin.

'You love him.'

Even though the answer to her mother's question was quite obviously yes, still she couldn't bring herself to say it out loud. Instead, she nodded.

'I'm in a mess, Mom. Over the last few months I've poured all my energy into hating him. I wouldn't know *how* to love him.'

Cecilia frowned. 'Why not?'

Marla looked at her mother. The woman called herself a sex therapist. Did she *really* not know? She sighed heavily.

'Because all I know of love and marriage is what I've learned from you.'

Cecilia laid a hand over Marla's on the table, and sat in silence for a minute or two. 'You think I like being this way, Marla?'

Marla chewed her lip. 'I don't know, Mom.' She shrugged. 'I guess you're just not the settling kind.'

Cecilia threw her hands up in the air, with an exasperated laugh.

'Is that really what you think of me?'

Marla didn't answer, and instead reached for her wine glass.

Cecilia rubbed her chin.

'I was too young when I married your father,' she said, quietly. 'We were a terrible match, but I loved him too much to see it at the time.'

Marla looked up and waited. Her mother never talked about the past.

'And then when he . . .'

Cecilia waved her heavily ringed hand around to infer intimacies she'd never shared with her daughter.

'When he *what*, Mom?'

Cecilia studied the scrubbed pine tabletop and sighed.

'He was a good father, Marla, but he wasn't a very good husband. Not long after our first wedding anniversary he slept with his research assistant. And our cleaner.' Her eyes clouded. 'The nanny was the last straw.'

Marla stared at her mother in shock. She'd been too young at the time to understand the goings-on in the grown-up world around her, and from that day to this her mother had never spoken a bad word about her father.

'I never knew.'

Cecilia nodded and patted Marla's hand. 'Good. And I wouldn't be telling you now if I didn't think it would help you to hear it.'

Marla looked at her mother with new eyes, and finally saw behind the confident, self-centred, butterfly facade.

'I spent the next however-many years ricocheting from one man to the next, always trying to fill the hole your father left in my heart.'

Regret rang clear in her mother's small voice.

'And did you?'

Please say yes, because I can't live with this hole in mine.

Cecilia sighed. 'You know what, honey? I lost sight of what love was after a while, and even when I finally found it again I somehow managed to let it slip through my fingers.'

Marla suddenly remembered the way her mother had lit up when she saw Robert again that night at Franco's.

'It's not too late, is it?' she whispered.

'For me? It probably is, yes.' Cecilia's smile was bitter-sweet. 'But not for you, Marla. Gabriel is a fine man. If you love him, be brave and grab him.'

Marla was lost for words. She'd invested so much time and effort into making sure she didn't tread in her mother's footsteps, but all along her mother had been trying to recapture the only true love she'd ever known.

Who knew? If her father had been a faithful man, her parents might have stayed together, saving her mother from a lifetime of discontent.

And Marla from a lifetime of confusion.

Her head ached.

All of her long-held beliefs about love and marriage were on shifting sands, and somewhere in amongst it all, she knew that she might have missed her one chance for happiness.

CHAPTER FORTY-ONE

'If I hear "White Christmas" one more time I'm going to make like Van Gogh and cut my ears off.'

Jonny swished down the aisle in his purple satin flares, to blast the Scissor Sisters in defiance of the season.

It was a little after midday on Christmas Eve, an hour since they'd waved off their final bride and groom of the year. Not that Jonny could complain that it had been a staid, traditional affair. Anything but; the only thing white about the wedding had been the snow that dusted the ground outside. The happy couple had made a surprisingly convincing Agnetha and Bjorn, and Marla's eyes ached from a morning surrounded by wall-to-wall flower power and kipper ties. Unlike Jonny, she was quite content to listen to the mellow sound of Bing Crosby; her ears ached from one too many renditions of Abba's 'I do, I do, I do, I do, I do'.

Emily looked up from her seat next to the aisle. She was dressed in a swirl-patterned maxi-dress that drew attention to her massive bump. She crossed her arms over the top of it and narrowed her eyes at Marla.

'I've always loved that dress. I'll never be skinny again,' she groused, eyeing Marla's emerald-green original seventies Biba dress.

'Rubbish. You can borrow it for the christening,' Marla laughed.

The dress had called out to her from a vintage shop window in New York a few years back and she'd fallen for its charms, despite the fact that the scoop neck displayed more cleavage than she was used to and the Lurex material clung to her rib cage. But the colour suited her hair, and the silver sparkle shot through it added enough pizzazz to give her the perfect excuse to wear her silver salsa-dancing sandals.

Since she'd opened the chapel, it had become her go-to dress for their seventies-themed weddings, of which there were a surprising number. Abba had a lot to answer for. She'd played up her eyes with smoky-green shadows and kohl pencil that morning, and voilà, the chapel had itself a bona fide seventies landlady.

'Sherry!'

Cecilia trilled as she tottered along the aisle in a gold lamé dress, a tray of schooner glasses balanced in her hands. She loved spending Christmas in England, and felt strongly that sherry was an integral part of the festivities.

Jonny helped himself to one of the glasses and poured its contents into the nearest plant pot.

'Sherry is for coffin dodgers.'

He arched his brows in challenge at Cecilia and reached behind the lectern for his secret bottle of Jack Daniel's.

'What?' he shrugged, round-eyed and innocent. 'It's my communion wine.'

Jonny didn't have a religious bone in his body, but he was more than happy to cherry-pick theological traditions to suit his needs. Those that involved alcohol, mostly.

Emily took the glass of orange juice from Cecilia's tray.

'Just leave me here until I've had the baby. I can't get up.'

'Not long now, sweetie.' Jonny stood behind her and massaged her shoulders.

Emily sighed and leaned back against him. 'You have magic hands.'

'You should see the rest of me, darlin',' he muttered, with a suggestive wiggle of his fingers.

'Er, I don't think so,' Emily laughed.

'Me neither, actually,' Jonny cackled. 'You'd never look at poor old Tom in the same light again.'

He winked and knocked back the rest of his JD, then glanced across at Marla.

'Ready, boss?'

Marla nodded and cast an apologetic smile at her mother as she replaced her untouched glass of sherry back on the tray.

'Sorry, Mom. Jonny and I better dash if we're going to get those glitter balls back to the hire company. Someone from the County Hotel is collecting them at four for their Christmas Day celebrations.'

She nodded towards the stack of glittering orbs lined up by the chapel door. Jonny flung his full-length military coat on and turned the collar up as he went out into the snow to load them into the car.

Marla passed the chapel keys to her mother.

'You just need to lock the front door, the back's already bolted. I'll see you at home in a couple of hours.'

She dropped a kiss on her mother's cheek and turned to Emily.

'Happy Christmas, Em. Give Tom a kiss from me.'

She leaned down and hugged her friend carefully around her bump.

'Have fun tomorrow. Last one with just the two of you.'

Emily held on tight. 'You try to have fun, too, okay?'

She looked up at Marla through suspiciously damp lashes.

'Just go home and relax. You shouldn't even be here.'

Emily had remained steadfast in her refusal to slow down, even though the baby was due in just a few weeks. She laughed off Marla's concerns and patted her bump.

'I will. This turkey's almost cooked.'

An icy blast hit Marla as she stepped outside onto the slippery path. She snuggled her chin down into her cashmere scarf and picked her way through the fresh snow to the car as Jonny loaded up the boot with the disco balls.

Inside, she whacked the heaters on full blast and blew on her frozen fingers. The snow on the windscreen melted away, revealing the desolate, boarded-up funeral parlour across from them. It looked particularly sorry for itself against the pretty backdrop of the village snow scene, with the charmingly ramshackle fairy lights strung from lamppost to lamppost. The funeral parlour cowered, as if it had no business being there; much the same way as its owner had felt at the end, thanks to Marla.

She hadn't laid eyes on Gabe since the day she'd thrown his love back in his face, but Ruth the florist had reliably informed her that *she'd* heard from Dan's mother's sister's cleaner that he'd gone home to Dublin. Marla's heart had iced over at the news.

Jonny slammed the boot door down and slid into the passenger seat, bringing an unwelcome gust of frozen air into the car with him.

'*Ker*ist! Dunno about glitter balls, but *my* poor balls shrivelled up like walnuts out there!'

He pulled off his leather gloves and clamped his hands over the heater vents.

Marla laughed and patted his satin-clad knee.

'Don't worry, still bigger than Rupert's, then.'

Jonny high-fived her with an evil snicker.

'So indiscreet, Ms Jacobs! I love you.'

Marla blushed. He was right. It *had* been an indiscreet comment, but if anyone deserved it, then it was Rupert. She usually played her cards close to her chest when it came to her personal life. Even Jonny had no clue about her relationship with Gabe.

If you could call it that, she thought, with a heavy heart.

She crawled along the High Street at ten miles an hour to avoid sliding towards the last-minute shoppers and Christmas Eve revellers spattering the pavements.

'Why the big sigh?' Jonny asked.

Marla frowned. She wasn't even aware that she *had* sighed.

'Would you want to spend Christmas Day with my mother?'

Jonny grinned.

'Just thank your lucky stars that creepy Brynn isn't here anymore.'

He pulled a macabre face. 'He'd have brought a whole new meaning to the term *stuffing the turkey*!'

Marla laughed softly and turned off the radio when she heard the opening bars of 'White Christmas', to prevent Jonny from reaching for the nearest sharp object.

'So, come on then, ladybird.' He rubbed his hands on his thighs like a market trader. 'What are you hoping for in your Christmas stocking?'

'Well . . . my mom always went traditional with oranges and walnuts at the bottom, but you've kinda just put me off.'

Marla eased the car to a stop at a red light.

'Let me take a wild guess.' He drummed his fingers on the dashboard. 'A tall, dark Irish undertaker?'

Marla turned to him sharply, but the all-too-knowing sparkle in his eye silenced the denial on her lips.

'How did you know?'

'Oh, come on! You two are like Romeo and Juliet, star-crossed lovers kept apart by the brides on one side and the widows on the other.'

'*Really?*' Marla squeaked, as she slid the car into first gear and moved off again. She hadn't even properly acknowledged her feelings to herself, yet it seemed that Jonny had known all along.

'Really,' Jonny confirmed.

Out on the pavement, a couple were wrapped in each other's arms, a bunch of mistletoe clutched tightly in the girl's hand. Marla's heart thumped against the sides of its ice tomb, desperate for escape.

'I think I love him, Jonny,' she whispered, and steered the car into a parking space.

The enormity of saying the 'L' word out loud required all of her attention.

'No shit, Sherlock! I know you do.'

Marla gulped in a great lungful of air as she brushed away tears. Tears of relief at having finally admitted it, and of fear that she'd left it too late.

'But he's gone. I sent him away. Oh God, what if he's changed his mind about me?'

'Don't be stupid. He's an undertaker.'

Marla squinted at him. 'So?'

'So he's reliable and serious, of course. And I happen to know that right at this very moment he's back on these shores.'

Marla stared at Jonny in silence, hardly daring to hope, willing him to continue.

'Come on Marla, work with me, sister! Ask me where he is!'

'Where is he?' she whispered.

Jonny tipped his head to one side and arched his eyebrows at her. 'How much do you want to know?'

Marla grabbed him by the lapels of his winter coat.

'That's more like it!' he laughed. 'Word on the street is that he's spending Christmas at his horny henchman's house so he can finalise the sale of the funeral parlour.'

Marla's heart soared at the knowledge that Gabe was close by, then nose-dived again. He was only here to tie up loose ends before he disappeared for good.

'What am I going to do?' she asked, as much to herself as to Jonny.

Her eyes focused on the street outside and spotted a doorway to the side of the hairdressers, which had a neon sign flashing in the window. For once, she'd asked a question and been given the answer. Life-altering decisions deserved to be marked. Maybe there was something in this praying thing after all.

'Don't answer that. I know exactly what to do.' Laughter bubbled up inside her as she jumped out of the car. 'Come on! Get out.'

She yanked Jonny's door open.

'I need you to hold my hand.'

CHAPTER FORTY-TWO

Gabe wandered along Beckleberry High Street with his head bowed against the snow and his hands shoved deep into his jean pockets.

Ahead of him loomed the boarded-over windows and smoke-damaged walls of the burnt-out funeral parlour. He couldn't look. Melanie hadn't only torched the bricks and mortar of his career. She'd taken with it his hopes and dreams, his achievements to date, and his plans for the future.

'Time to grow up, Gabe.'

If nothing else, he'd certainly achieved that. Maybe not in the successful, admirable way that would have made his father proud, but his naïve, rose-tinted glasses had gone up in smoke along with his business.

He didn't let his mind linger on the funeral parlour. He wasn't here for that today. He turned before he reached it and walked up the chapel path instead. He wasn't surprised to find the front door unlocked. Marla wasn't likely to let the small matter of Christmas keep her away from work.

'Marla?'

His voice echoed around the cold chamber of the chapel. He hesitated, and reached inside his coat to double-check the small parcel was still there.

The fast click-clack of heels against stone told him that she'd heard him, but it wasn't Marla who appeared through the stone archway seconds later.

It was her mother, dressed in a ridiculous gold dress, a look of complete panic on her face.

'Thank God!' she squawked, and crossed herself towards the stained-glass window. 'Who ever said this place was deconsecrated was wrong. This way.'

She turned and dashed back through the archway. Gabe glanced backwards in confusion, in case someone else had come in after him, but found no one. He scratched his head and followed her.

The reason for Cecilia's odd behaviour became obvious when he reached the kitchen and caught sight of Emily, heavily pregnant and doubled-up over the table. Relief flooded her face when she saw Gabe. Whether it was because her contraction had ended or because he was there, he wasn't entirely sure.

'I can't drive her to the hospital because I've had a glass of sherry,' Cecilia wailed.

Emily gulped and held up four fingers behind her back to Gabe, the almost empty bottle of sherry on the kitchen table verifying Emily's estimations.

Great. One in labour, one half-cut, and Marla nowhere to be seen.

Gabe sighed. As usual in Beckleberry, things weren't going to plan but life as an undertaker had taught him to stay cool in a crisis, and Gabe could see that Emily badly needed someone to take charge. He put his arm around her shoulders.

'How far apart are your contractions?'

He might be more accustomed to dealing with death rather than birth, but he'd grown up in a huge Irish family where pregnant women and babies were part of the fabric of life.

'About four minutes, I think?'

'Okay.'

Gabe thought fast. He wasn't sure, but four minutes sounded urgent and the hospital was at least twenty minutes away on a normal day. And today wasn't a normal day. It was Christmas Eve, and there was a snowstorm outside.

'Do you have a car, Cecilia?'

Cecilia put down the sherry glass she'd just refilled and shook her head.

'I do.' Emily groaned as another contraction started to build. 'The keys are in here.' She shoved her handbag across the table at him.

'Right then. Good. Here's what we're going to do. Cecilia? You lock up and fetch Emily's coat.'

Marla's mother shot off, and Gabe put both hands on Emily's shoulders.

'Okay, Emily.' He locked his gaze on hers. 'We're going to get you to the hospital. You just try to stay as calm as you can, and breathe through the contractions when they come.'

She nodded, and clutched his elbows as she panted through the pain.

'Thank you,' she managed, as the contraction eased. 'I'm so glad you're here, Gabe.'

He smiled and helped her put on the coat Cecilia proffered.

'Can you walk?'

'I think so.'

Gabe opened the back door and stepped outside, then held his hand out to help Emily down the step.

'Careful, it's slippery out here.'

Together they negotiated the snowy pathway. Another contraction hit as they reached Emily's Nissan Micra.

'That's it sweetheart, you're doing great.'

Gabe held her up as her fingers squeezed his hard enough to snap the bones.

'Has anyone called Tom?' he muttered over his shoulder to Cecilia.

'Answerphone,' she whispered back, with an exaggerated roll of her eyes.

Gabe thrust Emily's bag at Cecilia as she climbed into the back of the car. 'Emily's mobile is in there. Keep trying. Tell him to meet us at the hospital.'

He glanced at Emily, who he'd finally managed to manoeuvre into the passenger seat in between contractions.

'And tell him he'd better make it quick.'

Marla and Jonny collapsed into the car in a fit of euphoric giggles.

'That was inspired,' Jonny said, as his phone started to jingle out a Christmas version of 'YMCA'.

'You are a walking, talking cliché,' Marla laughed as she turned the key in the ignition, then gasped as the clock glowed neon-blue on the dashboard.

'We're going to have to step on it if the County Hotel

are going to get their glitter balls,' she said, as Jonny hung up the phone.

He shook his head. 'Forget about the glitter balls. That was your mother. Emily's gone into labour at the chapel.'

'Oh my God! With just my mother for company?'

Marla gripped the wheel in horror at the idea of her mother as a midwife. She couldn't imagine anyone less competent. Jonny laid a hand over hers on the gear stick as she threw the car into reverse.

'Wait. They're not at the chapel anymore. They're on their way to the hospital.'

'In the name of all that is holy, tell me my mother isn't driving.'

Marla could barely breathe. Her mother couldn't drive on the left if her life depended on it, let alone the lives of Emily and her unborn child.

'Your mother isn't driving.'

She sagged with relief and flicked on the wipers to clear the fresh snow from the windscreen. 'Who is then?'

Jonny pursed his lips and rubbed his hands together with excitement.

'Angel Gabriel.'

Gabe pushed Emily's Micra as hard as he dared through the snowy lanes towards the hospital. He was well aware that every four minutes had become more like every two minutes, and Cecilia's constant nasal chatter from the back seat was doing more to hype Emily up than calm her down.

Emily bent double as a particularly sharp contraction took grip of her. Concentrating hard on the pattern of the floor mat in an effort to tune out Cecilia's voice, she noticed a brown envelope slide out from beneath the seat as Gabe went around a corner. Picking it up as the pain eased, she recognised it straight away. Brown. Official. Medical. It was the envelope that the snotty doctor's receptionist had given her all those months back. Peeling open the top, she saw the words 'semen analysis results' and shoved it back inside again. *No way.* She didn't want to read it now, or ever. All of the major players in the drama knew their roles, and the uncertainty was the key to keeping everyone in their place. Maybe one day, much further down the road, the time would arise when the facts needed to be known, but that day wasn't today. Today was the day that she was going to give birth, and she and Tom had a lifetime of love ready to welcome this precious child into their hearts and their homes. Ripping the letter into shreds as she straightened up, Emily opened the window and hurled the pieces out into the snowstorm.

'Whoa! Are you too hot?' Gabe said, concerned.

Emily wound the window up and closed the icy blast out, watching the slips of paper disappear. 'Sorry. I just needed some air.'

At last the lights of the hospital loomed into view through the swipes of the windscreen wipers, and Gabe screeched to a halt outside Maternity. He dashed inside to grab a wheelchair from the foyer, then dashed back and flung Emily's door open.

'Ready?'

She nodded with a wince of pain and held her arms out to him.

Gabe had never known relief like the moment when a flurry of nurses crowded in and took charge of Emily. One look at her contorted face had been enough to galvanise them into action. In a blink, Cecilia, Gabe and Emily were hurried down a corridor into a room full of scary-looking lights and metal equipment strapped to the walls. A small woman in a dark blue uniform looked him over expectantly.

'Right then, Dad. Let's get Emily up on the bed so we can check what's going on down there.'

'Oh, I'm not the father,' Gabe said, thoroughly alarmed.

'No, I am.'

Everyone turned at the sound of a new voice in the room.

'Thanks Gabe. I'll take it from here.'

Emily burst into noisy tears.

'Tom. Thank God.'

Snowflakes settled on Gabe's shoulders as he leaned against the wall outside the maternity unit. He was frozen, but it was preferable to the cloying heat of the waiting area and having Cecilia snoozing on his shoulder.

Why did things never go as he expected them to around here?

This was the first time he'd set foot near Beckleberry since the day after the fire, and already his well-laid plans had been ripped to shreds. His phone bipped in his pocket, and he grinned as he scanned the predictable message from Dan. Everything else in his life might shift like quicksand, but Dan would always be Jack the Lad.

Pub. Now. Wall 2 Wall totty.

In the hot pub, which was packed out with tinsel-draped revellers, Dan felt his mobile vibrate in the back pocket of his jeans. He reached down for it without disturbing Trisha, the comely barmaid, who at that very moment was in the process of delivering his Christmas snog with considerable tonsil-probing skill.

He flicked the message onto the screen and squinted at it over her naked shoulder.

Sorry Bud. Sink a Guinness for me. Mercy dash to the hospital with Emily.

Dan read it twice over then shrugged Trisha off unapologetically and shouldered his way through the crowd, his jacket and cigarettes forgotten on the table behind him.

He had to get to the hospital.

Gabe stood in the shadows and watched Marla skate across the snowy car park towards him. He shook his head at her thoroughly unsuitable choice of footwear. Did the woman possess anything else except high heels? Her hair swirled around her pink cheeks, and her laugh danced on the crystal-cold air as she clung to Jonny's arm – not that he was much of an anchor for her in those ridiculous cowboy boots.

He liked Jonny a lot, but at that moment he'd have loved nothing more than for the man to disappear in a puff of smoke. For it to be *his* arm that Marla clutched, and *his* jokes that brought out that big laugh.

She drew closer, and he could so easily have stepped out of the darkness and called her name, but fear held him still as she rushed by. Besides, it was bloody freezing. Romantic as the notion was, he didn't want to say what he needed in an icy car park.

* * *

Marla spotted her mother straight away. She was difficult to miss, snoring and resplendent in her gold dress, with her shoes kicked off underneath her chair. She was cuddled up against the water cooler, and behind her, a rather sparsely decorated Christmas tree flashed in time with the piped Christmas carols.

'Christ. It seems the world's oldest fairy has fallen off the top of the tree,' Jonny tittered, but Marla was too distracted to laugh with him. Her eyes skittered around the room in search of a familiar dark head, her entire body braced with the anticipation of seeing Gabe again. The disappointment of his absence felt rather like the entire hospital had crumbled on her head.

She touched her mother's shoulder.

'Mom?'

Cecilia woke up and detached herself from the side of the water cooler in an undignified manner that involved drool and lopsided hair.

'Marla, darling, you're here.'

Her eyes slid from Marla to Jonny, and then flickered around reception.

'Where's Gabriel gone?'

Jonny glanced at Marla's stricken expression and came to her rescue.

'I was just about to ask you the same question.'

Cecilia frowned. 'Oh. Well, he *was* here, and then . . .'

'You fell into a drunken stupor and have no idea when he left?' Jonny supplied in a sympathetic voice, and batted his eyelids at Cecilia with a knowing smirk.

Marla sank down into the seat next to her mother and dropped her head in her hands.

She was too late.

It had been too much to expect that he'd still be here, and the flame of hope within her fizzled out.

He'd gone.

On the other side of the glass entrance doors, Gabe watched Marla drop down dejectedly next to her mother.

What was wrong?

Had something happened to Emily, or the baby?

He couldn't stand it any longer.

He knocked the snow out of his hair and went inside.

CHAPTER FORTY-THREE

'Marla.'

God, she had to get a grip. Jonny had even started to sound like Gabe in her head now. Marla peeled her hands away from her eyes and looked down at the feet in front of her.

Hmmm.

They definitely weren't Jonny's cowboy boots, and the purple satin trousers had been replaced by faded jeans that hugged in all the right places. She forced her eyes to skim past the crotch area, even though they wanted to linger.

Gabe's leather jacket clung to him, and snowflakes clung to it.

Lucky snowflakes.

Marla licked her dry lips and finally looked up into his face.

Still beautiful. But did he look a little gaunt?

Neither Jonny nor Cecilia moved a muscle, nor said a word.

'Is everything okay with the baby?'

Marla frowned, too dumbstruck by his presence to know the answer to any question more difficult than her own name.

What baby?

Again, Jonny rushed to her aid. 'No news yet, dude.' He reached down and yanked Cecilia onto her feet. 'Come on. Let's go and find you some coffee.'

'My shoes . . .' Cecilia grumbled and tried to bend to retrieve them, but Jonny, who had her tucked firmly under one arm, frog-marched her down the corridor.

Marla's throat constricted with nerves as Gabe sat down next to her.

'You came back,' she said.

'Yes.'

'How have you been?'

He studied her face for a few seconds before he answered. 'Okay.'

'Will you be leaving again soon?'

'Depends. Will you be done with the small talk soon?'

'Yes.'

'Thank God for that.'

He glanced around the waiting area with its constant ebb and flow of people.

'Come on. Let's go and find somewhere more quiet.'

Dan jumped out of the taxi he'd just paid an extortionate fare for and watched in relief as Gabe and Marla left the reception area.

How the hell would he have explained his presence here to them, when he couldn't even explain it to himself?

*   *   *

Cecilia leaned against the side of the drinks machine as Jonny stabbed at the buttons.

'Well, let's just hope those two stop pissing around and get their act together,' she grumbled under her breath.

Jonny stared at her in amazement. Firstly, he'd never heard her swear before, and secondly, he hadn't thought she possessed the perceptive powers to have noticed what was going on with her daughter.

'What?' She arched her eyebrows. 'I'm her mother. I gave birth to the girl. Well, almost, anyway.'

'Almost?' Jonny's mind boggled.

Cecilia waved her arm around in an airy fashion.

'Heck, Jonny, I've told you enough times that I'm built like a Barbie doll down there. She'd never have got out.'

Jonny shoved his fingers in his ears and closed his eyes before she could say any more.

'La la la! Stop talking, I can't hear you.'

Cecilia rolled her eyes and waited for him to stop humming and open his eyes.

'All I was going to say, if you'd let me finish,' she shot him the daggers, 'is that I'm hopeful for an Irish extension to the family.'

'Still match-making, I see.'

Jonny jumped at the rich voice behind him, and turned to see a vaguely familiar guy in doctor's whites smiling at Cecilia.

'Robert!'

Jonny noted the way Cecilia turned pink and straightened her shoulders, and the dishy doc slotted into place in his head as the ex-husband from Franco's.

'Cecilia, we must stop meeting like this.'

Something in Robert's twinkling eyes told Jonny that he didn't actually mean those words at all, and for the second time in half an hour he felt like a third wheel.

'I'll just go and check how Emily's doing,' he muttered, and left Cecilia in the capable-looking hands of her suave ex-husband.

'You have a beautiful son.'

The midwife wrapped a towel around the tiny, gunky-but-perfect child, before placing him in his mother's outstretched arms. Tom stood beside Emily and smoothed a damp strand of hair back from her brow.

'You were amazing.' He kissed her forehead and gazed down at the baby. 'Hey there little guy.'

He reached out, and the baby's miniature fists curled around one of Tom's fingers and held on fast.

Emily couldn't keep still after the nurses had finished their work. The birth had been quick and mercifully straightforward, and she still couldn't quite believe that she'd actually brought their baby safely into the world. The midwives melted away and Tom gathered them both into his arms.

'My family,' he whispered.

Emily leaned on his chest as tears slid down her cheeks onto the towel wrapped around her new boy.

Tears of joy, and tears of love.

A little while later, Emily belted her dressing gown around her already-deflating waistline and shuffled out of the en-suite on her way back to the bed. She was relieved to have been to the loo and not lost her insides down the bowl, as she'd feared she might. Good old Mother Nature.

Tom had nipped outside to share their happy news with the others, and to grab the camera that had been on permanent standby in the glove-box of his car for at least a month. He'd forgotten all about it in his panic to get to Emily's side.

She froze, statue-still, in the bathroom doorway. There was a man standing next to the baby's crib, and it wasn't Tom.

It was Dan.

'Hello, baby,' he whispered. Emily's less than strong legs wobbled with fear when he stepped closer.

What was he going to do?

She'd have to intervene if he reached out to pick him up, she knew that much.

But he didn't. He just shoved his hands deeper into his pockets and watched the tiny child swaddled in pale blue.

'A boy, huh? Wow. Well, that's good.' Emily heard the catch in his voice. 'That's really good.'

Dan pressed his hand against the outside of the maternity cot.

'Listen, bud. You be a good boy for your mum and dad, okay?' he whispered. Emily stepped back and held her breath, suddenly feeling like an intruder.

These were Dan's only few seconds with the son that, God willing, she'd have in her life forever. She watched silently as Dan looked at his child, then touched his fingers to his lips and placed them back on the glass.

'Right then. I better go. You didn't see me, right?' Dan tapped the side of his nose and winked at his son.

Emily dipped back into the bathroom, and gripped the sink as the sound of his footsteps receded. Her reflection in the bathroom mirror gazed back at her, familiar yet somehow different. She wasn't sure what it was exactly, but she wasn't the same person as she'd been yesterday.

She was a mother.

'Hey there, handsome.'

Jonny glanced up from his iPhone at the Love God who'd just joined him in the smoking shelter.

Tall.

Blond.

Muscles.

Come to Papa.

'Not many people could pull those trousers off, but you totally do.'

They both looked down at Jonny's purple satin trousers, and he wondered if it would be too forward to tell this Love God that he was more than welcome to pull the aforementioned trousers off any time he fancied. He decided that, on balance, it probably was, so he accepted the proffered cigarette instead. A pleasant electric shock rippled through his fingers when he cupped his hands around the flame of Love God's lighter.

'So. Do you come here often?' Over the years, Jonny had come to realise that sometimes the old lines were the best.

Love God took a long drag on his cigarette. 'I'm a nurse, so you could say that.'

Jonny blew out an elegant plume of smoke. 'What kind of a nurse smokes?'

'A lonely one.'

Jonny cast his eyes to the skies and wondered if Santa

had just dropped his Christmas present off right here in the smoking shelter.

He grinned and shuffled closer. 'Well, as it happens, I've been feeling a little under the weather myself lately . . .'

Emily gathered her sleepy son into her arms and nuzzled her face against his to breathe in his delicious, new baby scent.

Yes, baby, I'm going to love you forever.

She settled herself onto the window ledge to give him his first ever glimpse of the outside world. 'It's snowing,' she whispered against his forehead. 'You'll love this when you're a big boy. Your crazy daddy's already talking about buying a sledge.' She smiled at the image of them all in bobble hats and wellies in years to come.

Down below, she spotted Tom slip-sliding his way across the car park with the camera clutched in his hands. She lifted her hand to tap the glass, but her knuckles stilled as another figure emerged out into the splash of light that spilled from the foyer.

Dan.

They were the only two people out there, and on a direct collision course. They couldn't miss each other if they tried.

She watched in agony as Tom lifted his head. Dan's steps slowed, his hands still bunched up in his jean pockets. 'Keep walking Tom, please keep walking,' Emily whispered, and the baby snuffled into her neck, content against her shoulder.

Tom stopped walking.

It was like watching a silent movie. She could see the serious, guarded look on Tom's face as he spoke. Dan looked away for a few seconds, and then in slow motion, pulled his hand out of his pocket and held it out towards Tom. She saw Tom falter as he tried to decide how to play it. She didn't need to hear their conversation to know what was going on inside his head at that moment.

In every way that mattered this was Tom's child, and her heart ached with love as he reached out and accepted Dan's hand. They lingered for a moment longer before Dan touched his fingers against his forehead in silent salute and disappeared into the darkness.

Emily stroked the baby's velvet-soft head as she waited for Tom to come back upstairs, humbled beyond words by his love, and his strength.

He'd changed today, too. He was a father.

CHAPTER FORTY-FOUR

Marla followed Gabe into a deserted, private room and perched on the slippery edge of a hard hospital mattress. The room smelled strongly of turps, and paint-splattered ladders were leaning against the wall, but at least they were alone. She badly wished that she was wearing something a little less cleavage-revealing than the Biba dress, and that the snow hadn't turned her hair into a wild bird's nest.

Gabe, in contrast, looked lethal.

In theory, it should have been far easier to be around him now that she'd finally admitted to herself that she loved him. She could just fall into his arms and confess all. Job done.

So why did she feel suddenly as awkward as a tongue-tied schoolgirl?

She'd been desperate to see him for weeks, and now that he was in the same room she could barely meet his eyes, let alone profess her undying love or swoon in the hope that he'd catch her.

It didn't help that he looked so brooding and dangerous.

If he were auditioning for Heathcliff, he'd win the role hands down.

Romeo? Not so much.

'Nice dress.'

Marla instinctively glanced down at the low neckline to make sure she hadn't had a Janet Jackson-style wardrobe malfunction.

She knew it was her turn to speak, but it felt a little pre-emptive for 'I love you'.

'Thank you for driving Emily here.'

Gabe nodded and reverted back to brooding silence.

Okay. Small talk wasn't going to work, but then in fairness he'd made that clear once this evening already.

'So . . . why were you at the chapel, Gabe?'

'I was looking for you.'

'You were?'

He nodded. 'I never said goodbye.'

Marla's heart spluttered. No, no, no. Don't say it now.

'And I have something for you.'

He reached into his pocket and placed a white gift box with red ribbons on the bed next to Marla, and then glanced at his watch.

'It's five to midnight. You can open it in five minutes.'

Marla swallowed. So she had five little minutes to convince him to stay forever.

'I have a gift for you, too.' She licked her lips.

'Really?' He stepped closer, a wary flare of hope in his eyes.

She nodded. 'Yup. You can have it in six minutes.'

Well, that should convince him to stay an extra minute, at least.

'So what shall we do to pass the time?' she asked.

She was completely into this game now. She had nothing to lose except him, and she wasn't about to let that happen twice in her lifetime.

A small smile curved the corners of his mouth, and the guarded expression in his eyes cleared; he became as easy to read as A.B.C.

Or L.U.S.T., as seemed to be the case.

'Witch.' His hands found her waist and tugged her onto her feet.

'Can I cast a spell over you to make you stay this time?' she whispered.

His mouth was so close that she could have touched his lips with the tip of her tongue, but he didn't kiss her. His beautiful eyes were full of questions.

'Am I reading this wrong, Marla? Will you go back to hating me again tomorrow?'

'I could never hate you.' Her fingers curled around the neckline of his leather jacket in case he tried to move his warmth away from her.

'You did a very good impression of it for a long time.'

'I'm sorry. I was an idiot.'

Gabe nodded.

'You're not supposed to agree.'

He looked at his watch.

'Thirty seconds.'

She closed her eyes as he reached out and held her face in his hands, his breath mingled with hers. Thank God. Her stomach twisted with pleasure in anticipation of his kiss.

Frustration spiked through her as his lips touched her forehead instead, before moving down to brush her closed eyelids. Her lips begged to be kissed, but it was her cheek-bone that received his attentions next.

'Fifteen seconds,' he murmured as his tongue touched her ear, and the erotic impact made her swoon against him. He laughed softly and sank his teeth into her earlobe.

'Ten.'

Butterfly kisses along her jaw.

This has to be it. Please, please, please . . . She parted her lips, but he turned her face to kiss her other ear.

'Five.'

Her temple.

'Four.'

Her other temple.

'Three.'

The little space between her eyebrows.

'Two.'

The tip of her nose.

I'm going to die if one is not my mouth.

Actually, physically, die, and then all this build-up will have been for nothing.

'One.'

The warmth of his mouth covered hers, the briefest slide of his tongue against hers for a few blissful, all-too-fleeting seconds.

'Merry Christmas, Marla.'

CHAPTER FORTY-FIVE

Jonny stuck his head around the nearest doorway and was surprised to find a rather young and swarthy Santa with his trousers around his ankles, and a nurse on her knees personally delivering his Christmas gift.

'Looks like the kids will have to wait a little longer for their presents this year,' Jonny tittered, and grabbed Love God's hand.

'Let's try somewhere else.'

'In here,' Love God hissed. 'It's been painted today so it'll be empty.'

Jonny pushed the door open to find Marla and Gabe so close together that you couldn't slide a sheet of paper between them.

He grinned and quietly clicked the door. He shook his head. 'Occupied.'

Love God groaned and nodded towards a door at the far end of the corridor.

'There's always the cleaners' cupboard?'

'Sounds like a good place to get dirty.' Jonny grinned and flung open the door. They both yelped in shock at the sight of Cecilia and dishy doctor Robert engaged in a passionate snog.

Jonny slammed the door shut and leaned on it. 'For the love of God!' he howled. 'Could all of the straight people get out of the fucking closets, please? Gay men coming through!'

Love God laughed and pressed Jonny up against the door. 'Looks like there's no room at the inn.'

Jonny decided privacy was overrated anyway as Love God slipped his arms around him and copped a feel of his satin-clad bum cheeks.

'You can open your present now.'

Marla picked up the small box, chewing her lip as she pulled on the red spotted ribbon. It was heavy for a little box. Gabe had already proved himself a thoughtful gift-giver with the picnic extravaganza, so she had no idea what to expect. An ivory box nestled inside the outer wrapping paper.

'It's like pass the parcel.'

Her fingers shook as she flicked open the top of the box and peeped inside. It looked like glass, but she couldn't tell from the top. Something cool and heavy fell into her hand as she tipped the box carefully upside down.

She gasped softly at the beautiful little snow globe; a tiny red and white striped lighthouse peeped through the swirl of snowflakes as they settled.

Gabe reached out and stroked a strand of Marla's hair. 'It reminded me of you.'

Oh, he was too good at this stuff. Ivan's words at Dora's

386

funeral had been one of the most moving things she'd ever heard. Gabe had clearly been similarly touched.

'What can I say? It's perfect.'

Gabe's suddenly serious eyes searched her face.

'Is it?'

Tears prickled behind her eyelids, and she placed the snow globe slowly back into its box and set it down on the mattress next to her.

'That day in the chapel, when I said I didn't love you . . .' she faltered, but she forced herself on because she could tell that he was holding his breath. She didn't want him keeling over now that she was finally ready to admit her feelings.

'I was wrong, but it took you leaving for me to see it. And by then it was too late, because you'd gone and I couldn't tell you.'

He picked her hands up and bumped his thumbs over her knuckles.

'I hated every minute of not being near you.'

She pulled him close.

'Then come back. Rebuild the funeral parlour. We'll find a way to make it work.' Her voice cracked with the effort of not crying. 'Just come home. Please?'

He shook his head, and fear speared her heart. He wasn't coming back. He reached out and stroked her cheek.

'I'm not rebuilding the funeral parlour, Marla.'

She stared at him, dry-mouthed. 'Are you going back to Dublin?'

'Not if I have something to stay for.'

He'd asked the question once before, but this time she answered from her heart.

'Stay for me. Stay because I love you, Gabe.'

She couldn't hold the tears in any longer, but it didn't matter anymore. She'd said what she needed to, and he was kissing her like a drowning man. She wound her arms around his neck and melted against him.

Soft and pliant, against his firmness and warmth.

He brushed away her tears with his fingertips, and for several heavenly moments they dispensed of the need for words altogether.

Gabe came up for air and licked the hollow of her neck.

'Say it again.'

'Say what?'

She half laughed and half gasped as he slid a hand up her skirt and stroked the back of her thigh.

'You know what. Say it, or I'm going to take this ridiculous dress off.'

He played with the zipper at the back of her dress with his free hand.

'I love you, Gabriel Ryan.'

'I love you, too, Marla. Very much.'

He kicked up the heat when he kissed her again, and she slid a hand down between them to his crotch.

'I love you more,' she said, as he rocked against her fingers with an appreciative groan. His hand slid from her thigh to cup her bottom, and as she arched, pain irritated her hipbone, reminding her of something she still needed to do.

'Wait.' She pulled her head back. 'I nearly forgot to give you *your* present.'

He grumbled in frustration when she pushed him back a couple of steps, then perked up again when she hitched her skirt right up on one side. She gathered the slinky material up to knicker level, too excited to be bothered that she was flashing her underwear in a hospital side ward. Gabe's eyes were threatening to fall out of his head as she stood in front of him in her high heels, and Marla thanked the fashion gods that only her black La Perla lace briefs sat perfectly underneath the Biba dress.

'This is hands down the best present anyone has ever given me in my life.' He reached out to touch her, but Marla smacked his fingers away.

'I'm not your present, idiot.' She hitched the dress higher and revealed the white gauze square taped over her hipbone with surgical tape.

A deep frown of concern furrowed across Gabe's forehead.

'Oh God. Are you hurt?'

Marla nodded and tried to keep her face straight. 'It hurt like hell at the time, yeah.'

'What did you do?'

'Take it off and have a look for yourself,' Marla said.

'Jesus. Please tell me we're talking about your knickers.'

She cuffed him on the arm with her free hand and then reached down and peeled the tape back herself. 'There. Look.' She beckoned him closer.

Gabe dropped on his haunches until his head was level with her hip, close enough to get a bird's-eye view of the small lighthouse that had been freshly tattooed there that afternoon. She laid a hand on his shoulder to steady herself, and felt gentle laughter ripple through him as he shook his head. They had been on exactly the same page.

'It reminded me of you,' she murmured. 'Like Ivan and

Dora. People need someone to share their lives with. I guess I never really realised it was true for me too. We all need rocks to stand our lighthouses on.'

He dipped his dark head to place a kiss on her tender skin with infinite care.

When he straightened, the laughter in his eyes had been replaced with a fierce, burning look of love. She wound her arms around him and breathed him in; delicious and familiar and all hers.

He hitched her up onto the bed and glanced over his shoulder.

'Do you reckon there's a lock on that door?'

FIVE YEARS LATER ~ EVERYONE LOVES A GOOD WEDDING...

The sun rose early over Beckleberry on midsummers day, a low-slung rose pink haze streaked with delicate wisps of golden cloud that would melt away as soon as the sun gathered its strength.

Kev the Elvis impersonator carried buckets of creamy roses into the shop for Ruth the florist, taking the chance to smack the rounded cheek of her bottom as she bent double to pick out the most fragrant sweet peas from the delivery that had just arrived. She straightened, swatting affectionately at his hand as he leaned in to place a smacker on her lips. Their romance had taken everyone by surprise, Ruth and Kev most of all. A misplaced New Years eve peck on the cheek that had landed on her lips was all that it had taken for them to see each other in a whole new light, and he'd flourished like one of her freshly watered blooms under her attention. Not that today was their wedding day. All weddings were special of course, but the whole village seemed to be caught up in the romance of today's ceremony.

Two of their own were coming together at midday in the chapel, and they were all set to make it a day to remember.

'Baby blue or lavender?' Jonny stood in his skin tight Calvin Klein budgie-smugglers, his hands on his lean, suntanned hips. Two almost identical suits hung on the doors of the gilt armoire in front of him, both impressive enough to guarantee he'd stand out from the crowd.

'Lavender,' Sean said, propped up in bed with an early morning cup of coffee resting on his equally impressive chest. 'It goes with your eyes.'

Jonny twirled around with a cynical look on his face. 'I'm not Elizabeth fucking Taylor, Sean, pay attention. This is crucial.'

Sean threw the silver sheet back to reveal his impressive erection. 'No, Jonny. *This* is crucial. Get that delightful ass of yours over here.'

Jonny licked his lips, all thoughts of lavender and blue chased from his mind by the sight of something altogether more enticing. 'Love God,' he murmured, sidling over to the big baroque bed and beneath the held back covers. Sean laughed softly at the term of endearment, and Jonny caught his breath as the sun glinted off his wedding ring. Jonny hadn't taken the ring off since the moment Sean slid it into place less than six months after they'd met in that snowy smoking shelter five Christmas eve's ago. Their wedding had almost raised the roof of the chapel, and they'd remained scandalously happy from that day forward.

Yes. They'd already had their special day. Today belonged to two people they held as close as family in their hearts. And they'd be there centre-stage to help make sure it went with a bang, just as soon as they'd taken care of the love-bomb going off right there in their own bedroom

Marla leaned her back against her garden gate, a china cup of ginger tea cradled in her hands as she breathed in the pure early morning air. She could already feel the warmth of the sun kissing her bare arms as she watched Vinnie mooch around in the flowerbeds for his tennis ball. She didn't reprimand him. It didn't matter. The garden of the big old cottage was delightfully ramshackle, and these days Marla didn't feel quite so hung up on everything being so orderly and white. Hell, she was even wearing red striped wellies with her broderaise-anglais slip. Contentment could do that kind of thing to a girl.

She still couldn't believe her luck. Buying the rambling cottage on the edge of the village a couple of years back had been a no brainer for them, and it had been the final piece of their jigsaw. For god's sake, it even had yellow roses rambling around the door. Marla had loved it at first sight, just as Gabe had loved Marla from the moment he'd set eyes on her.

Gabriel Ryan. She glanced up at the low-slung white washed bedroom window frame over the doorway, knowing he was in there, sprawled naked across their crisp cotton sheets. He of the dark gypsy curls and come-to-bed eyes, the man who'd spent the last five years filling her heart and her life to the brim with a depth of love and happiness she hadn't believed existed outside of romance novels. The summer had been kind to them so far, sprinkling gold dust over his skin, rendering him even more beautiful to Marla's eyes. And to every other woman's, too; Marla loved the way he turned heads in every room he entered, and she loved him even more for not even being aware of it.

Vinnie, having finally retrieved his well-chewed tennis ball from the shrubbery, rolled his gangly little frame across the lawn towards her and dropped the ball expectantly on the toe of her wellington boot. A valentine's gift from Gabe, the leggy black lab pup had quickly wriggled his way into the fabric of Marla and Gabe's lives. Gabe had presented the fat little puppy in a basket tied with sky blue ribbons, blissfully unaware that Marla would present him with an even more unexpected gift later that very same day.

Tears had filled his expressive dark eyes when she'd told him he was going to be a father.

She rested her cup on the garden wall as the postman ambled down the lane rummaging around in his bag.

'Postcard for you,' he grinned, holding it out over the gate. 'Sounds like Dan's enjoying himself as usual.'

Marla smiled and shook her head as the postman wiggled his eyebrows and carried on down the lane. She was pretty much used to the nature of village life these days, to the way everyone knew everyone else's business.

The postcard had found its way to Beckleberry from the other side of the world, a jaunty outline of Australia set against the national flag. Marla smiled, knowing that Gabe would be glad to hear an update on Dan's big trip to Oz with Sandie, the receptionist from the funeral parlour.

Gabe's best friend had fallen in lust at first sight with the Australian ex-ballroom dancing champion, and Marla and Gabe had a sneaking suspicion that lust was turning steadily into love. The pair had flown out to Australia a few weeks previously for Sandie to show him around her homeland and introduce him to her folks. Marla flipped the card over.

G'day dudes!

Having a fucking awesome time! Weathers warm, the beers are cold and Sandie is bendy as hell.

Wish you were here. A bit. Not all that much. Too busy shagging.

Dan x

Oh, Sandie says to say Hi and she misses you! Blah blah blah!

Marla laughed. It was typical Dan, flippant with an underscore of affection. Sandie had been a welcome addition to all of their lives with her antipodean sunshine smile and can-do attitude. She'd slid seamlessly into the role of receptionist at Gabe's new funeral parlour at the far end of Beckleberry High St.

She picked up the teacup and laid a hand on the swell of her belly. At almost five months pregnant her body had well and truly started to bloom, and she finally had that impressive cleavage that she'd always wished for, albeit temporarily. Gabe made it easy to accept the changes to her figure, adoring her in their bed, loving her curves with his hands and his mouth, spooning his body around hers when he slept, his splayed hand protective and warm over her stomach.

Marla walked up the garden path with Vinnie dancing around her heels.

Today was the culmination of a love story, and she had tingles just thinking of how perfect it was going to be. She glanced at her watch as she opened the old wooden front door, counting the hours until she needed to be standing up at the front of the chapel.

*   *   *

395

The day started early over at Emily and Tom's, too. As on most other mornings, Adam had crashed into their bedroom a little after five am and burrowed his stout little body between his parents, his sandy hair tickling Tom's nose as he dozed back off.

Emily stroked his rounded cheek, still baby soft even though he'd turned five at Christmas. He was a strikingly beautiful child, a laugh always on his lips and mischief never far from his mind. Tom instinctively gathered Adam against him as he slept, and Emily stroked her fingertips lightly over his knuckles. *Her boys.*

Tucking the quilt around them, she slid from the bed and padded across the landing to the nursery, pushing the door ajar to check on ten-month-old Isadora. As dark haired as her mother, the baby slept blissfully on her back, a tiny fist curled around one of the bars of her cot. A small silk and tulle ballerina bridesmaid dress hung on her dresser in anticipation of the day that lay ahead.

Adam's arrival in their family had taught Tom and Emily many things, one of those things being that they adored being parents and wanted to give Adam a sibling. The tests that had been a cause of such heartache first time around had seemed so much less arduous with a child to love already, and with the help of medical miracles they'd welcomed Isadora into their hearts last autumn.

If Emily had been asked to choose one word to sum up her feelings as she gazed down at her sleeping daughter, it would have been blessed.

On the flip side of the world, Dan looked on as Sandie performed lazy lengths of her parent's swimming pool.

Her folks were out of town for a couple of days, leaving Dan and Sandie alone in the sparkling villa and a fridge full of beers. He glanced at his watch, and a quick calculation told him it was just around breakfast time in Buckleberry. His heart twisted a little, but only a little. He wished the happy couple nothing but good times ahead, but all the same he was glad to be oceans away from England today.

The water rippled as Sandie stepped out of the water, Bond-girl-esque, and his heart twisted back into shape and expanded a little as she stepped out of her wet bikini. He picked up a fresh towel and opened it wide.

'Come here, baby.'

The bells of the chapel rang out clear and true across the village, calling them all to gather and bear witness. Come, come and see the love.

'Stop fidgeting with your shirt collar,' Sean chided Jonny gently as they lounged together in the chapel doorway. 'Anyone would think you're nervous.'

Jonny scanned the street outside for cars. 'It's alright for you, you just have to sit there and look devastating. I've got to conduct the ceremony for two of our best friends. What if I fuck it up?'

'Jonny. You're good at everything you do, and you love these people. You won't fuck up.' Sean fixed his husband with the look, the one guaranteed to put the brakes on Jonny's tendency towards hysterics. 'Now. Big breaths.'

Jonny's eye's glittered with laughter as he glanced down at his chest and then back up at Sean. 'Yeth. And I'm only thicksteen.'

Sean rolled his eyes. 'The old ones are the best,' he muttered, letting his fingers linger against Jonny's adams apple as he straightened his collar properly for him. 'Look lively. I spy wedding guests.'

By ten to twelve, the chapel was packed, women in summer dresses showing off sun-pinked shoulders, and men in open necked shirts. Informal and relaxed had been the happy couple's requested dress code, the same approach they'd applied to their choice of decoration for the chapel. Vases of delicate sweet peas, peonies and vintage cream tea-roses filled the deep chapel windowsills, their petals fringed with palest pink.

Gabe and Tom sat in the front row, their heads close together in conversation.

'You've definitely got the ring?'

'Same place it was last time you checked, bud.'

They both glanced up as Jonny stepped up to the lectern with a discreet nod towards Sean to start the music, and a hush fell as the opening bars of "On Days Like These," lilted from the sound system. The congregation stood in excited acknowledgment of the appearance of four people in the doorway.

Marla, beautiful in a nude pink silk and lace dress that skimmed her curves, her red hair in lush waves around her shoulders. A simple circlet of burnished gold leaves scattered with diamonds lent her the appearance of a beautiful woodland nymph, an image made all the more earthly by the presence of baby Isadora on her hip.

At the front of the chapel, Gabe caught his breath. He'd loved Marla Jacobs from the moment he'd first laid eyes on her, but never so much as in that moment with the sun framing her face like a halo.

A few steps ahead of her, Emily moved slowly, radiant in floor length cafe-au-lait lace, hand in hand with the proudest five-year-old boy in the land. Adam had a look of concentration on his face, the expression of someone trying hard not to make a mistake. Imperceptibly, Emily squeezed his fingers in reassurance and sent him the most discreet of winks, making him beam and puff his chest out with pride.

Tom stood at the front of the chapel, finding it hard to see his family through the film of tears in his eyes. Emily shone, from her glossy dark set waves to the tips of her toes. He loved this woman, and she loved him back. Nothing else mattered.

They'd danced to the same song on the beach on their wedding night, barefoot and tipsy on local rum. Back then he'd never imagined that their marriage would be such a rollercoaster. Not that he'd have changed anything with the benefit of a crystal ball, except maybe taken care to fasten Emily's seatbelt a little tighter. He'd almost let her fall. He wouldn't make that mistake twice in one lifetime.

As the procession reached the front of the chapel, Adam's eyes flickered to Gabe, who gave him a thumbs up and a nod, the secret signal he'd agreed with the little boy to give his mum and dad his own special surprise.

On Gabe's nod, Adam lifted his mothers hand formally to his lips and pressed a kiss against the back of it, and then held it out towards Tom, an official handover. Tom swallowed the ball of love in his throat as he accepted his wife's hand from their child. Adam watched on with round, solemn blue eyes as Tom mirrored his actions, raising Emily's hand to his lips. He heard Emily's small intake of breath, and lifted his eyes to hers as his mouth brushed her skin.

The familiar scent of her favourite perfume. The feel of her hand in his. The look in her eyes at that very moment. He wanted to commit every second of the day to memory.

Gabe mussed Adam's hair in approval for a job well done as he came to sit beside him. The little boy looked up with a gap-toothed grin, and Gabe looked down into Dan's laughing eyes. His best friend had never breathed a word, but Gabe had long since realised that Adam was his son. He was in no doubt that Tom knew the truth too, and his faith in love was only deepened by the fact that they'd all somehow made their peace with it. The fabric of life wasn't made up of plain cotton and simple running stitch. It was fine velvet next to the coarsest hessian, stitched together with embroidery silk here and rough twine there. Rough and smooth. Beautiful, unexpected and unique.

He turned and dropped a kiss on Marla's shoulder as she sat beside him with Isadora on her knees, noticing the way the sun had sprinkled freckles on her fair skin.

As the last notes of the music faded, Tom straightened from kissing Emily's hand and impulsively drew her against him, his lips lingering on hers.

Happiness soared like a bird in Emily's chest. If she could have pressed pause right at that moment, she would have, because she knew with complete certainty that she could never be any happier. Had she have had the chance to look at that freeze-framed scene, she'd have seen the reverential way that Tom's hand cradled her face, his other hand on the base of her back as she arched into him.

As it was, she felt the fleeting perfection of the moment as Tom's lips moved over hers, his thumb brushing the tear from her cheek.

She wanted to kiss him forever. Everyone else in the place faded. There was just Tom. Tom's warm hands, Tom's lips, Tom's heart beating steady against hers.

And then there was Jonny, coughing dramatically at the lectern.

'Easy tigers, there's kids in the room,' he said, and things swam back into focus as a small laugh rippled around the chapel.

Tom and Emily drew apart a little, their hands still clasped as Jonny welcomed everyone to their vow renewal ceremony.

'Tom and Emily have written their own words for todays ceremony,' Jonny said, looking expectantly at Tom, who cleared his throat and reached for a piece of paper from his pocket. He looked down at it for a few seconds in silence, and then gazed up at Emily.

'Em. Emily. My beautiful, lovely Emily. I've spent so long trying to decide what to say to you today. I wrote this speech...' he shrugged, folding the piece of paper back up and putting it away again. 'And now it doesn't seem enough.'

He held both of his wife's hands in his own.

He shook his head, a look of wonder in his eyes as he gazed at Emily.

'I don't know what I did to earn you, and lord knows I've been an idiot sometimes, but we're still here, aren't we?' His thumbs stroked over Emily's knuckles as he spoke in the pin-drop silent room. 'Everything I've learned of love I've learned from you. I've learned that when you love someone, *really* love someone, it's not all hearts and flowers. Sometimes it's the hardest thing in the world, and the only thing that could be harder is to not love them anymore. So you do. You love them through it all, and afterwards you look at them and you think thank god.'

Emily's fingers tightened around Tom's as he carried on speaking.

'I think thank god I didn't walk away, because I'd have missed out on all of this, and I'd never have known life could be this good, or that I'd ever get the chance to stand here with you like this again in our lifetime.'

Marla's eyes slid to Gabe's profile as she listened to her friends in awe. She knew his features intimately enough that she'd be able to draw him with her eyes closed. And there, at last, after almost a decade of presiding over other people's weddings, Marla Jacob's finally got it.

Marriage wasn't about the wedding day, or the details, or even about the couple stood at the altar. It was about love, that collective, all encompassing, abiding emotion that kept the earth turning and bought wars to an end. About romantic love, about the love between a parent and the child they'd lay down their life for, about the bond between loyal, lifelong friends.

Gabe had asked her to marry him countless times over the years, and every time she'd said an affectionate no.

Not because she didn't love him. She loved him with all of her heart; she just didn't need a bit of paper to say so.

But sitting there listening to Tom speak, knowing that Gabe wanted to be her husband, she changed. She wanted his ring on her finger, his name after hers. After their babies. She smiled, smoothing a hand over Isadora's infant curls as Emily started to speak.

'You said something to me a few years ago, Tom. You said "I don't know what the future holds, I just want it to hold you." It was the most beautiful thing I'd ever heard. I knew it and I didn't tell you at the time, and I've always regretted it, so I'm telling you now. For better, for worse, we said in our wedding vows. You're my better in every way. Better at forgiveness, better at risotto, better at loving. You're the best man ever, and I'm the luckiest girl.'

Tom smiled, smoothing Emily's hair behind her ear.

'Our vows seemed so easy back then, didn't they?' he said. 'Two clueless kids dancing around on a paradise beach saying words that were too big for them. Not anymore. I've watched you lose your guts most mornings through two pregnancies, and I've watched you nurse our children every time they're ill. When I say in sickness and in health today, I understand what it means.' He paused for a moment to gather himself together.

'For richer for poorer, we said. I thought at the time that it spoke of money... of the bigger house we dreamed of, or the perfect job just over the horizon. I know better now. None of that stuff matters.' Tom slid the eternity ring onto Emily's finger beside her wedding ring and then lifted her palm flat over his heart. He didn't care who heard him, as long as the woman standing in front of him did. 'You've made me a rich man, Emily. In here, I'm a fucking millionaire.'

Jonny wiped the back of his hands over his chiseled cheekbones as Tom tugged his bride-again into the circle of his arms and kissed her. He'd worried over nothing. He'd barely needed to speak, and it was easily the most romantic ceremony he'd ever presided over.

The jubilant peal of wedding bells rang out as Tom turned and beckoned to Adam to join them as they hugged. Gabe handed Isadora over to Emily as the family of four made their way up the aisle to clapping and cheers from their friends and loved ones. They were picture perfect, Tom's arm slung around Emily's shoulders, his other hand clasped in Adam's, the baby on Emily's hip.

As the guests spilled out into the gardens behind the chapel, they discovered the enchanted tea-party scene that Jonny, Sean, Marla and Gabe had painstakingly created for their friends. The sun's haze cast an idyllic glow over proceedings as the champagne flowed into vintage cut-crystal flutes and tea was poured into a variety of pretty, mismatched china teacups. Conversation and laughter drifted around the gardens, underscored with melodies picked out by the steel drum duo Jonny had insisted on sourcing because Emily had mentioned it as one of her over-riding memories of their beachside wedding.

'And suddenly those hours on ebay buying tea-cups feels worth it,' Jonny said, his hand on Sean's leg beneath the long, gingham covered trestle table set beneath the oak tree. He'd known the exact bohemian glamour look he'd wanted to create for Emily, and had pulled out all of the stops.

Sean reached out for a sandwich from one of the several piled high cake stands running down the centre of the table. Ruth had set jam jars of wild flowers between the stands, and a deep victoria sponge sat on top of a cream vanity case in the centre, ruby jam and cream oozing between its layers.

'Peanut butter and jam?' Sean said, peeling his sandwich apart and peering inside.

Jonny shrugged. 'Gabe insisted. His favourite, apparently.'

'He's full of surprises, that man,' Sean murmured. They both watched Gabe laugh as he handed champagne glasses to Cecilia and Robert, who looked more loved up than teenagers with his hand resting on her bottom. It was a toss up who fancied Gabe more, Jonny or Sean; they both harboured a healthy dose of lust for the local undertaker.

Across the lawn, Tom and Emily slow-danced beneath a candelabra Jonny had strung from the bough of a tree, lost in their own world.

'Happy?' he murmured against her ear.

Emily didn't have the words to tell him just how happy he made her, so she put all of her emotions into kissing him instead.

'Me too, beautiful,' he murmured a few minutes later, his voice thick with love. 'Me too.'

* * *

Gabe walked through the cool, empty chapel in search of Marla. He'd spotted her heading inside a few minutes before, probably to escape the heat of the midsummer sunshine.

'Marla?' A perplexed frown furrowed his brow at the answering silence. He walked the length of the aisle, letting out a slow sigh of relief as he caught sight of her sitting out in the small, shady front garden.

'Too warm?' he said, handing her the glass of iced water he'd poured for her in the chapel kitchen.

'Playing hooky for five minutes.' She smiled as Gabe dropped down alongside her on the grass. Marla leaned her shoulder against the pale grey headstone next to her.

'They'd have enjoyed today, wouldn't they?' she said, nodding towards Dora and Ivan's headstone. Gabe laughed softly.

'Dora would have run the show while Ivan ate all of the sandwiches and drank too much champagne.'

Marla laced her fingers with Gabe's in the quiet garden, both of them thinking of the larger than life elderly couple who'd been so instrumental in all of their lives and love affairs.

Ivan without Dora just hadn't made any sense, and no one had been that surprised when he'd gone to sleep and not woke up again within four months of losing his wife.

It seemed fitting that their ashes be buried together in the chapel gardens he'd tended so carefully.

Gabe unpinned the corsage from his shirt and laid it at the foot of the stone.

'To them,' he said, and Marla loved him most of all in

that moment. She untied the corsage from her wrist and laid it beside Gabe's on the grass.

She traced her fingertip over the outline of a lighthouse etched into the stone beside Dora and Ivan's names. 'And to us.'

She turned her body towards Gabe's, hip to hip, eye to eye.

'Marry me?' she said, suddenly breathless.

Gabe's dark brown eyes filled with gentle humour. He'd asked her so many times that he knew she couldn't be serious. And then as he watched her face and realised she wasn't joking, the laughter left his eyes and he reached out a hand to cup her cheek.

'You mean it?' he said, smoothing his thumb over her bottom lip. Marla nodded, never taking her eyes from his face, loving the small, incredulous smile that touched his lips. He looked down for a second as he took her words in, his dark lashes sweeping his cheek. He was so incredibly beautiful that he made her heart hurt.

He leaned in and kissed her then, loving her mouth with his own. Gabe tasted of everything she adored, and even now five years down the line and pregnant with his child, he only had to look her way across a crowded room and she melted. He held her heart in his hands, and it felt safer than it ever had in her own. His tongue brushed slow and languid over hers as she stroked her fingers over his sun-warm dark hair, holding him to her.

'Be my wife, Marla Jacobs,' he murmured against her lips, his hand sweeping a slow tingle down her spine. 'Wear my ring. Have my babies. Let me love you forever.'

It was a dizzyingly perfect proposal. Marla closed her

eyes as Gabe kissed her again, the sounds of the wedding reception carrying towards them on the breeze.

Caught up in each other, neither of them noticed the workmen unloading new shop signs from a van outside the vacant premises next door.